D0941940

A
Garland Series

VICTORIAN
FICTION

*NOVELS OF FAITH
AND DOUBT*

*A collection of 121 novels
in 92 volumes, selected by
Professor Robert Lee Wolff,
Harvard University,
with a separate introductory volume
written by him
especially for this series.*

THE CLEVER WOMAN OF THE FAMILY

Charlotte M. Yonge

Two volumes in one

Garland Publishing, Inc., New York & London

1975

Bibliographical note:

this facsimile has been made from a copy in the
Harvard University Library
(EC85.y8033.865c)

Library of Congress Cataloging in Publication Data

Yonge, Charlotte Mary, 1823-1901.
    The clever woman of the family.

    (Victorian fiction : Novels of faith and doubt)
    Reprint of the 1865 ed. published by Macmillan,
London.
    I. Title. II. Series.
PZ3.Y8Cℓ15 [PR5912]   823'.8   75-1523
ISBN 0-8240-1595-9

Printed in the United States of America

THE

CLEVER WOMAN OF THE FAMILY.

THE

CLEVER WOMAN OF THE FAMILY.

BY THE

AUTHOR OF "THE HEIR OF REDCLYFFE."

IN TWO VOLUMES.

VOL. I.

London and Cambridge:

MACMILLAN AND CO.

1865.

LONDON :
R. CLAY SON, AND TAYLOR, PRINTERS,
BREAD STREET HILL.

CONTENTS.

CHAPTER VII.

CHAPTER VIII.

CHAPTER IX.

CHAPTER X.

CHAPTER XI.

CHAPTER XII.

CHAPTER XIII.

CHAPTER XIV.

CLEVER WOMAN OF THE FAMILY.

CHAPTER I.

IN SEARCH OF A MISSION.

" Thou didst refuse the daily round
    Of useful, patient love,
And longedst for some great emprise
    Thy spirit high to prove."—C. M. N.

" Che mi sedea con l'antica Rachele."—DANTE.

" IT is very kind in the dear mother."

" But what, Rachel? Don't you like it? She so enjoyed choosing it for you."

"Oh yes, it is a perfect thing in its way. Don't say a word to her ; but if you are consulted for my next birthday present, Grace, couldn't you suggest that one does cease to be a girl."

"Only try it on, Rachel dear, she will be pleased to see you in it. '

" Oh yes, I will bedizen myself to oblige her. I do assure you I am not ungrateful. It is beautiful in itself, and shows how well nature can be imitated; but it is meant for a mere girl, and this is the very day I had fixed for hauling down the flag of youth."

" Oh, Rachel."

" Ah, ha ! If Rachel be an old maid, what is Grace ? Come, my dear, resign yourself ! There is nothing more unbecoming than want of perception of the close of young-ladyhood."

" Of course I know we are not quite young girls now," said Grace, half perplexed, half annoyed.

" Exactly. From this moment we are established as the maiden sisters of Avonmouth, husband and wife to one another, as maiden pairs always are."

" Then thus let me crown our bridal," quoth Grace, placing on her sister's head the wreath of white roses.

"Treacherous child ! " cried Rachel, putting up her hands and tossing her head, but her sister held her still.

" You know brides always take liberties. . Please, dear, let it stay till the mother has been in, and pray don't talk before her of being so very old."

" No, I'll not be a shock to her. We will silently assume our immunities, and she will acquiesce if they come upon her gradually."

Grace looked somewhat alarmed, being perhaps in some dread of immunities, and aware that Rachel's silence would in any one else have been talkativeness.

" Ah, mother dear, good morning," as a pleasant placid-looking lady entered, dressed in black, with an air of feeble health, but of comely middle age.

Birthday greetings, congratulations, and thanks followed, and the mother looked critically at the position of the wreath, and Rachel for the first time turned to the glass and met a set of features of an irregular, characteristic cast, brow low and broad, nose *retroussé*, with large, singularly sensitive nostrils quivering like those of a high-bred horse at any emotion, full pouting lips, round cheeks glowing with the freshest red, eyes widely opened, dark deep grey and decidedly prominent, though curtained with thick black lashes. The glossy chestnut hair partook of the redundance and vigour of the whole being, and the roses hung on it gracefully though not in congruity with the thick winter dress of blue and black tartan, still looped up over the dark petticoat and hose, and stout high-heeled boots, that like the grey cloak and felt hat bore witness to the early walk. Grace's countenance and figure were in the same style, though without so much of mark or animation; and her dress was of like description, but less severely plain.

"Yes, my dear, it looks very well; and now you will oblige me by not wearing that black lace thing, that looks fit for your grandmother."

"Poor Lovedy Kelland's aunt made it, mother, and it was very expensive, and wouldn't sell."

"No wonder, I am sure, and it was very kind in you to take it off their hands; but now it is paid for, it can't make much difference whether you disfigure yourself with it or not."

"Oh yes, dear mother, I'll bind my hair when you bid me do it, and really these buds do credit to the makers. I wonder whether they cost them as dear in health as lace does," she added, taking off the flowers and examining them with a grave sad look.

"I chose white roses," proceeded the well-pleased mother, "because I thought they would suit either of the silks you have now, though I own I should like to see you in another white muslin."

"I have done with white muslin," said Rachel, rousing

from her reverie. "It is an affectation of girlish simplicity not becoming at our age."

"Oh Rachel!" thought Grace in despair; but to her great relief in at that moment filed the five maids, the coachman, and butler; and the mother began to read prayers.

Breakfast over, Rachel gathered up her various gifts, and betook herself to a room on the ground floor with all the appliances of an ancient schoolroom. Rather dreamily she took out a number of copy-books, and began to write copies in them in large text hand.

"And this is all I am doing for my fellow-creatures," she muttered half aloud. "One class of half-grown lads, and those grudged to me! Here is the world around one mass of misery and evil! Not a paper do I take up but I see something about wretchedness and crime, and here I sit with health, strength, and knowledge, and able to do nothing, *nothing*—at the risk of breaking my mother's heart! I have pottered about cottages and taught at schools in the *dilettante* way of the young lady who thinks it her duty to be charitable; and I am told that it is my duty, and that I may be satisfied. Satisfied, when I see children cramped in soul, destroyed in body, that fine ladies may wear lace trimmings! Satisfied with the blight of the most promising buds! Satisfied, when I know that every alley and lane of town or country reeks with vice and corruption, and that there is one cry for workers with brains and with purses! And here am I, able and willing, only longing to task myself to the uttermost, yet tethered down to the merest mockery of usefulness by conventionalities. I am a young lady forsooth! —I must not be out late; I must not put forth my views;

I must not choose my acquaintance ; I must be a mere helpless, useless being, growing old in a ridiculous fiction of prolonged childhood, affecting those graces of so-called sweet seventeen that I never had—because, because why ? Is it for any better reason than because no mother can bear to believe her daughter no longer on the lists for matrimony ? Our dear mother does not tell herself that this is the reason, but she is unconsciously actuated by it. And I have hitherto given way to her wish. I mean to give way still in a measure ; but I am five and twenty, and I will no longer be withheld from some path of usefulness ! I will judge for myself, and when my mission has declared itself, I will not be withheld from it by any scruple that does not approve itself to my reason and conscience. If it be only a domestic mission—say the care of Fanny, poor dear helpless Fanny ; I would that I knew she was safe,—I would not despise it, 1 would throw myself into it, and regard the training her and forming her boys as a most sacred office. It would not be too homely for me. But I had far rather become the founder of some establishment that might relieve women from the oppressive task-work thrown on them in all their branches of labour. Oh, what a worthy ambition !"

"Rachel !" called Grace. " Come, there's a letter, a letter from Fanny herself for you. Make haste, mamma is so nervous till you read it."

No exhortation was needed to make Rachel hurry to the drawing-room, and tear open the black-edged letter with the Australian stamp.

" All is right, mamma. She has been very ill, but is fast recovering, and was to sail by the *Voluta.* Why, she may be here any day."

"Any day! My dear Grace, see that the nurseries are well aired."

"No, mother, she says her party is too large, and wants us to take a furnished house for her to come into at once—Myrtlewood if possible. Is it let, Grace?"

"I think I saw the notice in the window yesterday."

"Then, I'll go and see about it at once."

"But, my dear, you don't really mean that poor dear Fanny thinks of coming anywhere but to us?" said her mother, anxiously.

"It is very considerate of her," said Grace, "with so many little children. You would find them too much for you, dear mother. It is just like Fanny to have thought of it. How many are there, Rachel?"

"Oh! I can't tell. They got past my reckoning long ago. I only know they are all boys, and that this baby is a girl."

"Baby! Ah, poor Fanny, I feared that was the reason she did not come sooner.

"Yes, and she has been very ill; she always is, I believe, but there is very little about it. Fanny never could write letters; she only just says: 'I have not been able to attempt a letter sooner, though my dear little girl is five weeks old to-day. Think of the daughter coming at last, too late for her dear father, who had so wished for one. She is very healthy, I am thankful to say; and I am now so much better, that the doctor says I may sail next week. Major Keith has taken our cabins, in the *Voluta*, and soon after you receive this, I hope to be showing you my dear boys. They are such good, affectionate fellows; but I am afraid they would be too much for my dear aunt, and our party is so large ; so the Major and I both think it will be the best way for you to take a house for me for six months. I should like Myrtlewood best, if it is to be had. I have told Conrade all about it, and how pretty it is; and it is so near you that I think there I can be happy as ever I can be again in this world, and have your advice for the dear children.' "

" Poor darling ! she seems but a child herself."

" My age—five and twenty," returned Rachel. " Well, I shall go and ask about the house. Remember, mother, this influx is to bring no trouble or care on you; Fanny Temple is my charge from henceforth. My mission has come to seek me," she added, as she quitted the room, in eager excitement of affection, emotion, and importance, for Fanny had been more like a sister than a cousin.

Grace and Rachel Curtis were the daughters of the squire of the Homestead ; Fanny, of his brother, an officer in the army. Left at home for education, the little girl had spent her life, from her seventh to her sixteenth year, as absolutely one with her cousins, until she was summoned to meet her father at the Cape, under the escort of his old friend, General Sir Stephen Temple. She found Colonel Curtis sinking under fatal disease, and while his relations were preparing to receive, almost to maintain, his widow and daughter, they were electrified by the tidings that the gentle little Fanny, at sixteen, had become the wife of Sir Stephen Temple, at sixty.

From that time little had been known about her ; her mother had continued with her, but the two Mrs. Curtises had never been congenial or intimate ; and Fanny was never a full nor willing correspondent, feeling perhaps the difficulty of writing under changed circumstances. Her husband had

been in various commands in the colonies, without returning
to England ; and all that was known of her was a general
impression that she had much ill-health and numerous children, and was tended like an infant by her bustling mother
and doting husband.   More than half a year back, tidings
had come of the almost sudden death of her mother ; and
about three months subsequently, one of the officers of Sir
Stephen's staff had written to announce that the good old
general had been killed by a fall from his horse, while on a
round of inspection at a distance from home.   The widow
was then completely prostrated by the shock, but promised to
write as soon as she was able ; and this was the fulfilment of
that promise, bringing the assurance that Fanny was coming
back with her little ones to the home of her childhood.

Of that home, Grace and Rachel were the joint-heiresses,
though it was owned by the mother for her life.   It was an
estate of farm and moorland, worth some three or four thousand
a year, and the house was perched on a beautiful promontory,
running out into the sea, and inclosing one side of a bay,
where a small fishing-village had recently expanded into a
quiet watering-place, esteemed by some for its remoteness from
railways, and for the calm and simplicity that were yearly
diminished by its increasing popularity.   It was the family
fashion to look down from their crag at the new esplanade
with pity and contempt for the ruined loneliness of the
pebbly beach ; and as Mrs. Curtis had not health to go often
into society, she had been the more careful where she trusted
her daughters.   They belonged to the county by birth and
tradition, and were not to be mixed up with the fleeting
residents of the watering-place, on whom they never called,
unless by special recommendation from a mutual friend ; and

the few permanent inhabitants chanced to be such, that a visit to them was in some degree a condescension. Perhaps there was more of timidity and caution than of pride in the mother's exclusiveness, and Grace had always acquiesced in it as the natural and established state of affairs, without any sense of superiority, but rather of being protected. She had a few alarms as to the results of Rachel's new immunities of age, and though never questioning the wisdom of her clever sister's conclusions, dreaded the effect on the mother, whom she had been forbidden to call mamma. " At their age it was affecting an interesting childishness."

Rachel had had the palm of cleverness conceded to her ever since she could recollect, when she read better at three years old than her sister at five, and ever after, through the days of education, had enjoyed, and exceeded in, the studies that were a toil to Grace. Subsequently, while Grace had contented herself with the ordinary course of unambitious feminine life, Rachel had thrown herself into the process of self-education with all her natural energy, and carried on her favourite studies by every means within her reach, until she considerably surpassed in acquirements and reflection all the persons with whom she came in frequent contact. It was a homely neighbourhood, a society well born, but of circumscribed interests and habits, and little connected with the great progressive world, where, however, Rachel's sympathies all lay, necessarily fed, however, by periodical literature, instead of by conversation or commerce with living minds.

She began by being stranded on the ignorance of those who surrounded her, and found herself isolated as a sort of pedant ; and as time went on, the narrowness of interests chafed her, and in like manner left her alone. As she grew

past girlhood, the *cui bono* question had come to interfere
with her ardour in study for its own sake, and she felt the
influence of an age eminently practical and sifting, but with
small powers of acting.   The quiet Lady Bountiful duties
that had sufficed her mother and sister were too small and
easy to satisfy a soul burning at the report of the great cry
going up to heaven from a world of sin and woe.   The
examples of successful workers stimulated her longings to be
up and doing, and yet the ever difficult question between
charitable works and filial deference necessarily detained her,
and perhaps all the more because it was not so much the fear
of her mother's authority as of her horror and despair, that
withheld her from the decisive and eccentric steps that she
was always feeling impelled to take.   Gentle Mrs. Curtis
had never been a visible power in her house, and it was
through their desire to avoid paining her that her government had been exercised over her two daughters ever since
their father's death, which had taken place in Grace's seven-
teenth year.   Both she and Grace implicitly accepted Rachel's
superiority as an unquestionable fact, and the mother, when
traversing any of her clever daughter's schemes, never disputed either her opinions or principles, only entreated that
these particular developments might be conceded to her own
weakness ; and Rachel generally did concede.   She could
not act ; but she could talk uncontradicted, and she hated
herself for the enforced submission to a state of things that
she despised.

This twenty-fifth birthday had long been anticipated as
the turning point when this submissive girlhood ought to
close, and the privileges of acting as well as thinking for
herself ought to be assumed.   Something to do was her cry,

and on this very day that something seemed to be cast in her
way. It was not ameliorating the condition of the masses,
but it was educating those who might ameliorate them ; and
Rachel gladly hailed the prospect of a vocation that might
be conducted without pain to her mother.

Young children of her own class were not exactly what
her dream of usefulness had devised ; but she had already a
decided theory of education, and began to read up with all
her might, whilst taking the lead in all the details of house
taking, servant hiring, &c. ; to which her regular occupations
of night school in the evening and reading to the lacemakers
by day, became almost secondary. In due time the arrival
of the ship was telegraphed, a hurried and affectionate note
followed, and, on a bright east-windy afternoon, Rachel
Curtis set forth to take up her mission. A telegram had
announced the arrival of the *Voluta*, and the train which
would bring the travellers to Avonchester. The Homestead
carriage was sent to meet them, and Rachel in it, to give her
helpless cousin assistance in this beginning of English habits.
A roomy fly had been engaged for nurses and children, and
Mrs. Curtis had put under the coachman's charge a parcel of
sandwiches, and instructed him to offer all the appliances for
making her own into an invalid carriage.

Full of warm tenderness to those who were to be dependent on her exertions, led by her good sense, Rachel paced
the platform till the engine rushed up, and she looked along
the line of windows, suddenly bewildered. Doors opened,
but gentlemen alone met her disappointed eye, until close to
her a soft voice said, " Rachel ! " and she saw a figure in
deep black close to her ; but her hand had been hardly
clasped before the face was turned eagerly to a tall, bearded

man, who was lifting out little boy after little boy, apparently in an endless stream, till at last a sleeping baby was brought out in the arms of a nurse.

" Good-bye. Thank you, oh, thank you. You will come soon. Oh, do come on now."

" Do come on now," was echoed by many voices.

" I leave you in good hands. Good-bye."

" Good-bye. Conrade dear, see what Cyril is doing ; never mind, Wilfred, the Major will come and see us ; run on with Coombe." This last was a respectable military-looking servant, who picked up a small child in one hand and a dressing-case in the other, and awaited orders.

There was a clinging to the Major by all the children, only ended by his finally precipitating himself into the carriage, and being borne off. Then came a chorus — " Mamma, let me go with you ;" " I'll go with mamma ;" " Me go with mamma ;" according to the gradations of age.

While Coombe and mamma decided the question by lifting the lesser ones into the fly, Rachel counted heads. Her mission exceeded her expectations. Here was a pair of boys in knickerbockers, a pair in petticoats, a pair in pelisses, besides the thing in arms. When the fly had been nearly crammed, the two knickerbockers and one pelisse remained for the carriage, quite against Rachel's opinion ; but " Little Wilfred can sit on my lap, he has not been well, poor little man," was quite conclusive ; and when Rachel suggested lying back to rest, there was a sweet, low laugh, and, " Oh, no thank you, Wilfred never tires me."

Rachel's first satisfaction was in seeing the veil disclose the face of eight years back ; the same soft, clear, olive skin ; delicate, oval face, and pretty deep-brown eyes, with the same imploring, earnest sweetness; no signs of having grown older; no sign of wear and tear, climate, or exertion; only the widow's dress and the presence of the great boys enhancing her soft youthfulness. The smile was certainly changed; it was graver, sadder, tenderer, and only conjured up by maternal affection or in grateful reply; and the blitheness of the young brow had changed to quiet pensiveness, but more than ever there was an air of dependence almost beseeching protection; and Rachel's heart throbbed with Britomart's devotion to her Amoret.

"Why wouldn't the Major come, mamma?"

"He will soon come, I hope, my dear."

Those few words gave Rachel a strong antipathy to the Major.

Then began a conversation under difficulties, Fanny trying to inquire after her aunt, and Rachel to detail the arrangements made for her at Myrtlewood, while the two boys were each accommodated with a window; but each moment they were claiming their mother's attention, or rushing across the ladies' feet to each other's window, treating Rachel's knees as a pivot, and vouchsafing not the slightest heed to her attempts at intelligent pointing out of the new scenes.

And Fanny made no apology, but seemed pleased, ready with answers and with eyes, apparently ignorant that Rachel's toes were less insensible than her own, and her heavy three-years-old Wilfred asleep on her lap all the time.

"She feeble, helpless, sickly!" thought Rachel, "I should have been less tired had I walked the twenty miles!"

She gave up talking in despair, and by the time the young gentlemen had tired themselves into quiescence, and began to eat the provisions, both ladies were glad to be allowed a little silence.

Coming over the last hill, Conrade roused at his mother's summons to look out at "home," and every word between them showed how fondly Avonmouth had been remembered far away.

"The sea!" said Fanny, leaning forwards to catch sight of the long grey line; "it is hard to believe we have been on it so long, this seems so much more my own."

"Yes," cried Rachel, "you are come to your own home, for us to take care of you."

"I take care of mamma! Major Keith said so," indignantly exclaimed Conrade.

"There's plenty of care for you both to take," said Fanny, half-smiling, half-sobbing. "The Major says I need not be a poor creature, and I will try. But I am afraid I shall be on all your hands."

Both boys drummed on her knee in wrath at her presuming to call herself a poor creature—Conrade glaring at Rachel as if to accuse her of the calumny.

"See the church," said Lady Temple, glad to divert the storm, and eagerly looking at the slender spire surmounting the bell-turret of a small building in early-decorated style, new, but somewhat stained by sea-wind, without having as yet acquired the tender tints of time. "How beautiful!" was her cry. "You were beginning the collection for it when I went away! How we used to wish for it."

"Yes, we did," said Rachel, with a significant sigh; but her cousin had no time to attend, for they were turning in a pepper-box lodge. The boys were told that they were arrived, and they were at the door of a sort of overgrown

Swiss cottage, where Mrs. Curtis and Grace stood ready to receive them.

There was a confusion of embraces, fondlings, and tears, as Fanny clung to the aunt who had been a mother to her—perhaps a more tender one than the ruling, managing spirit, whom she had hardly known in her childhood; but it was only for a moment, for Wilfred shrieked out in an access of shyness at Grace's attempt to make acquaintance with him; Francis was demanding, "Where's the orderly?" and Conrade looking brimful of wrath at any one who made his mother cry. Moreover, the fly had arrived, and the remainder had to be produced, named, and kissed—Conrade and Francis, Leoline and Hubert, Wilfred and Cyril, and little Stephana the baby. Really the names were a study in themselves, and the cousins felt as if it would be hopeless to endeavour to apply them.

Servants had been engaged conditionally, and the house was fully ready, but the young mother could hardly listen to her aunt's explanations in her anxiety that the little ones should be rested and fed, and she responded with semi-comprehending thanks, while moving on with her youngest in her arms, and as many hanging to her dress as could get hold of it. Her thanks grew more emphatic at the sight of cribs in inviting order, and all things ready for a meal.

"I don't drink tea with nurse," was Conrade's cry, the signal for another general outcry, untranquillized by soothings and persuasions, till the door was shut on the younger half of the family, and those who could not open it remained to be comforted by nurse, a soldier's widow, who had been with them from the birth of Conrade.

The Temple form of shyness seemed to consist in ignoring

strangers, but being neither abashed nor silenced, only resenting or avoiding all attempts at intercourse; and as the boys
rushed in and out of the rooms, exploring, exclaiming, and
calling mamma, to the interruption of all that was going on,
only checked for a few minutes by her uplifted hand and
gentle hush, Grace saw *her* mother so stunned and bewildered that she rejoiced in the fear of cold that had decided
that Rachel alone should spend the evening there.   Fanny
made some excuses; she longed to see more of her aunt, but
when they were a little more settled,—and as a fresh shout
broke out, she was afraid they were rather unruly,—she must
come and talk to her at the dear Homestead.   So kind of
Rachel to stay—not that the boys seemed to think so, as they
went racing in and out, stretching their ship-bound legs, and
taking possession of the minute shrubbery, which they scorned
for the want of gum-trees and parrots.

   " You won't mind, Rachel dear, I must first see about
baby;" and Rachel was left to reflect on her mission, while
the boys' feet cantered up and down the house, and one or
other of them would look in, and burst away in search of
mamma.

   Little more satisfactory was the rest of the evening, for the
boys took a great deal of waiting on at tea, and then some of
the party would not go to sleep in strange beds without long
persuasions and comfortings, till Fanny looked so weary that
it was plain that no conversation could have been hoped from
her, even if the baby had been less vociferous.   All that
could be done for her was to wish her good-night, and promise
to come down early.

   Come early !   Yes, Rachel might come, but what was the
use of that when Fanny was at the mercy of so many

claimants? She looked much better than the day before, and her sweet, soft welcome was most cordial and clinging. " Dear Rachel, it is like a dream to have you so near. I felt like the old life come back again to hear the surge of the sea all night, and know I should see you all so soon again."

" Yes, it is a great satisfaction to have you back in your old home, under our wing. I have a great deal to tell you about the arrangements."

" Oh yes ; thank you——"

" Mamma ! " roared two or three voices.

" I wanted to explain to you——" But Fanny's eye was roaming, and just then in burst two boys. " Mamma, nurse won't undo the tin box, and my ship is in it that the Major gave me."

" Yes, and my stuffed duck-bill, and I want it, mamma."

" My dear Con, the Major would not let you shout so loud about it, and you have not spoken to Aunt Rachel."

The boys did present their hands, and then returned to the charge. " Please order nurse to unpack it, mamma, and then Coombe will help us to sail it."

" Excuse me, dear Rachel," said Fanny, " I will first see about this."

And a very long seeing it was, probably meaning that she unpacked the box herself, whilst Rachel was deciding on the terrible spoiling of the children, and preparing a remonstrance.

" Dear Rachel, you have been left a long time."

" Oh, never mind that ; but, Fanny, you must not give way to those children too much ; they will be always—— Hark ! was that the door-bell ?"

It was, and the visitor was announced as " Mr. Touchett ;"

a small, dark, thin young clergyman he was, of a nervous manner, which, growing more nervous as he shook hands with Rachel, became abrupt and hesitating.

" My call is—is early, Lady Temple ; but I always pay my respects at once to any new parishioner—resident, I mean—in case I can be of any service."

" Thank you, I am very much obliged," said Fanny, with a sweet, gracious smile and manner that would have made him more at ease at once, if Rachel had not added, " My cousin is quite at home here, Mr. Touchett."

" Oh yes," he said, " so—so I understood."

" I know no place in England so well ; it is quite a home to me, so beautiful it is," continued Fanny.

" And you see great changes here."

" Changes so much for the better," said Fanny, smiling her winning smile again.

" One always expects more from improvements than they effect," put in Rachel, severely.

" You have a large young party," said Mr. Touchett, looking uneasily towards Lady Temple.

" Yes, I have half a dozen boys and one little girl."

" Seven ! " Mr. Touchett looked up half incredulous at the girlish contour of the gentle face, then cast down his eyes as if afraid he had been rude.   " Seven ! It is—it is a great charge."

" Yes, indeed it is," she said earnestly ; " and I am sure you will be kind enough to give your influence to help me with them—poor boys."

" Oh ! oh ! " he exclaimed. " anything I can do——" in such a transport of eager helpfulness that Rachel coldly said, " We are all anxious to assist in the care of the children."

He coloured up, and with a sort of effort at self-assertion, blurted out, " As the clergyman of the parish——," and there halted, and was beginning to look foolish, when Lady Temple took him up in her soft, persuasive way. " Of course we shall look to you so much, and you will be so kind as to let me know if there is any one I can send any broth to at any time."

" Thank you ; you are very good ; " and he was quite himself again. " I shall have the pleasure of sending you down a few names."

" I never did approve the broken victual system," began Rachel ; " it creates dependence."

" Come here, Hubert," said Fanny, beckoning a boy she saw at a distance, " come and shake hands with Mr. Touchett." It was from instinct rather than reason ; there was a fencing between Rachel and the curate that made her uncomfortable, and led her to break it off by any means in her power ; and though Mr. Touchett was not much at his ease with the little boy, this discussion was staved off. But again Mr. Touchett made bold to say that in case Lady Temple wished for a daily governess, he knew of a very desirable young person, a most admirable pair of sisters, who had met with great reverses ; but Rachel snapped him off shorter than ever. " We can decide nothing yet ; I have made up my mind to teach the little boys at present."

" Oh, indeed ! "

" It is very kind," said the perplexed Lady Temple.

" I beg your pardon ; I only thought, in case you were wishing for some one, that Miss Williams will be at liberty shortly."

" I do not imagine Miss Williams is the person to deal with

little boys," said Rachel. " In fact, I think that home teaching is always better than hired."

" I am so much obliged," said Fanny, as Mr. Touchett, after this defeat, rose up to take leave, and she held out her hand, smiled, thanked, and sent him away so much sweetened and gratified, that Rachel would have instantly begun dissecting him, but that a whole rush of boys broke in, and again engrossed their mother; and in the next lull, the uppermost necessity was of explaining about the servants who had been hired for the time, one of whom was a young woman whose health had given way over her lace pillow, and Rachel was eloquent over the crying evils of the system (everything was a system with Rachel) that chained girls to an unhealthy occupation in their early childhood, and made an overstocked market and underpaid workers—holding Fanny fast to listen by a sort of fascination in her overpowering earnestness, and great fixed eyes, which, when once their grasp was taken, would not release the victim; and this was a matter of daily occurrence on which Rachel felt keenly and spoke strongly.

" It is very sad. If you want to help the poor things, I will give anything I can."

" Oh, yes, thank you; but it is doleful merely to help them to linger out the remnant of a life consumed upon these cobwebs of vanity. It is the fountainhead that must be reached—the root of the system !"

Fanny saw, or rather felt, a boy making signs at the window, but durst not withdraw her eyes from the fascination of those eager ones. " Lace and lacemakers are facts," continued Rachel; " but if the middle men were exploded, and the excess of workers drafted off by some wholesome outlet, the price would rise, so that the remainder would be at leisure to fulfil the domestic offices of womanhood."

There was a great uproar above.

" I beg your pardon, dear Rachel," and away went Fanny.

" I do declare," cried Rachel, when Grace, having despatched her home-cares, entered the room a quarter of an hour after ; " poor Fanny's a perfect slave. One can't get in a word edgeways."

Fanny at last returned, but with her baby ; and there was no chance for even Rachel to assert herself while this small queen was in presence. Grace was devoted to infants, and there was a whole court of brothers vying with one another in picking up her constantly dropped toys, and in performing antics for her amusement. Rachel, desirous to be gracious and resigned, attempted conversation with one of the eldest pair, but the baby had but to look towards him, and he was at her feet.

On her departure, Rachel resumed the needful details of the arrangements respecting the house and servants, and found Lady Temple as grateful and submissive as ever, except that, when advised to take Myrtlewood for a term of seven years, she replied, that the Major had advised her not to bind herself down at once.

" Did you let him think we should quarrel ? "

" Oh, no, my dear ; but it might not agree with the children."

" Avonmouth ! Grace, do you hear what heresy Fanny has been learning ? Why, the proportion of ozone in the air here has been calculated to be five times that of even Aveton ! "

" Yes, dearest," said poor Fanny, very humbly, and rather

scared, "there is no place like Avonmouth, and I am sure the Major will think so when he has seen it."

" But what has he to do with your movements ?"

" Sir Stephen wished——" murmured Fanny.

"The Major is military secretary, and always settles our head-quarters, and no one interferes with him," shouted Conrade.

Rachel, suspicious and jealous of her rival, was obliged to let Fanny pass on to the next item, where her eager acceptance of all that was prescribed to her was evidently meant as compensation for her refractoriness about the house.

Grace had meanwhile applied herself to keeping off the boys, and was making some progress in their good graces, and in distinguishing between their sallow faces, dark eyes, and crisp, black heads. Conrade was individualized, not only by superior height, but by soldierly bearing, bright pride glancing in his eyes, his quick gestures, bold, decided words, and imperious tone towards all, save his mother—and whatever he was doing, his keen, black eye was always turning in search of her, he was ever ready to spring to her side to wait on her, to maintain her cause in rough championship, or to claim her attention to himself. Francis was thick-set, round-shouldered, bullet-headed and dull-eyed, in comparison, not aggressive, but holding his own, and not very approachable ; Leoline, thin, white-cheeked, large-eyed and fretful-lipped, was ready to whine at Conrade's tyranny and Francis's appropriations, but was graceful for Grace's protection, and more easy of access than his elders ; and Hubert was a handsome, placid child, the good boy, as well as the beauty of the family. The pair in the nursery hardly came on the stage, and the two elders would be quite sufficient for Mrs. Curtis, with whom the afternoon was to be spent.

The mother, evidently, considered it a very long absence, but she was anxious to see both her aunt and her own home, and set out, leaning on Rachel's arm, and smiling pleased though sad recognition of the esplanade, the pebbly beach, bathing machines and fishing boats, and pointing them out to her sons, who, on their side, would only talk of the much greater extent of Melbourne.

Within the gates of the Homestead, there was a steep, sharp bit of road, cut out in the red sandstone rock, and after a few paces she paused to rest with a sigh that brought Conrade to her side, when she put her arm round his neck, and leant on his shoulder; but even her two supporters could not prevent her from looking pale and exhausted.

"Never mind," she said, "this salt wind is delightful. How like old times it is!" and she stood gazing across the little steep lawn at the grey sea, the line of houses following the curve of the bay, and straggling up the valley in the rear, and the purple headlands projecting point beyond point, showing them to her boys, and telling their names.

"It is all ugly and cold," said Francis, with an ungracious shiver. "I shall go home to Melbourne when I'm a man."

"And you will come, mamma?" added Conrade.

He had no answer, for Fanny was in her aunt's arms; and, like mother and daughter, they clung to each other—more able to sympathize—more truly one together than the young widow could be with either of the girls.

As soon as Fanny had rested and enjoyed the home atmosphere downstairs, she begged to visit the dear old rooms, and carried Conrade through a course of recognitions through

the scarcely altered apartments. Only one had been much
changed, namely, the schoolroom, which had been stripped
of the kindly old shabby furniture that Fanny tenderly recollected, and was decidedly bare ; but a mahogany box stood
on a stand on one side ; there was a great accession of books,
and writing implements occupied the plain deal table in the
centre.

"What have you done to the dear old room—do you not
use it still ?" asked Fanny.

"Yes, I work here," said Rachel.

Vainly did Lady Temple look for that which women call
work.

"I have hitherto ground on at after-education and self-
improvement," said Rachel ; "now I trust to make my preparation available for others. I will undertake any of your
boys if you wish it."

"Thank you ; but what is that box ?"—in obedience to a
curious push and pull from Conrade.

"It is her dispensary," said Grace.

"Yes," said Rachel, "you are weak and nervous, and I
have just the thing for you."

"Is it homœopathy ?"

"Yes, here is my book. I have done great things in my
district, and should do more but for prejudice. There, this
globule is the very thing for your case ; I made it out last
night in my book. That is right, and I wanted to ask you
some questions about little Wilfred."

Fanny had obediently swallowed her own globule, but
little Wilfred was a different matter, and she retreated from
the large eyes and open book, saying that he was better, and
that Mr. Frampton should look at him ; but Rachel was not

to be eluded, and was in full career of elucidation to the
meanest capacity, when a sharp skirmish between the boys
ended the conversation, and it appeared that Conrade had
caught Francis just commencing an onslaught on the globules,
taking them for English sweetmeats of a minute description.

The afternoon passed with the strange heaviness well
known to those who find it hard to resume broken threads
after long parting. There was much affection, but not full
certainty what to talk about, and the presence of the boys
would have hindered confidence, even had they not incessantly occupied their mother. Conrade, indeed, betook himself to a book, but Francis was only kept out of mischief by
his constantly turning over pictures with him ; however, at
dark, Coombe came to convey them home, and the ladies of
the Homestead experienced a sense of relief. Rachel immediately began to talk of an excellent preparatory school.

" I was thinking of asking you," said Fanny, " if there is
any one here who would come as a daily governess."

" Oh !" cried Rachel, " these two would be much better
at school, and I would form the little ones, who are still
manageable."

" Conrade is not eight years old yet," said his mother in
an imploring tone, " and the Major said I need not part with
him till he has grown a little more used to English ways."

" He can read, I see," said Grace, " and he told me he had
done some Latin with the Major."

" Yes, he has picked up a vast deal of information, and on
the voyage the Major used to teach him out of a little pocket
Virgil. The Major said it would not be of much use at
school, as there was no dictionary ; but that the discipline
and occupation would be useful, and so they were. Conrade

will do anything for the Major, and indeed so will they all."

Three Majors in one speech, thought Rachel; and by way of counteraction she enunciated, " I could undertake the next pair of boys easily, but these two are evidently wanting school discipline."

Lady Temple feathered up like a mother dove over her nest.

" You do not know Conrade. He is so trustworthy and affectionate, dear boy, and they are both always good with me. The Major said it often hurts boys to send them too young."

" They are very young, poor little fellows," said Mrs. Curtis.

" And if they are forward in some things they are backward in others," said Fanny. " What Major Keith recommended was a governess, who would know what is generally expected of little boys."

" I don't like half measures," muttered Rachel. " I do not approve of encouraging young women to crowd the overstocked profession of governesses."

Fanny opened her brown eyes, and awaited the words of wisdom.

" Is it not a flagrant abuse," continued Rachel, " that whether she have a vocation or not, every woman of a certain rank, who wishes to gain her own livelihood, must needs become a governess ? A nursery maid must have a vocation, but an educated or half-educated woman has no choice ; and educator she must become, to her own detriment, and that of her victims."

" I always did think governesses often much to be pitied," said Fanny, finding something was expected of her.

"What's the use of pity if one runs on in the old groove? We must prevent the market from being drugged, by diverting the supply into new lines."

"Are there any new lines?" asked Fanny, surprised at the progress of society in her absence.

"Homœopathic doctresses," whispered Grace; who, dutiful as she was, sometimes indulged in a little fun, which Rachel would affably receive unless she took it in earnest, as in the present instance.

"Why not—I ask why not? Some women have broken through prejudice, and why should not others? Do you not agree with me, Fanny, that female medical men—I mean medical women—would be an infinite boon?"

"It would be very nice if they would never be nervous."

"Nerves are merely a matter of training. Think of the numbers that might be removed from the responsibility of incompetently educating! I declare that to tempt a person into the office of governess, instead of opening a new field to her, is the most short-sighted indolence."

"I don't want to tempt any one," said Fanny. "She ought to have been out before and be experienced, only she must be kind to the poor boys. I wanted the Major to inquire in London, but he said perhaps I might hear of some one here."

"That was right, my dear," returned her aunt. "A gentleman, an officer, could not do much in such a matter."

"He always does manage whatever one wants."

At which speech Rachel cast a glance towards her mother, and saw her look questioning and perplexed.

"I was thinking," said Grace, "that I believe the people

at the Cliff Cottages are going away, and that Miss Williams
might be at liberty."

" Didn't I know that Grace would come out with Miss
Williams?" exclaimed Rachel. " A regular eruption of the
Touchettomania. We have had him already advertising
her."

" Miss Williams!" said Mrs. Curtis. " Yes, she might
suit you very well. I believe they are very respectable
young women, poor things! I have always wished that
we could do more for them."

" Who?" asked Fanny.

" Certain pets of Mr. Touchett's," said Rachel; "some
cf the numerous ladies whose mission is that curatolatry
into which Grace would lapse but for my strenuous
efforts."

"I don't quite know why you call them his pets," said
Grace, " except that he knew their antecedents, and told us
about them."

" Exactly, that was enough for me. I perfectly understand
the meaning of Mr. Touchett's recommendations; and if
what Fanny wants is a commonplace sort of upper nursemaid, I dare say it would do." And Rachel leant back,
applied herself to her wood carving, and virtually retired
from the discussion.

" One sister is a great invalid," said Grace, " quite a
cripple, and the other goes out as a daily governess. They
are a clergyman's daughters, and once were very well off, but
they lost everything through some speculation of their brother.
I believe he fled the country under some terrible suspicion
of dishonesty; and though no one thought they had anything
to do with it, their friends dropped them because they would

not give him up, nor believe him guilty, and a little girl of his lives with them."

" Poor things ! " exclaimed Lady Temple. " I should very much like to employ this one. How very sad."

" Mrs. Grey told me that her children had never done so well with any one," said Mrs. Curtis. " She wanted to engage Miss Williams permanently, but could not induce her to leave her sister, or even to remove her to London, on account of her health."

" Do you know her, Grace ? " asked Fanny.

" I have called once or twice, and have been very much pleased with the sick sister ; but Rachel does not fancy that set, you see. I meet the other at the Sunday school ; I like her looks and manner very much, and she is always at the early service before her work."

" Just like a little mauve book ! " muttered Rachel.

Fanny absolutely stared. " You go, don't you, Rachel ? How we used to wish for it ! "

" You have wished and we have tried," said Rachel, with a sigh.

" Yes, Rachel," said Grace ; " but with all drawbacks, all disappointments in ourselves, it is a great blessing. We would not be without it."

" I could not be satisfied in relinquishing it voluntarily," said Rachel, " but I am necessarily one of the idle. Were I one of the occupied, *laborare est orare* would satisfy me, and that poor governess ought to feel the same. Think of the physical reaction of body on mind, and tell me if you could have the barbarity of depriving that poor jaded thing of an hour's sleep, giving her an additional walk, fasting, in all weathers, and preparing her to be savage with the children."

"Perhaps it refreshes her, and hinders her from being cross."

"Maybe she thinks so; but if she have either sense or ear, nothing would so predispose her to be cross as the squeaking of Mr. Touchett's penny-whistle choir."

"Poor Mr. Touchett," sighed Mrs. Curtis; "I wish he would not make such ambitious attempts."

"But you like the choral service," said Fanny, feeling as if everything had turned round. "When all the men of a regiment chant together you cannot think how grand it is, almost finer than the cathedral."

"Yes, where you can do it," said Rachel, "but not where you can't."

"I wish you would not talk about it," said Grace.

"I must, or Fanny will not understand the state of parties at Avonmouth."

"Parties! Oh, I hope not."

"My dear child, party spirit is another word for vitality. So you thought the church we sighed for had made the place all we sighed to see it, and ourselves too. Oh! Fanny, is this what you have been across the world for?"

"What is wrong?" asked Fanny, alarmed.

"Do you remember our axiom? Build your church, and the rest will take care of itself. You remember our scraping and begging, and how that good Mr. Davison helped us out and brought the endowment up to the needful point for consecration, on condition the incumbency was given to him. He held it just a year, and was rich, and could help out his bad health with a curate. But first he went to Madeira, and then he died, and there we are, a perpetual curacy of £70 a year, no resident gentry but ourselves, a fluctuating population mostly sick, our poor demoralized by them, and either crazed by dissent, or heathenized by their former distance from church. Who would take us? No more Mr. Davisons! There was no more novelty, and too much smartness to invite self-devotion. So we were driven from pillar to post till we settled down into this Mr. Touchett, as good a being as ever lived, working as hard as any two, and sparing neither himself nor any one else."

Fanny looked up prepared to admire.

" But he has two misfortunes. He was not born a gentleman, and his mind does not measure an inch across."

" Rachel, my dear, it is not fair to prejudice Fanny ; I am sure the poor man is very well-behaved."

" Mother ! would you be calling the ideal Anglican priest, poor man ? "

" I thought he was quite gentlemanlike," added Fanny.

" Gentlemanlike ! ay, that's it," said Rachel, " just so like as to delight the born curatolatress, like Grace and Miss Williams."

" Would it hurt the children ? " asked Fanny, hardly comprehending the tremendous term.

" Yes, if it infected you," said Rachel, intending some playfulness. " A mother of contracted mind forfeits the allegiance of her sons."

" Oh, Rachel, I know I am weak and silly," said the gentle young widow, terrified, " but the Major said if I only tried to do my duty by them I should be helped."

" And I will help you, Fanny," said Rachel. " All that is requisite is good sense and firmness, and a thorough sense of responsibility."

" That is what is so dreadful. The responsibility of all

those dear fatherless boys, and if—if I should do wrong by
them."

Poor Fanny fell into an uncontrollable fit of weeping at
the sense of her own desolation and helplessness, and Mrs.
Curtis came to comfort her, and tell her affectionately of
having gone through the like feelings, and of the repeated
but most comfortable words of promise to the fatherless and
the widow—words that had constantly come before the
sufferer, but which had by no means lost their virtue by
repetition, and Fanny was soothed with hearing instances of
the special Providence over orphaned sons, and their love
and deference for their mother. Rachel, shocked and distressed at the effect of her sense, retired out of the conversation, till at the announcement of the carriage for Lady
Temple, her gentle cousin cheered up, and feeling herself
to blame for having grieved one who only meant aid and
kindness, came to her and fondly kissed her forehead, saying,
" I am not vexed, dear Rachel, I know you are right. I am
not clever enough to bring them up properly, but if I try
hard, and pray for them, it may be made up to them. And
you will help me, Rachel dear," she added, as her readiest
peace-offering for her tears, and it was the most effectual, for
Rachel was perfectly contented as long as Fanny was dependent on her, and allowed her to assume her mission,
provided only that the counter influence could be averted,
and this Major, this universal referee, be eradicated from her
foolish clinging habits of reliance before her spirits were
enough recovered to lay her heart open to danger.

But the more Rachel saw of her cousin, the more she
realized this peril. When she went down on Monday
morning to complete the matters of business that had been

slurred over on the Saturday, she found that Fanny had not the slightest notion what her own income was to be. All she knew was that her General had left everything unreservedly to herself, except £100 and one of his swords to Major Keith, who was executor to the will, and had gone to London to "see about it," by which word poor Fanny expressed all the business that her maintenance depended on. If an old general wished to put a major in temptation, could he have found a better means of doing so? Rachel even thought that Fanny's incapacity to understand business had made her mistake the terms of the bequest, and that Sir Stephen must have secured his property to his children; but Fanny was absolutely certain that this was not the case, for she said the Major had made her at once sign a will dividing the property among them, and appointing himself and her Aunt Curtis their guardians. "I did not like putting such a charge on my dear aunt," said Fanny, "but the Major said I ought to appoint a relation, and I had no one else! And I knew you would all be good to them, if they had lost me too, when baby was born."

"We would have tried," said Rachel, a little humbly, "but oh! I am glad you are here, Fanny!"

Nothing could of course be fixed till the Major had "seen about it." After which he was to come to let Lady Temple know the result; but she believed he would first go to Scotland to see his brother. He and his brother were the only survivors of a large family, and he had been on foreign service for twelve years, so that it would be very selfish to wish him not to take full time at home. "Selfish," thought Rachel; "if he will only stay away long enough, you shall learn, my dear, how well you can do without him!"

The boys had interrupted the conversation less than the previous one, because the lesser ones were asleep, or walking out, and the elder ones having learnt that a new week was to be begun steadily with lessons, thought it advisable to bring themselves as little into notice as possible; but fate was sure to pursue them sooner or later, for Rachel had come down resolved on testing their acquirements, and deciding on the method to be pursued with them; and though their mamma, with a certain instinctive shrinking both for them and for herself, had put off the ordeal to the utmost by listening to all the counsel about her affairs, it was not to be averted.

"Now, Fanny, since it seems that more cannot be done at present, let us see about the children's education. Where are their books?"

"We have very few books," said Fanny, hesitating; "we had not much choice where we were."

"You should have written to me for a selection."

"Why—so we would, but there was always a talk of sending Conrade and Francis home. I am afraid you will think them very backward, dear Rachel, especially Francie; but it is not their fault, dear children, and they are not used to strangers," added Fanny, nervously.

"I do not mean to be a stranger," said Rachel.

And while Fanny, in confusion, made loving protestations about not meaning *that*, Rachel stepped out upon the lawn, and in her clear voice called "Conrade, Francis!" No answer. She called "Con-rade" again, and louder, then turned round with "where can they be—not gone down on the beach?"

"Oh, dear no, I trust not," said the mother, flurried,

and coming to the window with a call that seemed to Rachel's ears like the roar of a sucking dove.

But from behind the bushes forth came the two young gentlemen, their black garments considerably streaked with the green marks of laurel climbing.

"Oh, my dears, what figures you are! Go to Coombe and get yourselves brushed, and wash your hands, and then come down, and bring your lesson books."

Rachel prognosticated that these preparations would be made the occasion of much waste of time; but she was answered, and with rather surprised eyes, that they had never been allowed to come into the drawing-room without looking like little gentlemen.

"But you are not living in state here," said Rachel; "I never could enter into the cult some people, mamma especially, pay to their drawing-room."

"The Major used to be very particular about their not coming to sit down untidy," said Fanny. "He said it was not good for anybody."

Martinet! thought Rachel, nearly ready to advocate the boys making no toilette at any time; and the present was made to consume so much time that, urged by her, Fanny once more was obliged to summon her boys and their books.

It was not an extensive school library—a Latin grammar, an extremely dilapidated spelling-book, and the fourth volume of Mrs. Marcet's "Little Willie." The other three—one was unaccounted for, but Cyril had torn up the second, and Francis had thrown the first overboard in a passion. Rachel looked in dismay. "I don't know what can be done with these!" she said.

"Oh, then we'll have holidays till we have got books,

mamma," said Conrade, putting his hands on the sofa, and imitating a kicking horse.

" It is very necessary to see what kind of books you ought to have," returned Rachel. " How far have you gone in this ? "

" I say, mamma," reiterated Conrade, " we can't do lessons without books."

"Attend to what your Aunt Rachel says, my dear; she wants to find out what books you should have."

" Yes, let me examine you."

Conrade came most inconveniently close to her; she pushed her chair back; he came after her. His mother uttered a remonstrating, " My dear ! "

"I thought she wanted to examine me," quoth Conrade. " When Dr. M'Vicar examines a thing, he puts it under a microscope."

It was said gravely, and whether it were malice or simplicity, Rachel was perfectly unable to divine, but she thought anyway that Fanny had no business to laugh, and explaining the species of examination that she intended, she went to work. In her younger days she had worked much at schools, and was really an able and spirited teacher, liking the occupation ; and laying hold of the first book in her way, she requested Conrade to read. He obeyed, but in such a detestable gabble that she looked up appealingly to Fanny, who suggested, " My dear, you can read better than that." He read four lines, not badly, but then broke off, " Mamma, are not we to have ponies ? Coombe heard of a pony this morning; it is to be seen at the ' Jolly Mariner,' and he will take us to look at it."

" The ' Jolly Mariner ! ' It is a dreadful place, Fanny ; you never will let them go there ? "

"My dear, the Major will see about your ponies when he comes."

"We will send the coachman down to inquire," added Rachel.

"He is only a civilian, and the Major always chooses our horses," said Conrade.

"And I am to have one too, mamma," added Francis. "You know I have been out four times with the staff, and the Major said I could ride as well as Con!"

"Reading is what is wanted now, my dear, go on."

Five lines more; but Francis and his mother were whispering together, and of course Conrade stopped to listen. Rachel saw there was no hope but in getting him alone, and at his mother's reluctant desire, he followed her to the dining-room; but there he turned dogged and indifferent, made a sort of feint of doing what he was told, but whether she tried him in arithmetic, Latin, or dictation, he made such ludicrous blunders as to leave her in perplexity whether they arose from ignorance or impertinence. His spelling was phonetic to the highest degree, and though he owned to having done sums, he would not, or did not answer the simplest question in mental arithmetic. "Five apples and eight apples, come, Conrade, what will they make?"

"A pie."

That was the hopeful way in which the examination proceeded, and when Rachel attempted to say that his mother would be much displeased, he proceeded to tumble head over heels all round the room, as if he knew better; which performance broke up the *séance*, with a resolve on her part that when she had the books she would not be so beaten. She tried Francis, but he really did know next to nothing, and

whenever he came to a word above five letters long stopped
short, and when told to spell it, said, "Mamma never made
him spell;" also muttering something depreciating about
civilians.

Rachel was a woman of perseverance. She went to the
bookseller's, and obtained a fair amount of books, which she
ordered to be sent to Lady Temple's. But when she came
down the next morning, the parcel was nowhere to be found.
There was a grand interrogation, and at last it turned out to
have been safely deposited in an empty dog-kennel in the
back yard. It was very hard on Rachel that Fanny giggled
like a school-girl, and even though ashamed of herself and
her sons, could not find voice to scold them respectably. No
wonder, after such encouragement, that Rachel found her
mission no sinecure, and felt at the end of her morning's
work much as if she had been driving pigs to market, though
the repetition was imposing on the boys a sort of sense of fate
and obedience, and there was less active resistance, though
learning it was not, only letting teaching be thrown at them.
All the rest of the day, except those two hours, they ran wild
about the house, garden, and beach—the latter place under
the inspection of Coombe, whom, since the "Jolly Mariner"
proposal, Rachel did not in the least trust ; all the less when
she heard that Major Keith, whose soldier-servant he had
originally been, thought very highly of him. A call at
Myrtlewood was formidable from the bear-garden sounds, and
delicate as Lady Temple was considered to be, unable to walk
or bear fatigue, she never appeared to be incommoded by the
uproar in which she lived, and had even been seen careering
about the nursery, or running about the garden, in a way that
Grace and Rachel thought would tire a strong woman.   As

to be affectionate and grateful, and to be pretty and gracious at the dinner parties. Even in her mother's short and sudden illness, the one thought of both the patient and the General had been to spare Fanny, and she had been scarcely made aware of the danger, and not allowed to witness the suffering. The chivalrous old man who had taken on himself the charge of her, still regarded the young mother of his children as almost as much of a baby herself, and devoted himself all the more to sparing her trouble, and preventing her from feeling more thrown upon her by her mother's death. The notion of training her to act alone never even occurred to him, and when he was thrown from his horse, and carried into a wayside-hut to die, his first orders were that no hurried message might be sent to her, lest she might be startled and injured by the attempt to come to him. All he could do for her was to leave her in the charge of his military secretary, who had long been as a son to him. Fanny told her aunt with loving detail all that she had heard from Major Keith of the brave old man's calm and resigned end—too full of trust even to be distressed with alarms for the helpless young wife and children, but committing them in full reliance to the care of their Father in heaven, and to the present kindness of the friend who stood by his pillow.

The will, which not only Rachel but her mother thought strangely unguarded, had been drawn up in haste, because Sir Stephen's family had outgrown the provisions of a former one, which had besides designated her mother, and a friend since dead, as guardians. Haste, and the conscious want of legal knowledge, had led to its being made as simple as possible, and as it was, Sir Stephen had scarcely had the power to sign it.

It was Major Keith who had borne the tidings to the poor
little widow, and had taken the sole care of the boys during
the sad weeks of utter prostration and illness.   Female
friends were with her, and tended her affectionately, but if
exertion or thought were required of her, the Major had to
be called to her sofa to awaken her faculties, and she always
awoke to attend to his wishes, as though he were the channe
of her husband's.   This state of things ended with the birth
of the little girl, the daughter that Sir Stephen had so
much wished for, coming too late to be welcomed by him, but
awakening her mother to tearful joy and renewed powers of
life.   The nine months of little Stephana's life had been a
time of continual change and variety, of new interests and
occupations, and of the resumption of a feeling of health
which had scarcely been tasted since the first plunge into
warm climates.   Perhaps it was unreasonable to expect to
find Fanny broken down ; and she talked in her own simple
way with abundant overflowing affection of her husband ;
but even Mrs. Curtis thought it was to her more like the loss
of her own father than of the father of her children ; and
though not in the least afraid of anything unbecoming in her
gentle, retiring Fanny, still felt that it was more the charge
of a girl than of a widow, dreaded the boys, dreaded their
fate, and dreaded the Major more.

During this drive, Grace and Rachel had the care of the
elder boys, whom Rachel thought safer in her keeping than
in Coombe's.   A walk along the cliffs was one resource for
their amusement, but it resulted in Conrade's climbing into
the most break-neck places, by preference selecting those
that Rachel called him out of, and as all the others thought
it necessary to go after him, the jeopardy of Leoline and

Hubert became greater than it was possible to permit ; so Grace took them by the hands, and lured them home with promises of an introduction to certain white rabbits at the lodge. After their departure, their brothers became infinitely more obstreperous. Whether it were that Conrade had some slight amount of consideration for the limbs of his lesser followers, or whether the fact were—what Rachel did not remotely imagine—that he was less utterly unmanageable with her sister than with herself, certain it is that the brothers went into still more intolerable places, and treated their guardian as ducklings treat an old hen. At last they quite disappeared from the view round a projecting point of rock, and when she turned it, she found a battle royal going on over an old lobster-pot—Conrade hand to hand with a stout fisher-boy, and Francis and sundry amphibious creatures of both sexes exchanging a hail of stones, water-smoothed brick-bats, cockle-shells, fishes' backbones, and other un-savoury missiles. Abstractedly, Rachel had her theory that young gentlemen had better scramble their way among their poor neighbours, and become used to all ranks ; but when it came to witnessing an actual skirmish when she was respon-sible for Fanny's sons, it was needful to interfere, and in equal dismay and indignation she came round the point. The light artillery fled at her aspect, and she had to catch Francis's arm in the act of discharging after them a cuttle-fish's white spine, with a sharp " For shame ; they are running away ! Conrade, Zack, have done !"

Zack was one of her own scholars, and held her in respect. He desisted at once, and with a touch of his rough forelock, looked sheepish, and said, " Please, ma'am, he was meddling with our lobster-pot."

" I wasn't doing any harm," said Conrade. " I was just looking in, and they all came and shied stones at us."

" I don't care how the quarrel began," said Rachel. " You would not have run into it if you had been behaving properly. Zack was quite right to protect his father's property, but he might have been more civil. Now shake hands, and have done with it."

" Not shake hands with a low boy," growled Francis. But happily Conrade was of a freer spirit, and in spite of Rachel's interference, had sense enough to know himself in the wrong. He held out his hand, and when the ceremony had been gone through, put his hands in his pockets, produced a shilling, and said, " There, that's in case I did the thing any harm." Rachel would have preferred Zachary's being above its acceptance, but he was not, and she was thankful that a wood path offered itself, leading through the Homestead plantations away from the temptations and perils of the shore.

That the two boys, instead of listening to her remonstrance, took to punching and kicking one another, was a mitigated form of evil for which she willingly compounded, having gone through so much useless interference already, that she felt as if she had no spirit left to keep the peace, and that they must settle their little affairs between themselves. It was the most innocent diversion in which she could hope to see them indulge. She only desired that it might last them past a thrush's nest, in the hedge between the park and plantation, a somewhat treasured discovery of Grace's. No such good luck. Either the thrush's imprudence or Grace's visits had made the nest dangerously visible, and it was proclaimed with a shout. Rachel, in hot haste, warned them against taking birds'-nests in general, and that in particular.

" Nests are made to be taken," said Francis.

" I've got an egg of all the Australian birds the Major could get me," said Conrade, " and I mean to have all the English ones."

" Oh, one egg ; there's no harm in taking that ; but this nest has young birds."

The young birds must of course be seen, and Rachel stood by with despairing frowns, commands, and assurances of their mother's displeasure, while they peeped in, tantalized the gaping yellow throats, by holding up their fingers, and laid hands on the side of the nest, peeping at her with laughing, mischievous eyes, enjoying her distress. She was glad at last to find them coming away without the nest, and after crossing the park, arrived at the house, tired out, but with two hours of the boys still on her hands. They, however, were a little tired, too ; and, further, Grace had hunted out the old bowls, much to the delight of the younger ones. This sport lasted a good while, but at last the sisters, who had relaxed their attention a little, perceived that Conrade and Hubert were both missing, and on Rachel's inquiry where they were, she received from Francis that elegant stock answer, " in their skins." However, they came to light in process of time, the two mothers returned home, and Mrs. Curtis and Grace had the conversation almost in their own hands. Rachel was too much tired to do anything but read the new number of her favourite " Traveller's Magazine," listening to her mother with one ear, and gathering additional impressions of Sir Stephen Temple's imprudence, and the need of their own vigilance. To make Fanny feel that she could lean upon some one besides the military secretary, seemed to be the great object, and she was so confiding and affectionate with her own kin, that there were great hopes. Those boys were an infliction, no doubt, but, thought Rachel, "there is always an ordeal at the beginning of one's mission. I am mastering them by degrees, and should do so sooner if I had them in my own hands, and no more worthy task can be done than training human beings for their work in this world; so I must be willing to go through a little while I bring them into order, and fit their mother for managing them."

She spent the time before breakfast the next morning in a search among the back numbers of the " Traveller's Magazine " for a paper upon "Educational Laws," which she thought would be very good reading for Fanny. Her search had been just completed when Grace returned home from church, looking a good deal distressed. " My poor thrushes have not escaped, Rachel," she said; " I came home that way to see how they were going on, and the nest is torn out, one poor little fellow lying dead below it."

" Well, that is much worse than I expected !" burst out Rachel. " I did think that boy Conrade would at least keep his promises." And she detailed the adventure of the previous day, whence the conclusion was but too evident. Grace, however, said in her own sweet manner that she believed boys could not resist a nest, and thought it mere womanhood to intercede for such lawful game. She thought it would be best to take no notice, it would only distress Fanny, and make " the mother " more afraid of the boys than she was already, and she doubted the possibility of bringing it home to the puerile conscience.

" That is weak ! " said Rachel. " I received the boy's word, and it is my business to deal with the breach of promise."

So down went Rachel, and finding the boys rushing about the garden, according to their practice, before her arrival, she summoned Conrade, and addressed him with, " Well, Conrade, I knew that you were violent and disobedient, but I never expected you to fail in your honour as a gentleman."

" I'll thrash any one who says I have," hotly exclaimed Conrade.

" Then you must thrash me. You gave your word to me not to take your Aunt Grace's thrush's nest."

" And I didn't," said Conrade, boldly.

But Rachel, used to flat denials at the village-school, was not to be thus set aside. " I am shocked at you, Conrade," she said. " I know your mamma will be exceedingly grieved. You must have fallen into very sad ways to be able to utter such a bold untruth. You had better confess at once, and then I shall have something to tell her that will comfort her."

Conrade's dark face looked set as iron.

" Come ; tell me you are sorry you took the nest, and have broken your word, and told a falsehood."

Red colour flushed into the brown cheek, and the hands were clenched.

" There is not the smallest use in denying it. I know you took it when you and Hubert went away together. Your Aunt Grace found it gone this morning, and one of the poor little birds dead below. What have you done with the others ? "

Not a word.

" Then I grieve to say I must tell all to your mother."

There was a sort of smile of defiance, and he followed her. For a moment she thought of preventing this, and preparing Fanny in private, but recollecting that this would give him the opportunity of preparing Hubert to support his false-hood, she let him enter with her, and sought Lady Temple in the nursery.

" Dear Fanny, I am very sorry to bring you so much vexation. I am afraid it will be a bitter grief to you, but it is only for Conrade's own sake that I do it. It was a cruel thing to take a bird's-nest at all, but worse when he knew that his Aunt Grace was particularly fond of it ; and, be-sides, he had promised not to touch it, and now, saddest of all, he denies having done so."

" Oh, Conrade, Conrade !" cried Fanny, quite confounded, " You can't have done like this !"

" No, I have not," said Conrade, coming up to her, as she held out her hand, positively encouraging him, as Rachel thought, to persist in the untruth.

" Listen, Fanny," said Rachel. " I do not wonder that you are unwilling to believe anything so shocking, but I do not come without being only too certain." And she gave the facts, to which Fanny listened with pale cheeks and tearful eyes, then turned to the boy, whose hand she had held all the time, and said, " Dear Con, do pray tell me if you did it."

" I did not," said Conrade, wrenching his hand away, and putting it behind his back.

" Where's Hubert ?" asked Rachel, looking round, and much vexed when she perceived that Hubert had been within hearing all the time, though to be sure there was some little hope to be founded upon the simplicity of five years old.

" Come here, Hubert dear," said his mother ; " don't be frightened ; only come and tell me where you and Con went yesterday, when the others were playing at bowls."

Hubert hung his head, and looked at his brother.

" Tell," quoth Conrade. " Never mind her, she's only a civilian."

" Where did you go, Hubert ?"

" Con showed me the little birds in their nest."

" That is right, Hubert, good little boy. Did you or he touch the nest ?"

" Yes." Then, as Conrade started, and looked fiercely at him, " Yes you did, Con, you touched the inside to see what it was made of."

" But what did you do with it ?" asked Rachel.

" Left it there, up in the tree," said the little boy.

" There, Rachel !" said the mother, triumphantly.

" I don't know what you mean," said Rachel, angrily, "only that Conrade is a worse boy than I had thought him, and has been teaching his little brother falsehood."

The angry voice set Hubert crying, and little Cyril, who was very soft-hearted, joined in chorus, followed by the baby, who was conscious of something very disagreeable going on in her nursery. Thereupon, after the apparently most important business of comforting Miss Temple had been gone through, the court of justice adjourned, Rachel opening the door of Conrade's little room, and recommending solitary imprisonment there till he should be brought to confession. She did not at all reckon on his mother going in with him, and shutting the door after her. It was not the popular notion of solitary confinement, and Rachel was obliged to retire, and wait in the drawing-room for a quarter of an hour before Fanny came down; and then it was to say—

"Do you know, Rachel dear, I am convinced that it must be a mistake. Conrade assures me he never touched the nest."

"So he persists in it?"

"And indeed, Rachel dear, I cannot help believing him. If it had been Francie, now; but I never knew Conrade tell an untruth in his life."

"You never knew, because you always believe him."

"And it is not only me, but I have often heard the Major say he could always depend on Conrade's word."

Rachel's next endeavour was at gentle argument. "It must be dreadful to make such a discovery, but it was far worse to let deceit go on undetected; and if only they were firm——" At that moment she beheld two knickerbocker boys prancing on the lawn.

"Didn't you lock the door? Has he broken out? How audacious!"

"I let him come out," said Fanny; "there was nothing to shut him up for. I beg your pardon, dear Rachel; I am very sorry for the poor little birds and for Grace, but I am sure Conrade did not take it."

"How can you be so unreasonable, Fanny?—the evidence," and Rachel went over it all again.

"Don't you think," said Fanny, "that some boy may have got into the park?"

"My dear Fanny, I am sorry for you; it is quite out of the question to think so; the place is not a stone's-throw from Randall's lodge. It will be the most fatal thing in the world to let your weakness be imposed on in this way. Now that the case is clear, the boy must be forced to confession, and severely punished."

Fanny burst into tears.

" I am very sorry for you, Fanny. I know it is very painful ; I assure you it is so to me. Perhaps it would be best if I were to lock him up, and go from time to time to see if he is come to a better mind."

She rose up.

" No, no, Rachel !" absolutely screamed Fanny, starting up, " my boy hasn't done anything wrong, and I won't have him locked up ! Go away ! If anything is to be done to my boys, I'll do it myself : they haven't got any one but me. Oh, I wish the Major would come !"

" Fanny, how can you be so foolish ?—as if I would hurt your boys !"

" But you won't believe Conrade—my Conrade, that never told a falsehood in his life !" cried the mother, with a flush in her cheeks and a bright glance in her soft eyes. " You want me to punish him for what he hasn't done."

" How much alike mothers are in all classes of life," thought Rachel, and much in the way in which she would have brought Zack's mother to reason by threats of expulsion from the shoe-club, she observed, " Well Fanny, one thing is clear, while you are so weak as to let that boy go on in his deceit, unrepentant and unpunished, I can have no more to do with his education."

" Indeed," softly said Fanny, " I am afraid so, Rachel. You have taken a great deal of trouble, but Conrade declares he will never say a lesson to you again, and I don't quite see how to make him after this."

" Oh, very well ; then there's an end of it.   I am sorry for you, Fanny."

And away walked Rachel, and as she went towards the gate two artificial *jets d'eau*, making a considerable curve in the air, alighted, the one just before her, the other, better aimed, in the back of her neck.   She had too much dignity to charge back upon the offenders, but she went home full of the story of Fanny's lamentable weakness, and prognostications of the misery she was entailing on herself.   Her mother and sister were both much concerned, and thought Fanny extremely foolish ; Mrs. Curtis consoling herself with the hope that the boys would be cured and tamed at school, and begging that they might never be let loose in the park again.   Rachel could not dwell much longer on the matter, for she had to ride to Upper Avon Park to hold council on the books to be ordered for the book-club ; for if she did not go herself, whatever she wanted especially was always set aside as too something or other for the rest of the subscribers.

Mrs. Curtis was tired, and stayed at home ; and Grace spent the afternoon in investigations about the harrying of the thrushes, but, alas ! without coming a bit nearer the truth.   Nothing was seen or heard of Lady Temple till, at half-past nine, one of the midges, or diminutive flies used at Avonmouth, came to the door, and Fanny came into the drawing-room—wan, tearful, agitated.

" Dear Rachel, I am so afraid I was hasty ; I could not sleep without coming to tell you how sorry I am."

" Then you are convinced ?   I knew you would be."

" Oh, yes, I have just been sitting by him after he was gone to bed.   He never goes to sleep till I have done that, and he always tells me if anything is on his mind. I could not ask him again, it would have been insulting him; but he went over it all of himself, and owned he ought not to have put a finger on the edge of the nest, but he wanted so to see what it was lined with; otherwise he never touched it. He says, poor boy, that it was only your being a civilian that made you not able to believe him. I am sure you must believe him now."

Mrs. Curtis began, in her gentle way, about the difficulty of believing one's children in fault, but Lady Temple was entirely past accepting the possibility of Conrade's being to blame in this particular instance. It made her bristle up again, so that even Rachel saw the impossibility of pressing it, and trusted to some signal confutation to cure her of her infatuation. But she was as affectionate as ever, only wanting to be forgiven for the morning's warmth, and to assure dear Aunt Curtis, dear Grace, and dearest Rachel in particular, that there was no doing without them, and it was the greatest blessing to be near them.

" Oh! and the squirting, dear Rachel! I was so sorry when I found it out; it was only Francie and Leo. I was very angry with them for it, and I should like to make them ask pardon, only I don't think Francie would. I'm afraid they are very rude boys. I must write to the Major to find me a governess that won't be very strict with them, and if she could be an officer's daughter, the boys would respect her so much more."

CHAPTER III.

MACKAREL LANE.

" For I would lonely stand
  Uplifting my white hand,
  On a mission, on a mission,
  To declare the coming vision."
                    ELIZABETH BARRETT BROWNING.

" WELL, Grace, all things considered, perhaps I had better walk down with you to Mackarel Lane, and then I can form a judgment on these Williamses without committing Fanny."

" Then you do not intend to go on teaching?"

" Not while Conrade continues to brave me, and is backed up by poor Fanny."

" I might speak to Miss Williams after church, and bring her in to Myrtlewood for Fanny to see."

" Yes, that might do in time; but I shall make up my mind first. Poor Fanny is so easily led that we must take care what influences fall in her way."

" I always wished you would call."

" Yes, and I would not by way of patronage to please Mr. Touchett, but this is for a purpose; and I hope we shall find both sisters at home."

Mackarel Lane was at right angles to the shore, running up the valley of the Avon; but it soon ceased to be fishy, and became agricultural, owning a few cottages of very humble gentility, which were wont to hang out boards to attract lodgers of small means. At one of these Grace rang, and obtained admittance to a parlour with crazy French windows opening on a little strip of garden. In a large wheeled chair, between the fire and the window, surrounded by numerous little appliances for comfort and occupation, sat the invalid Miss Williams, holding out her hand in welcome to the guests.

" A fine countenance! what one calls a fine countenance ! " thought Rachel. " Is it a delusion of insipidity as usual ? The brow is good, massive, too much for the features, but perhaps they were fuller once ; eyes bright and vigorous, hazel, the colour for thought ; complexion meant to be brilliant brunette, a pleasant glow still ; hair with threads of grey. I hope she does not affect youth ; she can't be less than one or two and thirty ! Many people set up for beauties with far less claim. What is the matter with her ? It is not the countenance of deformity—accident, I should say. Yes, it is all favourable except the dress. What a material ! what a pattern ! Did she get it second-hand from a lady's-maid ? Will there be an incongruity in her conversation to match ? Let us see. Grace making inquiries—Quite at my best—Ah ! she is not one of the morbid sort, never thinking themselves better."

" I was afraid, I had not seen you out for some time."

" No ; going out is a troublesome business, and sitting in the garden answers the same purpose."

" Of air, perhaps, but hardly of change or of view."

" Oh ! I assure you there is a wonderful variety," she answered, with an eager and brilliant smile.

" Clouds and sunsets ? " asked Rachel, beginning to be interested.

" Yes, differing every day. Then I have the tamarisk and its inhabitants. There has been a tom-tit's nest every year since we came, and that provides us with infinite amusement. Besides the sea-gulls are often so good as to float high enough for me to see them. There is a wonderful charm in a circum-scribed view, because one is obliged to look well into it all."

" Yes ; eyes and no eyes apply there," said Rachel.

" We found a great prize, too, the other day. Rosie ! " At the call a brown-haired, brown-eyed child of seven, look-ing like a little fawn, sprang to the window from the outside. " My dear, will you show the sphynx to Miss Curtis ? "

The little girl daintily brought a box covered with net, in which a huge apple-green caterpillar, with dashes of bright colour on his sides, and a horny spike on his tail, was feasting upon tamarisk leaves. Grace asked if she was going to keep it. " Yes, till it buries itself," said the child. " Aunt Ermine thinks it is the elephant sphynx."

" I cannot be sure," said the aunt; " my sister tried to find a figure of it at Villars', but he had no book that gave the caterpillars. Do you care for those creatures ? "

" I like to watch them," said Grace, " but I know nothing about them scientifically ; Rachel does that."

" Then can you help us to the history of our sphynx ? " asked Miss Williams, with her pleasant look.

" I will see if I have his portrait," said Rachel, " but I doubt it. I prefer general principles to details."

" Don't you find working out details the best way of entering into general principles ? "

It was new to Rachel to find the mention of a general principle received neither with a stare nor a laugh ; and she gathered herself up to answer, " Naming and collecting is not science."

" And masonry is not architecture, but you can't have architecture without it."

" One can have broad ideas without all the petty work of flower botanists and butterfly naturalists."

" Don't you think the broad ideas would be rather of the hearsay order, at least to most people, unless their application were worked out in the trifle that came first to hand ? "

" Experimental philosophy," said Rachel, in rather a considering tone, as if the notion, when presented to her in plain English, required translation into the language of her thoughts.

" If you like to call it so," said Miss Williams, with a look of arch fun. " For instance, the great art of mud pie taught us the porous nature of clay, the expansive power of steam, etc. etc."

" You had some one to improve it to you ? "

" Oh dear no. Only afterwards, when we read of such things we remembered how our clay manufactures always burst in the baking unless they were well dried first."

" Then you had the rare power of elucidating a principle ? "

" No, not I. My brother had ; but I could only perceive the confirmation."

" This reminds me of an interesting article on the Edgeworth system of education in the 'Traveller's Review.' I will send it down to you."

" Thank you, but I have it here."

" Indeed ; and do you not think it excellent, and quite agree with it ? "

" Yes, I quite agree with it," and there was an odd look
in her bright transparent eyes that made Grace speculate
whether she could have heard that agreement with the Invalid
in the " Traveller's Review " was one of the primary articles
of faith acquired by Rachel.

But Grace, though rather proud of Rachel's falling under
the spell of Miss Williams' conversation, deemed an examination rather hard on her, and took the opportunity of
asking for her sister.

" She is generally at home by this time ; but this is her
last day at Cliff Cottages, and she was to stay late to help in
the packing up."

" Will she be at home for the present ? " asked Grace.

" Yes, Rose and I are looking forward to a festival of her."

Grace was not at all surprised to hear Rachel at once
commit herself with " My cousin, Lady Temple," and rush
into the matter in hand as if secure that the other Miss
Williams would educate on the principles of the Invalid ;
but full in the midst there was a sound of wheels and a ring
at the bell. Miss Williams quietly signed to her little attendant to put a chair in an accessible place, and in walked
Lady Temple, Mrs. Curtis, and the middle brace of boys.

" The room will be too full," was Grace's aside to her
sister, chiefly thinking of her mother, but also of their
hostess ; but Rachel returned for answer, " I must see about
it ; " and Grace could only remove herself into the verandah,
and try to attract Leoline and Hubert after her, but failing in
this, she talked to the far more conversible Rose about the
bullfinch that hung at the window, which loved no one but
Aunt Ermine, and scolded and pecked at every one else ;
and Augustus, the beloved tame toad, that lived in a hole

under a tree in the garden. Mrs. Curtis, considerate and tender-hearted, startled to find her daughter in the field, and wishing her niece to begin about her own affairs, talked common-place by way of filling up the time; and Rachel had her eyes free for a range of the apartment. The foundation was the dull, third-rate lodging-house, the superstructure told of other scenes. One end of the room was almost filled by the frameless portrait of a dignified clergyman, who would have had far more justice done to him by greater distance; a beautifully-painted miniature of a lady with short waist and small crisp curls, was the centre of a system of photographs over the mantel-piece; a large crayon sketch showed three sisters between the ages of six and sixteen, sentimentalizing over a flower-basket; a pair of water-colour drawings represented a handsome church and comfortable parsonage; and the domestic gallery was completed by two prints—one of a middle-aged county-member, the other one of Chalon's ladylike matrons in watered-silk aprons. With some difficulty Rachel read on the one the autograph, J. T. Beauchamp, and on the other the inscription, the Lady Alison Beauchamp. The table-cover was of tasteful silk patchwork, the vase in the centre was of red earthenware, but was encircled with real ivy leaves gummed on in their freshness, and was filled with wild flowers; books filled every corner; and Rachel felt herself out of the much-loathed region of common-place, but she could not recover from her surprise at the audacity of such an independent measure on the part of her cousin; and under cover of her mother's civil talk, said to Fanny, " I never expected to see you here."

" My aunt thought of it," said Fanny, "and as she seems to find the children too much——"

She broke off, for Mrs. Curtis had paused to let her introduce the subject, but poor Fanny had never taken the initiative, and Rachel did it for her by explaining that all had come on the same errand, to ask if Miss Williams would undertake the lessons of her nephews ; Lady Temple softly murmured under her veil something about hopes and too much trouble ; an appointment was made for the following morning, and Mrs. Curtis, with a general sensation of an oppressive multitude in a small room, took her leave, and the company departed, Fanny, all the way home, hoping that the other Miss Williams would be like her sister, pitying the cripple, wishing that the sisters were in the remotest degree military, so as to obtain the respect of the boys, and wondering what would be the Major's opinion.

"So many ladies ! " exclaimed little Rose. " Aunt Ermine, have they made your head ache ? "

"No, my dear, thank you, I am only tired. If you will pull out the rest for my feet, I will be quiet a little, and be ready for tea when Aunt Ailie comes."

The child handily converted the chair into a couch, arranging the dress and coverings with the familiarity of long use, and by no means shocked by the contraction and helplessness of the lower limbs, to which she had been so much accustomed all her life that it never even occurred to her to pity Aunt Ermine, who never treated herself as an object of compassion. She was thanked by a tender pressure on her hair, and then saying—

"Now I shall wish Augustus good night ; bring Violetta home from her play in the garden, and let her drink tea, and go to bed."

Ah, Violetta, purchased with a silver groat, what was not

your value in Mackarel Lane ? Were you not one of its most considered inhabitants, scarcely less a child of Aunt Ermine and Aunt Alison than their Rosebud herself ?

Murmur, murmur, rippled the child's happy low-toned monologue directed to her silent but sufficient playmate, and so far from disturbing the aunt, that more than one smile played on her lips at the quaint fancies, and at the well of gladness in the young spirit, which made day after day of the society of a cripple and an old doll, one constant song of bliss, one dream of bright imaginings. Surely it was an equalization of blessings that rendered little lonely Rose, motherless and well nigh fatherless, poor, with no companion but a crippled aunt, a bird and a toad, with scarcely a toy, and never a party of pleasure, one of the most joyous beings under the sun, free from occasions of childish troubles, without collisions of temper, with few contradictions, and with lessons rather pleasure than toil. Perhaps Ermine did not take into account the sunshiny content and cheerfulness that made herself a delightful companion and playfellow, able to accept the child as her solace, not her burthen.

Presently Rose looked up, and meeting the bright pleasant eyes, observed—" Violetta has been very good, and said all her lessons quite perfect, and she would like to sit up till her Aunt Ailie comes home. Do you think she may ? "

" Will she not be tired to-morrow ? "

" Oh, then she will be lazy, and not get up when she is called, till I pull all the clothes off, and that will be fun."

" Or she may be fretful now ? "

A series of little squeaks ensued, followed by " Now, my love ; that is taking a very unfair advantage of my promise.

You will make your poor Aunt Ermine's head ache, and I shall have to send you to bed."

" Would not a story pass away the time ? "

" You tell it, Aunt Ermine ; your stories are always the best. And let there be a fairy in it ! "

The fairy had nearly performed her part, when the arrival took place, and Rose darted forward to receive Aunt Ailie's greeting kiss.

" Yes, Rosie—yes, Violetta ; what do you think I have got for you ? "

And out came a doll's chair with a broken leg, condemned by the departing pupils, and granted with a laugh to the governess's request to take it to her little niece ; but never in its best days had the chair been so prized. It was introduced to Violetta as the reward of virtue for having controlled her fretfulness, and the repair of its infirmity was the first consideration that occupied all the three. After all, Violetta's sitting posture was, as Alison observed, an example of the inclined plane, but that was nothing to Rose, and the *séance* would have been indefinitely prolonged, but for considerations for Violetta's health.

The sisters were alike, and Alison had, like her elder, what s emphatically called countenance, but her features were less chiselled, and her dark straight brows so nearly met that, as Rose had once remarked, they made a bridge of one arch instead of two. Six years younger, in full health, and daily battling with the world, Alison had a remarkable look of concentration and vigour, her upright bearing, clear decided speech, and glance of kindness won instant respect and reliance, but her face missed the radiant beamy brightness of her sister's ; her face was sweet and winning, but it was not habitual with her, and there was about her a look as if some terrible wave of grief or suffering had swept over her ere yet the features were fully fixed, and had thus moulded her expression for life. But playfulness was the tone that reigned around Ermine's couch at ordinary moments, and beside her the grave Alison was lively, not with effort, but by infection.

"There," she said, holding up a cheque; "now we'll have a jubilee, and take you down under the East cliff, and we'll invest a shilling in 'Ivanhoe,' and Rose and Violetta shall open their ears!"

"And you shall have a respectable Sunday mantle."

"Oh, I dare say Julia will send us a box."

"Then you will have to put a label on your back, 'Second-hand!' or her velvet will be a scandal. I can't wear out that at home like this flagrant, flowery thing, that I saw Miss Curtis looking at as rather a disreputable article. There's preferment for you, Ailie! What do you think of a general's widow with six boys? She is come after you. We had a great invasion—three Curtises and this pretty little widow, and various sons!"

"Will she stay?"

"Most likely, for she is a relation of Mrs. Curtis, and comes to be near her. You are to call for inspection at eleven o'clock to-morrow, so I fear your holiday will be short."

"Well, the less play the less anxiety. How many drives will the six young gentlemen be worth to you?"

"I am afraid it will be at the cost of tough work to you; she looked to me too sweet a creature to have broken her sons in, but I should think she would be pleasant to deal with."

" If she be like Miss Curtis, I am sure she will."

" Miss Curtis ? My old friend you mean. She was rather suppressed to-day, and I began to comprehend the reason of the shudder with which Mr. Touchett speaks of the dogmatical young lady."

" I hope she did not overwhelm you ! "

" Oh, no ! I rather liked her; she was so earnest and spirited, I could fancy enjoying a good passage at arms with her if these were old times. But I hope she will not take the direction of your school-room, though she *is* an admirer of the educational papers in the 'Traveller.' "

And here the discussion was ended by the entrance of little Rose with the preliminaries of the evening meal, after which she went to bed, and the aunts took out books, work, and writing materials.

Alison's report the next day was—" Well, she is a very sweet creature. There is something indescribably touching in her voice and eyes, so soft and wistful, especially when she implores one not to be hard on those great scrambling boys of hers."

" So she is your fate ? "

" Oh, yes ; if there had been ten more engagements offered, I could not have helped accepting hers, even if it had not been on the best terms I have ever had."

" What ? "

" Seventy—for the hours between nine and five. Pretty well for a journeyman hack, is it not ? Indeed, the pretty thing's only fear seemed to be that she was requiring too much, and offering too little. No, not her *only* fear, for there is some major in the distance to whose approval everything must be subject—uncle or guardian, I suppose ; but he seemed to be rather an object of jealousy to the younger Miss Curtis, for every hint of wishing to wait for the Major made her press on the negotiations."

"Seventy ! I hope you will make it do, Ailie. It would be a great relief."

"And spare your brains not a little. Yes, I do trust to keeping it, for Lady Temple is delightful ; and as to the boys, I fancy it is only taming they want. The danger is, as Miss Rachel told me, whether she can bear the sight of the process. I imagine Miss Rachel herself has tried it, and failed."

"Past amateur work," said Ermine, smiling. "It really is lucky you had to turn governess, Ailie, or there would have been a talent thrown away."

"Stay till I have tried," said Alison, who had, however, had experience enough not to be much alarmed at the prospect. Order was wont to come with her presence, and she hardly knew the aspect of tumultuous idleness or insubordination to unenforced authority ; for her eye and voice in themselves brought cheerful discipline without constraint, and upheld by few punishments, for the strong influence took away the spirit of rebellion.

After her first morning's work she came home full of good auguries ; the boys had been very pleasant with her after the first ten minutes, and Conrade had gained her heart by his attention to his mother. He had, however, examined her minutely whether she had any connexion with the army, and looked grave on her disavowal of any relationship with soldiers ; Hubert adding, " You see, Aunt Rachel is only a civilian, and she hasn't any sense at all." And when Francis had been reduced to the much disliked process of spelling unknown words, he had muttered under his breath, "She was only a civilian." To which she had rejoined that " At least she knew thus much, that the first military duty was obedience," and Francis's instant submission proved that she had made a good shot. Of the Major she had heard much more. Everything was referred to him, both by mother and children, and Alison was the more puzzled as to his exact connexion with them. "I sometimes suspect," she said, " that he may have felt the influence of those winsome brown eyes and caressing manner, as I know I should if I were a man. I wonder how long the old general has been dead? No, Ermine, you need not shake your head at me. I don't mean even to let Miss Curtis tell me if she would. I know confidences from partizan relations are the most mischief-making things in the world."

In pursuance of this principle Alison, or Miss Williams, as she was called in her vocation, was always reserved and discreet, and though ready to talk in due measure, Rachel always felt that it was the upper, not the under current that was proffered. The brow and eyes, the whole spirit of the face, betokened reflection and acuteness, and Rachel wanted to attain to her opinions ; but beyond a certain depth there was no reaching. Her ways of thinking, her views of the children's characters, her estimate of Mr. Touchett—nay, even her tastes as to the Invalid's letters in the " Traveller's Review," remained only partially revealed, in spite of Rachel's best efforts at fishing, and attempting to set the example. " It really seemed," as she observed to Grace, " as if the more I talk, the less she says." At which Grace gave way to a small short laugh, though she owned the force of Rachel's maxim, that to bestow confidence was the way to provoke it ;

and forbore to refer to a certain delightful afternoon that
Rachel, in her childhood, had spent alone with a little girl
whom she had never discovered to be deaf and dumb. Still
Rachel had never been able to make out why Grace, with no
theories at all, got so many more confidences than she did.
She was fully aware of her sister's superior attractiveness to
common-place people, and made her welcome to stand first
with the chief of their kindred, and most of the clergy and
young ladies around. But it was hard that where Rachel
really liked and met half-way, the intimate confidence should
always be bestowed upon Grace, or even the mother. She
had yet to learn that the way to draw out a snail is not to
grasp its horns, and that halfway meeting is not to launch
one's self to the opposite starting point. Either her inquiries
were too point blank to invite detailed replies, or her own
communications absorbed her too much to leave room for a
return. Thus she told Miss Williams the whole story of the
thrush's nest, and all her own reflections upon the character-
istics it betokened ; and only afterwards, on thinking over
the conversation, perceived that she had elicited nothing but
that it was very difficult to judge in such cases, not even any
decided assent to her own demonstrations. It was true that
riots and breaches of the peace ceased while Miss Williams
was in the house, and learning and good manners were
being fast acquired ; but until Conrade's duplicity should be
detected, or the whole disposition of the family discussed
with herself, Rachel doubted the powers of the instructress.
It was true that Fanny was very happy with her, and only
regretted that the uncertainty of the Major's whereabouts precluded his being informed of the newly-found treasure ; but
Fanny was sure to be satisfied as long as her boys were happy

and not very naughty, and she cared very little about people's minds.

If any one did "get on" with the governess it was Grace, who had been the first acquaintance in the family, and met her often in the service of the parish, as well as in her official character at the Homestead. It so chanced that one Sunday afternoon they found themselves simultaneously at the door of the school-house, whence issued not the customary hum, but loud sounds of singing.

"Ah!" said Grace, "Mr. Touchett was talking of getting the choir master from Avoncester and giving up an afternoon to practice for Easter, but he never told me it was to be to-day."

On inquiry, it appeared that notice had been given in the morning, but not till after Miss Williams had gone home to fetch her little niece, and while Rachel was teaching her boys in the class-room out of hearing. It was one of the little bits of bad management that were sure to happen wherever poor Mr. Touchett was concerned; and both ladies feeling it easy to overlook for themselves, were thankful that it had not befallen Rachel. Alison Williams, thinking it far to walk either to the Homestead or Myrtlewood before church, proposed to Grace to come home with her, an offer that was thankfully accepted, with merely the scruple whether she should disturb the invalid.

"Oh, no, it would be a great pleasure; I always wish we could get more change and variety for her on Sunday."

"She is very self-denying to spare you to the school."

"I have often wished to give it up, but she never will let me. She says it is one of the few things we can do, and I see besides that it brings her fresh interests. She knows about all my class, and works for them, and has them to see her; and I am sure it is better for her, though it leaves her more hours alone with Rose."

" And the Sunday services are too long for her?"

" Not so much that, as that she cannot sit on those narrow benches unless two are put close together so that she can almost lie, and there is not room for her chair in the aisle on a Sunday. It is the greatest deprivation of all."

" It is so sad, and she is so patient and so energetic," said Grace, using her favourite monosyllable in peace, out of Rachel's hearing.

" You would say so, indeed, if you really knew her, or how she has found strength and courage for me through all the terrible suffering."

" Then does she suffer so much?"

" Oh, no, not now! That was in the first years."

" It was not always so."

" No, indeed! You thought it deformity! Oh, no, no! she was so beautiful."

" That she is still. I never saw my sister so much struck with any one. There is something so striking in her bright glance out of those clear eyes."

" Ah! if you had only seen her bloom before——"

" The accident?"

" I burnt her," said Alison, almost inaudibly.

" You! you, poor dear! How dreadful for you."

" Yes, I burnt her," said Alison, more steadily. " You ought not to be kind to me without knowing about it. It was an accident of course, but it was a fit of petulance. I threw a match without looking where it was going."

" It must have been when you were very young."

" Fourteen. I was in a naughty fit at her refusing to go to

the great musical meeting with us. We always used to go to stay at one of the canon's houses for it, a house where one was dull and shy; and I could not bear going without her, nor understand the reason."

"And was there a reason?"

"Yes, poor dear Ermine. She knew he meant to come there to meet her, and she thought it would not be right; because his father had objected so strongly, and made him exchange into a regiment on foreign service."

"And you did not know this?"

"No, I was away all the time it was going on, with my eldest sister, having masters in London. I did not come home till it was all over, and then I could not understand what was the matter with the house, or why Ermine was unlike herself, and papa restless and anxious about her. They thought me too young to be told, and the atmosphere made me cross and fretful, and papa was displeased with me, and Ermine tried in vain to make me good; poor patient Ermine, even then the chief sufferer!"

"I can quite imagine the discomfort and fret of being in ignorance all the time."

"Dear Ermine says she longed to tell me, but she had been forbidden, and she went on blaming herself and trying to make me enjoy my holidays as usual, till this dreadful day, when I had worried her intolerably about going to this music meeting, and she found reasoning only made me worse. She still wrote her note of refusal, and asked me to light the taper; I dashed down the match in a frenzy of temper and——"

She paused for breath, and Grace squeezed her hand.

"We did not see it at first, and then she threw herself

down and ordered me not to come near. Every one was
there directly, I believe, but it burst out again and again, and
was not put out till they all thought she had not an hour to
live. There was no pain, and there she lay, all calmness,
comforting us all, and making papa and Edward promise to
forgive me—me, who only wished they would kill me! And
the next day he came; he was just going to sail, and they
thought nothing would hurt her then. I saw him while he
was waiting, and never did I see such a fixed deathly face.
But they said she found words to cheer and soothe him."

"And what became of him?"

"We do not know. As long as Lady Alison lived (his
aunt) she let us hear about him, and we knew he was recovering from his wound. Then came her death, and then
my father's, and all the rest, and we lost sight of the Beauchamps. We saw the name in the Gazette as killed at Lucknow, but not the right Christian name nor the same rank;
but then, though the regiment is come home, we have heard
nothing of him, and though she has never spoken of him to
me, I am sure Ermine believes he is dead, and thinks of him
as part of the sunshine of the old Beauchamp days—the
sunshine whose reflection lasts one's life."

"He ought to be dead," said Grace.

"Yes, it would be better for her than to hear anything else
of him! He had nothing of his own, so there would have
been a long waiting; but his father and brother would not
hear of it, and accused us of entrapping him, and that
angered my father. For our family is quite good, and we
were very well off then. My father had a good private
fortune besides the Rectory at Beauchamp; and Lady Alison,
who had been like a mother to us ever since our own died,

quite thought that the prospect was good enough, and I believe got into a great scrape with her family for having promoted the affair."

" Your squire's wife ? "

" Yes, and Julia and Ermine had come every day to learn lessons with her daughters. I was too young; but as long as she lived we were all like one family. How kind she was! How she helped us through those frightful weeks ! "

" Of your sister's illness ? It must have lasted long ? "

" Long ? Oh longer than long ! No one thought of her living. The doctors said the injury was too extensive to leave any power of rallying; but she was young and strong, and did not die in the torture, though people said that such an existence as remained to her was not worth the anguish of struggling back to it. I think my father only prayed that she might suffer less, and Julia stayed on and on, thinking each day would be the last, till Dr. Long could not spare her any longer; and then Lady Alison nursed her night after night and day after day, till she had worn herself into an illness, and when the doctors spoke of improvement, we only perceived worse agony. It was eight months before she was even lifted up in bed, and it was years before the burns ceased to be painful or the constitution at all recovered the shock ; and even now weather tells on her, though since we have lived here she has been far better than I ever dared to hope."

" Then you consider her still recovering ? "

" In general health she is certainly greatly restored, and has strength to attempt more, but the actual injury, the contraction, can never be better than now. When we lived at Richmond she had constantly the best advice, and we were told that nothing more could be hoped for."

"I wonder more and more at her high spirits. I suppose that was what chiefly helped to carry her through?"

"I have seen a good many people," said Alison, pausing, "but I never did see any one so happy! Others are always wanting something; she never is. Every enjoyment seems to be tenfold to her what it is to other people; she sees the hopeful side of every sorrow. No burthen is a burthen when one has carried it to her."

As Alison spoke, she pushed open the narrow green door of the little lodging-house, and there issued a weak, sweet sound of voices: "The strain upraise of joy and praise." It was the same that had met their ears at the school-door, but the want of body in the voices was fully compensated by the heartfelt ring, as if here indeed was praise, not practice.

"Aunt Ailie! O Aunt Ailie!" cried the child, as the room-door opened and showed the little choir, consisting of herself, her aunt, and the small maid of the house, "you should not have come; you were not to hear us till Trinity Sunday."

Explanations were given, and Miss Curtis was welcomed, but Alison, still too much moved for ordinary conversation, slipped into the bedroom adjoining, followed by her sister's quick and anxious eye, and half-uttered inquiry.

"I am afraid it is my fault," said Grace; "she has been telling me about your accident."

"Poor Ailie," said Ermine, "she never *will* receive kindness without having that unlucky story out! It is just one of the things that get so cruelly exaggerated by consequences. It was one moment's petulance that might have caused a fright and been forgotten ever after, but for those chemicals. Ah! I see, she said nothing about them, because they were

Edward's. They were some parcels for his experiments, gun cotton and the like, which were lying in the window till he had time to take them upstairs. We had all been so long threatened with being blown up by his experiments that we had grown callous and careless, and it served us right!" she added, stroking the child's face as it looked at her, earnest to glean fresh fragments of the terrible half-known tale of the past. "Yes, Rosie, when you go and keep house for papa on the top of the Oural Mountains, or wherever it may be, you are to remember that if Aunt Ermine had not been in a foolish, inattentive mood, and had taken his dangerous goods out of the way, she might have been trotting to church now like other people. But poor Ailie has always helped herself to the whole blame, and if every childish fit of temper were the root of such qualities, what a world we should have here!"

"Ah! no wonder she is devoted to you."

"The child was not fifteen, had never known cross or care, but from that moment she never was out of my room if it was possible to be in; and when nurse after nurse was fairly worn out, because I could not help being so distressing, there was always that poor child, always handy and helpful, growing to be the chief dependence, and looking so piteously imploring whatever was tried, that it really helped me to go through with it. Poor Ailie," she added with an odd turn of playfulness, "I always fancied those frowns of anxiety made her eyebrows grow together. And ever since we came here, we know how she has worked away for her old cinder and her small Rosebud, don't we?" she added, playfully squeezing the child's cheeks up into a more budding look, hiding deeper and more overcoming feelings by the sportive action. And as her sister came back, she looked up and shook her head at her, saying,—

" You gossiping Ailie, to go ripping up old grievances. I am going to ask Miss Curtis not to let the story go any further, now you have relieved your mind of it."

" I did tell Lady Temple," said Alison ; " I never think it right not to let people know what sort of person they have to teach their children."

And Grace, on feeling her way, discovered that Lady Temple had been told the bare fact in Miss Williams's reserved and business-like manner, but with nothing of the affair that had led to it. She merely looked on it in the manner fully expressed by—" Ah, poor thing ; how sad for her ! " as a shocking secret, never to be talked of or thought about. And that voluntary detailed relation from Alison could only be regarded as drawn forth by Grace's own individual power of winning confidence, and the friendliness that had so long subsisted between them. Nor indeed was the reserve regarding the cause of the present reduced circumstances of the sisters at all lessened ; it was only known that their brother had ruined them by a fraudulent speculation, and had then fled to the Continent, leaving them burthened with the maintenance of his child, but that they refused to believe in his guilt, and had thus incurred the displeasure of other relatives and friends. Alison was utterly silent about him. Ermine seemed to have a tender pleasure in bringing in a reference to his ways as if all were well, and it were a matter of course to speak of " Edward ; " but it was plain that Ermine's was an outspoken nature. This might, however, be only because the one had been a guarded, sheltered invalid, while the other had gone forth among

strangers to battle for a livelihood, and moreover, the elder
sister had been fully grown and developed before the shock
which had come on the still unformed Alison.

At any rate, nobody but Grace " got on " with the governess,
while the invalid made friends with all who visited her, and
most signally with Rachel, who, ere long, esteemed her enlivenment a good work, worthy of herself. The charity of sitting
with a twaddling, muffatee-knitting old lady was indisputable,
but it was perfectly within Grace's capacity ; and Rachel believed herself to be far more capable of entertaining the sick
Miss Williams, nor was she mistaken. When excited or
interested, most people thought her oppressive ; but Ermine
Williams, except when unwell, did not find her so, and even
then a sharp debate was sometimes a cure for the nervous
ailments induced by the monotony of her life. They seemed
to have a sort of natural desire to rub their minds one against
the other, and Rachel could not rest without Miss Williams's
opinion of all that interested her—paper, essay, book, or
event ; but often, when expecting to confer a favour by the
loan, she found that what was new to her was already well
known in that little parlour, and even the authorship no
mystery. Ermine explained this by her correspondence with
literary friends of her brother's, and country-bred Rachel, to
whom literature was still an oracle unconnected with living
agencies, listened, yes, absolutely listened to her anecdotes of
sayings and doings, far more like clever memoirs than the
experiences of the banks of the Avon. Perhaps there was this
immediate disadvantage, that hearing of a more intellectual
tone of society tended to make Rachel less tolerant of that
which surrounded her, and especially of Mr. Touchett. It was
droll that, having so long shunned the two sisters under the

impression that they were his *protégées* and worshippers, she
found that Ermine's point of view was quite the rectorial
one, and that to venerate the man for his office sake was
nearly as hard to Ermine as to herself, though the office was
more esteemed.

Alison, the reserved, had held her tongue on his antecedents;
but Ermine was drawn into explaining that his father had
been a minor canon, who had eked out his means with a
combination of chaplaincies and parts of curacies, and by
teaching at the school where his son was educated. Indignant
at the hack estimation in which his father had been held, the
son, far more justly viewing both the dignity and duty of his
office, was resolved to be respected ; but bred up in second-
rate society, had neither weight, talent, nor manners to veil
his aggressive self-assertion, and he was at this time especially
trying to the Curtises.

Cathedral music had been too natural to him for the
endurance of an unchoral service, and the prime labour of
his life was to work up his choir ; but he was musical by
education rather than nature, and having begun his career
with such mortal offence to the native fiddlers and singers as
to impel them into the arms of dissent, he could only supply
the loss from the school by his own voice, of which he was
not chary, though using it with better will than taste.   The
staple of his choir were Rachel's scholars.   Her turn had
always been for boys, and her class on Sunday mornings and
two evenings in the week had long been in operation before
the reign of Mr. Touchett.   Then two lads, whose paternal
fiddles had seceded to the Plymouth Brethren, were suspended
from all advantages by the curate, and Rachel was with
difficulty withheld from an explosion ; but even this was less

annoying than the summons at the class-room door every Sunday morning, that, in the midst of her lesson, carried off the chief of her scholars to practise their chants.   Moreover, the blame of all imperfect lessons was laid on the " singing for the parson," and all faults in the singing by the tasks for Miss Rachel ; and one night, the excellent Zack excused his failure in geography by saying that Mr. Touchett had thrown away his book, and said that it was no better than sacrilege, omitting, however, to mention that he had been caught studying it under his surplice during the lessons.

At last, with his usual fatality, the curate fixed the grand practice for the Saturday evenings that were Rachel's great days for instruction in the three R's, and for a sort of popular lecture.   Cricket was to succeed the singing, and novelty carried the day; but only by the desertion of her scholars did Rachel learn the new arrangement, and she could hardly credit the assertion that the curate was not aware that it was her day.   In fact, it was the only one when the fisher lads were sure not to be at sea, and neither party would yield it. Mr. Touchett was determined not to truckle to dictation from the great house ; so when Rachel declared she would have nothing to do with the boys unless the Saturdays were conceded to her, he owned that he thought the clergyman had the first right to his lads, and had only not claimed them before out of deference for the feelings of a well-meaning parishioner.

Both parties poured out their grievances to the same auditor, for Mr. Touchett regarded Ermine Williams as partly clerical, and Rachel could never be easy without her sympathy.   To hear was not, however, to make peace, while each side was so sore, so conscious of the merits of its own case, so blind to those of the other. One deemed praise in its highest form the prime object of his ministry ; the other found the performance indevotional, and raved that education should be sacrificed to wretched music. But that the dissension was sad and mischievous, it would have been very diverting ; they were both so young in their incapacity of making allowances, their certainty that theirs was the theory to bring in the golden age, and even in their magnanimity of forgiveness ; and all the time they thought themselves so very old. " I am resigned to disappointments ; I have seen something of life."—" You forget, Miss Williams, that my ministerial experience is not very recent."

There was one who would have smoothed matters far better than any, who, like Ermine, took her weapons from the armoury of good sense ; but that person was entirely unconscious how the incumbent regarded her soft eyes, meek pensiveness, motherly sweetness, and, above all, the refined graceful dignity that remained to her from the leading station she had occupied. Her gracious respect towards her clergyman was a contrast as much to the deferential coquetry of his admirers as to the abruptness of his foe, and her indifference to parish details had even its charm in a world of fussiness ; he did not know himself how far a wish of hers would have led him, and she was the last person to guess. She viewed him, like all else outside her nursery, as something out of the focus of her eye ; her instinct regarded her clergyman as necessarily good and worthy, and her ear heard Rachel railing at him ; it sounded hard, but it was a pity Rachel should be vexed and interfered with. In fact, she never thought of the matter at all ; it was only part of that outer kind of dreamy stage-play at Avonmouth, in which she let herself be moved about at her cousin's bidding. One part of her life had passed away from her, and what remained to her was among her children; her interests and intelligence seemed contracted to Conrade's horizon, and as to everything else, she was subdued, gentle, obedient, but slow and obtuse.

Yet, little as he knew it, Mr. Touchett might have even asserted his authority in a still more trying manner. If the gentle little widow had not cast a halo round her relatives, he could have preached that sermon upon the home-keeping duties of women, or have been too much offended to accept any service from the Curtis family; and he could have done without them, for he had a wide middle-class popularity; his manners with the second-rate society, in which he had been bred, were just sufficiently superior and flattering to recommend all his best points, and he obtained plenty of subscriptions from visitors, and of co-operation from inhabitants. Many a young lady was in a flutter at the approach of the spruce little figure in black, and so many volunteers were there for parish work, that districts and classes were divided and subdivided, till it sometimes seemed as if the only difficulty was to find poor people enough who would submit to serve as the *corpus vile* for their charitable treatment.

For it was not a really poor population. The men were seafaring, the women lacemaking, and just well enough off to make dissent doubly attractive as an escape from some of the interfering almsgiving of the place. Over-visiting, criticism of dress, and inquisitorial examinations had made more than one Primitive Methodist, and no severe distress had been so recent as to render the women tolerant of troublesome weekly inspections. The Curtis sisters were, however, regarded as

an exception; they were viewed as real gentlefolks, not only
by their own tenants, but by all who were conscious of their
hereditary claims to respect; they did not care whether hair
were long or short, and their benefits were more substantial
and reliable than could be looked for from the casual visitors
and petty gentry around, so that sundry houses that were
forbidden ground to district visitors, were ready to grant them
a welcome.

One of these belonged to the most able lacemaker in the
place, a hard-working woman, who kept seven little pupils
in a sort of cupboard under the staircase, with a window into
the back garden, " because," said she, " they did no work if
they looked out into the front, there were so many gapsies;"
these gapsies consisting of the very scanty traffic of the
further end of Mackarel Lane. For ten hours a day did
these children work in a space just wide enough for them
to sit, with the two least under the slope of the stairs,
permitted no distraction from their bobbins, but invaded by
their mistress on the faintest sound of tongues. Into this
hotbed of sprigs was admitted a child who had been a
special favourite at school, an orphan niece of the head
of the establishment. The two brothers had been lost
together at sea; and while the one widow became noted
for her lace, the other, a stranger to the art, had maintained herself by small millinery, and had not sacrificed her
little girl to the Moloch of lace, but had kept her at school
to a later age than usual in the place. But the mother
died, and the orphan was at once adopted by the aunt, with
the resolve to act the truly kind part by her, and break
her in to lacemaking. That determination was a great blow
to the school visitors; the girls were in general so young,

or so stupefied with their work, that an intelligent girl like
Lovedy Kelland was no small treasure to them; there were
designs of making her a pupil teacher in a few years, and
offers and remonstrances rained in upon her aunt. But they
had no effect; Mrs. Kelland was persuaded that the child
had been spoilt by learning, and in truth poor Lovedy was
a refractory scholar; she was too lively to bear the confinement patiently; her mind was too much awake not to rebel
against the dulness, and her fingers had not been brought
into training early enough. Her incessant tears spoilt her
thread, and Mrs. Kelland decided that "she'd never get her
bread till she was broke of her buke;" which breaking was
attempted by a summary pawning of all poor Lovedy's reward
books. The poor child confided her loss to her young lady
teacher at the Sunday school; the young lady, being new,
young, and inflammable, reproached Mrs. Kelland with dishonesty and tyranny to the orphan, and in return was nearly
frightened out of her wits by such a scolding as only such
a woman as the lace mistress could deliver. Then Mr.
Touchett tried his hand, and though he did not meet with
quite so much violence, all he heard was that she had "given
Lovedy the stick for being such a little töd as to complain,
when she knew the money for the bukes was put safe away
in her money-box. She was not going to the Sunday schule
again, not she, to tell stories against her best friends!" And
when the next district visitor came that way, the door was
shut in her face, with the tract thrown out at the opening,
and an intimation in Mrs. Kelland's shrill voice, that no
more bukes were wanted; she got plenty from Miss Curtis.

These bukes from Miss Curtis were sanatory tracts, which
Rachel was constantly bestowing, and which on Sundays

Mrs. Kelland spelt through, with her finger under the line, in happy ignorance whether the subject were temporal or spiritual, and feeling herself in the exemplary discharge of

Sunday duty. Moreover, old feudal feeling made Rachel be unmolested when she came down twice a week, opened the door of the blackhole under the stairs, and read aloud something religious, something improving, and a bit of a story, following it up by mental arithmetic and a lesson on objects, which seemed to Mrs. Kelland the most arrant non-sense in the world, and to her well-broken scholars was about as interesting as the humming of a blue-bottle fly; but it was poor Lovedy's one enjoyment, though making such havoc of her work that it was always expiated by extra hours, not on her pillow, but at it.

These visits of Rachel were considered to encourage the Kelland refractoriness, and it was officially intimated that it would be wise to discontinue them, and that "it was thought better" to withdraw from Mrs. Kelland all that direct patron-age of her trade, by which the ladies had enabled her to be in some degree independent of the middle-men, who absorbed so much of the profit from the workers. Grace and Rachel, sufficiently old inhabitants to remember the terrible wreck that had left her a struggling widow, felt this a hard, not to say a vindictive decision. They had long been a kind of agents for disposing of her wares at a distance; and, feeling that the woman had received provocation, Grace was not disposed to give her up, while Rachel loudly averred that neither Mr. Touchett nor any of his ladies had any right to interfere, and she should take no notice.

"But," said Grace, "can we run counter to our clergy-man's direct wishes?"

" Yes, when he steps out of his province. My dear Grace, you grew up in the days of curatolatry, but it won't do ; men are fallible even when they preach in a surplice, and you may be thankful to me that you and Fanny are not both led along in a string in the train of Mr. Touchett's devotees ! "

" I wish I knew what was right to do," said Grace, quietly ; and she remained wishing it after Rachel had said a great deal more ; but the upshot of it was, that one day when Grace and Fanny were walking together on the esplanade, they met Mr. Touchett, and Grace said to him, " We have been thinking it over, and we thought, perhaps, you would not wish us not to give any orders to Mrs. Kelland. I know she has behaved very ill ; but I don't see how she is to get on, and she has this child on her hands."

" I know," said Mr. Touchett ; " but really it was flagrant."

" Oh," said Lady Temple, gently, " I dare say she didn't mean it, and you could not be hard on a widow."

" Well," said Mr. Touchett, " Miss Brown was very much put out, and—and—it is a great pity about the child ; but I never thought myself that such strong measures would do any good."

" Then you will not object to her being employed ? "

" No, not at all. From a distance, it is not the same thing as close at home ; it won't be an example."

" Thank you," said Grace ; and " I am so glad," said Lady Temple ; and Mr. Touchett went on his way, lightened of his fear of having let his zealous coadjutors oppress the hard-working, and far more brightened by the sweet smile of requital, but all the time doubtful whether he had been weak. As to the victory, Rachel only laughed, and said,

" If it made Grace more comfortable, it was well, except for that acknowledgment of Mr. Touchett's jurisdiction."

A few days after, Rachel made her appearance in Mackarel Lane, and announced her intention of consulting Ermine Williams under seal of secresy. " I have an essay that I wish you to judge of before I send it to the ' Traveller.' "

" Indeed ! " said Ermine, her colour rising. " Would it not be better——"

" Oh, I know what you mean, but don't scruple on that score. At my age, with a mother like mine, it is simply to avoid teasing and excitement that I am silent."

" I was going to say I was hardly a fair——"

" Because of your different opinions ? But those go for nothing. You are a worthy antagonist, and enter into my views as my mother and sister cannot do, even while you oppose them."

" But I don't think I can help you, even if——"

" I don't want help ; I only want you to judge of the composition. In fact, I read it to you that I may hear it myself."

Ermine resigned herself.

" ' Curatolatry is a species——' "

" I beg your pardon."

" Curatolatry. Ah ! I thought that would attract attention."

" But I am afraid the scholars would fall foul of it."

" Why, have not they just made Mariolatry ? "

" Yes ; but they are very severe on hybrids between Latin and Greek."

" It is not worth while to boggle at trifles when one has an expressive term," said Rachel ; " if it turns into English, that is all that is wanted."

" Would it not be rather a pity if it should turn into English ? Might it not be hard to brand with a contemptuous name what does more good than harm ? "

" That sickly mixture of flirtation and hero worship, with a religious daub as a salve to the conscience."

" Laugh it down, and what do you leave ? In Miss Austen's time silly girls ran to balls after militiamen ; now, if they run to schools and charities more for the curate's sake than they quite know, is not the alternative better ? "

" It is greater humbug," said Rachel. " But I knew you would not agree, at least beforehand ; it is appreciation that I want."

Never did Madame de Genlis make a cleverer hit than in the reading of the Genius Phanor's tragedy in the Palace of Truth. Comically absurd as the inconsistency is of transporting the *lecture* of a Parisian academician into an enchanted palace, full of genii and fairies of the remotest possible connexion with the Arab *jinn*, the whole is redeemed by the truth to nature of the sole dupe in the Palace of Truth being the author reading his own works. Ermine was thinking of him all the time. She was under none of the constraint of Phanor's auditors, though she carried a perpetual palace of truth about with her ; she would not have had either fears or compunctions in criticising, if she could. The paper was in the essay style, between argument and sarcasm, something after the model of the Invalid's Letters ; but it was scarcely lightly touched enough, the irony was wormwood, the gravity heavy and sententious, and where there was a just thought or happy hit, it seemed to travel in a road-waggon, and be lost in the rumbling of the wheels. Ermine did not restrain a smile, half of amusement, half of relief, at the self-antidote the paper contained; but the smile passed with the authoress as a tribute to her satire.

"In this age," she said, "we must use those lighter weapons of wit, or no one will attend."

"Perhaps," said Ermine, "if I approve your object, I should tell you you don't use them lightly."

"Ah! but I know you don't approve it. You are not lay woman enough to be impartial, and you belong to the age that was trying the experiment of the hierarchy modified; I to that which has found it will not do. But at least you understand my view; I have made out my case."

"Yes, I understand your view; but——"

"You don't sympathize. Of course not; but when it receives its full weight from the printer's hands, you will see that it will tell. That bit about the weak tea fumes I thought of afterwards, and I am afraid I did not read it well."

"I remember it; but forgive me if I say first I think the whole is rather too—too lengthy to take."

"Oh, that is only because manuscript takes long to read aloud. I counted the words, so I can't be mistaken; at least I counted twenty lines, and multiplied; and it is not so long as the Invalid's last letter about systematic reading."

"And then comes my question again, Is good to come of it?"

"That I can't expect you to see at this time; but it is to be the beginning of a series, exposing the fallacies of woman's life as at present conducted; and out of these I mean to point the way to more consistent, more independent, better combined exertion. If I can make myself useful with my pen, it will compensate for the being debarred from so many more obvious outlets. I should like to have as much influence over people's minds as that Invalid for instance, and by earnest effort I know I shall attain it."

" I—I—" half-laughing and blushing, "I hope you will, for I know you would wish to use it for good ; but, to speak plainly, I doubt about the success of this effort, or—or if it ought to succeed."

" Yes, I know you do," said Rachel. " No one ever can judge of a manuscript. You have done all I wished you to do, and I value your sincerity. Of course I did not expect praise, since the more telling it is on the opposite side, the less you could like it. I saw you appreciated it."

And Rachel departed, while Rose crept up to her aunt, asking, "Aunt Ermine, why do you look so very funny ? It was very tiresome. Are not you glad it is over ? "

" I was thinking, Rose, what a difficult language plain English is sometimes."

" What, Miss Rachel's ? I couldn't understand one bit of her long story, except that she did not like weak tea."

" It was my own that I meant," said Ermine. " But, Rose, always remember that a person who stands plain speaking from one like me has something very noble and generous in her. Were you here all the time, Rosie ? I don't wonder you were tired."

" No, Aunt Ermine, I went and told Violetta and Augustus a fairy tale out of my own head."

" Indeed ; and how did they like it ? "

" Violetta looked at me all the time, and Augustus gave three winks, so I think he liked it."

" Appreciated it ! " said Aunt Ermine.

CHAPTER IV.

THE HERO.

" And which is Lucy's? Can it be
That puny fop, armed *cap-à-pie*,
Who loves in the saloon to show
The arms that never knew a foe."—SCOTT.

" MY lady's compliments, ma'am, and she would be much obliged if you would remain till she comes home," was Coombe's reception of Alison. "She is gone to Avoncester with Master Temple and Master Francis."

" Gone to Avoncester!" exclaimed Rachel, who had walked from church to Myrtlewood with Alison.

" Mamma is gone to meet the Major!" cried three of the lesser boys, rushing upon them in full cry; then Leoline, facing round, "Not the major, he is lieutenant-colonel now—Colonel Keith, hurrah!"

" What—what do you mean? Speak rationally, Leoline, if you can."

" My lady sent a note to the Homestead this morning," explained Coombe. "She heard this morning that Colonel Keith intended to arrive to-day, and took the young gentlemen with her to meet him."

Rachel could hardly refrain from manifesting her displeasure, and bluntly asked what time Lady Temple was likely to be at home.

" It depended," Coombe said, " upon the train ; it was not certain whether Colonel Keith would come by the twelve or the two o'clock train."

And Rachel was going to turn sharply round, and dash home with the tidings, when Alison arrested her with the question—

" And who is Colonel Keith ?"

Rachel was too much wrapped up in her own view to hear the trembling of the voice, and answered, " Colonel Keith ! why, the Major ! You have not been here so long without hearing of the Major ?"

" Yes ; but I did not know. Who is he ?" And a more observant person would have seen the governess's gasping effort to veil her eagerness under her wonted self-control.

" Don't you know who the Major is ?" shouted Leoline. " He is our military secretary."

" That's the sum total of my knowledge," said Rachel. " I don't understand his influence, nor know where he was picked up."

" Nor his regiment ?"

" He is not a regimental officer ; he is on our staff," said Leoline, whose imagination could not attain to an earlier condition than " on our staff."

" I shall go home, then," said Rachel, " and see if there is any explanation there."

" I shall ask the Major not to let Aunt Rachel come here," observed Hubert, as she departed ; it was well it was not before.

" Leoline," anxiously asked Alison, " can you tell me the Major's name ?"

"Colonel Keith—Lieutenant-Colonel Keith," was all the answer.

"I meant his Christian name, my dear."

"Only little boys have Christian names!" they returned, and Alison was forced to do her best to tame herself and them to the duties of the long day of anticipation so joyous on their part, so full of confusion and bewildered anxiety on her own. She looked in vain, half stealthily, as often before, for a recent Army List or Peerage. Long ago she had lost the Honourable Colin A. Keith from among the officers of the —th Highlanders, and though in the last Peerage she had laid hands on he was still among the surviving sons of the late Lord Keith, of Gowanbrae, the date had not gone back far enough to establish that he had not died in the Indian war. It was fear that predominated with her; there were many moments when she would have given worlds to be secure that the new comer was not the man she thought of, who, whether constant or inconstant, could bring nothing but pain and disturbance to the calm tenour of her sister's life. Everything was an oppression to her; the children, in their wild, joyous spirits and gladsome inattention, tried her patience almost beyond her powers; the charge of the younger ones in their mother's absence was burthensome, and the delay in returning to her sister became wellnigh intolerable, when she figured to herself Rachel Curtis going down to Ermine with the tidings of Colonel Keith's arrival, and her own discontent at his influence with her cousin. Would that she had spoken a word of warning; yet that might have been merely mischievous, for the subject was surely too delicate for Rachel to broach with so recent a friend. But Rachel had bad taste for anything! That the

little boys did not find Miss Williams very cross that day
was an effect of the long habit of self-control, and she could
hardly sit still under the additional fret, when, just as tea
was spread for the school-room party, in walked Miss Rachel,
and sat herself down, in spite of Hubert, who made up
a most coaxing, entreating face, as he said, "Please, Aunt
Rachel, doesn't Aunt Grace want you very much?"

"Not at all. Why, Hubert?"

"Oh, if you would only go away, and not spoil our fun
when the Major comes."

For once Rachel did laugh, but she did not take the hint,
and Alison obtained only the satisfaction of hearing that she
had at least not been in Mackarel Lane. The wheels sounded
on the gravel, out rushed the boys; Alison and Rachel sat in
strange, absolute silence, each forgetful of the other, neither
guarding her own looks, nor remarking her companion's.
Alison's lips were parted by intense listening; Rachel's teeth
were set to receive her enemy. There was a chorus of voices
in the hall, and something about tea and coming in warned
both to gather up their looks before Lady Temple had
opened the door, and brought in upon them not one foe, but
two! Was Rachel seeing double? Hardly that, for one was
tall, bald, and bearded, not dangerously young, but on that
very account the more dangerously good-looking; and the
other was almost a boy, slim and light, just of the empty
young officer type. Here, too, was Fanny, flushed, excited,
prettier and brighter than Rachel had seen her at all, waving
an introduction with head and hand; and the boys hanging
round the Major with deafening exclamations of welcome, in
which they were speedily joined by the nursery detachment.
Those greetings, those observations on growth and looks,

those glad, eager questions and answers, were like the welcome of an integral part of the family; it was far more intimate and familiar than had been possible with the Curtises after the long separation, and it was enough to have made the two spectators feel out of place, if such a sensation had been within Rachel's capacity, or if Alison had not been engaged with the tea. Lady Temple made a few explanations, *sotto voce*, to Alison, whom she always treated as though in dread of not being sufficiently considerate. "I do hope the children have been good; I knew you would not mind; I could not wait to see you, or I should have been too late to meet the train, and then he would have come by the coach; and it is such a raw east wind. He must be careful in this climate."

"How warm and sunshiny it has been all day," said Rachel, by way of opposition to some distant echo of this whisper.

"Sunshiny, but treacherous," answered Colonel Keith; "there are cold gusts round corners. This must be a very sheltered nook of the coast."

"Quite a different zone from Avoncester," said the youth.

"Yes, delightful. I told you it was just what would suit you," added Fanny, to the colonel.

"Some winds are very cold here," interposed Rachel. "I always pity people who are imposed upon to think it a Mentone near home. They are choking our churchyard."

"Very inconsiderate of them," muttered the young man.

"But what made you come home so late, Fanny?" said Rachel.

Alison suspected a slight look of wonder on the part of both the officers at hearing their general's wife thus called to account; but Fanny, taking it as a matter of course, answered, "We found that the —th was at Avoncester. I had no idea of it, and they did not know I was here; so I went to call upon Mrs. Hammond, and Colonel Keith went to look for Alick, and we have brought him home to dine."

Fanny took it for granted that Rachel must know who Alick was, but she was far from doing so, though she remembered that the —th had been her uncle's regiment, and had been under Sir Stephen Temple's command in India at the time of the mutiny. The thought of Fanny's lapsing into military society was shocking to her. The boys were vociferating about boats, ponies, and all that had been deferred till the Major's arrival, and he was answering them kindly, but hushing the extra outcry less by word than sign; and his own lowered voice and polished manner—a manner that excessively chafed her as a sort of insult to the blunt, rapid ways that she considered as sincere and unaffected, a silkiness that no doubt had worked on the honest, simple general, as it was now working on the weak young widow. Anything was better than leaving her to such influence, and in pursuance of the intention that Rachel had already announced at home, she invited herself to stay to dinner; and Fanny eagerly thanked her, for making it a little less ·dull for Colonel Keith and Alick. It was so good to come down and help. Certainly Fanny was an innocent creature, provided she was not spoilt, and it was a duty to guard her innocence.

Alison Williams escaped to her home, sure of nothing but that her sister must not be allowed to share her uncertainties; and Lady Temple and her guests sat down to dinner. Rachel meant to have sat at the bottom and carved, as belonging to the house; but Fanny motioned the Colonel to the place, observing, "It is so natural to see you there! One only wants poor Captain Dent at the other end. Do you know whether he has his leave ? "

Wherewith commenced a discussion of military friends— who had been heard of from Australia, who had been met in England, who was promoted, who married, who retired, &c., and all the quarters of the —th since its return from India two years ago ; Fanny eagerly asking questions and making remarks, quite at home and all animation, absolutely a different being from the subdued, meek little creature that Rachel had hitherto seen. Attempts were made to include Miss Curtis in the conversation by addressing anecdotes to her, and asking if she knew the places named ; but she had been to none, and the three old friends quickly fell into the swing of talk about what interested them. Once, however, she came down on them with, " What conclusion have you formed upon female emigration ? "

> " ' His sister she went beyond the seas,
>   And died an old maid among black savagees.'

That's the most remarkable instance of female emigration on record, isn't it ? " observed Alick.

" What ; her dying an old maid ? " said Colonel Keith. " I am not sure. Wholesale exportations of wives are spoiling the market."

" I did not mean marriage," said Rachel, stoutly. " I am particularly anxious to know whether there is a field open to independent female labour."

" All the superior young women seemed to turn nursery-maids," said the Colonel.

" Oh," interposed Fanny, " do you remember that nice girl of ours who *would* marry that Orderly-Sergeant O'Donoghoe ? I have had a letter from her in such distress."

" Of course, the natural termination," said Alick, in his lazy voice.

" And I thought you would tell me how to manage sending her some help," proceeded Fanny.

" I could have helped you, Fanny. Won't an order do it ? "

" Not quite," said Fanny, a shade of a smile playing on her lip. " It is whether to send it through one of the officers or not. If Captain Lee is with the regiment, I know he would take care of it for her."

So they plunged into another regiment, and Rachel decided that nothing was so wearisome as to hear triflers talk shop.

There was no opportunity of calling Fanny to order after dinner, for she went off on her progress to all the seven cribs, and was only just returning from them when the gentlemen came in, and then she made room for the younger beside her on the sofa, saying, " Now, Alick, I do so want to hear about poor, dear little Bessie ; " and they began so low and confidentially, that Rachel wondered if her alarms were to be transferred from the bearded colonel to the dapper boy, or if, in very truth, she must deem poor Fanny a general coquette. Besides, a man must be contemptible who wore gloves at so small a party, when she did not.

She had been whiling away the time of Fanny's absence by looking over the books on the table, and she did not regard the present company sufficiently to desist on their account. Colonel Keith began to turn over some numbers of the " Traveller " that lay near him, and presently looked up, and said, " Do you know who is the writer of this ? "

" What is it ? Ah ! one of the Invalid's essays. They strike every one ; but I fancy the authorship is a great secret."

" You do not know it ? "

" No, I wish I did. Which of them are you reading ? ' Country Walks.' That is not one that I care about, it is a mere hash of old recollections ; but there are some very sensible and superior ones, so that I have heard it sometimes doubted whether they are man's or woman's writing. For my part, I think them too earnest to be a man's ; men always play with their subject."

" Oh, yes," said Fanny, " I am sure only a lady could have written anything so sweet as that about flowers in a sick-room ; it so put me in mind of the lovely flowers you used to bring me one at a time, when I was ill at Cape Town."

There was no more sense to be had after those three once fell upon their reminiscences.

That night, after having betrayed her wakefulness by a movement in her bed, Alison Williams heard her sister's voice, low and steady, saying, " Ailie, dear, be it what it may, guessing is worse than certainty."

" Oh, Ermine, I hoped—I know nothing—I have nothing to tell."

" You dread something," said Ermine ; " you have been striving for unconcern all the evening, my poor dear ; but surely you know, Ailie, that nothing is so bad while we share it."

" And I have frightened you about nothing."

" Nothing ! nothing about Edward ?"

" Oh, no, no !"

" And no one has made you uncomfortable ?"

" No."

" Then there is only one thing that it can be, Ailie, and you need not fear to tell me that. I always knew that if he lived I must be prepared for it, and you would not have hesitated to tell me of his death."

" It is not that, indeed it is not, Ermine, it is only this—that I found to-day that Lady Temple's major has the same name."

" But you said she was come home. You must have seen him."

" Yes, but I should not know him. I had only seen him once, remember, twelve years ago, and when I durst not look at him."

" At least," said Ermine, quickly, " you can tell me what you saw to-day."

" A Scotch face, bald head, dark beard, grizzled hair."

" Yes I am grey, and he was five years older ; but he used not to have a Scotch face. Can you tell me about his eyes ?"

" Dark," I think.

" They were very dark blue, almost black. Time and climate must have left them alone. You may know him by those eyes, Ailie. And you could not make out anything about him ?"

" No, not even his Christian name nor his regiment. I had only the little ones and Miss Rachel to ask, and they knew nothing. I wanted to keep this from you till I was sure, but you always find me out."

" Do you think I couldn't see the misery you were in all the evening, poor child ? But now you have had it out, sleep, and don't be distressed."

" But, Ermine, if you——"

" My dear, I am thankful that nothing is amiss with you or Edward. For the rest, there is nothing but patience.

Now, not another word ; you must not lose your sleep, nor take away my chance of any."

How much the sisters slept they did not confide to one another ; but when they rose, Alison shook her head at her sister's heavy eyelids, and Ermine retorted with a reproachful smile at certain dark tokens of sleeplessness under Alison's eyes.

" No, not the flowered flimsiness, please," she said, in the course of her toilette, " let me have the respectable grey silk." And next she asked for a drawer, whence she chose a little Nuremberg horn brooch for her neck. " I know it is very silly," she said, " but I can't quite help it. Only one question, Ailie, that I thought of too late. Did he hear your name ?"

" I think not, Lady Temple named nobody. But why did you not ask me last night ?"

" I thought beginning to talk again would destroy your chance of sleep, and we had resolved to stop."

" And, Ermine, if it be, what shall I do ?"

" Do as you feel right at the moment," said Ermine, after a moment's pause. " I cannot tell how it may be. I have been thinking over what you told me about ' the Major' and Lady Temple."

" Oh, Ermine, what a reproof this is for that bit of gossip."

" Not at all, my dear, the warning may be all the better for me," said Ermine, with a voice less steady than her words. " It is not what, under the circumstances, I could think likely in the Colin whom I knew ; but were it indeed so, then, Ailie, you had better say nothing about me, unless he found you out. We would get employment elsewhere."

" And I must leave you to the suspense all day."

" Much better so. The worst thing we could do would be to go on talking about it. It is far better for me to be left with my dear little unconscious companion."

Alison tried to comfort herself with this belief through the long hours of the morning, during which she only heard that mamma and Colonel Keith were gone to the Homestead, and she saw no one till she came forth with her troop to the midday meal.

And there, at sight of Lady Temple's content and calm, satisfied look, as though she were once more in an accustomed atmosphere, and felt herself and the boys protected, and of the Colonel's courteous attention to her and affectionate authority towards her sons, it was an absolute pang to recognise the hue of eye described by Ermine ; but still Alison tried to think them generic Keith eyes, till at length, amid the merry chatter of her pupils, came an appeal to " Miss Williams," and then came a look that thrilled through her, the same glance that she had met for one terrible moment twelve years before, and renewing the same longing to shrink from all sight or sound. How she kept her seat and continued to attend to the children she never knew, but the voices sounded like a distant Babel ; and she did not know whether she were most relieved, disappointed, or indignant when she left the dining-room to take the boys for their walk. Oh, that Ermine could be hid from all knowledge of what would be so much harder to bear than the death in which she had long believed !

Harder to bear? Yes, Ermine had already been passing through a heart sickness that made the morning like an age. Her resolute will had struggled hard for composure, cheerfulness, and occupation ; but the little watchful niece had seen through the endeavour, and had made her own to the sleepless night and the headache. The usual remedy was a drive in a wheeled chair, and Rose was so urgent to be allowed to go and order one, that Ermine at last yielded, partly because she had hardly energy enough to turn her refusal graciously, partly because she would not feel herself staying at home for the vague hope ; and when the child was out of sight, she had the comfort of clasping her hands, and ceasing to restrain her countenance, while she murmured, " Oh, Colin, Colin, are you what you were twelve years back ? Is this all dream, all delusion, and waste of feeling, while you are lying in your Indian grave, more mine than you can ever be living ! Be as it may,—

> " ' Calm me, my God, and keep me calm
>   While these hot breezes blow ;
>   Be like the night dew's cooling balm
>   Upon earth's fevered brow.
>   Calm me, my God, and keep me calm,
>   Soft resting on Thy breast ;
>   Soothe me with holy hymn and psalm,
>   And bid my spirit rest.' "

CHAPTER V.

MILITARY SOCIETY.

> " My trust
> Like a good parent did beget of him
> A falsehood in its contrary as great
> As my trust was, which had indeed no limit."—TEMPEST.

ROSE found the wheeled chair, to which her aunt gave the preference, was engaged, and shaking her little discreet head at " the shakey chair" and " the stuffy chair," she turned pensively homeward, and was speeding down Mackarel Lane, when she was stayed by the words, " My little girl !" and the grandest and most bearded gentleman she had ever seen, demanded, " Can you tell me if Miss Williams lives here ?"

" My aunt ?" exclaimed Rose, gazing up with her pretty, frightened-fawn look.

" Indeed !" he exclaimed, looking eagerly at her, " then you are the child of a very old friend of mine ! Did you never hear him speak of his old school-fellow, Colin Keith ?"

" Papa is away," said Rose, turning back her neck to get a full view of his face from under the brim of her hat.

" Will you run on and ask your aunt if she would like to see me ?" he added.

Thus it was that Ermine heard the quick patter of the child's steps, followed by the manly tread, and the words sounded in her ears, " Aunt Ermine, there's a gentleman,

and he has a great beard, and he says he is papa's old friend !
And here he is."

Ermine's beaming eyes as absolutely met the new comer
as though she had sprung forward. " I thought you would
come," she said, in a voice serene with exceeding bliss.

" I have found you at last," as their hands clasped ; and
they gazed into each other's faces in the untroubled repose of
the meeting, exclusive of all else.

Ermine was the first to break silence. "Oh, Colin, you
look worn and altered."

" You don't; you have kept your sunbeam face for me
with the dear brown glow I never thought to have seen
again. Why did they tell me you were an invalid, Ermine ?"

" Have you not seen Alison ?" she asked, supposing he
would have known all.

" I saw her, but did not hear her name, till just now at
luncheon, when our looks met, and I saw it was not another
disappointment."

" And she knows you are come to me ?"

" It was not in me to speak to her till I had recovered
you ! One can forgive, but not forget."

" You will do more when you know her, and how she has
only lived and worked for me, dear Ailie, and suffered far more
than I——"

" While I was suffering from being unable to do anything
but live for you," he repeated, taking up her words ; " but
that is ended now——" and as she made a negative motion
of her head, " have you not trusted to me ?"

" I have thought you not living," she said ; " the last I
know was your letter to dear Lady Alison, written from the
hospital at Cape Town, after your wound. She was ill

even when it came, and she could only give it to Ailie for me."

" Dear good aunt, she got into trouble with all the family for our sake ; and when she was gone no one *would* give me any tidings of you."

" It was her last disappointment that you were not sent home on sick leave. Did you get well too fast ? "

" Not exactly ; but my father, or rather, I believe, my brother, intimated that I should be welcome only if I had laid aside a certain foolish fancy, and as lying on my back had not conduced to that end, I could only say I would stay where I was."

" And was it worse for you ? I am sure, in spite of all that tanned skin, that your health has suffered.   Ought you to have come home ? "

" No, I do not know that London surgeons could have got at the ball," he said, putting his hand on his chest, " and it gives me no trouble in general.   I was such a spectacle when I returned to duty, that good old Sir Stephen Temple, always a proverb for making his staff a refuge for the infirm, made me his aide-de-camp, and was like a father to me."

" Now I see why I never could find your name in any list of the officers in the moves of the regiment !   I gave you quite up when I saw no Keith among those that came home from India.   I did believe then that you were the Colonel Alexander Keith whose death I had seen mentioned, though I had long trusted to his not being honourable, nor having your first name."

" Ah ! he succeeded to the command after Lady Temple's father.   A kind friend to me he was, and he left me in charge of his son and daughter.   A very good and gallant fellow is that young Alick. I must bring him to see you some day——"

" Oh ! I saw his name ; I remember ! I gloried in the doings of a Keith ; but I was afraid he had died, as there was no such name with the regiment when it came home."

" No, he was almost shattered to pieces ; but Sir Stephen sent him up the hills to be nursed by Lady Temple and her mother, and he was sent home as soon as he could be moved. I was astonished to see how entirely he had recovered."

" Then you went through all that Indian war ? "

" Yes ; with Sir Stephen."

" You must show me all your medals ! How much you have to tell me ! And then——?"

" Just when the regiment was coming home, my dear old chief was appointed to the command in Australia, and insisted on my coming with him as military secretary. He had come to depend on me so much that I could not well leave him ; and five years there was the way to promotion and to claiming you at once. We were just settled there, when what I heard made me long to have decided otherwise, but I could not break with him then. I wrote to Edward, but had my letter returned to me."

" No wonder ; Edward was abroad, all connexion broken."

" I wrote to Beauchamp, and he knew nothing, and I could only wait till my chief's time should be up. You know how it was cut short, and how the care of the poor little widow detained me till she was fit for the voyage. I came and sought you in vain in town. I went home, and found my brother lonely and dispirited. He has lost his son, his daughters are married, and he and I are all the brothers left out of the six ! He was urgent that I should come and live with him and marry. I told him I would, with all my heart, when I had found you, and he saw I was too much in earnest to be opposed. Then I went to Beauchamp, but Harry knew nothing about any one. I tried to find out your sister and Dr. Long, but heard they were gone to Belfast."

" Yes, they lost a good deal in the crash, and did not like retrenching among their neighbours ; so they went to Ireland, and there they have a flourishing practice."

" I thought myself on my way there," he said, smiling ; " only I had first to settle Lady Temple, little guessing who was her treasure of a governess! Last night I had nearly opened on another false scent ; I fell in with a description that I could have sworn was yours, of the heather behind the parsonage. I made a note of the publisher in case all else had failed."

" I'm glad you knew the scent of the thyme ! "

" Then it was no false scent ?"

" One must live, and I was thankful to do anything to lighten Ailie's burthen. I wrote down that description that I might live in the place in fancy ; and one day, when the contribution was wanted and I was hard up for ideas, I sent it, though I was loth to lay open that bit of home and heart."

" Well it might give me the sense of meeting you ! And in other papers of the series I traced your old self more ripened."

" The editor was a friend of Edward's, and in our London days he asked me to write letters on things in general, and when I said I saw the world through a key-hole, he answered that a circumscribed view gained in distinctness. Most kind and helpful he has been, and what began between sport and need to say out one's mind has come to be a resource for which we are very thankful. He sends us books for reviewal, and that is pleasant and improving, not to say profitable."

" Little did I think you were in such straits ! " he said, stroking the child's head, and waiting as though her presence were a restraint on 'nquiries, but she eagerly availed herself of the pause. " Aunt Ermine, please what shall I say about the chairs ? Will you have t.e nice one and Billy when they come home ? I was to take the answer, only you did talk *so* that I could not ask ! "

" Thank you, my dear ; I don't want chairs nor anything else while I can talk *so*," she answered, smiling. " You had better take a run in the garden when you come back ; " and Rose replied with a nod of assent that made the colonel smile and say, " Good-bye then, my sweet Lady Discretion, some day we will be better acquainted."

" Dear child," said Ermine, " she is our great blessing, and some day I trust will be the same to her dear father. Oh, Colin ! it is too much to hope that you have not believed what you must have heard ! And yet you wrote to him."

" Nay, I could not but feel great distrust of what I heard, since I was also told that his sisters were unconvinced ; and besides, I had continually seen him at school the victim of other people's faults."

" This is best of all," exclaimed Ermine, with glistening eyes, and hand laid upon his ; " it is the most comfortable word I have heard since it happened. Yes, indeed, many a time before I saw you, had I heard of ' Keith' as the friend who saw him righted. Oh, Colin ! thanks, thanks for believing in him more than for all ! "

" Not believing, but knowing," he answered—" knowing both you and Edward. Besides, is it not almost invariable that the inventor is ruined by his invention—a Prospero by nature ? "

" It was not the invention," she answered ; " that throve as long as my father lived."

" Yes, he was an excellent man of business."

" And he thought the concern so secure that there was no danger in embarking all the available capital of the family in it ; and it did bring us in a very good income.

" I remember that it struck me that the people at home would find that they had made a mistake after all, and missed a fortune for me ! It was an invention for diminishing the fragility of glass under heat ; was it not ? "

" Yes, and the manufacture was very prosperous, so that my father was quite at ease about us. After his death we made a home for Edward in London, and looked after him when he used to be smitten with some new idea and forgot all sublunary matters. When he married we went to live at Richmond, and had his dear little wife very much with us, for she was a delicate tender creature, half killed by London. In process of time he fell in with a man named Maddox, plausible and clever, who became a sort of manager, especially while Edward was in his trances of invention ; and at all times knew more about his accounts than he did himself. Nothing but my father's authority had ever made him really look into them, and this man took them all off his hands. There was a matter about the glass that Edward was bent on ascertaining, and he went to study the manufacture in Bohemia, taking his wife with him, and leaving Rose with us.   Shortly after, Dr. Long and Harry Beauchamp received letters asking for a considerable advance, to be laid out on the materials that this improvement would require. Immediately afterwards came the crash."

" Exactly what I heard. Of course the letters were written in ignorance of what was impending."

" Colin, they were never written at all by Edward! He denied all knowledge of them. Alison saw Dr. Long's, most ingeniously managed—foreign paper and all—but she could swear to the forgery——"

" You suspect this Maddox?"

" Most strongly! He knew the state of the business; Edward did not. And he had a correspondence that would have enabled so ingenious a person easily to imitate Edward's letters. I do not wonder at their having been taken in; but how Julia—how Harry Beauchamp could believe— what they do believe. Oh, Colin! it will not do to think about it!"

" Oh, that I had been at home! Were no measures taken?"

" Alas! alas! we urged Edward to come home and clear himself; but that poor little wife of his was terrified beyond measure, imagined prisons and trials. She was unable to move, and he could not leave her; she took from him an unhappy promise not to put himself in what she fancied danger from the law, and then died, leaving him a baby that did not live a day. He was too broken-hearted to care for vindicating himself, and no one—no one would do it for him!"

Colonel Keith frowned and clenched the hand that lay in his grasp till it was absolute pain, but pain that was a relief to feel. " Madness, madness!" he said. " Miserable! But how was it at home—— ? Did this Maddox stand his ground ? "

" Yes, if he had fled, all would have been clear, but he doctored the accounts his own way, and quite satisfied Dr. Long and Harry. He showed Edward's receipt for the 600l. that had been advanced, and besides, there was a large sum not accounted for, which was, of course, supposed to have been invested abroad by Edward—some said gambled away—as if he had not had a regular hatred of all sorts of games."

" Edward with his head in the clouds ! One notion is as likely as the other.—Then absolutely nothing was done ! "

" Nothing ! The bankruptcy was declared, the whole affair broken up ; and certainly if every one had not known Edward to be the most heedless of men, the confusion would have justified them in thinking him a dishonest one. Things had been done in his name by Maddox that might have made a stranger think him guilty of the rest, but to those who had ever known his abstraction, and far more his real honour and uprightness, nothing could have been plainer."

" It all turned upon his absence."

" Yes, he must have borne the brunt of what had been done in his name, I know ; that would have been bad enough ; but in a court of justice, his whole character would have been shown, and besides, a prosecution for forgery of his receipt would have shown what Maddox was sufficiently to exculpate him."

" And you say the losers by the deception would not believe in it ? "

" No, they only shook their heads at our weak sisterly affection."

" I wish I could see one of those letters. Where is Maddox now ? "

" I cannot tell. He certainly did not go away immediately after the settlement of accounts, but it has not been possible to us to keep up a knowledge of his movements, or something might have turned up to justify Edward. Oh, what it is to be helpless women ! You are the very first person, Colin, who has not looked at me pityingly, like a creature to be forborne with an undeniable delusion ! "

" They must be very insolent people, then, to look at that brow and eyes, and think even sisterly love could blind them," he said. " Yes, Ermine, I was certain that unless Edward were more changed than I could believe, there must be some such explanation. You have never seen him since ? "

" No ; he was too utterly broken by the loss of his wife to feel anything else. For a long time we heard nothing, and that was the most dreadful time of all ! Then he wrote from a little German town, where he was getting his bread as a photographer's assistant. And since that he has cast about the world, till just now he has some rather interesting employment at the mines in the Oural Mountains, the first thing he has really seemed to like or care for."

" The Oural Mountains ! that is out of reach. I wish I could see him. One might find some means of clearing him. What directed your suspicion to Maddox ? "

" Chiefly that the letters professed to have been sent in a parcel to him to be posted from the office. If it had been so, Edward and Lucy would certainly have written to us at the same time. I could have shown, too, that Maddox had written to me the day before to ascertain where Edward was, so as to be sure of the date. It was a little country village, and I made a blunder in copying the spelling from Lucy's writing. Ailie found that very blunder repeated in Dr. Long's letter, and we showed him that Edward did not write it so. Besides, before going abroad, Edward had lost the seal-ring with his crest, which you gave him. You remember the Saxon's head?"

" I remember! You all took it much to heart that the engraver had made it a Saracen's head, and not a long-haired Saxon."

" Well, Edward had renewed the ring, and taken care to make it a Saxon. Now Ailie could get no one to believe her, but she is certain that the letter was sealed with the old Saracen, not the new Saxon. But—but—if you 'had but been there——"

" Tell me you wished for me, Ermine."

" I durst not wish anything about you," she said, looking up through a mist of tears.

" And you, what fixed you here ? "

" An old servant of ours had married and settled here, and had written to us of her satisfaction in finding that the clergyman was from Hereford. We thought he would recommend Ailie as daily governess to visitors, and that Sarah would be a comfortable landlady. It has answered very well ; Rose deserves her name far more than when we brought her here, and it is wonderful how much better I have been since doctors have become a mere luxury."

" Do you, can you really mean that you are supporting yourselves ?"

" All but twenty-five pounds a year, from a legacy to us, that Mr. Beauchamp would not let them touch. But it has been most remarkable, Colin," she said, with the dew in her eyes, " how we have never wanted our daily bread, and how happy we have been ! If it had not been for Edward, this would in many ways have been our happiest time. Since the old days the little frets have told less, and Ailie has been infinitely happier and brighter since she has had to work instead of only to watch me. Ah, Colin, must I not own to having been happy? Indeed it was very much because peace had come when the suspense had sunk into belief that I might think of you as——, where you would not be grieved by the sight of what I am now——"

As she spoke, a knock, not at the house, but at the room-door, made them both start, and impel their chairs to a more ordinary distance, just as Rachel Curtis made her entrance, extremely amazed to find, not Mr. Touchett, but a much greater foe and rival in that unexpected quarter. Ermine, the least disconcerted, was the first to speak. " You are surprised to find a visitor here," she said, " and indeed only now, did we find out that ' our military secretary,' as your little cousins say, was our dear old squire's nephew."

There was a ring of gladness in the usually patient voice that struck even Rachel, though she was usually too eager to be observant, but she was still unready with talk for the occasion, and Ermine continued : " We had heard so much of the Major before-hand, that we had a sort of Jupiter-like expectation of the coming man. I am not sure that I shall not go on expecting a mythic major !"

Rachel, never understanding playfulness, thought this both audacious and unnecessary, and if it had come from any one else, would have administered a snub, but she felt the invalid sacred from her weapons.

" Have you ever seen the boys ?" asked Colonel Keith. " I am rather proud of Conrade, my pupil ; he is so chivalrous towards his mother."

" Alison has brought down a division or two to show me. How much alike they are."

" Exactly alike, and excessively unruly and unmanageable," said Rachel. " I pity your sister."

" More unmanageable in appearance than in reality," said the colonel : " there's always a little trial of strength against the hand over them, and they yield when they find it is really a hand. They were wonderfully good and considerate when it was an object to keep the house quiet."

Rachel would not encourage him to talk of Lady Temple, so she turned to Ermine on the business that had brought her, collecting and adapting old clothes for emigrants.— It was not exactly gentlemen's pastime, and Ermine tried to put it aside and converse, but Rachel never permitted any petty consideration to interfere with a useful design, and as there was a press of time for the things, she felt herself justified in driving the intruder off the field and out-staying him. She succeeded ; he recollected the desire of the boys that he should take them to inspect the pony at the " Jolly Mariner," and took leave with—" I shall see you to-morrow."

" You knew him all the time !" exclaimed Rachel, pausing in her unfolding of the Master Temples' ship wardrobe. " Why did you not say so ?"

" We did not know his name. He was always the ' Major.' "

" Who, and what is he ?" demanded Rachel, as she knelt before her victim, fixing those great prominent eyes, so like those of Red Riding Hood's grandmother, that Ermine involuntarily gave a backward impulse to her wheeled chair, as she answered the readiest thing that occurred to her,—

" He is brother to Lord Keith of Gowan-brae."

" Oh," said Rachel, kneeling on meditatively, " that accounts for it. So much the worse. The staff is made up of idle honourables."

" Quoth the ' Times !' " replied Ermine ; " but his appointment began on account of a wound, and went on because of his usefulness——"

" Wounded ! I don't like wounded heroes," said Rachel ; " people make such a fuss with them that they always get spoilt."

" This was nine years ago, so you may forget it if you like," said Ermine, diversion suppressing displeasure.

" And what is your opinion of him ? " said Rachel, edging forward on her knees, so as to bring her inquisitorial eyes to bear more fully.

" I had not seen him for twelve years," said Ermine, rather faintly.

" He must have had a formed character when you saw him last. The twelve years before five-and-forty don't alter the nature."

" Five-and-forty ! Illness and climate have told ; but I did not think it was so much. He is only thirty-six——"

" That is not what I care about," said Rachel ; " you are both of you so cautious that you tell me what amounts to nothing ! You should consider how important it is to me to know something about the person in whose power my cousin's affairs are left."

" Have you not sufficient guarantee in the very fact of her husband's confidence ? ".

" I don't know. A simple-hearted old soldier always means a very foolish old man."

" Witness the Newcomes," said Ermine, who, besides her usual amusement in tracing Rachel's dicta to their source, could only keep in her indignation by laughing.

" General observation," said Rachel, not to be turned from her purpose. " I am not foolishly suspicious, but it is not pleasant to see great influence and intimacy without some knowledge of the person exercising it."

" I think," said Ermine, bringing herself with difficulty to answer quietly, " that you can hardly understand the terms they are on without having seen how much a staff officer becomes one of the family."

" I suppose much must be allowed for the frivolity and narrowness of a military set in a colony. Imagine my one attempt at rational conversation last night. Asking his views on female emigration, absolutely he had none at all ; he and Fanny only went off upon a nursemaid married to a sergeant !"

" Perhaps the bearings of the question would hardly suit mixed company."

" To be sure there was a conceited young officer there ; for as ill luck will have it, my uncle's old regiment is quartered at Avoncester, and I suppose they will all be coming after Fanny. It is well they are no nearer, and as this colonel says he is going to Belfast in a day or two, there will not be much provocation to them to come here. Now this great event of the Major's coming is over, we will try to put Fanny upon a definite system, and I look to you and your sister as a great assistance to me, in counteracting the follies and nonsenses that her situation naturally exposes her to. I have been writing a little sketch of the dangers of indecision, that I thought of sending to the 'Traveller.' It would strike Fanny to see there what I so often tell her; but I can't get an answer about my paper on ' Curatocult,' as you made me call it."

"Did I ?"

" You said the other word was of two languages. I can't think why they don't insert it ; but in the meantime I will bring down my ' Human Reeds,' and show them to you. I have only an hour's work on them ; so I'll come to-morrow afternoon."

" I think Colonel Keith talked of calling again—thank you," suggested Ermine in despair.

" Ah, yes ; one does not want to be liable to interruptions in the most interesting part. When he is gone to Belfast——"

" Yes, when he is gone to Belfast !" repeated Ermine, with an irresistible gleam of mirth about her lips and eyes, and at that moment Alison made her appearance. The looks of the sisters met, and read one another so far as to know that the meeting was over, and for the rest they endured, while Rachel remained, little imagining the trial her presence had been to Alison's burning heart-sick anxiety and doubt How could it be well ? Let him be loveable, let him be constant, that only rendered Ermine's condition the more pitiable ; and the shining glance of her eyes was almost more than Alison could bear. So happy as the sisters had been together, so absolutely united, it did seem hard to disturb that calm life with hopes and agitations that must needs be futile; and Alison, whose whole life and soul were in her sister, could not without a pang see that sister's heart belonging to another, and not for hopeful joy, but pain and grief. The yearning of jealousy was sternly reproved and forced down, and told that Ermine had long been Colin Keith's, that the perpetrator of the evil had the least right of any one to murmur that her own monopoly of her sister was interfered with; that she was selfish, unkind, envious; that she had only to hate herself and pray for strength to bear the punishment, without alloying Ermine's happiness while it lasted. How it could be so bright Alison knew not, but so it was she recognised by every tone of the voice, by every smile on the lip, by even the upright vigour with which Ermine sat in her chair and undertook Rachel's tasks of needlework.

And yet, when the visitor rose at last to go, Alison was almost unwilling to be alone with her sister, and have that power of sympathy put to the test by those clear eyes that were wont to see her through and through. She went with Rachel to the door, and stood taking a last instruction, hearing it not at all, but answering, and relieved by the delay, hardly knowing whether to be glad or not that when she returned Rose was leaning on the arm of her aunt's chair with her most eager face. But Rose was to be no protection, for what was passing between her and her aunt?

"O auntie, I am so glad he is coming back. He is just like the picture you drew of Robert Bruce for me. And he is so kind. I never saw any gentleman speak to you in such a nice soft voice."

Alison had no difficulty in smiling as Ermine stroked the child's hair, kissed her, and looked up with an arch, blushing, glittering face that could not have been brighter those long twelve years ago.

And then Rose turned round, impatient to tell her other aunt her story. " O aunt Ailie, we have had such a gentleman here, with a great brown beard like a picture. And he is papa's old friend, and kissed me because I am papa's little girl, and I do like him so very much. I went where I could look at him in the garden, when you sent me out, aunt Ermine."

" You did, you monkey?" said Ermine, laughing, and blushing again. " What will you do if I send you out next time? No, I won't then, my dear, for *all* the time, I should like you to see him and know him."

" Only, if you want to talk of anything very particular," observed Rose.

" I don't think I need ask many questions," said Alison, smiling being happily made very easy to her. " Dear Ermine, I see you are perfectly satisfied——"

" O Ailie, that is no word for it ! Not only himself, but to find him loving Rose for her father's sake, undoubting of him through all. Ailie, the thankfulness of it is more than one can bear."

" And he is the same !" said Alison.

" The same—no, not the same. It is more, better, or I am able to feel it more. It was just like the morrow of the day he walked down the lane with me and gathered honeysuckles, only the night between has been a very, very strange time."

" I hope the interruption did not come very soon."

" I thought it was directly, but it could not have been so soon, since you are come home. We had just had time to tell

what we most wanted to know, and I know a little more of
what he is. I feel as if it were not only Colin again, but
ten times Colin. O Ailie, it must be a little bit like the
meetings in heaven!"

" I believe it is so with you," said Alison, scarcely able to
keep the tears from her eyes.

" After sometimes not daring to dwell on him, and then
only venturing because I thought he must be dead, to have
him back again with the same looks, only deeper—to find that
he clung to those weeks so long ago, and, above all, that there
was not one cloud, one doubt about the troubles—Oh, it is
too, too much."

Ermine lent back with clasped hands. She was like one
weary with happiness, and fain to rest in the sense of newly-
won peace. She said little more that evening, and if spoken
to, seemed like one wakened out of a dream, so that more
than once she laughed at herself, begged her sister's pardon,
and said that it seemed to her that she could not hear anything for the one glad voice that rang in her ear, " Colin is
come home." That was sufficient for her, no need for any
other sympathy, felt Alison, with another of those pangs
crushed down. Then wonder came—whether Ermine could
really contemplate the future, or if it were absolutely lost in
the present?

Colonel Keith went back to be seized by Conrade and
Francis, and walked off to the pony inspection, the two
boys, on either side of him, communicating to him the great
grievance of living in a poky place like this, where nobody
had ever been in the army, nor had a bit of sense, and Aunt
Rachel was always bothering, and trying to make mamma
think that Con told stories.

"I don't mind that," said Conrade, stoutly ; "let her try !"

"Oh, but she wanted mamma to shut you up," added Francis.

"Well, and mamma knows better," said Conrade, "and it made her leave off teaching me, so it was lucky. But I don't mind that ; only don't you see, Colonel, they don't know how to treat mamma ! They go and bully her, and treat her like—like a subaltern, till I hate the very sight of it."

"My boy," said the Colonel, who had been giving only half attention ; "you must make up your mind to your mother not being at the head of everything, as she used to be in your father's time. She will always be respected, but you must look to yourself as you grow up to make a position for her !"

"I wish I was grown up !" ·sighed Conrade ; "how I would give it to Aunt Rachel ! But why must we live here to have her plaguing us ?"

Questions that the Colonel was glad to turn aside by means of the ponies, and by a suggestion that, if a very quiet one were found, and if Conrade would be very careful, mamma might, perhaps, go out riding with them. The motion was so transcendant that, no sooner had the ponies been seen, than the boys raced home, and had communicated it at the top of their voices to mamma long before their friend made his appearance. Lady Temple was quite startled at the idea. "Dear papa," as she always called her husband, "had wished her to ride, but she had seldom done so, and now——" The tears came into her eyes.

"I think you might," said the Colonel, gently ; "I could find you a quiet animal, and to have you with Conrade would be such a protection to him," he added, as the boys had rushed out of the room.

"Yes; perhaps, dear boy. But I could not begin alone; it is so long since I rode. Perhaps when you come back from Ireland."

"I am not going to Ireland."

"I thought you said——" said Fanny looking up surprised; "I am very glad! But if you wished to go, pray don't think about us! I shall learn to manage in time, and I cannot bear to detain you."

"You do not detain me," he said, sitting down by her; "I have found what I was going in search of, and through your means."

"What—what do you mean? You were going to see Miss Williams this afternoon, I thought!"

"Yes, and it was she whom I was seeking." He paused, and added slowly, as if merely for the sake of dwelling on the words, "I have found her!"

"Miss Williams!" said Fanny, with perplexed looks.

"Miss Williams!—my Ermine whom I had not seen since the day after her accident, when we parted as on her death-bed!"

"That sister! Oh, poor thing, I am so glad! But I am sorry!" cried the much confused Fanny, in a breath; "were not you very much shocked?"

"I had never hoped to see her face in all its brightness again," he said. "Twelve years! It is twelve years that she has suffered, and of late she has been brought to this grievous state of poverty, and yet the spirit is as brave and cheerful as ever! It looks out of the beautiful eyes—more beautiful than when I first saw them,—I could see and think of nothing else!"

" Twelve years ! " repeated Fanny ; " is it so long since you saw her ? "

" Almost since I heard of her ! She was like a daughter to my aunt at Beauchamp, and her brother was my school-fellow. For one summer, when I was quartered at Hertford, I was with her constantly, but my family would not even hear of the indefinite engagement that was all we could have looked to, and made me exchange into the —th."

" Ah ! that was the way we came to have you ! I must tell you, dear Sir Stephen always guessed. Once when he had quite vexed poor mamma by preventing her from joking you in her way about young ladies, he told me that once, when he was young, he had liked some one who died or was married, I don't quite know which, and he thought it was the same with you, from something that happened when you withdrew your application for leave after your wound."

" Yes ! it was a letter from home, implying that my return would be accepted as a sign that I gave her up. So that was an additional instance of the exceeding kindness that I always received."

And there was a pause, both much affected by the thought of the good old man's ever ready consideration. At last Fanny said, " I am sure it was well for us ! What would *he* have done without you ?—and," she added, " do you really mean that you never heard of her all these years ? "

" Never after my aunt's death, except just after we went to Melbourne, when I heard in general terms of the ruin of the family and the false imputation on their brother."

" Ah ! I remember that you did say something about going home, and Sir Stephen was distressed, and mamma and I persuaded you because we saw he would have missed you so much, and mamma was quite hurt at your thinking of going. But if you had only told him your reason, he would never have thought of standing in your way."

"I know he would not, but I saw he could hardly find any one else just then who knew his ways so well. Besides, there was little use in going home till I had my promotion, and could offer her a home; and I had no notion how utter the ruin was, or that she had lost so much. So little did I imagine their straits that, but for Alison's look, I should hardly have inquired even on hearing her name."

"How very curious—how strangely things come round!" said Fanny; then with a start of dismay, "but what shall I do? Pray, tell me what you would like. If I might only keep her a little while till I can find some one else, though no one will ever be so nice; but indeed I would not for a moment, if you had rather not."

"Why so? Alison is very happy with you, and there can be no reason against her going on."

"Oh!" cried Lady Temple, with an odd sound of satisfaction, doubt, and surprise, "but I thought you would not like it."

"I should like, of course, to set them all at ease; but as I can do no more than make a home for Ermine and her niece, I can only rejoice that Alison is with you."

"But your brother!"

"If he does not like it, he must take the consequence of the utter separation he made my father insist on," said the Colonel sternly. "For my own part, I only esteem both sisters the more, if that were possible, for what they have done for themselves."

"Oh! that is what Rachel would like! She is so fond of

the sick—I mean of your—Miss Williams. I suppose I may not tell her yet."

" Not yet, if you please. I have scarcely had time as yet to know what Ermine wishes; but I could not help telling you."

" Thank you—I am so glad," she said, with sweet earnestness, holding out her hand in congratulation. " When may I go to her? I should like for her to come and stay here. Do you think she would?"

" Thank you, I will see. I know how kind you would be —indeed, have already been to her."

" And I am so thankful that I may keep Miss Williams! The dear boys never were so good. And perhaps she may stay till baby is grown up. Oh! how long it will be first! "

" She could not have a kinder friend," said the Colonel, smiling, and looking at his watch.

" Oh, is it time to dress? It is very kind of my dear aunt; but I do wish we could have stayed at home to-night. It is so dull for the boys when I dine out, and I had so much to ask you. One thing was about that poor little Bessie Keith. Don't you think I might ask her down here, to be near her brother?"

" It would be a very kind thing in you, and very good for her, but you must be prepared for rather a gay young lady."

" Oh, but she would not mind my not going out. She would have Alick, you know, and all the boys to amuse her; but, if you think it would be tiresome for her, and that she would not be happy, I should be very sorry to have her, poor child."

" I was not afraid for her," said Colonel Keith, smiling, " but of her being rather too much for you."

"Rachel is not too much for me," said Fanny, "and she and Grace will entertain Bessie, and take her out. But I will talk to Alick. He spoke of coming to-morrow. And don't you think I might ask Colonel and Mrs. Hammond to spend a day? They would so like the sea for the children."

"Certainly."

"Then perhaps you would write—oh, I forgot," colouring up, "I never can forget the old days; it seems as if you were on the staff still."

"I always am on yours, and always hope to be," he said, smiling, "though I am afraid I can't write your note to the Hammonds for you."

"But you won't go away," she said. "I know your time will be taken up, and you must not let me or the boys be troublesome; but to have you here makes me so much less lost and lonely. And I shall have such a friend in your Erminia. Is that her name?

"Ermine, an old Welsh name, the softest I ever heard. Indeed it is dressing time," added Colonel Keith, and both moved away with the startled precision of members of a punctual military household, still feeling themselves accountable to somebody.

CHAPTER VI.

ERMINE'S RESOLUTION.

" For as his hand the weather steers,
  So thrive I best 'twixt joys and tears,
  And all the year have some green ears."—H. VAUGHAN.

ALISON had not been wrong in her presentiment that the
second interview would be more trying than the first. The
exceeding brightness and animation of Ermine's countenance,
her speaking eyes, unchanged complexion, and lively manner
—above all, the restoration of her real substantial self—had
so sufficed and engrossed Colin Keith in the gladness of their
first meeting that he had failed to comprehend her helpless
state ; and already knowing her to be an invalid, not entirely
recovered from her accident, he was only agreeably surprised
to see the beauty of face he had loved so long, retaining all
its vivacity of expression. And when he met Alison the
next morning with a cordial brotherly greeting and inquiry
for her sister, her " Very well," and " not at all the worse for
the excitement," were so hearty and ready that he could not
have guessed that " well with Ermine meant something rather
relative than positive. Alison brought him a playful message
from her, that since he was not going to Belfast, she should
meet him with a freer conscience if he would first give her
time for Rose's lessons, and, as he said, he had lived long
enough with Messrs. Conrade and Co. to acknowledge the

wisdom of the message. But Rose had not long been at
leisure to look out for him before he made his appearance,
and walking in by right, as one at home ; and sitting down
in his yesterday's place, took the little maiden on his knee,
and began to talk to her about the lessons he had been told
to wait for. What would she have done without them ? He
knew some people who never could leave the house quiet
enough to hear one's-self speak if they were deprived of
lessons. Was that the way with her ? Rose laughed like a
creature, her aunt said, " to whom the notion of noise at
play was something strange and ridiculous ; necessity has
reduced her to Jacqueline Pascal's system with her *pen-
sionnaires,* who were allowed to play one by one without any
noise."

"But I don't play all alone," said Rose ; " I play with
you, Aunt Ermine, and with Violetta."

And Violetta speedily had the honour of an introduction,
very solemnly gone through, in due form ; Ermine, in the
languid sportiveness of enjoyment of his presence and his
kindness to the child, inciting Rose to present Miss Violetta
Williams to Colonel Keith, an introduction that he returned
with a grand military salute, at the same time as he shook
the doll's inseparable fingers. " Well, Miss Violetta, and
Miss Rose, when you come to live with me, I shall hope for
the pleasure of teaching you to make a noise."

" What does he mean ?" said Rose, turning round amazed
upon her aunt.

" I am afraid he does not quite know," said Ermine, sadly.

"Nay, Ermine," said he, turning from the child, and
bending over her, " you are the last who should say that.
Have I not told you that there is nothing now in our way—

no one with a right to object, and means enough for all we should wish, including her—— ? What is the matter ? " he added, startled by her look.

" Ah, Colin ! I thought you knew——"

" Knew what, Ermine ? " with his brows drawn together.

" Knew—what I am," she said ; " knew the impossibility. What, they have not told you ? I thought I was the invalid, the cripple, with every one."

" I knew you had suffered cruelly; I knew you were lame," he said, breathlessly ; " but—what——"

" It is more than lame," she said. " I should be better off if the fiction of the Queens of Spain were truth with me. I could not move from this chair without help. Oh, Colin ! poor Colin ! it was very cruel not to have prepared you for this ! " she added, as he gazed at her in grief and dismay, and made a vain attempt to find the voice that would not come. " Yes, indeed it is so," she said; " the explosion, rather than the fire, did mischief below the knee that poor nature could not repair, and I can but just stand, and cannot walk at all."

" Has anything been done—advice ? " he managed to utter.

" Advice upon advice, so that I felt it at last almost a compensation to be out of the way of the doctors. No, nothing more can be done ; and now that one is used to it, the snail is very comfortable in its shell. But I wish you could have known it sooner ! " she added, seeing him shade his brow with his hand, overwhelmed.

" What you must have suffered ! " he murmured.

" That is all over long ago ; every year has left that further behind, and made me more content. Dear Colin, for me there is nothing to grieve."

He could not control himself, rose up, made a long stride, and passed through the open window into the garden.

"Oh, if I could only follow him," gasped Ermine, joining her hands and looking up.

"Is it because you can't walk?" said Rose, somewhat frightened, and for the first time beginning to comprehend that her joyous-tempered aunt could be a subject for pity.

"Oh! this was what I feared!" sighed Ermine. "Oh, give us strength to go through with it." Then becoming awake to the child's presence—"A little water, if you please, my dear." Then, more composedly, "Don't be frightened, my Rose; you did not know it was such a shock to find me so laid by——"

"He is in the garden walking up and down," said Rose. "May I go and tell him how much merrier you always are than Aunt Ailie?"

Poor Ermine felt anything but merry just then, but she had some experience of Rose's powers of soothing, and signed assent. So in another second Colonel Keith was met in the hasty, agonized walk by which he was endeavouring to work off his agitation, and the slender child looked wistfully up at him from dark depths of half understanding eyes—"Please, please don't be so very sorry," she said. "Aunt Ermine does not like it. She never is sorry for herself——"

"Have I shaken her—distressed her?" he asked, anxiously.

"She doesn't like you to be sorry," said Rose, looking up. "And, indeed, she does not mind it; she is such a merry aunt! Please, come in again, and see how happy we always are——"

The last words were spoken so near the window that Ermine caught them, and said, "Yes, come in, Colin, and learn not to grieve for me, or you will make me repent of my selfish gladness yesterday."

"Not grieve!" he exclaimed, "when I think of the beautiful vigorous being that used to be the life of the place——" and he would have said more but for a deprecating sign of the hand.

"Well," she said, half smiling, "it is a pity to think even of a crushed butterfly; but indeed, Colin, if you can bear to listen to me, I think I can show you that it all has been a blessing even by sight, as well as, of course, by faith. Only remember the unsatisfactoriness of our condition—the never seeing or hearing from one another after that day when Mr. Beauchamp came down on us. Did not the accident win for us a parting that was much better to remember than that state of things? Oh, the pining, weary feel as if all the world had closed on me! I do assure you it was much worse than anything that came after the burn. Yes, if I had been well and doing like others, I know I should have fretted and wearied, pined myself ill perhaps, whereas I could always tell myself that every year of your absence might be a step towards your finding me well; and when I was forced to give up that hope for myself, why then, Colin, the never seeing your name made me think you would never be disappointed and grieved as you are now. It is very merciful the way that physical trials help one through those of the mind."

"I never knew," said the Colonel; "all my aunt's latter letters spoke of your slow improvement beyond hope."

"True, in her time, I had not reached the point where I stopped. The last time I saw her I was still upstairs; and, indeed, I did not half know what I could do till I tried."

"Yes," said he, brightened by that buoyant look so remarkable in her face; "and you will yet do more, Ermine. You have convinced me that we shall be all the happier together——"

"But that was not what I meant to convince you of——" she said, faintly.

"Not what you meant, perhaps; but what it did convince me was, that you—as you are, my Ermine—are ten thousand times more to me than even as the beautiful girl, and that there never can be a happier pair than we shall be when I am your hands and feet."

Ermine sat up, and rallied all her forces, choked back the swelling of her throat, and said, "Dear Colin, it cannot be! I trusted you were understanding that when I told you how it was with me."

He could not speak from consternation.

"No," she said; "it would be wrong in me to think of it for an instant. That you should have done so, shows—— O Colin, I cannot talk of it; but it would be as ungenerous in me to consent, as it is noble of you to propose it."

"It is no such thing," he answered; "it has been the one object and thought of my life, the only hope I have had all these years."

"Exactly so," she said, struggling again to speak firmly; "and that is the very thing. You kept your allegiance to the bright, tall, walking, active girl, and it would be a shame in the scorched cripple to claim it."

"Don't call yourself names. Have I not told you that you are more than the same?"

"You do not know. You are pleased because my face is not burnt, nor grown much older, and because I can talk and laugh in the same voice still." (Oh, how it quivered!) "But it would be a wicked mockery in me to pretend to be the wife you want. Yes, I know you think you do, but that is just because my looks are so deceitful, and you have kept on thinking about me ; but you must make a fresh beginning."

"You can tell me that," he said, indignantly.

"Because it is n t new to me," she said ; "the quarter of an hour you stood by me, with that deadly calm in your white face, was the real farewell to the young hopeful dream of that bright summer. I wish it was as calm now."

"I believed you dying then," answered he.

"Do not make me think it would have been better for you if I had been," she said, imploringly. "It was as much the end, and I knew it from the time my recovery stopped short. I would have let you know if I could, and then you would not have been so much shocked."

"So as to cut me off from you entirely?"

"No, indeed. The thought of seeing you again was too—too overwhelming to be indulged in ; knowing, as I did, that if you were the same to me, it must be at this sad cost to you," and her eyes filled with tears.

"It is you who make it so, Ermine."

"No ; it is the providence that has set me aside from the active work of life. Pray do not go on, Colin, it is only giving us both useless pain. You do not know what it costs me to deny you, and I feel that I must. I know you are only acting on the impulse of generosity. Yes, I will say so, though you think it is to please yourself," she added, with one of those smiles that nothing could drive far from her lips, and which made it infinitely harder to acquiesce in her denial.

" I will make you think so in time," he said.

" Then I might tell you, you had no right to please yourself," she answered, still with the same air of playfulness; "you have got a brother, you know—and—yes, I hear you growl; but if he is a poor old broken man out of health, it is the more reason you should not vex him, nor hamper yourself with a helpless commodity."

" You are not taking the way to make me forget what my brother has done for us."

" How do you know that he did not save me from being a strong-minded military lady? After all, it was absurd to expect people to look favourably on our liking for one another, and you know they could not be expected to know that there was real stuff in the affair. If there had not been, we should have thought so all the same, you know, and been quite as furious."

He could not help smiling, recollecting fury that, in the course of these twelve years, he had seen evinced under similar circumstances by persons who had consoled themselves before he had done pitying them. " Still," he said, gravely, " I think there was harshness."

" So do I, but not so much as I thought at that time, and —oh, surely that is not Rachel Curtis!" I told her I thought you would call."

" Intolerable!" he muttered between his teeth. " Is she always coming to bore you?"

" She has been very kind, and my great enlivenment," said Ermine, " and she can't be expected to know how little we want her. Oh, there, the danger is averted! She must have asked if you were here."

" I was just thinking that she was the chief objection

to Lady Temple's kind wish of having you at Myrtle-wood."

" Does Lady Temple know ? " asked Ermine, blushing.

" I could not keep it from one who has been so uniformly kind to me ; but I desired her not to let it go further till I should hear your wishes."

" Yes, she has a right to know," said Ermine; "but please, not a word elsewhere."

" And will you not come to stay with her ? "

" I ? Oh, no ; I am fit for no place but this. You don't half know how bad I am. When you have seen a little more of us, you will be quite convinced."

" Well, at least, you give me leave to come here."

" Leave ? When it is a greater pleasure than I ever thought to have again ; that is, while you understand that you said good-bye to the Ermine of Beauchamp Parsonage twelve years ago, and that the thing here is only a sort of ghost, most glad and grateful to be a friend—a sister."

" So," he said, " those are to be the terms of my admission."

" The only possible ones."

" I will consider them. I have not accepted them."

" You will," she said.

But she met a smile in return, implying that there might be a will as steadfast as her own, although the question might be waived for a time.

Meantime, Rachel was as nearly hating Colonel Keith as principle would allow, with " Human Reeds," newly finished, burning in her pocket, " Military Society " fermenting in her brain, and " Curatocult " still unacknowledged. Had he not had quite time for any rational visit ? Was he to devour

Mackarel Lane as well as Myrtlewood? She was on her way to the latter house, meeting Grace as she went, and congratulating herself that he could not be in two places at once, whilst Grace secretly wondered how far she might venture to build on Alison Williams's half confidence, and regretted the anxiety wasted by Rachel and the mother; though, to be sure, that of Mrs. Curtis was less uncalled for than her daughter's, since it was only the fear of Fanny's not being sufficiently guarded against misconstructions.

Rachel held up her hands in despair in the hall. "Six officers' cards!" she exclaimed.

"No, only six cards," said Grace; "there are two of each."

"That's enough," sighed Rachel; "and look there," gazing through the garden-door. "She is walking with the young puppy that dined here on Thursday, and they called Alick."

"Do you remember," said Grace, "how she used to chatter about Alick, when she first came to us, at six years old. He was the child of one of the officers. Can this be the same?"

"That's one of your ideas, Grace. Look, this youth could have been hardly born when Fanny came to us. No; he is only one of the idlers that military life has accustomed her to."

Rather against Grace's feeling, Rachel drew her on, so as to come up with Lady Temple and her friend in the midst of their conversation, and they heard the last words—

"Then you will give me dear Bessie's direction?"

"Thank you, it will be the greatest kindness——"

"Oh, Grace, Rachel, is it you?" exclaimed Fanny. "You have not met before, I think. Mr. Keith—Miss Curtis."

Very young indeed were both face and figure, fair and pale, and though there was a moustache, it was so light and silky as to be scarcely visible ; the hair, too, was almost flaxen, and the whole complexion had a washed-out appearance. The eyes, indeed, were of the same peculiar deep blue as the Colonel's, but even these were little seen under their heavy sleepy lids, and the long limbs had in every movement something of weight and slowness, the very sight of which fretted Rachel, and made her long to shake him. It appeared that he was come to spend the Sunday at Avonmouth, and Grace tried to extract the comfort for her mother that two gentlemen were better than one, and Fanny need not be on their minds for chaperonage for that day.

A party of garden-chairs on the lawn invited repose, and there the ladies seated themselves ; Fanny laying down her heavy crape bonnet, and showing her pretty little delicate face, now much fresher and more roseate than when she arrived, though her wide-spreading black draperies gave a certain dignity to her slight figure, contrasting with the summer muslins of her two cousins ; as did her hot-house plant fairness, with their firm, healthy glow of complexion ; her tender shrinking grace, with their upright vigour. The gentleman of the party leant back in a languid, easy posture, as though only half awake, and the whole was so quiet that Grace, missing the usual tumult of children, asked after them.

" The boys have gone to their favourite cove under the plantation. They have a fort there, and Hubert told me he was to be a hero, and Miss Williams a she-ro."

" I would not encourage that description of sport," said Rachel, willing to fight a battle in order to avert maternal anecdotes of boyish sayings.

" They like it so much," said Fanny, "and they learn so much now that they act all the battles they read about."

" That is what I object to," said Rachel ; " it is accustoming them to confound heroism with pugnacity."

" No, but Rachel dear, they do quarrel and fight among themselves much less now that this is all in play and good humour," pleaded Fanny.

" Yes, that may be, but you are cultivating the dangerous instinct, although for a moment giving it a better direction."

" Dangerous ? Oh, Alick ! do you think it can be ?" said Fanny, less easily borne down with a supporter beside her.

" According to the Peace Society," he answered, with a quiet air of courteous deference ; " perhaps you belong to it ?"

" No, indeed," answered Rachel, rather indignantly, " I think war the great purifier and ennobler of nations, when it is for a good and great cause ; but I think education ought to protest against confounding mere love of combat with heroism."

" Query, the true meaning of the word ?" he said, leaning back.

" *Heros*, yes from the same root as the German *herr*," readily responded Rachel, " meaning no more than lord and master ; but there can be no doubt that the progress of ideas has linked with it a much nobler association."

" Progress ! What, since the heroes were half divine !"

" Half divine in the esteem of a people who thought brute courage godlike. To us the word maintains its semi-divinity, and it should be our effort to associate it only with that which veritably has the god-like stamp."

" And that is——?"

"Doing more than one's duty," exclaimed Rachel, with a glistening eye.

" Very uncomfortable and superfluous, and not at all easy," he said, half shutting his already heavy eyes.

" Easy, no, that's the beauty and the glory——"

" Major Sherborne and Captain Lester in the drawing-room, my lady," announced Coombe, who had looked infinitely cheered since this military influx.

" You will come with me, Grace," said Fanny, rising. " I dare say you had rather not, Rachel, and it would be a pity to disturb you, Alick."

" Thank you ; it would be decidedly more than my duty."

" I am quite sorry to go, you are so amusing," said Fanny ; " but I suppose you will have settled about heroism by the time we come out again, and will tell me what the boys ought to play at."

Rachel's age was quite past the need of troubling herself at being left *tête-à-tête* with a mere lad like this ; and, besides, it was an opportunity not to be neglected of giving a young carpet knight a lesson in true heroism. There was a pause after the other two had moved off. Rachel reflected for a few moments, and then, precipitated by the fear of her audience falling asleep, she exclaimed—

" No words have been more basely misused than hero and heroine. The one is the mere fighting animal whose strength or fortune have borne him through some more than ordinary danger, the other is only the subject of an adventure, perfectly irrespective of her conduct in it."

" Bathos attends all high words," he said, as she paused, chiefly to see whether he was awake, and not like her dumb playfellow of old.

" This is not their natural bathos but their misuse. They ought to be reserved for those who in any department have passed the limits to which the necessity of their position constrained them, and done acts of self-devotion for the good of others. I will give you an instance, and from you own profession, that you may see I am not prejudiced ; besides, the hero of it is past praise or blame."

Encouraged by seeing a little more of his eyes, she went on. " It was in the course of the siege of Delhi, a shell came into a tent where some sick and wounded were lying. There was one young officer among them who could move enough to have had a chance of escaping the explosion, but instead of that he took the shell up, its fuse burning as it was, and ran with it out of the tent, then hurled it to a distance. It exploded, and of course was his death, but the rest were saved, and I call that a deed of heroism far greater than mounting a breach or leading a forlorn hope."

" Killed, you say ? " inquired Mr. Keith, still in the same lethargic manner.

" Oh yes, mortally wounded : carried back to die among the men he had saved."

" Jessie Cameron singing his dirge," mumbled this provoking individual, with something about the form of his cheek that being taken by Rachel for a derisive smile, made her exclaim vehemently, " You do not mean to undervalue an action like that in comparison with mere animal pugnacity in an advance."

" More than one's duty was your test," he said.

" And was not this more than duty ? Ah ! I see yours is a spirit of depreciation, and I can only say I pity you."

He took the trouble to lift himself up and make a little

bow of acknowledgment. Certainly he was worse than the Colonel; but Rachel, while mustering her powers for annihilating him, was annoyed by all the party in the drawing-room coming forth to join them, the other officers rallying young Keith upon his luxurious station, and making it evident that he was a proverb in the regiment for taking his ease. Chairs were brought out, and afternoon tea, and the callers sat down to wait for Colonel Keith to come in; Grace feeling obliged to stay to help Fanny entertain her visitors, and Rachel to protect her from their follies. One thing Grace began to perceive, that Lady Temple had in her former world been a person of much more consideration than she was made here, and seeing the polite and deferential manner of these officers to her, could only wonder at her gentle content and submission in meeting with no particular attention from anybody, and meekly allowing herself to be browbeaten by Rachel and lectured by her aunt.

A lecture was brewing up for her indeed. Poor Mrs. Curtis was very much concerned at the necessity, and only spurred up by a strong sense of duty to give a hint—the study of which hint cost her a whole sleepless night and a very weary Sunday morning. She decided that her best course would be to drive to Myrtlewood rather early on her way to church, and take up Fanny, gaining a previous conference with her alone, if possible. "Yes, my dear," she said to Grace, "I must get it over before church, or it will make me so nervous all through the service."

And Grace, loving her mother best, durst not suggest what it might do to Fanny, hoping that the service might help her to digest the hint.

Mrs. Curtis's regular habits were a good deal shocked to

find Fanny still at the breakfast table. The children had
indeed long finished, and were scattered about the room,
one of them standing between Colonel Keith's knees, repeating a hymn ; but the younger guest was still in the midst
of his meal, and owned in his usual cool manner that he
was to blame for the lateness, there was no resisting the
charms of no morning parade.

Her aunt's appearance made Fanny imagine it much later
than it really was, and she hurried off the children to be
dressed, and proceeded herself to her room, Mrs. Curtis
following, and by way of preliminary, asking when Colonel
Keith was going to Ireland.

" Oh ! " said Fanny, blushing most suspiciously under her
secret, " he is not going to Ireland now."

" Indeed ! I quite understood he intended it."

" Yes," faltered Fanny, " but he found that he need not."

"Indeed ! " again ejaculated poor perplexed Mrs. Curtis ;
" but then, at least, he is going away soon."

" He must go to Scotland by-and-by, but for the present
he is going into lodgings. Do you know of any nice ones,
dear aunt ? "

"Well, I suppose you can't help that ; you know, my
dear, it would never *do* for him to stay in this house."

" I never thought of that," said Fanny simply, the colour
coming in a fresh glow.

" No, my dear, but you see you are very young and inexperienced. I do not say you have done anything the least
amiss, or that you ever would mean it, only you will forgive
your old aunt for putting you on your guard."

Fanny kissed her, but with eyes full of tears, and cheeks
burning, then her candour drew from her—" It was he that

thought of getting a lodging. I am glad I did not persuade him not ; but you know he always did live with us."

" With *us*. Yes, my poor dear, that is the difference, and you see he feels it. But, indeed, my dear child, though he is a very good man, I dare say, and quite a gentleman all but his beard, you had better not encourage—— You know people are so apt to make remarks."

" I have no fear," said Fanny, turning away her head, conscious of the impossibility of showing her aunt her mistake.

" Ah ! my dear, you don't guess how ready people are to talk ; and you would not like—for your children's sake, for your husband's sake—that—that——"

" Pray, pray aunt," cried Fanny, much pained ; " indeed you don't know. My husband had confidence in him more than in any one. He told him to take care of me and look after the boys. I couldn't hold aloof from him without transgressing those wishes"—and the words were lost in a sob.

" My dear, indeed I did not mean to distress you. You know, I dare say—I mean——" hesitated poor Mrs. Curtis. " I know you must see a great deal of him. I only want you to take care—appearances are appearances, and if it was said you had all these young officers always coming about——"

" I don't think they will come. It was only just to call, and they have known me so long. It is all out of respect to my father and Sir Stephen," said Fanny, meekly as ever. " Indeed, I would not for the world do anything you did not like, dear aunt ; but there can't be any objection to my having Mrs. Hammond and the children to spend the day to-morrow."

Mrs. Curtis did not like it ; she had an idea that all

military ladies were dashing and vulgar, but she could not say there was any objection, so she went on to the head of poor Fanny's offending. "This young man, my dear, he seems to make himself very intimate."

"Alick Keith? Oh aunt!" said Fanny, more surprised than by all the rest; "don't you know about him? His father and mother were our greatest friends always; I used to play with him every day till I came to you. And then just as I married, poor Mrs. Keith died, and we had dear little Bessie with us till her father could send her home. And when poor Alick was so dreadfully wounded before Delhi, Sir Stephen sent him up in a litter to the hills for mamma and me to nurse. Mamma was so fond of him, she used to call him her son."

"Yes, my dear, I dare say you have been very intimate; but you see you are very young; and his staying here——"

"I thought he would be so glad to come and be with the colonel, who was his guardian and Bessie's," said Fanny; "and I have promised to have Bessie to stay with me, she was such a dear little thing——"

"Well, my dear, it may be a good thing for you to have a young lady with you, and if he *is* to come over, her presence will explain it. Understand me, my dear, I am not at all afraid of your—your doing anything foolish, only to get talked of is so dreadful in your situation, that you can't be too careful."

"Yes, yes, thank you, dear aunt," murmured the drooping and subdued Fanny, aware how much the remonstrance must cost her aunt, and sure that she must be in fault in some way, if she could only see how. "Please, dear aunt, help me, for indeed I don't know how to manage—tell me how to

be civil and kind to my dear husband's friends without—
without——"

Her voice broke down, though she kept from tears as an
unkindness to her aunt.

In very fact, little as she knew it, she could not have
defended herself better than by this humble question, throwing the whole guidance of her conduct upon her aunt.   If
she had been affronted, Mrs. Curtis could have been displeased; but to be thus set to prescribe the right conduct,
was at once mollifying and perplexing.

"Well, well, my dear child, we all know you wish to do
right; you can judge best.   I would not have you ungrateful
or uncivil, only you know you are living very quietly, and
intimacy—oh! my dear, I know your own feeling will direct
you.   Dear child! you have taken what I said so kindly.
And now let me see that dear little girl."

Rachel had not anticipated that the upshot of a remonstrance, even from her mother, would be that Fanny was to
be directed by her own feeling!

That same feeling took Lady Temple to Mackarel Lane later
in the day.   She had told the Colonel her intention, and
obtained Alison's assurance that Ermine's stay at Myrtlewood
need not be impracticable, and armed with their consent, she
made her timid tap at Miss Williams' door, and showed her
sweet face within it.

"May I come in?   Your sister and your little niece are
gone for a walk.   I told them I would come!   I did want
to see you!"

"Thank you," said Ermine, with a sweet smile, colouring
cheek, yet grave eyes, and much taken by surprise at being
seized by both hands, and kissed on each cheek.

" Yes, you must let me," said her visitor, looking up with her pretty imploring gesture ; " you know I have known him so long, and he has been so good to me ! "

" Indeed it is very kind in you," said Ermine, fully feeling the force of the plea expressed in the winning young face and gentle eyes full of tears.

" Oh, no, I could not help it. I am only so sorry we kept him away from you when you wanted him so much ; but we did not know, and he was Sir Stephen's right hand, and we none of us knew what to do without him ; but if he had only told——"

" Thank you, oh, thank you ! " said Ermine, " but indeed it was better for *him* to be away." Even her wish to console that pleading little widow could not make her say that his coming would not have been good for her. " It has been such a pleasure to hear he had so kind and happy a home all these years."

" Oh, you cannot think how Sir Stephen loved and valued him. The one thing I always did wish was, that Conrade should grow up to be as much help and comfort to his father, and now he never can ! But," driving back a tear, " it was so hard that you should not have known how distinguished and useful and good he was all those years. Only now I shall have the pleasure of telling you," and she smiled. She was quite a different being when free from the unsympathizing influence which, without her understanding it, had kept her from dwelling on her dearest associations.

" It will be a pleasure of pleasures," said Ermine, eagerly.

" Then you will do me a favour, a very great favour," said Lady Temple, laying hold of her hand again, " if you and your sister and niece will come and stay with me." And as Ermine commenced her refusal, she went on in the same coaxing way, with a description of her plans for Ermine's comfort, giving her two rooms on the ground floor, and assuring her of the absence of steps, the immunity from all teasing by the children, of the full consent of her sister, and the wishes of the Colonel; nay, when Ermine was still unpersuaded of the exceeding kindness it would be to herself. "You see I am terribly young, *really*," she said, "though I have so many boys, and my aunt thinks it awkward for me to have so many officers calling, and I can't keep them away because they are my father's and Sir Stephen's old friends ; so please do come and make it all right !"

Ermine was driven so hard, and so entirely deprived of all excuse, that she had no alternative left but to come to the real motive.

"I ought not," she said, "it is not good for him, so you must not press me, dear Lady Temple. You see it is best for him that nobody should ever know of what has been between us."

"What ! don't you mean——— ?" exclaimed Fanny, breaking short off.

"I cannot ! " said Ermine.

"But he would like it. He wishes it as much as ever."

"I know he does," said Ermine, with a troubled voice ; "but you see that is because he did not know what a wretched remnant I am, and he never has had time to think about any one else."

"Oh no, no."

"And it would be very unfair of me to take advantage of that, and give him such a thing as I am."

" Oh dear, but that is very sad ! " cried Fanny, looking much startled.

" But I am sure you must see that it is right."

" It may be right," and out burst Fanny's ready tears ; " but it is very, very hard and disagreeable, if you don't mind my saying so, when I know it is so good of you. And don't you mean to let him even see you, when he has been constant so long ? "

" No ; I see no reason for denying myself that ; indeed I believe it is better for him to grow used to me as I am, and be convinced of the impossibility."

" Well then, why will you not come to me ? "

" Do you not see, in all your kindness, that my coming to you would make every one know the terms between us, while no one remarks his just coming to me here as an old friend ? And if he were ever to turn his mind to any one else——"

" He will never do that, I am sure."

" There is no knowing. He has never been, in his own estimation, disengaged from me," said Ermine ; " his brother is bent on his marrying, and he ought to be perfectly free to do so, and not under the disadvantage that any report of this affair would be to him."

" Well, I am sure he never will," said Fanny, almost petulantly ; " I know I shall hate her, that's all."

Ermine thought her own charity towards Mrs. Colin Keith much more dubious than Lady Temple's, but she continued—

" At any rate you will be so very kind as not to let any one know of it. I am glad you do. I should not feel it right that you should not, but it is different with others."

" Thank you. And if you will not come to me, you will let me come to you, won't you ? It will be so nice to come

and talk him over with you. Perhaps I shall persuade you
some of these days after all. Only I must go now, for I
always give the children their tea on Sunday. But please
let your dear little niece come up to-morrow and play with
them; the little Hammonds will be there, she is just their
age."

Ermine felt obliged to grant this at least, though she was
as doubtful of her shy Rose's happiness as of the expedience
of the intimacy; but there was no being ungracious to the
gentle visitor, and no doubt Ermine felt rejoiced and elevated.
She did not need fresh assurances of Colin's constancy, but
the affectionate sister-like congratulations of this loving,
winning creature, showed how real and in earnest his intentions were. And then Lady Temple's grateful esteem for
him being, as it was, the reflection of her husband's, was no
small testimony to his merits.

"Pretty creature!" said Ermine to herself; "really if it
did come to that, I could spare him to her better than to any
one else. She has some notion how to value him."

Alison and Rose had, in the meantime, been joined by
Colonel Keith and the boys, whom Alick had early deserted
in favour of a sunny sandy nook. The Colonel's purpose was
hard on poor Alison; it was to obtain her opinion of her
sister's decision, and the likelihood of persistence in it. It
was not, perhaps, bad for either that they conversed under
difficulties, the boys continually coming back to them from
excursions on the rocks, and Rose holding her aunt's hand
all the time; but to be sure Rose had heard nearly all the
Colonel's affairs, and somehow mixed him up with Henry of
Cranstoun.

Very tenderly towards Alison herself did Colin Keith

speak. It was the first time they had ever been brought into
close contact, and she had quite to learn to know him. She
had regarded his return as probably a misfortune, but it was
no longer possible to do so when she heard his warm and considerate way of speaking of her sister, and saw him only desirous of learning what was most for her real happiness. Nay,
he even made a convert of Alison herself ! She did believe that
would Ermine but think it right to consent, she would be
happy and safe in the care of one who knew so well how to
love her.   Terrible as the wrench would be to Alison herself,
she thought he deserved her sister, and that she would be as
happy with him as earth could make her. But she did not
believe Ermine would ever accept him. She knew the strong,
unvarying resolution by which her sister had always held to
what she thought right, and did not conceive that it would
waver.   The acquiescence in his visits, and the undisguised
exultant pleasure in his society, were evidences to Alison not
of wavering or relenting, but of confidence in Ermine's own
sense of impossibility. She durst not give him any hope,
though she owned that he merited success. " Did she think
his visits bad for her sister ? " he then asked in the unselfishness that pleaded so strongly for him.

" No, certainly not," she answered eagerly, then made a
little hesitation that made him ask further.

" My only fear," she said candidly, " is, that if this is
pressed much on her, and she has to struggle with you and
herself too, it may hurt her health.   Trouble tells not on her
cheerfulness, but on her nerves."

" Thank you," he said, " I will refrain."

Alison was much happier than she had been since the first
apprehension of his return. The first pang at seeing Ermine's

heart another's property had been subdued ; the present state
of affairs was indefinitely prolonged, and she not only felt
trust in Colin Keith's consideration for her sister, but she
knew that an act of oblivion was past on her perpetration of
the injury. She was right. His original pitying repugnance
to a mere unknown child could not be carried on to the
grave, saddened woman devoted to her sister ; and in the
friendly brotherly tone of that interview, each understood
the other. And when Alison came home and said, " I have
been walking with Colin," her look made Ermine very
happy.

" And learning to know him."

" Learning to sympathize with him, Ermine," with steady
eyes and voice. " You are hard on him."

" Now, Ailie," said Ermine, " once for all, he is not to set
you on me, as he has done with Lady Temple. The more he
persuades me, the better I know that to listen would be an
abuse of his constancy. It would set him wrong with his
brother, and, as dear Edward's affairs stand, we have no right
to carry the supposed disgrace into a family that would believe
it, though he does not. If I were ever so well, I should not
think it right to marry. I shall not shun the sight of him ;
it is delightful to me, and a less painful cure to him than
sending him away would be. It is in the nature of things
that he should cool into a friendly kindly feeling, and I shall
try to bear it. Or if he does marry, it will be all right,
I suppose—" but her voice faltered, and she gave a sort of
broken laugh. " There," she said, with a recovered flash of
liveliness, " there's my resolution, to do what I like more
than anything in the world as long as I can ; and when it
is over I shall be helped to do without it ! "

" I can't believe——" broke out Alison.

" Not in your heart, but in your reason," said Ermine, endeavouring to smile. " He will hover about here, and always be kind, loving, considerate ; but a time will come that he will want the home happiness I cannot give.   Then he will not wear out his affection on the impossible literary cripple, but begin over again, and be happy.   And, Alison, if your love for me is of the sound, strong sort I know it is, you will help me through with it, and never say one word to make all this less easy and obvious to him."

CHAPTER VII.

WAITING FOR ROSE.

" Not envy, sure ! for if you gave me
  Leave to take or to refuse
  In earnest, do you think I'd choose
  That sort of new love to enslave me ? "—R. BROWNING.

So, instead of going to Belfast, here was Colonel Keith
actually taking a lodging and settling himself into it ; nay,
even going over to Avoncester on a horse-buying expedition,
not merely for the Temples, but for himself.

This time Rachel did think herself sure of Miss Williams'
ear in peace, and came down on her with two fat manuscripts
upon Human Reeds and Military Society, preluding, however,
by bitter complaints of the " Traveller " for never having
vouchsafed her an answer, nor having even restored " Curatocult," though she had written three times, and sent a
directed envelope and stamps for the purpose. The paper
must be ruined by so discourteous an editor, indeed she had
not been nearly so much interested as usual by the last few
numbers. If only she could get her paper back, she should
try the " Englishwoman's Hobby-horse," or some other paper
of more progress than that " Traveller." " Is it not very hard
to feel one's self shut out from the main stream of the work
of the world when one's heart is burning ? "

" I think you overrate the satisfaction."

" You can't tell ! You are contented with that sort of home peaceful sunshine that I know suffices many. Even intellectual as you are, you can't tell what it is to feel power within, to strain at the leash, and see others in the race."

" I was thinking whether you could not make an acceptable paper on the lace system, which you really know so thoroughly."

" The fact is," said Rachel, " it is much more difficult to describe from one's own observation than from other sources."

" But rather more original," said Ermine, quite overcome by the *naïveté* of the confession.

" I don't see that," said Rachel. " It is abstract reasoning from given facts that I aim at, as you will understand when you have heard my ' Human Reeds,' and my other—dear me, there's your door bell. I thought that Colonel was gone for the day."

" There are other people in the world besides the Colonel," Ermine began to say, though she hardly felt as if there were, and at any rate a sense of rescue crossed her. The persons admitted took them equally by surprise, being Conrade Temple and Mr. Keith.

" I thought," said Rachel, as she gave her unwilling hand to the latter, " that you would have been at Avoncester to-day."

" I always get out of the way of horse-dealing. I know no greater bore," he answered.

" Mamma sent me down," Conrade was explaining ; " Mr. Keith's uncle found out that he knew Miss Williams—no, that's not it, Miss Williams' uncle found out that Mr. Keith preached a sermon, or something of that sort, so mamma sent me down to show him the way to call upon her; but I need not stay now, need I?"

"After that elegant introduction and lucid explanation, I think you may be excused," returned Alick Keith.

The boy shook Ermine's hand with his soldierly grace, but rather spoilt the effect thereof by his aside, "I wanted to see the toad and the pictures our Miss Williams told me about, but I'll come another time;" and the wink of his black eyes, and significant shrug of his shoulders at Rachel, were irresistible. They all laughed, even Rachel herself, as Ermine, seeing it would be worse to ignore the demonstration, said, "The elements of aunt and boy do not always work together."

"No," said Rachel; "I have never been forgiven for being the first person who tried to keep those boys in order."

"And now," said Ermine, turning to her other visitor, "perhaps I may discover which of us, or of our uncles, preached a sermon."

"Mine, I suspect," returned Mr. Keith. "Your sister and I made out at luncheon that you had known my uncle, Mr. Clare, of Bishopsworthy."

"Mr. Clare! Oh yes," cried Ermine eagerly; "he took the duty for one of our curates once for a long vacation. Did you ever hear him speak of Beauchamp?"

"Yes, often; and of Dr. Williams. He will be very much interested to hear of you."

"It was a time I well remember," said Ermine. "He was an Oxford tutor then, and I was about fourteen, just old enough to be delighted to hear clever talk. And his sermons were memorable; they were the first I ever listened to."

" There are few sermons that it is not an infliction to listen to," began Rachel, but she was not heard or noticed.

" I assure you they are even more striking now in his blindness."

" Blindness! Indeed, I had not heard of that."

Even Rachel listened with interest as the young officer explained that his uncle, whom both he and Miss Williams talked of as a man of note, of whom every one must have heard, had for the last four years been totally blind, but continued to be an active parish priest, visiting regularly, preaching, and taking a share in the service, which he knew by heart. He had, of course, a curate, who lived with him, and took very good care of him.

" No one else?" said Rachel. " I thought your sister lived at Bishopsworthy."

" No, my sister lives, or has lived, at Little Worthy, the next parish, and as unlike it as possible. It has a railroad in it, and the cockneys have come down on it and 'villafied' it. My aunt, Mrs. Lacy Clare, has lived there ever since my sister has been with her; but now her last daughter is to be married, she wishes to give up housekeeping."

" And your sister is coming to Lady Temple," said Rachel, in her peculiar affirmative way of asking questions. " She will find it very dull here."

" With all the advantages of Avoncester at hand?" inquired Alick, with a certain gleam under his flaxen eyelashes that convinced Ermine that he said it in mischief. But Rachel drew herself up gravely, and answered—

" In Lady Temple's situation any such thing would be most inconsistent with good feeling."

" Such as the cathedral?" calmly, not to say sleepily,

inquired Alick, to the excessive diversion of Ermine, who saw that Rachel had never been laughed at in her life, and was utterly at a loss what to make of it.

" If you meant the cathedral," she said, a little uncertainly, recollecting the tone in which Mr. Clare had just been spoken of, and thinking that perhaps Miss Keith might be a curato-latress, " I am afraid it is not of much benefit to people living at this distance, and there is not much to be said for the imitation here."

" You will see what my sister says to it. She only wants training to be the main strength of the Bishops Worthy choir, and perhaps she may find it here."

Rachel was evidently undecided whether chants or marches were Miss Keith's passion, and, perhaps, which propensity would render the young lady the most distasteful to herself. Ermine thought it merciful to divert the attack by mentioning Mr. Clare's love of music, and hoping his curate could gratify it. " No," Mr. Keith said, " it was very unlucky that Mr. Lifford did not know one note from another; so that his vicar could not delude himself into hoping that his playing on his violin was anything but a nuisance to his companion, and in spite of all the curate's persuasions, he only indulged himself therewith on rare occasions." But as Ermine showed surprise at the retention of a companion devoid of this sixth sense, so valuable to the blind, he added —" No one would suit him so well. Mr. Lifford has been with him ever since his sight began to fail, and understands all his ways."

" Yes, that makes a great difference."

" And," pursued the young man, coming to something like life as he talked of his uncle, " though he is not quite all that a companion might be, my uncle says there would be no keeping the living without him, and I do not believe there would, unless my uncle would have me instead."

Ermine laughed and looked interested, not quite knowing what other answer to make. Rachel lifted up her eyebrows in amazement.

" Another advantage," added Alick, who somehow seemed to accept Ermine as one of the family, " is, that he is no impediment to Bessie's living there, for, poor man, he has a wife, but insane."

" Then your sister will live there ? " said Rachel. " What an enviable position, to have the control of means of doing good that always falls to the women of a clerical family."

" Tell her so," said the brother, with his odd, suppressed smile.

" What, she does not think so ? "

" Now," said Mr. Keith, leaning back, " on my answer depends whether Bessie enters this place with a character for chanting, croquet, or crochet. Which should you like worst, Miss Curtis ? "

" I like evasions worst of all," said Rachel, with a flash of something like playful spirit, though there was too much asperity in it.

" But you see, unfortunately, I don't know," said Alick Keith, slowly. " I have never been able to find out, nor she either. I don't know what may be the effect of example," he added. Ermine wondered whether he were in mischief or earnest, and suspected a little of both.

" I shall be very happy to show Miss Keith any of my ways," said Rachel, with no doubts at all ; " but she will find me terribly impeded here. When does she come ? "

" Not for a month or six weeks, when the wedding will be over. It is high time she saw something of her respected guardian."

" The colonel ? "

" Yes;" then to Ermine, " Every one turns to him with reliance and confidence. I believe no one in the army received so many last charges as he has done, or executes them more fully."

"And," said Ermine, feeling pleasure colour her cheek more deeply than was convenient, " you are relations."

" So far away that only a Scotsman would acknowledge the cousinship."

" But do not you call yourself Scotch ? " said Ermine, who had for years thought it glorious to do so.

" My great grandfather came from Gowanbrae," said Alick ; " but our branch of the family has lived and died in the —th Highlanders for so many generations that we don't know what a home is out of it. Our birthplaces—yes, and our graves—are in all parts of the world."

" Were you ever in Scotland ? "

" Never ; and I dread nothing so much as being quartered there. Just imagine the trouble it would be to go over the pedigree of every Keith I met, and to dine with them all upon haggis and sheeps' head ! "

" There's no place I want to see as much as Scotland," said Rachel.

" Oh, yes ! young ladies always do."

" It is not for a young lady reason," said Rachel, bluntly. " I want to understand the principle of diffused education, as there practised. The only other places I should really care to see are the Grand Reformatory for the Destitute in Holland, and the Hospital for Cretins in Switzerland."

" Scotch pedants, Dutch thieves, Swiss *goîtres*—I will bear your tastes in mind," said Mr. Keith, rising to take leave.

" Really," said Rachel, when he was gone, " if he had not that silly military tone of joking, there might be something tolerable about him if he got into good hands. He seems to have some good notions about his sister. She must be just out of the school-room, at the very turn of life, and I will try to get her into my training and show her a little of the real beauty and usefulness of the career she has before her. How late he has stayed ! I am afraid there is no time for the manuscripts."

And though Ermine was too honest to say she was sorry, Rachel did not miss the regret.

Colonel Keith came the next day, and under his arm was a parcel, which was laid in little Rose's arms, and, when unrolled, proved to contain a magnificent wax doll, no doubt long the object of unrequited attachment to many a little Avoncestrian, a creature of beauteous and unmeaning face, limpid eyes, hair that could be brushed, and all her members waxen, as far as could be seen below the provisional habiliment of pink paper that enveloped her. Little Rose's complexion became crimson, and she did not utter a word, while her aunt, colouring almost as much, laughed and asked where were her thanks.

" Oh ! " with a long gasp, " it can't be for me ! "

" Do you think it is for your aunt ? " said the colonel.

" Oh, thank you ! But such a beautiful creature for me ! " said Rose, with another gasp, quite oppressed. " Aunt Ermine, how shall I ever make her clothes nice enough ? "

" We will see about that, my dear. Now take her into the verandah and introduce her to Violetta."

" Yes ;" then pausing and looking into the fixed eyes, " Aunt Ermine, I never saw such a beauty, except that one the little girl left behind on the bench on the esplanade, when Aunt Ailie said I should be coveting if I went on wishing Violetta was like her."

" I remember," said Ermine, " I have heard enough of that *ne plus ultra* of doll ! Indeed, Colin, you have given a great deal of pleasure, where the materials of pleasure are few. No one can guess the delight a doll is to a solitary imaginative child."

" Thank you," he said, smiling.

" I believe I shall enjoy it as much as Rose," added Ermine, " both for play and as a study. Please turn my chair a little this way, I want to see the introduction to Violetta. Here comes the beauty, in Rose's own cloak."

Colonel Keith leant over the back of her chair and silently watched, but the scene was not quite what they expected. Violetta was sitting in her " slantingdicular " position on her chair placed on a bench, and her little mistress knelt down before her, took her in her arms, and began to hug her.

" Violetta, darling, you need not be afraid ! There is a new beautiful creature come, and I shall call her Colinette, and we must be very kind to her, because Colonel Keith is so good, and knows your grandpapa ; and to tell you a great secret, Violetta, that you must not tell Colinette or anybody, I think he is Aunt Ermine's own true knight."

" Hush !" whispered the colonel, over Ermine's head, as he perceived her about to speak.

" So you must be very good to her, Violetta, and you shall help me make her clothes ; but you need not be afraid I ever could love any one half or one quarter as much as you, my own dear child, not if she were ten times as beautiful, and so come and show her to Augustus. She'll never be like you, dear old darling."

" It is a study," said the colonel, as Rose moved off with a doll in either hand ; " a moral that you should take home."

Ermine shook her head, but smiled, saying, " Tell me, does your young cousin know——"

" Alick Keith ? Not from me, and Lady Temple is perfectly to be trusted ; but I believe his father knew it was for no worse reason that I was made to exchange. But never mind, Ermine, he is a very good fellow, and what is the use of making a secret of what even Violetta knows ?"

There was no debating the point, for her desire of secrecy was prompted by the resolution to leave him unbound, whereas his wish for publicity was with the purpose of binding himself, and Ermine was determined that discussion was above all to be avoided, and that she would, after the first explanation, keep the conversation upon other subjects. So she only answered with another reproving look and smile, and said, " And now I am going to make you useful. The editor of the ' Traveller ' is travelling, and has left his work to me. I have been keeping some letters for him to answer in his own hand, because mine betrays womanhood ; but I have just heard that he is to stay about six weeks more, and people must be put out of their misery before that. Will you copy a few for me ? Here is some paper with the office stamp."

" What an important woman you are, Ermine."

" If you had been in England all this time, you would see how easy the step is into literary work ; but you must not betray this for the Traveller's sake or Ailie's."

"Your writing is not very womanish," said the colonel, as she gave him his task. "Or is this yours? It is not like that of those verses on Malvern hills that you copied out for me, the only thing you ever gave me."

"I hope it is more to the purpose than it was then, and it has had to learn to write in all sorts of attitudes."

"What's this?" as he went on with the paper; "your manuscript entitled 'Curatocult.' Is that the word? I had taken it for the produce of Miss Curtis's unassisted genius."

"Have you heard her use it?" said Ermine, disconcerted, having by no means intended to betray Rachel.

"Oh yes! I heard her declaiming on Sunday about what she knows no more about than Conrade! A detestable, pragmatical, domineering girl! I am thankful that I advised Lady Temple only to take the house for a year. It was right she should see her relations, but she must not be tyrannized over."

"I don't believe she dislikes it."

"She dislikes no one! She used to profess a liking for a huge Irishwoman, whose husband had risen from the ranks; the most tremendous woman I ever saw, except Miss Curtis."

"You know they were brought up together like sisters."

"All the worse, for she has the habit of passive submission. If it were the mother it would be all right, and I should be thankful to see her in good keeping, but the mother and sister go for nothing, and down comes this girl to battle every suggestion with principles picked up from every catchpenny periodical, things she does not half understand, and enunciates as if no one had even heard of them before."

"I believe she seldom meets any one who has. I mean to

whom they are matters of thought. I really do like her vigour and earnestness."

" Don't say so, Ermine ! One reason why she is so intolerable to me is that she is a grotesque caricature of what you used to be."

" You have hit it ! I see why I always liked her, besides that it is pleasant to have any sort of visit, and a good scrimmage is refreshing; she is just what I should have been without papa and Edward to keep me down, and without the civilizing atmosphere at the park."

" Never."

" No, I was not her equal in energy and beneficence ; and I was younger when you came. But I feel for her longing to be up and doing, and her puzzled chafing against constraint and conventionality, though it breaks out in very odd effervescences."

" Extremely generous of you when you must be bored to death with her interminable talk."

" You don't appreciate the pleasure of variety ! Besides, she really interests me, she is so full of vigorous crudities. I believe all that is unpleasing in her arises from her being considered as the clever woman of the family ; having no man nearly connected enough to keep her in check, and living in society that does not fairly meet her. I want you to talk to her, and take her in hand."

" Me ! Thank you, Ermine ! Why, I could not even stand her talking about you, though she has the one grace of valuing you."

" Then you ought, in common gratitude, for there is no little greatness of soul in patiently coming down to Mackarel Lane to be snubbed by one's cousin's governess's sister."

" If you will come up to Myrtlewood, you don't know what you may do."

" No, you are to set no more people upon me, though Lady Temple's eyes are very wistful."

" I did not think you would have held out against her."

" Not when I had against you? No, indeed, though I never did see anybody more winning than she is in that meek, submissive gentleness! Alison says she has cheered up and grown like another creature since your arrival."

" And Alexander Keith's. Yes, poor thing, we have brought something of her own old world, where she was a sort of little queen in her way. It is too much to ask me to have patience with these relations, Ermine. If you could see the change from the petted creature she was with her mother and husband, almost always the first lady in the place, and latterly with a colonial court of her own, and now, ordered about, advised, domineered over, made nobody of, and taking it as meekly and sweetly as if she were grateful for it! I verily believe she is! But she certainly ought to come away."

" I am not so sure of that. It seems to me rather a dangerous responsibility to take her away from her own relations, unless there were any with equal claims."

" They are her only relations, and her husband had none. Still to be under the constant yoke of an overpowering woman with unfixed opinions seems to be an unmitigated evil for her and her boys; and no one's feelings need be hurt by her fixing herself near some public school for her sons' education. However, she is settled for this year, and at the end we may decide."

With which words he again applied himself to Ermine's

correspondence, and presently completed the letter, offering to direct the envelope, which she refused, as having one already directed by the author. He rather mischievously begged to see it that he might judge of the character of the writing, but this she resisted."

However, in four days' time there was a very comical twinkle in his eye, as he informed her that the new number of the "Traveller" was in no favour at the Homestead, "there was such a want of original thought in it." Ermine felt her imprudence in having risked the betrayal, but all she did was to look at him with her full, steady eyes, and a little twist in each corner of her mouth, as she said, "Indeed! Then we had better enliven it with the recollections of a military secretary," and he was both convinced of what he guessed, and also that she did not think it right to tell him; "But," he said, "there is something in that girl, I perceive, Ermine; she does think for herself, and if she were not so dreadfully earnest that she can't smile, she would be the best company of any of the party."

" I am so glad you think so ! I shall be delighted if you will really talk to her, and help her to argue out some of her crudities. Indeed she is worth it. But I suppose you will hardly stay here long enough to do her any good."

"What, are you going to order me away?"

"I thought your brother wanted you at home."

"It is all very well to talk of an ancestral home, but when it consists of a tall, slim house, with blank walls and pepper-box turrets, set down on a bleak hill side, and every one gone that made it once a happy place, it is not attractive. More-over, my only use there would be to be kept as a tame heir, the person whose interference would be most resented, and I don't recognise that duty."

"You are a gentleman at large, with no obvious duty," said Ermine, meditatively.

"What, none?" bending his head, and looking earnestly at her.

"Oh, if you come here out of duty—" she said archly, and with her merry laugh. "There, is not that a nice occasion for picking a quarrel? And seriously," she continued, "perhaps it might be good for you if we did. I am beginning to fear that I ought not to keep you lingering here without purpose or occupation."

"Fulfil my purpose, and I will find occupation."

"Don't say that."

"This once, Ermine. For one year I shall wait in the hope of convincing you. If you do not change your mind in that time, I shall look for another staff appointment, to last till Rose is ready for me."

The gravity of this conclusion made Ermine laugh. "That's what you learnt of your chief," she said.

"There would be less difference in age," he said. "Though I own I should like my widow to be less helpless than poor little Lady Temple. So," he added, with the same face of ridiculous earnest, "if you continue to reject me yourself, you will at least rear her with an especial view to her efficiency in that capacity."

And as Rose at that critical moment looked in at the window, eager to be encouraged to come and show Colinette's successful toilette, he drew her to him with the smile that had won her whole heart, and listening to every little bit of honesty about "my work" and "Aunt Ermine's work," he told her that he knew she was a very managing domestic character, perfectly equal to the charge of both young ladies.

" Aunt Ermine says I must learn to manage, because some day I shall have to take care of papa."

" Yes," with his eyes on Ermine all the while, " learn to be a useful woman ; who knows if we shan't all depend on you by-and-by ? "

" Oh do let me be useful to you," cried Rose ; " I could hem all your handkerchiefs, and make you a kettle-holder."

Ermine had never esteemed him more highly than when he refrained from all but a droll look, and uttered not one word of the sportive courtship that is so peculiarly unwholesome and undesirable with children. Perhaps she thought her colonel more a gentleman than she had done before, if that were possible ; and she took an odd, quaint pleasure in the idea of this match, often when talking to Alison of her views of life and education, putting them in the form of what would become of Rose as Lady Keith ; and Colin kept his promise of making no more references to the future. On moving into his lodgings, the hour for his visits was changed, and unless he went out to dinner, he usually came in the evening, thus attracting less notice, and moreover rendering it less easy to lapse into the tender subject, as Alison was then at home, and the conversation was necessarily more general.

The afternoons were spent in Lady Temple's service. Instead of the orthodox dowager britchska and pair, ruled over by a tyrannical coachman, he had provided her with a herd of little animals for harness or saddle, and a young groom, for whom Coombe was answerable. Mrs. Curtis groaned and feared the establishment would look flighty ; but for the first time Rachel became the colonel's ally. " The worst despotism practised in England," she said, " is that of coachmen, and it is well that Fanny should be spared ! The coachman who lived here when mamma was married, answered her request to go a little faster, ' I shall drive *my* horses as I plazes, and I really think the present one is rather worse in deed, though not in word."

Moreover, Rachel smoothed down a little of Mrs. Curtis's uneasiness at Fanny's change of costume at the end of her first year of widowhood, on the ground that Colonel Keith advised her to ride with her sons, and that this was incompatible with weeds. " And dear Sir Stephen did so dislike the sight of them," she added, in her simple, innocent way, as if she was still dressing to please him.

" On the whole, mother," said Rachel, " unless there is more heart-break than Fanny professes, there's more coquetry in a pretty young thing wearing a cap that says ' come pity me,' than in going about like other people."

" I only wish she could help looking like a girl of seventeen," sighed Mrs. Curtis. " If that colonel were but married ; or the other young man ! I'm sure she will fall into some scrape ; she does not know how, out of sheer innocence."

" Well, mother, you know I always mean to ride with her, and that will be a protection."

" But, my dear, I am not sure about your riding with these gay officers ; you never used to do such things."

" At my age, mother, and to take care of Fanny."

And Mrs. Curtis, in her uncertainty whether to sanction the proceedings and qualify them, or to make a protest—

dreadful to herself, and more dreadful to Fanny,—yielded
the point when she found herself not backed up by her
energetic daughter, and the cavalcade almost daily set forth
from Myrtlewood, and was watched with eyes of the greatest
vexation, if not by kind Mrs. Curtis, by poor Mr. Touchett,
to whom Lady Temple's change of dress had been a grievous
shock. He thought her so lovely, so interesting, at first ;
and now, though it was sacrilege to believe it of so gentle
and pensive a face, was not this a return to the world ?
What had she to do with these officers ? How could her
aunt permit it ? No doubt it was all the work of his great
foe, Miss Rachel.

It was true that Rachel heartily enjoyed these rides.
Hitherto she had been only allowed to go out under the
escort of her tyrant the coachman, who kept her in very
strict discipline. She had not anticipated anything much
more lively with Fanny, her boys, and ponies ; but Colonel
Keith had impressed on Conrade and Francis that they were
their mother's prime protectors, and they regarded her bridle-
rein as their post, keeping watch over her as if her safety
depended on them, and ready to quarrel with each other if
the roads were too narrow for all three to go abreast. And
as soon as the colonel had ascertained that she and they were
quite sufficient to themselves, and well guarded by Coombe
in the rear, he ceased to regard himself as bound to their
company, but he and Rachel extended their rides in search
of objects of interest. She liked doing the honours of the
county, and achieved expeditions which her coachman had
hitherto never permitted to her, in search of ruins, camps,
churches, and towers. The colonel had a turn for geology,
though a wandering life even with an Indian baggage-train

had saved him from incurring her contempt for collectors; but he knew by sight the character of the conformations of rocks, and when they had mounted one of the hills that surrounded Avonmouth, discerned by the outline whether granite, gneiss, limestone, or slate formed the grander height beyond, thus leading to schemes of more distant rides to verify the conjectures, which Rachel accepted with the less argument, because sententious dogmatism was not always possible on the back of a skittish black mare.

There was no concealing from herself that she was more interested by this frivolous military society than by any she had ever previously met. The want of comprehension of her pursuits in her mother's limited range of acquaintance had greatly conduced both to her over-weening manner and to her general dissatisfaction with the world, and for the first time she was neither succumbed to, giggled at, avoided, nor put down with a grave, prosy reproof. Certainly Alick Keith, as every one called him, nettled her extremely by his murmured irony, but the acuteness of it was diverting in such a mere lad, and showed that if he could only once be roused, he might be capable of better things. There was an excitement in his unexpected manner of seeing things that was engaging as well as provoking; and Rachel never felt content if he were at Myrtlewood without her seeing him, if only because she began to consider him as more dangerous than his elder namesake, and so assured of his position that he did not take any pains to assert it, or to cultivate Lady Temple's good graces; he was simply at home and perfectly at ease with her.

Colonel Keith's tone was different. He was argumentative where his young cousin was sarcastic. He was reading some

of the books over which Rachel had strained her capacities
without finding any one with whom to discuss them, since
all her friends regarded them as poisonous ; and even Ermine
Williams, without being shaken in her steadfast trust, was so
haunted and distressed in her lonely and unvaried life by the
echo of these shocks to the faith of others, that absolutely as
a medical precaution she abstained from dwelling on them.
On the other hand Colin Keith liked to talk and argue out
his impressions, and found in Rachel the only person with
whom the subject could be safely broached, and thus she for
the first time heard the subjects fairly handled.   Hitherto
she had never thought that justice was done to the argument
except by a portion of the press, that drew conclusions which
terrified while they allured her, whereas she appreciated the
candour that weighed each argument, distinguishing principle
from prejudice, and religious faith from conventional construction, and in this measurement of minds she felt the
strength and acuteness of powers superior to her own.   He
was not one of the men who prefer unintellectual women.
Perhaps clever men, of a profession not necessarily requiring
constant brain work, are not so much inclined to rest the mind
with feminine empty chatter, as are those whose intellect is
more on the strain.   At any rate, though Colonel Keith was
attentive and courteous to every one, and always treated Lady
Temple as a prime minister might treat a queen, his tendency
to conversation with Rachel was becoming marked, and she
grew increasingly prone to consult him.   The interest of
this new intercourse quite took out the sting of disappointment, when again Curatocult came back, "declined with
thanks."   Nay, before making a third attempt she hazarded
a question on his opinion of female authorship, and much to

her gratification, and somewhat to her surprise, heard that he thought it often highly useful and valuable.

"That is great candour. Men generally grudge whatever they think their own privilege."

"Many things can often be felt and expressed by an able woman better than by a man, and there is no reason that the utterance of anything worthy to be said should be denied, provided it *is* worthy to be said."

"Ah! there comes the hit. I wondered if you would get through without it."

"It was not meant as a hit. Men are as apt to publish what is not worth saying as women can be, and some women are so conscientious as only to put forth what is of weight and value."

"And you are above wanting to silence them by palaver about unfeminine publicity?"

"There is no need of publicity. Much of the best and most wide-spread writing emanates from the most quiet, unsuspected quarters."

"That is the benefit of an anonymous press."

"Yes. The withholding of the name prevents well-mannered people from treating a woman as an authoress, if she do not proclaim herself one; and the difference is great between being known to write, and setting up for an authoress."

"Between fact and pretension. But write or not write, there is an instinctive avoidance of an intellectual woman."

"Not always, for the simple manner that goes with real superiority is generally very attractive. The larger and deeper the mind, the more there would be of the genuine humbleness and gentleness that a shallow nature is incapable of. The very word humility presupposes depth."

" I see what you mean," said Rachel.   " Gentleness is not feebleness, nor lowness lowliness.   There must be something held back."

" I see it daily," said Colonel Keith ; and for a moment he seemed about to add something, but checked himself, and took advantage of an interruption to change the conversation.

" Superior natures lowly and gentle ! " said Rachel to herself.   " Am I so to him, then, or is he deceiving himself ? What is to be done ?   At my age !   Such a contravention of my principles !   A soldier, an honourable, a title in prospect, Fanny's major !   Intolerable !   No, no !   My property absorbed by a Scotch peerage, when I want it for so many things !   Never.   I am sorry for him though.   It is hard that a man who can forgive a woman for intellect, should be thrown back on poor little Fanny ; and it is gratifying——. But I am untouched yet, and I will take care of myself.   At my age a woman who loves at all, loves with all the gathered force of her nature, and I certainly feel no such passion. No, certainly not ; and I am resolved not to be swept along till I have made up my mind to yield to the force of the torrent.   Let us see."

" Grace, my dear," said Mrs. Curtis, in one of her most confidential moments, " is not dear Rachel looking very well ? I never saw her dress so well put on."

" Yes, she is looking very handsome," said Grace.   " I am glad she has consented to have her hair in that new way, it is very becoming to her."

" I—I don't know that it is all the hair," said the mother, faltering, as if half ashamed of herself ; " but it seemed to me that we need not have been so uneasy about dear Fanny. I think, don't you ? that there may be another attraction.

To be sure, it would be at a terrible distance from us ; but so good and kind as he is, it would be such a thing for you and Fanny as well——"

Grace gave a great start.

" Yes, my dear," Mrs. Curtis gently prosed on with her speculation, " she would be a dreadful loss to us ; but you see, so clever and odd as she is, and with such peculiar ideas, I should be so thankful to see her in the hands of some good, sensible man that would guide her."

" But do you really think it is so, mother ? "

" Mind, my dear, it is nothing to build on, but I cannot help being struck, and just thinking to myself. I know you'll not say anything."

Grace felt much distressed after this communication had opened her eyes to certain little touches of softening and consciousness that sat oddly enough on her sister. From the first avowal of Colonel Keith's acquaintance with the Williamses, she had concluded him to be the nameless lover, and had been disappointed that Alison, so far from completing the confidence, had become more reserved than ever, leaving her to wonder whether he were indeed the same, or whether his constancy had survived the change of circumstances. There were no grounds on which to found a caution, yet Grace felt full of discomfort and distrust ; a feeling shared by Alison, who had never forgiven herself for her half confidence, and felt that it would be wiser to tell the rest, but was withheld by knowing that her motive would actuate her sister to a contrary course. That Colin should detach himself from her, love again, and marry, was what Ermine schooled herself to think fitting ; but Alison alternated between indignant jealousy for her sister, and the desire to warn Rachel

that she might at best win only the reversion of his heart.
Ermine was happy and content with his evening visits, and
would not take umbrage at the daily rides, nor the reports of
drawing-room warfare, and Alison often wavered between the
desire of preparing her, and the doubt whether it were not
cruel to inflict the present pain of want of confidence.   If
that were a happy summer to some at Avonmouth, it was a
very trying one to those two anxious, yet apparently un-
interested sisters, who were but lookers-on at the game that
affected their other selves.

At length, however, came a new feature into the quiet
summer life at Avonmouth.   Colin looked in on Ermine one
morning to announce, with shrugged shoulders, and a face
almost making game of himself, that his brother was coming !
Lord Keith had been called to London on business, and would
extend his journey to come and see what his brother was
doing.   "This comes of being the youngest of the family,"
observed Colin, meditatively.   "One is never supposed
capable of taking care of one's self.   With Keith I shall be
the gay extravagant young officer to the end of my days."

"You are not forgiving to your brother," said Ermine.

"You have it in your power to make me so," he said
eagerly.

"Then you would have nothing to forgive," she replied,
smiling.

Lady Temple's first thought was a renewal of her ardent
wish that Ermine should be at Myrtlewood ; and that Mackarel Lane, and the governessship should be as much as possible
kept out of sight.   Even Alison was on her side ; not that
she was ashamed of either, but she wished that Ermine should
see and judge with her own eyes of Colin's conduct, and also

eagerly hailed all that showed him still committed to her sister. She was proportionably vexed that he did not think it expedient to harass Ermine with further invitations.

"My brother knows the whole," he said, "and I do not wish to attempt to conceal anything."

"I do not mean to conceal," faltered Fanny, "only I thought it might save a shock—appearances—he might think better of it, if——"

"You thought only what was kind," answered the colonel, "and I thank you for it most warmly; but this matter does not depend on my brother's consent, and even if it did, Ermine's own true position is that which is most honourable to her."

Having said this, he was forced to console Fanny in her shame at her own kind attempt at this gentle little feminine subterfuge. He gratified her, however, by not interfering with her hospitable instincts of doing honour to and entertaining his brother, for whose sake her first approach to a dinner party was given; a very small one, but treated by her and her household as a far more natural occurrence than was any sort of entertainment at the Homestead. She even looked surprised, in her quiet way, at Mrs. Curtis's proffers of assistance in the *et ceteras*, and gratefully answered for Coombe's doing the right thing, without troubling herself further. Mrs. Curtis was less easy in her mind, her housewifely soul questioned the efficiency of her niece's establishment, and she was moreover persuaded that Lord Keith must be bent on inspecting his brother's choice, while even Rachel felt as if the toils of fate were being drawn round her, and let Grace embellish her for the dinner party, in an odd sort of mood, sometimes rejecting her attempts at decoration, sometimes vouchsafing a glance at the glass, chiefly to judge whether her looks were really as repellently practical and intellectual as she had been in the habit of supposing. The wreath of white roses, which she wore for the first time, certainly had a pleasing and softening effect, and she was conscious that she had never looked so well ; then was vexed at the solicitude with which her mother looked her over, and fairly blushed with annoyance at the good lady's evident satisfaction.

But, after all, Rachel, at her best, could not have competed with the grace of the quiet little figure that received them, the rich black silk giving dignity to the slender form, and a sort of compromise between veil and cap sheltering the delicate fair face ; and with a son on each side, Fanny looked so touchingly proud and well supported, and the boys were so exultant and admiring at seeing her thus dressed, that it was a very pretty sight, and struck the first arrived of her guests, Mr. Touchett, quite dumb with admiration. Colonel Hammond, the two Keiths, and their young kinsman, completed the party. Lord Keith of Gowanbrae was best described by the said young kinsman's words—" a long-backed Scotchman." He was so intensely Scottish that he made his brother look and sound the same, whereas ordinarily neither air nor accent would have shown the colonel's nation, and there was no definable likeness between them, except, perhaps, the baldness of the forehead ; but the remains of Lord Keith's hair were silvered red, whereas Colin's thick beard and scanty locks were dark brown, and with a far larger admixture of hoar-frost, though he was the younger by twenty years, and his brother's appearance gave the impression of a far greater age than fifty-eight ; there was the stoop of rheumatism, and a worn, thin look on

the face, with its high cheek bones, narrow lips, and cold
eyes, by no means winning. On the other hand, he was the
most finished gentleman that Grace and Rachel had ever
encountered ; he had all the gallant polish of manner that the
old Scottish nobility have inherited from the French of the
old *régime*—a manner that, though Colin possessed all its
essentials, had been in some degree rubbed off in the frank-
ness of his military life, but which the old nobleman retained
in its full perfection. Mrs. Curtis admired it extremely as a
specimen of the " old school," for which she had never ceased
to mourn ; and Rachel felt as if it took her breath away
by the likeness to Louis XIV. ; but, strange to say, Lady
Temple acted as if she were quite in her element. It might
be that the old man's courtesy brought back to her something
of the tender chivalry of her soldier husband, and that a sort
of filial friendliness had become natural to her towards an
elderly man, for she responded at once, and devoted herself to
pleasing and entertaining him. Their civilities were something
quite amusing to watch, and in the evening, with a complete
perception of his tastes, she got up a rubber for him.

" Can you bear it ? You will not like to play?" murmured
the colonel to her, as he rung for the cards, recollecting the
many evenings of whist with her mother and Sir Stephen.

" Oh ! I don't mind. I like anything like old times, and
my aunt does not like playing——"

No, for Mrs. Curtis had grown up in a family where cards
were disapproved, and she felt it a sad fall in Fanny to be
playing with all the skill of her long training, and receiving
grand compliments from Lord Keith on joint victories over
the two colonels. It was a distasteful game to all but the
players, for Rachel felt slightly hurt at the colonel's defection,

and Mr. Touchett, with somewhat of Mrs. Curtis's feeling that it was a backsliding in Lady Temple, suddenly grew absent in a conversation that he was holding with young Mr. Keith upon—of all subjects in the world—lending library books, and finally repaired to the piano, where Grace was playing her mother's favourite music, in hopes of distracting her mind from Fanny's enormity; and there he stood, mechanically thanking Miss Curtis, but all the time turning a melancholy eye upon the game. Alick Keith, meanwhile, sat himself down near Rachel and her mother, close to an open window, for it was so warm that even Mrs. Curtis enjoyed the air; and perhaps because that watching the colonel had made Rachel's discourses somewhat less ready than usual, he actually obtained an interval in which to speak! He was going the next day to Bishops Worthy, there to attend his cousin's wedding, and at the end of a fortnight to bring his sister for her visit to Lady Temple. This sister was evidently his great care, and it needed but little leading to make him tell a good deal about her. She had, it seemed, been sent home from the Cape at about ten years old, when the regiment went to India, and her brother, who had been at school, then was with her for a short time before going out to join the regiment.

"Why," said Rachel, recovering her usual manner, "you have not been ten years in the army!"

"I had my commission at sixteen," he answered.

"You are not six-and-twenty!" she exclaimed.

"You are as right as usual," was the reply, with his odd little smile; "at least till the 1st of August."

"My dear!" said her mother, more alive than Rachel to his amusement at her daughter's knowing his age better than he did himself, but adding, politely, "you are hardly come to the time of life for liking to hear that your looks deceived us."

"Boys are tolerated," he said, with a quick glance at Rachel; but at that moment something many-legged and tickling flitted into the light, and dashed over her face. Mrs. Curtis was by no means a strong-minded woman in the matter of moths and crane-flies, disliking almost equally their sudden personal attentions and their suicidal propensities, and Rachel dutifully started up at once to give chase to the father-long-legs, and put it out of window before it had succeeded in deranging her mother's equanimity either by bouncing into her face, or suspending itself by two or three legs in the wax of the candle. Mr. Keith seconded her efforts, but the insect was both lively and cunning, eluding them with a dexterity wonderful in such an apparently over-limbed creature, until at last it kindly rested for a moment with its wooden peg of a body sloping, and most of its thread-like members prone upon a newspaper, where Rachel descended on it with her pocket-handkerchief, and Mr. Keith tried to inclose it with his hands at the same moment. To have crushed the fly would have been melancholy; to have come down on the young soldier's fingers, awkward; but Rachel did what was even more shocking—her hands did descend on, what should have been fingers, but they gave way under her—she felt only the leather of the glove between her and the newspaper. She jumped and very nearly cried out, looking up with an astonishment and horror only half reassured by his extremely amused smile. "I beg your pardon; I'm so sorry——" she gasped confused.

"Inferior animals can dispense with a member more or

less," he replied, giving her the other corner of the paper, on which they bore their capture to the window, and shook it till it took wing, with various legs streaming behind it. "That venerable animal is apparently indifferent to having left a third of two legs behind him," and as he spoke he removed the already half drawn-off left-hand glove, and let Rachel see for a moment that it had only covered the thumb, forefinger, two joints of the middle, and one of the third ; the little finger was gone, and the whole hand much scarred. She was still so much dismayed that she gasped out the first question she had ever asked him—

"Where—— ? "

"Not under the handkerchief," he answered, picking it up as if he thought she wanted convincing. "At Delhi, I imagine."

At that moment, Grace, as an act of general beneficence certainly pleasing to her mother, began to sing. It was a stop to all conversation, for Mrs. Curtis particularly disliked talking during singing, and Rachel had to digest her discoveries at her leisure, as soon as she could collect herself after the unnatural and strangely lasting sensation of the solid giving way. So Grace was right, he was no boy, but really older than Fanny, the companion of her childhood, and who probably would have married her had not the general come in the way ! Here was, no doubt, the real enemy, while they had all been thinking of Colonel Keith. A man only now expecting his company ! It would sound more absurd. Yet Rachel was not wont to think how things would sound ! And this fresh intense dislike provoked her. Was it the unsuitability of the young widow remarrying ? "Surely, surely, it must not be that womanhood in its contemptible

side is still so strong that I want to keep all for myself!
Shame! And this may be the true life love, suppressed, now
able to revive! I have no right to be disgusted, I will
watch minutely, and judge if he will be a good guide and
father to the boys, though it may save the colonel trouble.
Pish! what have I to do with either? Why should I think
about them? Yet I must care for Fanny, I must dislike to
see her lower herself even in the eyes of the world. Would
it really be lowering herself? I cannot tell, I must think it
out. I wish that game was over, or that Grace would let one
speak."

But songs and whist both lasted till the evening was ended
by Lady Temple coming up to the curate with her winnings
and her pretty smile, " Please, Mr. Touchett, let this go
towards some treat for the school children. I should not like
to give it in any serious way, you know, but just for some
little pleasure for them."

If she had done it on purpose, she could not have better
freshly riveted his chains. That pensive simplicity, with the
smile of heartfelt satisfaction at giving pleasure to anybody,
were more and more engaging as her spirits recovered their
tone, and the most unsatisfactory consideration which Rachel
carried away that evening was that Alexander Keith being
really somewhat the senior, if the improvement in Fanny's
spirits were really owing to his presence, the objection on the
score of age would not hold. But, thought Rachel, Colonel
Keith being her own, what united power they should have
over Fanny. Pooh! she had by no means resigned herself to
have him, though for Fanny's sake it might be well, and was
there not a foolish prejudice in favour of married women,
that impeded the usefulness of single ones? However, if the

stiff, dry old man approved of her for her fortune's sake, that would be quite reason enough for repugnance.

The stiff old man was the pink of courtesy, and paid his respects in due order to his brother's friends the next day, Colin attending in his old *aide-de-camp* fashion. It was curious to see them together. The old peer was not at all ungracious to his brother ; indeed, Colin had been agreeably surprised by an amount of warmth and brotherliness that he had never experienced from him before, as if old age had brought a disposition to cling to the remnant of the once inconveniently large family, and make much of the last survivor, formerly an undesirable youngest favourite, looked on with jealous eyes and thwarted and retaliated on for former petting, as soon as the reins of government fell from the hands of the aged father.   Now, the elder brother was kind almost to patronizing, though evidently persuaded that Colin was a gay careless youth, with no harm in him, but needing to be looked after ; and as to the Cape, India, and Australia being a larger portion of the world than Gowanbrae, Edinburgh, and London, his lordship would be incredulous to the day of his death.

He paid his formal and gracious visits at Myrtlewood and the Homestead, and then supposed that his brother would wish him to call upon " these unfortunate ladies."   Colin certainly would have been vexed if he had openly slighted them ; but Alison, whom the brothers overtook on their way into Mackarel Lane, did not think the colonel looked in the most felicitous frame of mind, and thought the most charitable construction might be that he shared her wishes that she could be a few minutes in advance ; to secure that neither Rose's sports nor Colinette's toilette were very prominent.

All was right, however; Ermine's taste for the fitness of things had trained Rose into keeping the little parlour never in stiff array, but also never in a state to be ashamed of, and she herself was sitting in the shade in the garden, whither, after the first introduction, Colin and Rose brought seats; and the call, on the whole, went off extremely well. Ermine never let any one be condescending to her, and conducted the conversation with her usual graceful good breeding, while the colonel, with Rose on his knee, half talked to the child, half listened and watched.

As soon as he had deposited his brother at the hotel, he came back again, and in answer to Ermine's "Well," he demanded, "What she thought of his brother, and if he were what she expected?"

"Very much, only older and feebler. And did he communicate his views of Mackarel Lane? I saw him regarding me as a species of mermaid or syren, evidently thinking it a great shame that I have not a burnt face. If he had only known about Rose!"

"The worst of it is that he wants me to go home with him, and I am afraid I must do so, for now that he and I are the last in the entail, there is an opportunity of making an arrangement about the property, for which he is very anxious."

"Well, you know, I have long thought it would be very good for you."

"And when I am there I shall have to visit every one in the family;" and he looked into her eyes to see if she would let them show concern, but she kept up their brave sparkle as she still said, "You *know* you ought."

"Then you deliver me up to Keith's tender mercies till——"

"Till you have done your duty—and forgiven him."

" Remember, Ermine, I can't spend a winter in Scotland. A cold always makes the ball remind me of its presence in my chest, and I was told that if I spent a winter at home, it must be on the Devonshire coast."

" That ball is sufficient justification for ourselves, I allow," she said, that one little word *our* making up for all that had gone before.

" And meantime you will write to me—about Rose's education."

" To be sure, or what would be the use of growing old ? "

Alison felt savage all through this interview.   That perfect understanding and the playful fiction about waiting for Rose left him a great deal too free. Ermine might almost be supposed to want to get rid of him, and even when he took leave she only remained for a few minutes leaning her cheek on her hand, and scarcely indulged in a sigh before asking to be wheeled into the house again, nor would she make any remark, save " It has been too bright a summer to last for ever.   It would be very wrong to wish him to stay dangling here.   Let what will happen, he is himself."

It sounded far too like a deliberate resignation of him, and persuasion that if he went he would not return to be all he had been.   However, the departure was not immediate, Lord Keith had taken a fancy to the place and scenery, and wished to see all the lions of the neighbourhood, so that there were various expeditions in the carriages or on horseback, in which he displayed his grand courtesy to Lady Temple, and Rachel enjoyed the colonel's conversation, and would have enjoyed it still more if she had not been tracing a meaning in every attention that he paid her, and considering whether she was committing herself by receiving it.   She was glad he was going away that she might have time to face the subject, and make up her mind, for she was convinced that the object of his journey was to make himself certain of his prospects. When he said that he should return for the winter, and that he had too much to leave at Avonmouth to stay long away from it, there must be a meaning in his words.

Ermine had one more visit from Lord Keith, and this time he came alone. He was in his most gracious and courteous mood, and sat talking of indifferent things for some time, of his aunt Lady Alison, and of Beauchamp in the old time, so that Ermine enjoyed the renewal of old associations and names belonging to a world unlike her present one. Then he came to Colin, his looks and his health, and his own desire to see him quit the army.

Ermine assented to his health being hardly fit for the army, and restrained the rising indignation as she recollected what a difference the best surgical advice might have made ten years ago.

And then, Lord Keith said, a man could hardly be expected to settle down without marrying. He wished earnestly to see his brother married, but, unfortunately, charges on his estate would prevent him from doing anything for him ; and, in fact, he did not see any possibility of his—of his marrying, except a person with some means.

" I understand," said Ermine, looking straight before her, and her colour mounting.

" I was sure that a person of your great good sense would do so," said Lord Keith. " I assure you no one can be more sensible than myself of the extreme forbearance, discretion, and regard for my brother's true welfare that has been shown here."

Ermine bowed. He did not know that the vivid carmine that made her look so handsome was not caused by gratification at his praise, but by the struggle to brook it patiently.

" And now, knowing the influence over him that, most deservedly, you must always possess, I am induced to hope that, as his sincere friend, you will exert it in favour of the more prudent counsels."

" I have no influence over his judgment," said Ermine, a little proudly.

" I mean," said Lord Keith, forced to much closer quarters, " you will excuse me for speaking thus openly—that in the state of the case, with so much depending on his making a satisfactory choice, I feel convinced, with every regret, that you will feel it to be for his true welfare—as indeed I infer that you have already endeavoured to show him—to make a new beginning, and to look on the past as past."

There was something in the insinuating tone of this speech, increased as it was by the modulation of his Scottish voice, that irritated his hearer unspeakably, all the more because it was the very thing she had been doing.

" Colonel Keith must judge for himself," she said, with a cold manner, but a burning heart.

" I—I understand," said Lord Keith, " that you had most honourably, most consistently, made him aware that—that what once might have been desirable has unhappily become impossible."

" Well," said Ermine.

" And thus," he proceeded, " that the sincere friendship with which you still regard him would prevent any encouragement to continue an attachment, unhappily now hopeless and obstructive to his prospects."

Ermine's eyes flashed at the dictation. "Lord Keith," she said, " I have never sought your brother's visits nor striven to prolong them ; but if he finds pleasure in them after a life of disappointment and trouble, I cannot refuse nor discourage them."

" I am aware," said Lord Keith, rising as if to go, " that I have trespassed long on your time, and made a suggestion only warranted by the generosity with which you have hitherto acted."

" One may be generous of one's own, not of other people's," said Ermine.

He looked at her puzzled, then said, " Perhaps it will be best to speak categorically, Miss Williams. Let it be distinctly understood that my brother Colin, in paying his addresses to you, is necessarily without my sanction or future assistance."

" It might not be necessary, my lord. Good morning ;" and her courteous bow was an absolute dismissal.

But when Alison came home she found her more depressed than she had allowed herself to be for years, and on asking what was the matter was answered—

" Pride and perverseness, Ailie !" then, in reply to the eager exclamation, " I believe he was justified in all he said. But, Ailie, I have preached to Colin more than I had a right to do about forgiving his brother. I did not know how provoking he can be. I did not think it was still in me to fly out as I did !"

" He had no business to come here interfering and tormenting you," said Alison, hotly.

" I dare say he thought he had ! But one could not think of that when it came to threatening me with his giving no help to Colin if—— There was no resisting telling him how little we cared !"

" You have not offended him so that he will keep Colin away !"

" The more he tried, the more Colin would come ! No, I am not sorry for having offended him. I don't mind *him;* but Ailie, how little one knows ! All the angry and bitter feelings that I thought burnt out for ever when I lay waiting for death, are stirred up as hotly as they were long ago. The old self is here as strong as ever ! Ailie, don't tell Colin about this ; but to-morrow is a saint's day, and would you see Mr. Touchett, and try to arrange for me to go to the early service ? I think then I might better be helped to conquer this."

" But, Ermine, how can you ? Eight o'clock, you know."

" Yes, dearest, it will give you a great deal of trouble, but you never mind that, you know ; and I am so much stronger than I used to be, that you need not fear. Besides, I want help so much ! And it is the day Colin goes away !"

Alison obeyed, as she always obeyed her sister ; and Lord Keith, taking his constitutional turn before breakfast on the esplanade, was met by what he so little expected to encounter that he had not time to get out of the way—a Bath chair with Alison walking on one side, his brother on the other. He bowed coldly, but Ermine held out her hand, and he was obliged to come near.

" I am glad to have met you !" she said.

" I am glad to see you out so early," he answered, confused.

" This is an exception," she said, smiling and really look-ing beautiful. " Good-bye, I have thought over what passed yesterday, and I believe we are more agreed than perhaps I gave you reason to think."

There was a queenly air of dignified exchange of pardon in her manner of giving her hand and bending her head as she again said " Good-bye," and signed to her driver to move on.

Lord Keith could only say " Good-bye ;" then, looking after her, muttered, " After all, that is a remarkable woman."

CHAPTER VIII.

WOMAN'S MISSION DISCOVERED.

" But O unseen for three long years,
  Dear was the garb of mountaineers
  To the fair maid of Lorn."—LORD OF THE ISLES.

" ONLY nerves," said Alison Williams, whenever she was
pushed hard as to why her sister continued unwell, and her
own looks betrayed an anxiety that her words would not
confess. Rachel, after a visit on the first day, was of the
same opinion, and prescribed globules and enlivenment ; but
after a personal administration of the latter in the shape of a
discussion of Lord Keith, she never called in the morning
without hearing that Miss Williams was not up, nor in the
afternoon without Alison's meeting her, and being very sorry,
but really she thought it better for her sister to be quite
quiet.

In fact, Alison was not seriously uneasy about Ermine's
health, for these nervous attacks were not without precedent,
as the revenge for all excitement of the sensitive mind upon
the much-tried constitution. The reaction must pass off in
time, and calm and patience would assist in restoring her ;
but the interview with Lord Keith had been a revelation to
her that her affection was not the calm, chastened, mortified,
almost dead thing of the past that she had tried to believe it ;
but a young, living, active feeling, as vivid, and as little able

to brook interference as when the first harsh letter from Gowanbrae had fallen like a thunderbolt on the bright hopes of youth. She looked back at some verses that she had written, when first perceiving that life was to be her portion, where her own intended feelings were ascribed to a maiden who had taken the veil, believing her crusader slain, but who saw him return and lead a recluse life, with the light in her cell for his guiding star. She smiled sadly to find how far the imaginings of four and twenty transcended the powers of four and thirty; and how the heart that had deemed itself able to resign was chafed at the appearance of compulsion. She felt that the right was the same as ever; but it was an increased struggle to maintain the resolute abstinence from all that could bind Colin to her, at the moment when he was most likely to be detached, and it was a struggle rendered the more trying by the monotony of a life, scarcely varied except by the brainwork, which she was often obliged to relinquish.

Nothing, however, here assisted her so much as Lady Temple's new pony carriage which, by Fanny's desire, had been built low enough to permit of her being easily lifted into it. Inert, and almost afraid of change, Ermine was hard to persuade, but Alison, guessing at the benefit, was against her, and Fanny's wistful eyes and caressing voice were not to be gainsaid; so she suffered herself to be placed on the broad easy seat, and driven about the lanes, enjoying most intensely the new scenes, the peeps of sea, the distant moors, the cottages with their glowing orchards, the sloping harvest fields, the variety that was an absolute healing to the worn spirits, and moreover, that quiet conversation with Lady Temple, often about the boys, but more often about Colonel Keith.

Not only Ermine, but other inhabitants of Avonmouth
found the world more flat in his absence. Rachel's interest
was lessened in her readings after she had lost the pleasure
of discussion, and she asked herself many times whether the
tedium were indeed from love, or if it were simply from the
absence of an agreeable companion. " I will try myself," she
said to herself; "if I am heartily interested in my occupations by the end of the next week, then I shall believe
myself my own woman ! "

But in going back to her occupations, she was more than
ordinarily sensible of their unsatisfactoriness. One change
had come over her in the last few months. She did not so
much long for a wider field, as for power to do the few things
within her reach more thoroughly. Her late discussions had,
as it were, opened a second eye, that saw two sides of questions that she had hitherto thought had only one, and she
was restless and undecided between them, longing for some
impulse from within or without, and hoping, for her own
dignity and consistency's sake, that it was not only Colonel
Keith's presence which had rendered this summer the richest
in her life.

A test was coming for her, she thought, in the person of
Miss Keith. Judging by the brother, Rachel expected a tall
fair dreamy blonde, requiring to be taught a true appreciation
of life and its duties, and whether the training of this young
girl would again afford her food for eagerness and energy,
would, as she said to herself, show whether her affections
were still her own. Moreover, there was the great duty of
deciding whether the brother were worthy of Fanny !

It chanced to be convenient that Rachel should go to
Avoncester on the day of the arrival, and call at the station

for the traveller. She recollected how, five months previously, she had there greeted Fanny, and had seen the bearded apparition since regarded with so much jealousy, and now with such a strangely mixed feeling. This being a far more indifferent errand, she did not go on the platform, but sat in the carriage reading the report of the Social Science Congress, until the travellers began to emerge, and Captain Keith (for he had had his promotion) came up to her with a young lady who looked by no means like his sister. She was somewhat tall, and in that matter alone realized Rachel's anticipations, for she was black-eyed, and her dark hair was *crêpé* and turned back from a face of the plump contour, and slightly rosy complexion that suggested the patches of the last century ; as indeed Nature herself seemed to have thought when planting near the corner of the mouth a little brown mole, that added somehow to the piquancy of the face, not exactly pretty, but decidedly attractive under the little round hat, and in the point device, though simple and plainly coloured travelling dress.

" Will you allow me a seat ? " asked Captain Keith, when he had disposed of his sister's goods ; and on Rachel's assent, he placed himself on the back seat in his lazy manner.

" If you were good for anything, you would sit outside and smoke," said his sister.

" If privacy is required for swearing an eternal friendship, I can go to sleep instead," he returned, closing his eyes.

" Quite the reverse," quoth Bessie Keith ; " he has prepared me to hate you all, Miss Curtis."

" On the mutual aversion principle," murmured the brother.

" Don't you flatter yourself ! Have you found out, Miss

o 2

Curtis, that it is the property of this species always to go by contraries ? "

" To Miss Curtis I always appear in the meekest state of assent," said Alick.

" Then I would not be Miss Curtis. How horribly you must differ ! "

Rachel was absolutely silenced by this cross fire; something so unlike the small talk of her experience, that her mind could hardly propel itself into velocity enough to follow the rapid encounter of wits. However, having stirred up her lightest troops into marching order, she said, in a puzzled, doubtful way, " How has he prepared you to hate us ?—By praising us ? "

" Oh, no ; that would have been too much on the surface. He knew the effect of that," looking in his sleepy eyes for a twinkle of response. " No ; his very reserve said, I am going to take her to ground too transcendent for her to walk on, but if I say one word, I shall never get her there at all. It was a deep refinement, you see, and he really meant it, but I was deeper," and she shook her head at him.

" You are always trying which can go deepest ? " said Rachel.

" It is a sweet fraternal sport," returned Alick.

" Have you no brother ? " asked Bessie.

" No."

" Then you don't know what detestable creatures they are ; " but she looked so lovingly and saucily at her big brother, that Rachel, spite of herself, was absolutely fascinated by this novel form of endearment. An answer was spared her by Miss Keith's rapture at the sight of some soldiers in the uniform of her father's old regiment.

" Have a care, Bessie ; Miss Curtis will despise you," said her brother.

" Why should you think so ?" exclaimed Rachel, not desirous of putting on a forbidding aspect to this bright creature.

" Have I not been withered by your scorn ?"

" I—I——" Rachel was going to say something of her change of opinion with regard to military society, but a sudden consciousness set her cheeks in a flame and checked her tongue ; while Bessie Keith, with ease and readiness, filled up the blank. " What, Alick, you have brought the service into disrepute ! I am ashamed of you !"

" Oh, no !" said Rachel, in spite of her intolerable blushes, feeling the necessity of delivering her confession, like a cannon-ball among skirmishers ; " only we had been used to regard officers as necessarily empty and frivolous, and our recent experience has—has been otherwise." Her period altogether failed her.

" There, Alick, is that the effect of your weight of wisdom ? I shall be more impressed with it than ever. It has re-deemed the character of your profession. Captain Keith and the army."

" I am afraid I cannot flatter myself," said Alick ; and a sort of reflection of Rachel's burning colour seemed to have lighted on his cheek ; " its reputation has been in better hands."

" O Colonel Colin ! Depend upon it, he is not half as sage as you, Alick. Why, he is a dozen years older !—What, don't you know, Miss Curtis, that the older people grow the less sage they get ?"

" I hope not," said Rachel.

" Do you ! A contrary persuasion sustains me when I see people obnoxiously sage to their fellow-creatures."

" Obnoxious sageness in youth is the token that there is stuff behind," said Alick, with eagerness that set his sister laughing at him for fitting on the cap ; but Rachel had a sort of odd dreamy perception that Bessie Keith had unconsciously described her (Rachel's) own aspect, and that Alick was defending her, and she was silent and confused, and rather surprised at the assumption of the character by one who she thought could never even exert himself to be obnoxious. He evidently did not wish to dwell on the subject, but began to inquire after Avonmouth matters, and Rachel in return asked for Mr. Clare.

" Very well," was the answer ; " unfailing in spirits, every one agreed that he was the youngest man at the wedding."

" Having outgrown his obnoxious sageness," said Bessie. " There is nothing he is so adroit at as guessing the fate of a croquet-ball by its sound."

" Now Bessie," exclaimed Alick.

" I have not transgressed, have I ?" asked Bessie ; and in the exclamations that followed, she said, " You see what want of confidence is. This brother of mine no sooner saw you in the carriage than he laid his commands on me not to ask after your croquet-ground all the way home, and the poor word cannot come out of my mouth without——"

" I only told you not to bore Miss Curtis with the eternal subject, as she would think you had no more brains than one of your mallets," he said, somewhat energetically.

" And if we had begun to talk croquet, we should soon have driven him outside."

" But suppose I could not talk it," said Rachel, " and that we have no ground for it."

" Why, then,"—and she affected to turn up her eyes,— " I can only aver that the coincidence of sentiments is no doubt the work of destiny."

" Bessie !" exclaimed her brother.

" Poor old fellow ! you had excuse enough, lying on the sofa to the tune of tap and click ; but for a young lady in the advanced ranks of civilization to abstain is a mere marvel."

" Surely it is a great waste of time," said Rachel.

" Ah ! when I have converted you, you will wonder what people did with themselves before the invention."

" Woman's mission discovered !" quoth her brother.

" Also man's, unless he neglects it," returned Miss Elizabeth ; " I wonder, now, if you would play if Miss Curtis did."

" Wisdom never pledges itself how it will act in hypothetical circumstances," was the reply.

" Hypothetical," syllabically repeated Bessie Keith ; " did you teach him that word, Miss Curtis ? Well, if I don't bring about the hypothetical circumstances, you may call me hyperbolical."

So they talked, Rachel in a state of bewilderment, whether she were teased or enchanted, and Alexander Keith's quiet nonchalance not concealing that he was in some anxiety at his sister's reckless talk ; but, perhaps, he hardly estimated the effect of the gay, quaint manner that took all hearts by storm, and gave a frank careless grace to her nonsense. She grew graver and softer as she came nearer Avonmouth, and spoke tenderly of the kindness she had received at the time of her mother's death at the Cape, when she had been brought to the general's, and had there remained like a child of the house, till she had been sent home on the removal of the regiment to India.

" I remember," she said, " Mrs. Curtis kept great order. In fact, between ourselves, she was rather a dragon; and Lady Temple, though she had one child then, seemed like my companion and playfellow. Dear little Lady Temple, I wonder if she is altered!"

" Not in the least," returned both her companions at once, and she was quite ready to agree with them when the slender form and fair young face met her in the hall amid a cloud of eager boys. The meeting was a full renewal of the parting, warm and fond, and Bessie so comported herself on her introduction to the children, that they all became enamoured of her on the spot, and even Stephana relaxed her shyness on her behalf. That sunny gay good-nature could not be withstood, and Rachel, again sharing Fanny's first dinner after an arrival, no longer sat apart despising the military atmosphere, but listening, not without amusement, to the account of the humours of the wedding, mingled with Alick Keith's touches of satire.

" It was very stupid," said Bessie, " of none of those girls to have Uncle George to marry them. My aunt fancied he would be nervous, but I know he did marry a couple when Mr. Lifford was away; I mean him to marry me, as I told them all."

"You had better wait till you know whether he will," observed Alick.

" Will? Oh, he is always pleased to feel he can do like other people," returned Bessie; and I'll undertake to see that he puts the ring on the right—I mean the left finger. Because you'll have to give me away, you know, Alick ; so you can look after him."

" You seem to have arranged the programme pretty thoroughly," said Rachel.

" After four weddings at home, one can't but lay by a little experience for the future," returned Bessie ; "and after all, Alick need not look as if it must be for oneself. He is quite welcome to profit by it, if he has the good taste to want my uncle to marry him."

" Not unless I were very clear that he liked my choice," said Alick, gravely.

" Oh, dear ! Have you any doubts, or is that meant for a cut at poor innocent me, as if I could help people's folly, or as if *he* was not gone to Rio Janeiro," exclaimed Bessie, with a sort of meek simplicity and unconsciousness that totally removed all the unsatisfactoriness of the speech, and made even her brother smile while he looked annoyed ; and Lady Temple quietly changed the conversation. Alick Keith was obliged to go away early, and the three ladies sat long in the garden outside the window, in the summer twilight, much relishing the frank-hearted way in which this engaging girl talked of herself and her difficulties to Fanny as to an old friend, and to Rachel as belonging to Fanny.

" I am afraid that I was very naughty," she said, with a hand laid on Lady Temple's, as if to win pardon ; " but I never can resist plaguing that dear anxious brother of mine, and he did so dreadfully take to heart the absurdities of that little Charlie Carleton, as if any one with brains could think him good for anything but a croquet partner, that I could not help giving a little gentle titillation.

I saw you did not like it, dear Lady Temple, and I am sorry for it."

" I hope I did not vex you," said Fanny, afraid of having been severe.

" Oh, no, indeed ; a little check just makes one feel one is cared for," and they kissed affectionately : " you see when one has a very wise brother, plaguing him is irresistible. How little Stephana will plague hers, in self-defence, with so many to keep her in order."

" They all spoil her."

" Ah, this is the golden age. See what it will be when they think themselves responsible for her ! Dear Lady Temple, how could you send him home so old and so grave ? "

" I am afraid we sent him home very ill. I never expected to see him so perfectly recovered. I could hardly believe my eyes when Colonel Keith brought him to the carriage not in the least lame."

" Yes ; and it was half against his will. He would have been almost glad to be a lay curate to Uncle George, only he knew if he was fit for service my father would have been vexed at his giving up his profession."

" Then it was not his choice ! " said Rachel.

" Oh, he was born a soldier, like all the rest of us, couldn't help it. The —th is our home, and if he would only take my hint and marry, I could be with him there, now ! Lady Temple, do pray send for all the eligible officers—I don't know any of them now, except the two majors, and Alick suspects my designs, I believe, for he won't tell me anything about them."

" My dear ! " said Fanny, bewildered, " how you talk ; you know we are living a very quiet life here."

" Oh, yes, so Alick has told me," she said, with a pretty compunction in her tone ; " you must be patient with me," and she kissed Fanny's fingers again and spoke in a gentler way. " I am used to be a great chatter-box, and nobody protested but Alick."

" I wish you would tell me about his return, my dear ; he seemed so unfit to travel when your poor father came to the hills and took him away by dâk. It seemed so impossible he could bear the journey ; he could not stand or help himself at all, and had constant returns of fever ; but they said the long sea voyage was the only chance, and that in India he could not get vigour enough to begin to recover. I was very unhappy about him," said Fanny, innocently, whilst Rachel felt very vigilant, wondering if Fanny were the cause of the change his sister spoke of.

" Yes, the voyage did him good, but the tidings of papa's death came two months before him, and Uncle George's eyes were in such a state that he had to be kept in the dark, so that no one could go and meet the poor dear boy at Southampton but Mr. Lifford, and the shock of the news he heard brought the fever back, and it went on intermitting for weeks and weeks. We had him at Littleworthy at first, thinking he could be better nursed and more cheerful there, but there was no keeping the house quiet enough."

" Croquet ! " said Rachel.

" Everything ! " returned Bessie. " Four courtships in more or less progress, besides a few flirtations, and a house where all the neighbours were running in and out in a sociable way. Our loss was not as recent there as it was to him, and they were only nieces, so we could not have interfered with them ; besides, my aunt was afraid he would be dull, and

wanted to make the most of her conquering hero, and everybody came and complimented him, and catechised him
whether he believed in the Indian mutilations, when, poor
fellow, he had seen horrors enough never to bear to think of
them, except when the fever brought them all over again.
I am sure there was excuse enough for his being a little
irritable."

" My dear," exclaimed Fanny, quite hurt, " he was patience
itself while he was with us."

" That's the difference between illness and recovery, dear
Lady Temple ! I don't blame him. Any one might be
irritable with fresh undetected splinters of bone always
working themselves out, all down one side ; and doubts
which were worse, the fingers on, or the fingers off, and no
escape from folly or politeness, for he could not even use a
crutch. Oh, no, I don't blame him; I quite excuse the
general dislike he took to everything at poor dear Littleworthy. He viewed it all like that child in Mrs. Browning's
poem, ' seeing through tears the jugglers leap,' and we have
partaken of the juggler aspect to him ever since ! "

" I don't think he could ever be *very* irritable," said Fanny,
taking the accusation much to heart.

" Sister and recovery ! " lightly said Bessie ; " they encounter what no one else does ! He only pined for Bishopsworthy, and when we let him move there, after the first
month, he and my uncle were happy. I stayed there for a
little while, but I was only in the way, the dear good folks
were always putting themselves out on my account ; and as
to Alick, you can't think how the absence of his poor
" *souffre-douleur*," invigorated him. Every day I found him
able to put more point into his cutting compliments, and

reading to my uncle with more energy; till at last by the time the —th came home, he had not so much as a stiff leg to retire upon. Luckily, he and my uncle both cared too much for my poor father's wishes for him to do so without, though if any unlucky chance should take Mr. Lifford away from my uncle, he threatens coming to supply the vacancy, unless I should, and that is past hope."

" Your home is with your uncle," affirmed Rachel.

" Yes," she said, mournfully, " dear Littleworthy was too happy to last. It broke itself up by its own charms—all married and gone, and the last rose of summer in my poor person must float away. Jane wants her mother and not me, and my uncle will submit to me as cheerfully as to other necessary evils. It is not myself that I fear for; I shall be very happy with the dear uncle, but it will be a dreadful overthrow to his habits."

" I do not see why it need be," said Rachel.

" What! two old bachelors with a young lady turned in on them ! And the housekeeper—think of her feelings !"

" I do not think you need be uneasy, my dear," said Fanny. " Your brother is convinced that it will be the greatest pleasure and comfort to Mr. Clare to have you; and though there may be difficulties at first, I am sure anybody must be the happier for having you," and she caressed the upturned face, which responded warmly, but with a sigh.

" Alick is no judge ! He is the child of the house, and my uncle and Mr. Lifford don't feel complete without him. My uncle is as fond of me as can be, and he and I could get on beautifully; but then Mr. Lifford is impracticable."

" Impracticable ?" said Rachel, taking up the long word.

" He objects to your exerting yourself in the parish. I know what that is."

" Pray, Rachel," said Fanny, imploringly, " pray don't say anything against him ! I am very sorry he has annoyed you, but I do like him."

" Oh, does he play croquet ?" cried Bessie.

" I gather," said Rachel, in her impressive tone, a little disappointed, " that by impracticable you mean one who will not play croquet."

" You have hit it !" laughed Bessie. " Who will neither play at croquet, nor let one work except in his way. Well, there are hopes for you. I cure the curates of every cure I come near, except, of course, the cure that touches me most nearly. The shoemaker's wife goes the worst shod ! I'll tame yours."

" My dear, I can't have poor Mr. Touchett made game of."

" I won't make game of him, dear Lady Temple, only make him play a game."

" But you said Alick did not approve," said Fanny, with the dimmest possible ideas of what croquet was, and believing it a wicked flirtation trap that figured in " Punch."

" Oh, that's fudge on Master Alick's part ! Just the remains of his old miseries, poor fellow. What he wants is love ! Now he'll meet his fate some of these days ; and as he can't meet three Englishwomen without a mallet in hand, love and croquet will come together."

" Alick is very good," went on Lady Temple, not an-swering, but arguing with herself whether this opposition could be right. " Colonel Hammond gave me such an account of him, so valuable and excellent among the men, and doing all that is possible for their welfare, interesting himself about their library, and the regimental school and all. The colonel said he wished only that he was a little more easy and popular among the young officers ; but so many of his own standing were gone by the time he joined again, that he lives almost too much to himself, reads a good deal, and is most exemplary, but does not quite make his influence as available as it might be."

" That's just it," cried Bessie, eagerly ; " the boy is a lazy boy, and wants shaking up, or he'll get savage and no good. Can't you see, by the way he uses his poor little sister, what an awful don Captain Keith must be to a schoolboy of an ensign ? He must be taught toleration and hunted into amiability, or he'll be the most terrible Turk by the time he is a colonel; and you are the only person that can do it, dear Lady Temple."

Rachel did not much like this, but it was so prettily and playfully said that the pleasing impression was quite predominant ; and when Rachel took leave, it was with a sense of vexation that a person whom she had begun to esteem should be hard upon this bright engaging sister. Yet it might be well if Fanny took note of the admission that he could be irritable as well as stern, and sometimes mistaken in his judgments. What would the Colonel say to all this ? The Colonel—here he was coming back again into her imagination. Another symptom !

The brother left the field entirely to his sister for the present ; he was a good deal occupied after his leave, and other officers being away, he was detained at Avoncester, and meantime Bessie Keith took all hearts by storm with her gay good humour and eager sympathy. By the end of the first morning she had been to the stable with a swarm of boys, patted, and learnt the names of all, the ponies; she was on the warmest terms with the young spaniel, that, to the Curtises' vexation, one of the officers had given Conrade, and which was always getting into the way; she had won Alison by telling her of Mr. Clare's recollections of Ermine's remarkable beauty and intelligence, and charmed Ermine herself by his kind messages and her own sunshiny brightness; she had delighted Mrs. Curtis and Grace by appreciating their views and their flowers; she had discussed hymnals and chants with Mr. Touchett, and promised her services; she had given a brilliant object lesson at Mrs. Kelland's, and received one herself in lace-making; and had proved herself, to Rachel's satisfaction, equally practical and well-read. All the outer world was asking, " Have you seen the young lady with Lady Temple ? "

Nothing came amiss to her, from the antiquity of man to Stephana's first words; and whether she taught Grace new stitches, played cricket with Conrade, made boats for Cyril, prattled with Lady Temple, or studied with Rachel, all was done with grace, zest, and sympathy peculiarly her own. Two practisings at the school removed the leaden drawl, and lessened the twang of the choir; and Mr. Touchett looked quite exalted, while even Rachel owned that she had hardly believed her ears.

Rachel and she constituted themselves particular friends, and Grace kept almost aloof in the fear of disturbing them. She had many friends, and this was the first, except Ermine Williams, to whom Rachel had taken, since a favourite companion of her youth had disappointed her by a foolish marriage. Bessie's confidences had a vigour in them that even Rachel's half-way meetings could not check, and then the sharp, clever things she would say, in accordance with Rachel's views, were more sympathetic than anything she had met with. It was another new charm to life.

One great pleasure they enjoyed together was bathing. The Homestead possessed a little cove of its own under the rocks, where there was a bathing-house, and full perfection of arrangement for young ladies' aquatic enjoyment, in safety and absolute privacy. Rachel's vigorous strength and health had been greatly promoted by her familiarity with salt water, and Bessie was in ecstasies at the naiad performances they shared together on the smooth bit of sandy shore, where they dabbled and floated fearlessly. One morning, when they had been down very early to be beforehand with the tide, which put a stop to their enjoyment long before the breakfast hour, Bessie asked if they could not profit by their leisure to climb round the edge of the cliffs instead of returning by the direct path, and Rachel agreed, with the greater pleasure, that it was an enterprise she had seldom performed.

Very beautiful, though adventurous, was the walk—now on the brow of the steep cliff, looking down on the water or on little bays of shingle; now through bits of thicket that held out brambles to entangle the long tresses streaming on their shoulders; always in the brisk morning air, that filled them with strength and spirit, laughing, joking, calling to one another and to Conrade's little dog, that, like every other creature, had attached itself to Bessie, and had followed her from Myrtlewood that morning, to the vexation of Rachel, who had no love for dogs in their early youth.

They were beyond the grounds of the Homestead, but had to go a little further to get into the path, when they paused above a sort of dip or amphitheatre of rock around a little bay, whilst Rachel began telling of the smugglers' traditions that haunted the place—how much brandy and silk had there been landed in the time of the great French war, and how once, when hard pressed, a party of smugglers, taking a short cut in the moonlight midnight across the Homestead gardens, had encountered an escaped Guinea-pig, and no doubt taking it for the very rat without a tail, in whose person Macbeth's witch was to do, and to do, and to do, had been nearly scared out of their wits.

Her story was cut short by a cry of distress from the dog, and looking down, they perceived that the poor fellow had been creeping about the rocks, and had descended to the little cove, whence he was incapable of climbing up again. They called encouragingly, and pretended to move away, but he only moaned more despairingly, and leapt in vain.

"He has hurt his foot!" exclaimed Rachel; "I must go down after him. Yes, Don, yes, poor fellow, I'm coming."

"My dear Curtia, don't leap into the gulf!"

"Oh, it's no great height, and the tide will soon fill up this place."

"Don't! don't! You'll never be able to get up again."

But Rachel was already scrambling down, and, in effect, she was sure-footed and used to her own crags, nor was the distance much above thirty feet, so that she was soon safe on the shingle, to the extreme relief of poor Don, shown by grateful whines; but he was still evidently in pain, and Rachel thought his leg was broken. And how to get up the rock, with a spaniel that when she tried to lift it became apparently twice the size she had always believed it to be, and where both hands as well as feet were required, with the sea fast advancing too?

"My dear Rachel, you will only break your neck, too; it is quite vain to try!"

"If you could just come to that first rock, perhaps I could push him up to you!"

Bessie came to it, but screamed. "Oh, I'm not steady; I couldn't do it! Besides, it would hurt him so, and I know you would fall. Poor fellow, it is very sad; but indeed, Rachel, your life is more precious than a dog's!"

"I can't leave him to drown," said Rachel, making a desperate scramble, and almost overbalancing herself. "Here, if you could only get him by the scrough of his neck, it would not hurt him so much; poor Don, yes, poor fellow!" as he whined, but still showed his confidence in the touching manner of a sensible dog, knowing he is hurt for his good. Bessie made another attempt, but, unused to rocks, she was uneasy about her footing, and merely frightened herself. "Indeed," she said, "I had better run and call some one; I won't be long, and you are really quite safe."

"Yes, quite safe. If you were down here and I above I am sure we could do it easily."

"Ah! but I'm no cragswoman; I'll be back instantly."

"That way, that's the shortest; call to Zack or his father," cried Rachel, as the light figure quickly disappeared, leaving her a little annoyed at her predicament. She was not at all alarmed for herself, there was no real danger of drowning, she could at any moment get up the rock herself if she chose to leave the dog to its fate; but that she could not bear to think of, and she even thought the stimulus of necessity might prove the mother of invention, if succour should not come before that lapping flux and reflux of water should have crept up the shingly beach on which she stood; but she was anxious, and felt more and more drawn to the poor dog, so suffering, yet so patient and confiding. Nor did she like the awkwardness of being helped in what ought to be no difficulty at all to a native, and would not have been had her companion been Grace or even Conrade. Her hope was that her ally Zack would come, as she had directed Bessie towards the cottage ; but, behold, after a wearily long interval, it was no blue jacket that appeared, but a round black sea-side hat, and a sort of easy clerical-looking dress, that Bessie was fluttering before !

Few words were required, the stranger's height and length of arm did all that was needful, and Don was placed in safety with less pain and outcry than could have been hoped, Rachel ascending before the polite stranger had time to offer his assistance. The dog's hurt was, he agreed with Rachel, a broken leg, and his offer of carrying it home could not be refused, especially as he touched it with remarkable tenderness and dexterity, adding that with a splint or two, he thought he had surgery enough to set the limb.

They were much nearer the Homestead than to Myrtlewood, and as it had been already agreed that Bessie should breakfast there, the three bent their steps up the hill as fast as might be, in consideration of Mrs. Curtis's anxieties. Bessie in a state of great exultation and amusement at the romantic adventure, Rachel somewhat put out at the untoward mishap that obliged her to be beholden to one of the casual visitors, against whom her mother had such a prejudice.

Still, the gentleman himself was far from objectionable, in appearance or manner ; his air was that of an educated man, his dress that of a clergyman at large, his face keen. Rachel remembered to have met him once or twice in the town

within the last few days, and wondered if he could be a
person who had called in at the lace school and asked so
many questions that Mrs. Kelland had decided that he could
be after no good; he must be one of the Parliament folks
that they sent down to take the bread out of children's
mouths by not letting them work as many hours as was good
for them.   Not quite believing in a Government commission
on lace-making grievances, Rachel was still prepared to greet
a kindred spirit of philanthropy, and as she reflected more,
thought that perhaps it was well that an introduction had
been procured on any terms.

So she thawed a little, and did not leave all the civility to
Miss Keith, but graciously responded to the stranger's admiration of the views, the exquisite framings of the summer sea and
sky made by tree, rock, and rising ground, and the walks so
well laid out on the little headland, now on smooth turf, now
bordering slopes wild with fern and mountain ash, now amid
luxuriant exotic shrubs that attested the mildness of Avonmouth winters.

When they came near the front of the house, Rachel took
man and dog in through the open window of her own sitting-
room, and hastened to provide him with bandages and splints,
leaving Bessie to reassure Mrs. Curtis that no human limbs
were broken, and that no one was even wet to the skin ; nay,
Bessie had even the tact to spare Mrs. Curtis the romantic
colouring that deligh ed herself.   Grace had followed Rachel
to assist at the operation, and was equally delighted with its
neatness and tenderness, as well as equally convinced of the
necessity of asking the performer first to wash his hands and
then to eat his breakfast, both which kind proposals he accepted with diffident gratitude, first casting a glance around

the apartment, which, though he said nothing, conveyed that
he was profoundly struck with the tokens of occupation that
it contained.   The breakfast was, in the first place, a very
hungry one ; indeed, Bessie had been too ravenous to wait
till the surgery was over, and was already arrived at her
second egg when the others appeared, and the story had again
to be told to the mother, and her warm thanks given.   Mrs.
Curtis did not like strangers when they were only names, but
let her be brought in contact, and her good nature made her
friendly at once, above all in her own house.   The stranger
was so grave and quiet too, not at all presuming, and making
light of his services, but only afraid he had been trespassing
on the Homestead grounds.   These incursions of the season
visitors were so great a grievance at the Homestead that Mrs.
Curtis highly approved his forbearance, whilst she was
pleased with his tribute to her scenery, which he evidently
admired with an artistic eye.   Love of sketching had brought
him to Avonmouth ; and before he took leave, Mrs. Curtis
had accorded him that permission to draw in her little peninsula for which many a young lady below was sighing and
murmuring.   He thanked her with a melancholy look, confessing that in his circumstances his pencil was his toy and
his solace.

" Once again, that landscape painter ! " exclaimed Bessie,
with uplifted hands, as soon as both he and Mrs. Curtis were
out of earshot, " an adventure at last."

" Not at all," said Rachel, gravely ; " there was neither
alarm nor danger."

" Precisely ; the romance minus the disagreeables.   Only
the sea monster wanting.   Young Alcides, and rock—you
stood there for sacrifice, I was the weeping Dardanian dames."

Even Grace could not help laughing at the mischief of the one, and the earnest seriousness of the other.

"Now, Bessie, I entreat that you will not make a ridiculous story of a most simple affair," implored Rachel.

"I promise not to make one, but don't blame me if it makes itself."

"It cannot, unless some of us tell the story."

"What, do you expect the young Alcides to hold his tongue? That is more than can be hoped of mortal landscape painter."

"I wish you would not call him so. I am sure he is a clergyman."

"Landscape painter, I would lay you anything you please."

"Nay," said Grace, "according to you, that is just what he ought not to be."

"I do not understand what diverts you so much," said Rachel, growing lofty in her displeasure. "What matters it what the man may be?"

"That is exactly what we want to see," returned Bessie.

Poor Rachel, a grave and earnest person like her, had little chance with one so full of playful wit and fun as Bessie Keith, to whom her very dignity and susceptibility of annoyance made her the better game. To have involved the grave Rachel in such a parody of an adventure was perfectly irresistible to her, and to expect absolute indifference to it would, as Grace felt, have been requiring mere stupidity. Indeed, there was forbearance in not pushing Rachel further at the moment; but proceeding to tell the tale at Myrtlewood, whither Grace accompanied Bessie, as a guard against possible madcap versions capable of misconstruction.

"Yes," said Rachel to herself, "I see now what Captain

Keith regrets. His sister, with all her fine powers and abilities, has had her tone lowered to the hateful conventional style of wit that would put one to the blush for the smallest mishap. I hope he will not come over till it is forgotten, for the very sight of his disapproval would incite her further. I am glad the Colonel is not here. Here, of course, he is, in my imagination. Why should I be referring everything to him; I, who used to be so independent? Suppose this nonsense gave him umbrage? Let it. I might then have light thrown on his feelings and my own. At any rate, I will not be conscious. If this stranger be really worth notice, as I think he is, I will trample on her ridicule, and show how little I esteem it."

CHAPTER IX.

THE NEW SPORT.

" ' Sire,' I replied, ' joys prove cloudlets,
  Men are the merest Ixions.'
  Here the King whistled aloud, ' Let's,
  Heighho, go look at our lions ! '
  Such are the sorrowful chances
  If you talk fine to King Francis."—R. BROWNING.

THE day after Rachel's adventure with Don a card came into
the drawing-room, and therewith a message that the gentleman had availed himself of Mrs. Curtis's kind permission and
was sketching the Spinster's Needles, two sharp points of red
rock that stood out in the sea at the end of the peninsula,
and were specially appropriated by Rachel and Grace.

The card was written, not engraved, the name "Rd. R. H.
C. L. Mauleverer ; " and a discussion ensued whether the
first letters stood for Richard or for Reverend, and if he
could be unconscionable enough to have five initials.   The
sisters had some business to transact at Villars's, the Avonmouth deposit of literature and stationery, which was in the
hands of a somewhat aspiring genius, who edited the weekly
paper, and respected Miss Rachel Curtis in proportion to the
number of periodicals she took in, and the abstruseness of
the publications she inquired after.   The paper in its Saturday's dampness lay fresh on the counter, and glancing at the

new arrivals, Grace had the desired opportunity of pointing
to Mr. Mauleverer's name, and asking when he had come.
About a week since, said the obliging Mr. Villars, he appeared
to be a gentleman of highly literary and artistic tastes, a
philanthropist; indeed, Mr. Villars understood him to be a
clerical gentlemen who had opinions—

" Oh, Rachel, I am very sorry," said Grace.

" Sorry, what for?"

" Why, you and mamma seemed quite inclined to like
him."

" Well, and what have we heard?"

" Not much that is rational, certainly," said Grace, smiling;
" but we know what was meant."

" Granting that we do, what is proved against him?   No,
I will not say proved, but alleged.   He is one of the many
who have thought for themselves upon the perplexing problems of faith and practice, and has been sincere, uncompromising, self-sacrificing, in avowing that his mind is still
in that state of solution in which all earnest and original
minds must be ere the crystallizing process sets in.   Observe,
Grace, I am not saying for an instant that he is in the right.
All I do say is, that when depth of thought and candour
have brought misfortune upon a man, it is ungenerous, therefore, to treat him as if he had the leprosy."

" Indeed, Rachel, I think you have made more out of his
opinions than I did."

" I was only arguing on your construction of his opinions."

" Take care—!"   For they were at this moment reaching
a gate of Myrtlewood, and the sound of hoofs came close
behind them.   They were those of the very handsome chestnut, ridden by Alexander Keith, who jumped off his horse

with more alacrity than usual as they were opening the gate for him, and holding out his hand, eagerly said—

"Then I conclude there is nothing the matter?"

"Nothing at all," said Grace. "What did you hear?"

"Only a little drowning, and a compound fracture or two," said he, relapsing into his languid ease as he gave his bridle to a groom, and walked with them towards the house.

"There, how very annoying!" exclaimed Rachel, "though, of course, the smallest adventure does travel."

"I may venture to hope that neither are you drowned, nor my sister's leg broken, nor a celebrated professor and essayist 'in a high fever wi' pulling any of you out of the sea.'"

"There, Grace," exclaimed Rachel; "I told you he was something distinguished."

"My dear Rachel, if his celebrity be in proportion to the rest of the story."

"Then there really was a rescue!" exclaimed Captain Keith, now with much more genuine anxiety; and Rachel recollecting her desire that the right version should have the precedence, quickly answered, "There was no danger, only Don slipped down into that curved cove where we walked one day with the boys. I went down after him, but he had broken his leg. I could not get up with him in my arms, and Bessie called some one to help me."

"And why could not Bessie help you herself?"

"Oh! strangers can never climb on our slippery rocks as we can."

"Moreover, it would have spoilt the predicament," muttered the brother to himself; then turning round with a smile, "And is the child behaving herself?"

" Grace and Rachel answered in a eager duet how she was charming every one, so helpful, so kind, so everything."

" Ah !" he said with real satisfaction, apparent in the eyes that were so pleasant when open wide enough to be visible ; " I knew she always did better when I was not there."

They were by this time entering the hall, which, in the confident fashion of the sea-side, stood open ; and at the moment Fanny came tripping downstairs with her dress looped up, and a shady hat on her head, looking fearfully girlish, thought her cousins, though her attire was still rigidly black.

" Oh, I am so glad to see you ; Don is so much better, Rachel, and Conrade wants to thank you. He went up yesterday, and was so sorry you were out. Might it not have been dreadful, Alick ? I have been so wanting to tell you how very delightful that dear sister of yours is. All the boys are distracted about her. Come out please. She has been teaching the boys such a delightful game ; so much nicer than cricket, for I can play with them."

Alick and Rachel could not but exchange a glance, and at the same moment, emerging through the screen of shrubs on the lawn, Bessie Keith, Conrade, Francis, and Leoline, were seen each with a mallet in hand and a gay ball in readiness to be impelled through the hoops that beset the lawn.

" And you really are learning croquet !" exclaimed innocent Grace ; " well, it makes a beautiful ground."

" Croquet !" exclaimed poor Lady Temple, with startled eyes ; " you don't really mean that it is croquet ! O Bessie, Bessie !"

" Ah ! I didn't mean you to have come so soon," said the much amused Bessie, as she gave her hand in greeting.   " I meant the prejudice to be first conquered. See, dear Lady Temple, I'm not ashamed ; this whitey brown moustache is going to kiss me nevertheless and notwithstanding."

And so it certainly did, and smiled into the bargain, while the boys came clamouring up, and after thanks for Don's preservation, began loudly to beg mamma would come, they could not make up their sides without her ; but mamma was distressed and unhappy.

" Not now, my dears—I must—I must. Indeed I did not know."

" Now, Alick, I trust to your generosity," said Bessie, finding that they must be pacified. " Coming, Con—Come, Grace, come and convince Lady Temple that the pastime is not too wicked for you."

" Indeed, Alick," Lady Temple was saying. " I am very sorry, I won't allow it one moment if you think it is objectionable."

" But I don't," said Alick, smiling. " Far from it. It is a capital game for you and your boys."

" I thought—I thought you disapproved and could not bear it," said Lady Temple, wondering and wistful.

" Can't bear is not disapprove. Indeed," seeing that gentle earnest alone could console her, " there is no harm in the game itself. It is a wholly personal distaste, arising from my having been bored with it when I was ill and out of spirits."

" But is not there something about it in ' Punch ?'" she still asked, so anxiously, that it was impossible not to smile ; but there was not a particle of that subdued mockery that was often so perplexing in him, as he replied, " Certainly there is about its abuse as an engine for flirtation, which, to tell you the truth, was what sickened me with the sight at

Littleworthy; but that is not the line Con and Francie will take just yet. Why, my uncle is specially addicted to listening to croquet, and knows by the step and sound how each player is getting on, till he is quite an oracle in disputed hits."

"So Bessie told me," said Fanny, still feeling that she had been taken in and the brother unkindly used; "but I can't think how she could, when you don't like it."

"Nobody is bound to respect foolish prejudices," said Alick, still quite in earnest. "It would have been very absurd not to introduce it."

"Come, Alick," said Bessie, advancing, "have you absolved her, and may we begin? Would it not be a generous act of amnesty if all the present company united in a match?"

"Too many," said Alick; "odd numbers. I shall go down and call on Miss Williams. May I come back, Lady Temple, and have a holiday from the mess?"

"I shall be very glad; only I am afraid there is no dinner."

"So much the better. Only let me see you begin, or I shall never dare to express an opinion for the future."

"Mamma, do pray, pray begin; the afternoon is wasting like nothing!" cried Conrade of the much-tried patience. "And Aunt Rachel," he added, in his magnanimity, "you shall be my partner, and I'll teach you."

"Thank you, Conrade, but I can't; I promised to be at home at four," said Rachel, who had all this time been watching with curious interest which influence would prevail —whether Alick would play for Fanny's sake, or Fanny abstain for Alick's sake. She was best satisfied as it was, but she had still to parry Bessie Keith's persuasive determination. Why would she go home? it certainly was to inspect the sketches of the landscape-painter. " You heard, Alick, of the interesting individual who acted the part of Rachel's preserver," she added.

The very force of Rachel's resolution not to be put out of countenance served to cover her with the most uncomfortable blushes, all the more at the thought of her own unlucky exclamation. " I came here," said Alick, coolly, " to assist in recovering the beloved remains from a watery grave ;" and then, as Bessie insisted on hearing the Avoncester version, he gave it ; while Grace added the intelligence that the hero was a clergyman, sinking the opinions, as too vague to be mentioned, even had not the company been too flighty for a subject she thought serious and painful. " And he is at this moment sketching the Spinster's Needles !" said Bessie. " Well, I am consoled. With all your resolve to flatten down an adventure, fate is too strong for you. Something *will* come of it. Is not the very resolve that it shall not be an adventure a token ?"

" If any one should wish to forget it, it is you, I think, Bessie," said Alick. " Your admirable sagacity seems to have been at fault. I thought you prided yourself on your climbing."

" Up a slippery perpendicular——"

" I know the place," he gravely answered.

" Well," exclaimed Bessie, recovering herself, " I am not a mermaid nor even a dear gazelle, and, in my humble opinion, there was far more grace in preventing heroism from being ' unwept, unnoticed, and unsung,' than in perilling my own neck, craning down and strangling the miserable beast, by

pulling him up by the scrough of his neck! What an introduction would have been lost!"

"If you are going to play, Bessie," said her brother, "it
would be kind to take pity upon those boys."

"One achievement is mine," she said, dancing away backwards, her bright eyes beaming with saucy merriment, "the
great Alexander has bidden me to croquet."

"I am afraid," said her brother, turning to Rachel as she
departed, "that it was all her fault. Pray be patient with
her, she has had many disadvantages."

His incomprehensible irony had so often perplexed Rachel,
that she did not know whether his serious apologetic tone
were making game of her annoyance, and she answered not
very graciously, "Oh, never mind, it did not signify." And
at the same time came another urgent entreaty from the boys
that the two "aunts" would join the game, Conrade evidently
considering that partnership with him would seal the forgiveness Aunt Rachel had won by the rescue of Don.

Grace readily yielded, but Rachel pleaded her engagement;
and when the incorrigible Bessie declared that they perfectly
understood that nothing could compete with the sketch of
the Spinster's Needles, she answered, "I promised to write a
letter for my mother on business before post time. The
Burnaby bargain," she explained, to add further conviction.

"A business-like transaction indeed!" exclaimed Bessie,
much diverted with the name.

"Only a bit of land in trust for apprenticing poor children," said Rachel. "It was left by a Curtis many generations ago, in trust to the rector of the parish and the lord of
the manor; and poor Mr. Linton is so entirely effete, that it
is virtually in our hands. It is one of the vexations of my

life that more good cannot be done with it, for the fees are too small for superior tradespeople, and we can only bind them to the misery of lacemaking. The system belongs to a worn-out state of things."

The word system in Rachel's mouth was quite sufficient to send Bessie to her croquet, and the poor boys were at length rewarded for their unusual patience. Their mother had been enduring almost as much as they did in her dislike to see them tantalized, and she now threw herself into the game with a relish that proved that, as yet, at least, Conrade's approbation was more to her than Captain Keith's. It was very pretty to see her so pleased with her instructions, so eager about her own game, and yet so delighted with every hit of her boys; while Bessie was an admirable general, playing everybody's game as well as her own, and with such life and spirit, such readiness and good nature, that a far duller sport would have been delicious under her management.

"Poor Alick," said she, meeting him when he again strolled into the garden, while the boys were collecting the mallets and balls; "he did think he had one lawn in the world undefiled by those horrible hoops!" then as she met his smile of amusement and pardon; "but it was so exactly what they wanted here. It is so good for Lady Temple and her boys to have something they can do together."

The pleased affectionate smile was gone.

"I object to nothing but its being for her good," he said gravely.

"But now, does not it make her very happy, and suit her excellently?"

"May be so, but that is not the reason you introduced it."

" You have a shocking habit of driving one up into corners, Alick ; but it shall be purely, purely for my own selfish delight," and she clasped her hands in so droll an affectation of remorse, that the muscles round his eyes quivered with diversion, though the hair on his lip veiled what the corners of his mouth were about ; " if only," she proceeded, " you won't let it banish you. You must come over to take care of this wicked little sister, or who knows what may be the consequences."

" I kept away partly because I was busy, and partly because I believe you are such a little ape as always to behave worse when you have the semblance of a keeper ;" he said, with his arm fondly on her shoulder as they walked.

" And in the mean time fell out the adventure of the distinguished essayist."

" I am afraid," he returned, " that was a gratuitous piece of mischief, particularly annoying to so serious and thoughtful a person as Miss Rachel Curtis."

" Jealousy ?" exclaimed Bessie in an ecstatic tone.   " You see what you lost by not trusting me, to behave myself under the provocation of your presence."

" What ! the pleasure of boxing your ears for a coward !"

" Of seizing the happy opening ! I am very much afraid for you now, Alick," she proceeded with mock gravity. " What hope can a poor Captain of Highlanders, even if he does happen to be a wounded hero or two, have against a distinguished essayist and landscape painter, if it were a common case indeed ; but where Wisdom herself is concerned——"

" Military frivolity cannot hope," returned Alick, with a shake of his head, and a calm matter-of-fact acquiescent tone.

" Ah, poor Alick," pursued his sister, " you always were a discreet youth ; but to be connected with such a union of learning, social science, and homœopathy, soared beyond my utmost ambition. I suppose the wedding tour—supposing the happy event to take place—will be through a series of model schools and hospitals, ending in Hanwell."

" No," said Alick, equally coolly, "to the Dutch reformatory, and the Swiss cretin asylum."

She was exceedingly tickled at his readiness, and proceeded in a pretended sentimental tone, " I am glad you have revealed the secrets of your breast. I saw there was a powerful attraction and that you were no longer your own, but my views were humbler. I thought the profound respect with which you breathed the name of Avonmouth, was due to the revival of the old predilection for our sweet little——"

" Hush, Bessie," said her brother, roused for the first time into sternness, " this is more than nonsense. One word more of this, and you will cut me off from my greatest rest and pleasure."

" From the lawn where croquet waits his approbation," was on Bessie's tongue, but she did not say it. There were moments when she stood in fear of her brother. He paused, and as if perceiving that his vehemence was in itself suspicious, added, " Remember, I never met her from seven years old till after her marriage. She has been the kindest of friends in right of our fathers' old friendship. You know how her mother nursed me, and the sister she was to me. And Bessie, if your selfishness — I wish I could call it thoughtlessness—involves her innocent simplicity in any scrape, derogatory to what is becoming her situation, I shall find it very hard to forgive you, and harder still to forgive myself for letting you come here."

Bessie pouted for a moment, but her sweetness and good humour were never away. "There, you *have* given your wicked little sister a screed," she said, looking insinuatingly up at him. "Just as if I did not think her a darling, and would not for the world do anything to spoil her. Have not I been leading the most exemplary life, talking systems and visiting cottages with Rachel and playing with the boys, and singing with the clergyman; and here am I pounced on, as if I were come to be the serpent in this anti-croquet paradise."

"Only a warning, Bessie."

"You'll be better now you have had it out. I've seen you suppressing it all this time, for fear of frightening me away."

Every one knows how the afternoon croquet match on the Myrtlewood Lawn became an institution, though with some variation in the observers thereof, owing to the exigencies of calls, rides, and Ermine Williams's drive, which Lady Temple took care should happen at least twice a week. The most constant votaries of the mallet and hoop were, of course, the two elder boys, the next pair being distant worshippers only now and then admitted by special favour; but the ardour of their mother even exceeded that of Bessie Keith, and it was always a disappointment to her if she were prevented from playing. Grace and Alison Williams frequently took their share with enjoyment, though not with the same devotion; and visitors, civil and military, also often did their part, but the most fervent of all these was Mr. Touchett. Ever since that call of his, when, after long impatience of his shy jerks of conversation and incapacity of taking leave, Miss Keith had exclaimed, " Did you ever play at croquet ? do come, and we will teach you," he had been its most assiduous student. The first instructions led to an appointment for more, one contest to another, and the curate was becoming almost as regular a croquet player as Conrade himself, not conversing much but sure to be in his place ; and showing a dexterity and precision that always made Lady Temple pleased to have him on her side, and exclaim with delight at his hits as a public benefit to the cause, or thank him with real gratitude when he croqued her or one of her sons out of a difficulty.

Indeed that little lawn at Myrtlewood was a battle-field, of which Alison used to carry her sister amusing and charac- teristic sketches. The two leading players were Miss Keith and Mr. Touchett, who alone had any idea of tactics ; but what she did by intuition, sleight of hand or experience, he effected by calculation and generalship, and even when Con- rade claimed the command of his own side, the suggestions of the curate really guided the party. Conrade was a sort of Murat on the croquet field, bold, dashing, often making wonderful hits, but uncertain, and only gradually learning to act in combination. Alison was a sure-handed, skilful hitter, but did not aspire to leadership. Mamma tried to do what- ever her boys commanded, and often did it by a sort of dainty dexterity, when her exultation was a very pretty sight ; nor was Grace's lady-like skill contemptible, but having Francis as an ally was like giving a castle ; and he was always placed on the other side from Conrade, as it was quite certain that he would do the very reverse of whatever his brother advised. Now and then invitations were given for Rose Williams to join the game, but her aunts never accepted them. Ermine had long ago made up her mind against intimacies between her niece and any pupils of Alison's, sure that though starts of pleasure might result, they would be at the cost of ruffling, and, perhaps, perturbing the child's even stream of happiness—even girl-friendships might have been of doubtful effect where circumstances were so unequal ; but Lady Temple's household of boys appeared to Ermine by no means a desirable sphere for her child to be either teased or courted in. Violetta, Colinette, and Augustus were safer comrades, and Rose continued to find them sufficient, varied with the rare delight of now and then sharing her aunt's drive, and brightened by many a kind message in Colonel Keith's letters to her aunt, nay, occasionally a small letter to herself, or an enclosure of some pretty photograph for her much-loved scrap book, or some article for Colinette's use, sometimes even a new book ! She was never forgotten in his letters, and Ermine smiled her strange pensive smile of amusement at his wooing of the unconscious Rose.

CHAPTER X.

THE PHILANTHROPIST.

"Scorn not the smallness of daily endeavour,
  Let the great meaning enoble it ever,
  Droop not o'er efforts expended in vain,
  Work, as believing, that labour is gain."
  Queen Isabel, &c. by S. M.

THE sturdy recusant against Myrtlewood croquet continued to be Rachel Curtis, and yet it was not a testimony against the game so much as real want of time for it. She was always full of occupation, even while her active mind craved for more definite and extended labour; and when she came upon the field of strategy, it was always either with some business before her, or else so late that the champions were only assisting their several lags to bring the battle to an end.

If there had been a will there would have been a way, but, as she said, she saw enough to perceive that proficiency could only be attained at the cost of much time and study, and she did not choose to be inferior and mediocre. Also, she found occupations open to her elsewhere that had long been closed or rendered unpleasant. Mr. Touchett had become wonderfully pacific and obliging of late; as if the lawn tactics absorbed his propensities for offence and defence, he really seemed obliged for one or two bits of parish work that

she attended to ; finding that between him and his staff of
young ladies they were getting omitted. Somehow, too, an
unaccountable blight was passing over the activity of those
curatolatresses, as Rachel had been wont to call them ; they
were less frequently to be met with popping out of the
schools and cottages, and Rachel, who knew well all the real
poor, though refusing the bonds of a district, was continually
detecting omissions which she more often supplied than reported. There was even a smaller sprinkling at the weekly
services, and the odd thing was that the curate never seemed
to remark or be distressed by the change, or if any one spoke
of the thin congregation he would say, winter was the Avonmouth season, which was true enough, but the defaulters
were mostly his own peculiar followers, the female youth of
the professional and mercantile population.

Rachel did not trouble herself about the cause of all this,
indeed she was too much occupied with the gradual gliding
into somewhat of her original activity and importance in the
field thus left open to her. None the less, however, did she
feel the burden of life's problems ; the intercourse she had
enjoyed with Colonel Keith had excited her for a time, but
in the reaction, the old feelings returned painfully that the
times were out of joint ; the heavens above became obscure
and misty as before, the dark places of the earth looked
darker than ever, and those who lived at ease seemed to be
employed either in sport upon the outside of the dungeon
where the captives groaned, or in obstructing the way of
those who would fain have plunged in to the rescue.

Her new acquaintance, Mr. Mauleverer, was an example of
such prevention, which weighed much on her mind. He had
been perfectly unobtrusive, but Mrs. Curtis meeting him on

the second day of his sketching, had naturally looked at his drawing, and admired it so much that she brought her daughters to see it when in course of completion the next day. He had then asked whether there would be any objection to his making use of the sketches in the way of remunerative sale. Mrs. Curtis looked rather taken aback, it hardly agreed with her exclusive notions of privacy, and he at once apologized with such humility that she was touched, and felt herself doing him a wrong, whilst Rachel was angry at her scruple, yet uncomfortably thought of " that landscape painter," then said in her decided way, " you did not mean to object, mother ? "

" Oh, not for a moment, pray don't think of it," returned Mr. Mauleverer, in haste. " I would not think of the intrusion. It is only that these poor trifles are steps to one of the few means by which I can still hope to do even a little for my fellow creatures ; the greatest solace that remains to me."

" My mother did not mean to prevent anything," said Rachel eagerly ; " least of all any means of doing good."

" Indeed, I cannot but be aware that Miss Curtis is the last individual who would do so, except indeed by the good works she herself absorbs."

" You are too good, sir," returned Mrs. Curtis ; " I am sure I did not mean to object to anything for good. If it is for a charity, I am sure some of our friends would be very glad to take some sketches of our scenery ; they have been begging me this long time to have it photographed. I should like to have that drawing myself, it would please your aunt so much, my dear, if we sent it to her."

Mr. Mauleverer bowed, but Rachel was not sure whether he had not been insulted.

Next day he left at the door the drawing handsomely mounted, and looking so grand and meritorious that poor Mrs. Curtis became much troubled in mind whether its proper price might not be five or even ten guineas, instead of the one for which she had mentally bargained, or if this might not be the beginning of a series ; "which would be quite another thing, you know, my dear."

Rachel offered to go and talk to the artist, who was sketching in full view from the windows, and find out what value he set upon it.

"Perhaps, but I don't know, my dear. Won't it be odd ? Had you not better wait till Grace comes in, or till I can come down with you ? "

" No need at all, mother, I can do it much better alone, and at my age——"

So Rachel took a parasol and stepped out, looked at the outline newly produced, thanked and praised the drawing that had been received, adding that her mother would be glad to know what price Mr. Mauleverer set upon it. She was met by a profession of ignorance of its value, and of readiness to be contented with whatever might be conferred upon his project ; the one way in which he still hoped to be of service to his fellow creatures, the one longing of his life.

" Ah ! " said Rachel, greatly delighted with this congenial spirit, and as usual preferring the affirmative to the interrogative. " I heard you had been interesting yourself about Mrs. Kelland's lace school. What a miserable system it is ! "

" My inquiries have betrayed me then ? It is indeed a trying spectacle."

" And to be helpless to alleviate it," continued Rachel. " Over work, low prices and middle men perfectly batten on the lives of our poor girls here. I have thought it over again and again, and it is a constant burden on my mind."

"Yes, indeed. The effects of modern civilization are a constant burden on the compassion of every highly constituted nature."

"The only means that seems to me likely to mitigate the evil," continued Rachel, charmed at having the most patient listener who had ever fallen to her lot, "would be to commence an establishment where some fresh trades might be taught, so as to lessen the glut of the market, and to remove the workers that are forced to undersell one another, and thus oblige the buyers to give a fairly remunerative price."

"Precisely my own views. To commence an establishment that would drain off the superfluous labour, and relieve the oppressed, raising the whole tone of female employment."

"And this is the project you meant ? "

"And in which, for the first time, I begin to hope for success, if it can only receive the patronage of some person of influence."

"Oh, anything I can do !" exclaimed Rachel, infinitely rejoiced. "It is the very thing I have been longing for for years. What, you would form a sort of industrial school, where the children could be taught some remunerative labour, and it might soon be almost self-supporting ? "

"Exactly ; the first establishment is the difficulty, for which I have been endeavouring to put a few mites together."

"Every one would subscribe for such a purpose !" exclaimed Rachel.

"You speak from your own generous nature, Miss Curtis ; but the world would require patronesses to recommend."

"There could be no difficulty about that!" exclaimed Rachel; but at this moment she saw the Myrtlewood pony carriage coming to the door, and remembering that she had undertaken to drive out Ermine Williams in it, she was obliged to break off the conversation, with an eager entreaty that Mr. Mauleverer would draw up an account of his plan, and bring it to her the next day, when she would give her opinion on it, and consider of the means.

"My dear," said her mother, on her return, "how long you have been; and what am I to give for the water-colour?"

"Oh, I forgot all about the water-colour; but never mind what we give, mamma, it is all to go to an asylum for educating poor girls, and giving them some resource beyond that weary lace-making—the very thing I have always longed for. He is coming to settle it all with me to-morrow, and then we will arrange what to give."

"Indeed, my dear, I hope it will be something well managed. I think if it were not for those middle men, lace-making would not be so bad. But you must not keep poor Miss Williams waiting."

Ermine had never seen Rachael in such high spirits as when they set out through the network of lanes, describing her own exceeding delight in the door thus opening for the relief of the suffering over which she had long grieved, and launching out into the details of the future good that was to be achieved. At last Ermine asked what Rachel knew of the proposer.

"Captain Keith heard he was a distinguished professor and essayist."

"Then I wonder we have not heard his name," said

Ermine. "It is a remarkable one ; one might look in the
' Clergy List' at Villars's."

" Villars called him a clerical gentleman," mused Rachel.

" Then you would be sure to be able to find out something
about him before committing yourself."

" I can see what he is," said Rachel, " a very sensible,
accomplished man, and a great deal more ; not exactly a
finished gentleman. But that is no objection to his doing a
great work."

"None at all," said Ermine, smiling ; " but please forgive
me. We have suffered so much from trusting too implicitly,
that I never can think it safe to be satisfied without thorough
knowledge of a person's antecedents."

" Of course," said Rachel, " I shall do nothing without
inquiry. I will find out all about him, but I cannot see any
opening for distrust. Schemes of charity are not compatible
with self-seeking and dishonesty."

" But did I not hear something about opinions ? "

" Oh, as to that, it was only Villars. Besides, you are a
clergyman's daughter, and your views have a different colouring from mine. Modern research has introduced so many
variations of thought, that no good work would be done at
all if we required of our fellow-labourers perfect similarity of
speculative belief."

" Yet suppose he undertook to teach others ? "

" The simple outlines of universal doctrine and morality
which are required by poor children are not affected by
the variations to which investigation conducts minds of
more scope."

" I am afraid such variations may often reach the foundation."

"Now, Miss Williams, I am sure you must often have heard it observed how when it comes to real practical simple teaching of uninstructed people, villagers or may be heathens, the details of party difference melt away, and people find themselves in accordance."

"True, but there I think party differences in the Church, and even the variations between Christian sects are concerned, both being different ways of viewing the same truth. These may, like the knights in the old fable, find that both were right about the shield, both have the same foundation. But where the foundation is not the same, the results of the teaching will not agree."

"Every one agrees as to morality."

"Yes, but do all give a motive sufficient to enforce the self-denial that morality entails? Nay, do they show the way to the spiritual strength needful to the very power of being moral?"

"That is begging the question. The full argument is whether the full church, say Christian system, exactly as you, as we hold it, is needful to the perfection of moral observance. I don't say whether I assent, but the present question is whether the child's present belief and practice need be affected by its teacher's dogmatic or undogmatic system."

"The system for life is generally formed in childhood. Harvest depends on seed time."

"And after all," added Rachel, "we have no notion whether this poor man be not precisely of your own opinions, and from their fruits I am sure you ought to claim them."

"Their blossoms if you please," laughed Ermine. "We have not seen their fruits yet."

"And I shall take care the fruits are not nipped with the blight of suspicion," said Rachel, good-humouredly.

However, after driving Ermine home, and seeing her lifted out and carried into the house by her sister, Rachel did send the carriage back by the groom and betake herself to Villars's shop, where she asked for a sight of the "Clergy List." The name of Mauleverer caught her eye, but only one instance of it appeared, and he was a cathedral canon, his presentation dated in 1832, the time at which, judging from appearances, the object of her search might have been born; besides, he rejoiced in the simple name of Thomas. But Rachel's search was brought to an abrupt conclusion by the issue of Mr. Mauleverer himself from the reading-room within the shop. He bowed and passed by, but Rachel for the life of her could not hinder a burning colour from spreading to the very tips of her ears; so certain did she feel that she was insulting him by her researches, and that he perceived them. She felt absolutely ashamed to see him the next day, and even in her dreams was revolving speeches that might prove that though cautious and clear-sighted, she was neither suspicious nor narrow-minded.

He came when some morning visitors were at the Homestead, prosy neighbours whose calls were always a penance to Rachel; and the butler, either from the manner of the inquiry or not regarding him as drawing-room company, put him into the dining-room and announced, "Mr. Mauleverer to see Miss Rachel." Up jumped Miss Rachel, with "You'll excuse me, it is on business;" and went off highly satisfied that "the mother" was hindered by politeness from making any attempt at chaperonage either personally or through Grace; so unnecessary at her age, for since Colonel Keith's departure, Rachel's age had begun to grow on her again.

She held out her hand as if to atone for her search, but she found at once that it had been remarked.

" You were doing me the honour to look for my name in the 'Clergy List,' Miss Curtis," he said.

" Yes, one is apt——," faltered Rachel, decidedly out of countenance.

" I quite appreciate the motive. It is exactly in accord with Miss Curtis's prudence and good sense. I should wish to be fully explicit before any arrangements are made. I am unhappily not in orders, Miss Curtis. I know your liberality will regard the cause with leniency."

" Indeed," said Rachel, sufficiently restored to recall one of her premeditated reassurances. " I can fully appreciate any reluctance to become stringently bound to dogmatic enuncia- tions, before the full powers of the intellect have examined into them."

" You have expressed it exactly, Miss Curtis. Without denying an iota of them, I may be allowed to regret that our formularies are too technical for a thoughtful mind in the present age."

" Many have found it so," returned Rachel, thoughtfully, " who only needed patience to permit their convictions to ripen. Then I understand you, it was a rejection on negative not positive grounds?"

" Precisely ; I do not murmur, but it has been the blight of my life."

" And yet," said Rachel, consolingly, " it may enable you to work with more freedom."

" Since you encourage me to believe so, Miss Curtis, I will hope it, but I have met with much suspicion."

" I can well believe it," said Rachel ; " even some of the

most superior persons refuse to lay their hands to any task unless they are certified of the religious opinions of their coadjutors, which seems to me like a mason's refusing to work at a wall with a man who liked Greek architecture when he preferred Gothic !"

If Rachel had been talking to Ermine she might have been asked whether the dissimilarity might not be in the foundations, or in the tempering of the mortar, but Mr. Mauleverer only commended her liberal spirit, and she thought it high time to turn from this subject to the immediate one in hand. He had wished to discuss the plan with her, he said, before drawing it up, and in effect she had cogitated so much upon it that her ideas came forth with more than her usual fluency and sententiousness. The scheme was that an asylum should be opened under the superintendence of Mr. Mauleverer himself, in which young girls might be placed to learn handicrafts that might secure their livelihood, in especial, perhaps, wood engraving and printing. It might even be possible, in time, to render the whole self-supporting, suppose by the publication of a little illustrated periodical, the materials for which might be supplied by those interested in the institution.

If anything could add to Rachel's delight it was this last proposition. In all truth and candour, the relief to the victims to lace-making was her primary object, far before all besides, and the longing desire of her heart for years seemed about to be fulfilled ; but a domestic magazine, an outlet to all the essays on Curatocult, on Helplessness, on Female Folly, and Female Rights, was a development of the plan beyond her wildest hopes ! No dull editor to hamper, reject or curtail ! She should be as happy, and as well able to expand as the Invalid herself.

Mr. Mauleverer had brought a large packet of letters with him, in all manner of hands. There were some testimonials from a German university, and letters from German professors in a compromise between English and German hand, looking impossible to read, also the neat writing and thin wavy water-marked paper of American professors and philanthropists in high commendation of his ability and his scheme, and a few others that he said were of too private a nature to do more than show Miss Curtis in confidence, but on which she recognised some distinguished names of persons interested in Social Science. She would not wound his feelings by too close an inquiry, but she felt armed at all points against cavillers. Really, she began to think, it was a great pity Colonel Keith should cross her path again, she had so much on her hands that it would be a public misfortune if any one man's private domestic love should monopolize her; and yet, such was this foolish world, the Honourable Mrs. Colin Keith would be a more esteemed lady patroness than Miss Rachel Curtis, though the Curtises had been lords of the soil for many generations, and Colonel Keith was a mere soldier of fortune.

One disappointment Rachel had, namely, that Mr. Mauleverer announced that he was about to return to St. Norbert's, the very large and fashionable watering-place in the next ndentation of the coast. He had duties there, he said, and he had only come to Avonmouth for a brief holiday, a holiday that was to result in such happy effects. He lived in an exceedingly retired way, he said, being desirous of saving his small private means for his great object, and he gave Rachel his address at the chief printseller's of the place, where his letters were left for him, while he made excursions from time to time to study the picturesque, and to give lectures on behalf of philanthropical subjects. He offered such a lecture at Avonmouth, but Mr. Touchett would not lend either school-room, and space was nowhere else available. In the meantime a prospectus was drawn up, which Rachel undertook to get printed at Villars's, and to send about to all her friends, since a subscription in hand was the first desideratum.

Never since she had grown up to be a thinking woman had Rachel been so happy as with this outlet to her activity and powers of managing, "the good time coming at last." Eagerly she claimed sympathy, names and subscriptions. Her own immediate circle was always easily under her influence, and Lady Temple and Mrs. Curtis supplied the dignity of lady patronesses; Bessie Keith was immensely diverted at the development of "that landscape painter," and took every opportunity of impressing on Rachel that all was the result of her summons to the rescue. Ermine wished Rachel had found out who was the bishop's chaplain who rejected him, but allowed that it would have been an awkward question to ask, and also she wondered if he were a university man; but Mr. Touchett had been at a Hall, and never knew anybody, besides being so firmly convinced that Mr. Mauleverer was a pestiferous heretic, that no one, except Lady Temple, could have obtained a patient answer from him on that head—and even with her he went the length of a regret that she had given the sanction of her name to an undertaking by a person of whose history and principles nothing satisfactory was known. "Oh!" said Fanny, with her sweet look of asking pardon, "I am so sorry you think so; Rachel wished it so much, and it seems such a nice thing for the poor children."

"Indeed," said Mr. Touchett, well nigh disarmed by the look, "I am quite sensible of the kindness of all you do, I only ventured to wish there had been a little more delay, that we were more certain about this person."

"When Colonel Keith comes back he will find out all about him, I am sure," said Fanny, and Mr. Touchett, to whom seemed to have been transferred Rachel's dislike to the constant quoting of Colonel Keith, said no more.

The immediate neighbourhood did not very readily respond to the appeal to it in behalf of the lace-makers. People who did not look into the circumstances of their neighbours thought lace furnished a good trade, and by no means wished to enhance its price; people who did care for the poor had charities of their own, nor was Rachel Curtis popular enough to obtain support for her own sake; a few five pound notes, and a scanty supply of guineas and half guineas from people who were ready at any cost to buy off her vehement eyes and voice was all she could obtain, and with a subscription of twenty pounds each from her mother, Lady Temple, and Grace, and all that she could scrape together of her own, hardly seemed sufficient to meet the first expenses, and how would the future be provided for? She calculated how much she could spare out of her yearly income, and actually, to the great horror of her mother and the coachman, sold her horse.

Bessie Keith was the purchaser. It was an expense that she could quite afford, for she and her brother had been left very well off by their father—a prudent man, who, having been a widower during his Indian service, had been able to live inexpensively, besides having had a large amount of prize money. She had always had her own horse at Littleworthy, and now when Rachel was one day lamenting to her the difficulty of raising money for the Industrial Asylum, and declaring that she would part with her horse if she was sure of its falling into good hands, Bessie volunteered to buy it, it was exactly what would suit her, and she should delight in it as a reminder of dear Avonmouth. It was a pang, Rachel loved the pretty spirited creature, and thought of her rides with the colonel; but how weigh the pleasure of riding against the welfare of one of those hard-worked, half-stifled little girls, and besides, it might be best to have done with Colonel Keith now that her mission had come to find her. So the coachman set a purposely unreasonable value upon poor Meg, and Rachel reduced the sum to what had been given for it three years before; but Bessie begged her brother to look at the animal and give his opinion.

"Is that what you are after?" he exclaimed.

"Indeed, Alick, I thought it was the greatest kindness I could do her; she is so very eager about this plan, and so anxious to find poor Meg a good home."

"Purely to oblige her?"

"Of course, Alick, it was much more convenient to her than if she had had to send about to horse-dealers or to advertise. I doubt if she could have done it at all; and it is for her asylum, you know."

"Then give the coachman's sixty guineas at once."

"Ah, Alick, that's your infatuation!" and she put on a droll gesture of pity. "But excuse me, where would be the fine edge of delicacy in giving a manifestly fancy price? Come and look at her."

" I never meddle with horse-dealing."

" Stuff, as if you weren't the best-mounted man in the regiment. I shall send a note to Captain Sykes if you won't; he knows how to drive a bargain."

" And give a fancy price the other way. Well, Bessie, on one condition I'll go, and that is, that Meg goes to Bishops-worthy the day she is yours. I won't have her eating Lady Temple's corn, and giving her servants trouble."

" As if I should think of such a thing."

Captain Keith's estimate of the value of the steed precisely agreed with Rachel's demand of the original price. Bessie laughed, and said there was collusion.

" Now seriously, Alick, do you think her worth so much ? Isn't it a pity, when you know what a humbug poor Rachel is going to give it to ? " and she looked half comical, half saucy.

" If she were going to throw it into the sea, I don't see what difference that would make."

" Ah ! you are far too much interested. Nothing belonging to *her* can bear a vulgar price."

" Nothing belonging to me is to gain profit by her self-denial," said Alick, gravely. " You cannot do less than give her what she gave for it, if you enter on the transaction at all."

" You mean that it would look shabby. You see we womankind never quite know the code of the world on such matters," she said, candidly.

" There is something that makes codes unnecessary, Bessie," he said.

" Ah ! I can make allowances. It is a cruel stroke. I don't wonder you can't bear to see any one else on her palfrey ; above all, as a sacrifice to the landscape painter."

"Then spare my feelings, and send the mare to Bishops-worthy," said Alick, as usual too careless of the imputation to take the trouble to rebut it or to be disconcerted.

Bessie was much tickled at his acceptance, and laughed heartily.

"To be sure," she said, "it is past concealment now. You must have been very far gone, indeed, to have been taken in to suppose me to be making capital of her 'charitable purposes.'"

"Your acting is too like life," he said, not yet induced to laugh, and she rattled on with her droll, sham, sentimental air. "Is it the long words, Alick, or is it 'the great eyes, my dear;' or is it—oh, yes, I know what is the great attraction —that the Homestead doesn't possess a single spot where one could play at croquet!"

"Quite irresistible!" replied Alick, and Bessie retreated from the colloquy still not laughing at but with him ; that is, if the odd, quaint, inward mirth which only visibly lengthened his sleepy eyes, could be called a laugh.

Next time Captain Keith rode to Avonmouth he met the riding party on the road, Bessie upon Rachel's mare ; and it appeared that Lady Temple had considered it so dreadful that Meg should not share her hospitality, that it had been quite impossible to send her away. "So, Alick, your feelings must endure the dreadful spectacle."

Meanwhile Rachel was hard at work with the subscribers to the "Christian Knowledge Society." Beginning with the A's, and working down a page a day, she sent every member a statement of the wrongs of the lacemakers, and the plans of the industrial establishment, at a vast expense of stamps ; but then, as she calculated, one pound thus gained paid for two hundred and forty fruitless letters.

"And pray," said Alick, who had ridden on to call at the Homestead, " how do you reconcile yourself to the temptation to the postmen ? "

"They don't see what my letters are about ? "

"They must be dull postmen if they don't remark on the shower of envelopes that pass through their hands—ominous money-letters, all with the same address, and no detection remember. You don't know who will answer and who will not."

" I never thought of that," said Rachel ; " but risks must be run when any great purpose is in hand."

"The corruption of one postman *versus* the rescue of—how many children make a postman ? " asked Captain Keith, with his grave, considering look.

" The postman would be corrupt already," said Grace, as Rachel thought the last speech too mocking to be worthy of reply, and went on picking up her letters.

" There is another objection," added Captain Keith, as he watched her busy fingers. " Have you considered how you are frightening people out of the society ? It is enough to make one only subscribe as Michael Miserly or as Simon Skinflint, or something equally uninviting to applications."

" I shall ask you to subscribe by both names ! " said Rachel, readily. " How much for Simon Skinflint ? "

" Ten pounds. Stop—when Mr. Mauleverer gives him a reference."

" That's ungenerous. Will Michael Miserly make up for it ? "

" Yes, when the first year's accounts have been audited."

" Ah ! those who have no faith to make a venture can never effect any good."

"You evidently build on a great amount of faith from the public. How do you induce them to believe—do you write in your own name?"

"No, it makes mamma unhappy. I was going to put R.C., but Grace said people would think it meant Roman Catholic. Your sister thought I had better put the initials of Female Union for Lacemaker's Employment."

"You don't mean that Bessie persuaded you to put that?" exclaimed Alick Keith, more nearly starting up than Rachel had ever seen him.

"Yes. There is no objection, is there?"

"Oh, Rachel, Rachel, how could we have helped thinking of it?" cried Grace, nearly in a state of suffocation.

Rachel held up her printed appeal, where subscriptions were invited to the address of F. U. L. E., the Homestead, Avonmouth.

"Miss Curtis, though you are not Scottish, you ought to be well read in Walter Scott."

"I have thought it waste of time to read incorrect pictures of pseudo-chivalry since I have been grown up," said Rachel. "But that has nothing to do with it."

"Ah, Rachel, if we had been more up in our Scotch, we should have known what F. U. L. E. spells," sighed Grace.

A light broke in upon Rachel. "I am sure Bessie never could have recollected it," was her first exclamation. "But there," she continued, too earnest to see or stumble at straws, "never mind. It cannot be helped, and I dare say not one person in ten will be struck by it."

"Stay," said Grace, "let it be Englishwoman's Employment. See, I can very easily alter the L into an E."

Rachel would hardly have consented, but was forced to

yield to her mother's entreaties. However, the diligent trans-
formation of L's did not last long ; for three days after a
parcel was left at the Homestead containing five thousand
printed copies of the appeal, with the E rightly inserted.
Bessie laughed, and did not disavow the half reluctant thanks
for this compensation for her inadvertence or mischief, which-
ever it might be, laughing the more at Rachel's somewhat
ungrateful confession that she had rather the cost had gone
into a subscription for the F. U. E. E. As Bessie said to
herself, it was much better and more agreeable for all parties
that it should so stand, and she would consider herself in
debt to Alick for the amount. Indeed, she fully expected
him to send her in the bill, but in the meantime not one
word was uttered between the brother and sister on the
subject. They understood one another too well to spend
useless words.

Contrary to most expectation, there was result enough
from Rachel's solicitations to serve as justification for the
outlay in stamps. The very number of such missives that
fly about the world proves that there must be a great amount
of uninquiring benevolence to render the speculation anything but desperate, and Rachel met with very tolerable
success. Mr. Mauleverer called about once a week to report
progress on his side, and, in his character of treasurer, to
take charge of the sums that began to accumulate. But
Rachel had heard so much on all sides of the need of caution
in dealing with one so entirely a stranger, that she resolved
that no one should blame her for imprudence, and therefore
retained in her own name, in the Avoncester Bank, all the
sums that she received. Mr. Mauleverer declared himself
quite contented with this arrangement, and eagerly antici-

pated the apologies that Rachel was ashamed even to make to him.

Enough was collected to justify a beginning on a small scale. A house was to be taken where Mr. Mauleverer and a matron would receive the first pupils, teach them wood engraving, and prepare the earlier numbers of the magazine. When a little more progress had been made, the purchase of a printing-press might be afforded, and it might be struck off by the girls themselves, but in the meantime they must be dependent on the regular printer. On this account Mr. Mauleverer thought it best to open the establishment, not at Avonmouth, but at St. Norbert's, where he had acquaintance that would facilitate the undertaking.

Rachel was much disappointed. To be in and out constantly, daily teaching and watching the girls, and encouraging them by learning the employment herself, had been an essential portion of her vision. She had even in one of her most generous moods proposed to share the delight with the Williamses, and asked Ermine if she would not, if all things suited, become the resident matron. However, Mr. Mauleverer said that there was an individual of humbler rank, the widow of a National Schoolmaster, so anxious to devote herself to the work, that he had promised she should share it whenever he was in a condition to set the asylum on foot ; and he assured Rachel that she would find this person perfectly amenable to all her views, and ready to work under her. He brought letters in high praise of the late schoolmaster, and recommendations of his widow from the clergyman of the parish where they had lived ; and place and name being both in the " Clergy List," even Ermine and Alison began to feel ashamed of their incredulity, whilst as

to Grace, she had surrendered herself completely to the eager
delight of finding a happy home for the little children in
whom she was interested. Grace might laugh a little at
Rachel, but in the main her trust in her sister's superiority
always led her judgment, and in the absence of Colonel
Keith, Fanny was equally willing to let Rachel think for her
when her own children were not concerned.

Rachel did not give up her hopes of fixing the asylum
near her till after a considerable effort to get a house for it at
Avonmouth, but this was far from easy. The Curtises' unwillingness to part with land for building purposes enhanced
the price of houses, and in autumn and winter the place was
at its fullest, so that she could not even rent a house but at a
ruinous price. It would be the best way to build on Homestead land, but this would be impracticable until spring,
even if means were forthcoming, as Rachel resolved they
should be, and in the meantime she was obliged to acquiesce
in Mr. Mauleverer's assurance that a small house in an over-
built portion of St. Norbert's would be more eligible than
one in some inland parish. Anything was better than delay.
Mr. Mauleverer was to superintend from his lodgings.

Rachel went with Grace and her mother to St. Norbert's,
and inspected the house, an ordinary cheap one, built to
supply lodgings for the more economical class of visitors.
It was not altogether what Rachel wished, but must serve
till she could build, and perhaps it would be best to form
her experience before her plans. Mr. Mauleverer's own lodgings were near at hand, and he could inspect progress. The
furniture was determined upon—neat little iron beds for the
dormitories, and all that could serve for comfort and even
pleasure, for both Mr. Mauleverer and Rachel were strong

against making the place bare and workhouse-like, insulting poverty and dulling the spirit.

Grace suggested communication with the clergyman of the parish; but the North Hill turned out not to belong to St. Norbert's proper, being a part of a great moorland parish, whose focus was twelve miles off. A district was in course of formation, and a church was to be built; but in the meantime the new houses were practically almost pastorless, and the children and their matron must take their chance on the free seats of one of the churches of St. Norbert's. The staff of clergy there were so busy that no one liked to add extra parochial work to their necessary duties, and there was not sufficient acquaintance with them to judge how they would view Mr. Mauleverer's peculiarities. Clerical interference was just what Rachel said she did not want; it was an escape that she did not call it meddling.

One bit of patronage at least she could exercise; a married pair of former Homestead servants had set up a fuel store at St. Norbert's, receiving coal from the ships, and retailing it. They were to supply the F. U. E. E. with wood, coal, and potatoes; and this was a great ingredient in Mrs. Curtis's toleration. The mother liked anything that brought custom to Rossiter and Susan.

The establishment was at present to consist of three children : the funds were not sufficient for more. One was the child of the matron, and the other two were Lovedy Kelland and the daughter of a widow in ill health, whose family were looking very lean and ill cared for. Mrs. Kelland was very unwilling to give Lovedy up; she had always looked to receiving the apprentice fee from the Burnaby bargain for her as soon as the child was fourteen, and she had a strong

prejudice against any possible disturbance to the lace trade;
but winter would soon come and her sale was uncertain; her
best profit was so dependent on Homestead agency that it was
impolitic to offend Miss Curtis; and, moreover, Lovedy was
so excited by the idea of learning to make pictures to books
that she forgot all the lace dexterity she had ever learnt,
and spoilt more than she made, so that Mrs. Kelland was
reduced to accept the kind proposal that Lovedy should be
Lady Temple's nominee, and be maintained by her at the
F. U. E. E. at seven shillings a week.

Fanny, however, asked the clergyman's consent first, telling him, with her sweet, earnest smile, how sorry she was
for the little girl, and showing him the high testimonials to
Mrs. Rawlins. He owned that they were all that could be
wished, and even said at her request that he would talk to
Mr. Mauleverer. What the talk amounted to they never
knew; but when Fanny said "she hoped he had found
nothing unsatisfactory, the poor man must be so glad to be
of use;" Mr. Touchett replied with, "Indeed, it is an unfortunate situation;" and his opposition might therefore be
considered as suspended.

"Of course," cried Bessie, "we know by what witchery!"
But Alison Williams, her listener, turned on her such great
eyes of wilful want of comprehension, that she held her
peace.

Rachel and Grace united in sending Mary Morris, the
other child; they really could do nothing more, so heavily
had their means been drawn upon for the first expenses; but
Rachel trusted to do more for the future, and resolved
that her dress should henceforth cost no more than Alison
Williams's; indeed, she went through a series of assertions

by way of examining Alison on the expenses of her wardrobe.

The house was taken from Michaelmas, and a few days after, the two little victims, as Bessie laughingly called them, were taken over to St. Norbert's in the Homestead carriage, Lady Temple chaperoning the three young ladies to see the inauguration, and the height of Rachel's glory.

They were received by Mr. Mauleverer at the door, and slightly in the rear saw the matron, Mrs. Rawlings, a handsome pale woman, younger than they expected, but whose weeds made Fanny warm to her directly; but she was shy and retiring, and could not be drawn into conversation ; and her little Alice was only three years old, much younger than Rachel had expected as a pupil, but a very pretty creature with great black eyes.

Tea and cake were provided by way of an inauguration feast, and the three little girls sat up in an atmosphere of good cheer, strongly suggestive of school feasts, and were left in the midst, with many promises of being good, a matter that Lovedy seemed to think would be very easy in this happy place, with no lace to make.

Mrs. Rawlings, whose husband had been a trained schoolmaster, was to take the children to church, and attend to their religious instruction ; indeed, Mr. Mauleverer was most anxious on this head, and as Rachel already knew the scruples that withheld him from ordination were only upon the absolute binding himself to positive belief in minor technical points, that would never come in the way of young children.

Altogether, the neat freshness of the room, the urbanity of Mr. Mauleverer, the shy grief of the matron, all left a most pleasant impreseion.   Rachel was full of delight and triumph,

and Grace and Fanny quite enthusiastic; the latter even to
the being sure that the Colonel would be delighted, for the
Colonel was already beginning to dawn on the horizon, and
not alone. He had written, in the name of his brother, to
secure a cottage of gentility of about the same calibre as
Myrtlewood, newly completed by a speculator on one of the
few bits of ground available for building purposes. A name
was yet wanting to it; but the day after the negotiation was
concluded, the landlord paid the delicate compliment to his
first tenant by painting " Gowanbrae " upon the gate-posts in
letters of green. " Go and bray," read Bessie Keith as she
passed by; " for the sake of the chief of my name, I hope
that it is not an omen of his occupations here."

The two elder boys were with her; and while Francis,
slowly apprehending her meaning in part, began to bristle up
with the assurance that " Colonel Keith never brayed in his
life," Conrade caught the point with dangerous relish, and
dwelt with colonial disrespect, that alarmed his mother, on
the opinion expressed by some unguarded person in his hearing, that Lord Keith was little better than an old donkey.
" He is worse than Aunt Rachel," said Conrade, meditatively,
" now she has saved Don, and keeps away from the croquet."

Meantime Rachel studied her own feelings. A few weeks
ago her heart would have leapt at the announcement; but
now her mission had found her out, and she did not want
to be drawn aside from it. Colonel Keith might have many
perfections; but alike as Scotsman, soldier, and High-Church-
man, he was likely to be critical of the head of the F. U. E. E.,
and matters had gone too far now for her to afford to doubt,
or to receive a doubting master. Moreover, it would be
despicable to be diverted from a great purpose by a courtship

like any ordinary woman ; nor must marriage settlements
come to interfere with her building and endowment of the
asylum, and ultimate devotion of her property thereunto.
No, she would school herself into a system of quiet dis-
couragement, and reserve herself and her means as the
nucleus of the great future establishment for maintaining
female rights of labour.

CHAPTER XI.

LADY TEMPLE'S TROUBLES.

" The pheasant in the falcon's claw,
    He scarce will yield to please a daw."—SCOTT.

EARLY in the afternoon of a warm October day, the brothers
arrived at Avonmouth, and ten minutes after both were upon
the lawn at Myrtlewood, where croquet was still in progress.
Shouts of delight greeted the Colonel, and very gracefully
did Bessie Keith come to meet him, with the frank confiding
sweetness befitting his recent ward, the daughter of his friend.
A reassuring smile and monosyllable had scarcely time to pass
between him and the governess before a flood of tidings was
poured on him by the four elder boys, while their mother
was obliged to be mannerly, and to pace leisurely along with
the elder guest, and poor Mr. Touchett waited a little aloof,
hammering his own boot with his mallet, as if he found the
enchanted ground failing him. But the boys had no notion
of losing their game, and vociferated an inquiry whether the
Colonel knew croquet. Yes, he had several times played with
his cousins in Scotland. "Then," insisted Conrade, "he
must take mamma's place, whilst she was being devoured,
and how surprised she would be at being so helped on!"

"Not now; not to-day," he answered. "I may go to your
sister, Ailie? Yes, boys, you must close up your ranks
without me."

" Then please," entreated Hubert, "take him away," pointing to the engrosser of their mother.

" Do you find elder brothers so easily disposed of, Hubert?" said the Colonel. "Do you take Conrade away when you please?"

"I should punch him," returned Francis.

" He knows better," quoth Conrade in the same breath, both with infinite contempt for Hubert.

" And *I* know better," returned Colonel Keith; "never mind, boys, I'll come back in—in reasonable time to carry him off," and he waved a gay farewell.

"Surely you wish to go too," said Bessie to Alison, "if only to relieve them of the little girl! I'll take care of the boys. Pray go."

" Thank you," said Alison, surprised at her knowledge of the state of things, " but they are quite hardened to Rose's presence, and I think would rather miss her."

And in fact Alison did not feel at all sure that, when stimulated by Bessie's appreciation of their mischief, her flock might not in her absence do something that might put their mother in despair, and make their character for naughtiness irretrievable; so Leoline and Hubert were summoned, the one from speculations whether Lord Keith would have punched his brother, the other from amaze that there was anything our military secretary could not do, and Conrade and Francis were arrested in the midst of a significant contraction of the nostrils and opening of the mouth, which would have exploded in an "eehaw" but for Bessie's valiant undertaking to be herself and Lady Temple both at once.

Soon Colonel Keith was knocking at Ermine's door, and

Rose was clinging to him, glowing and sparkling with shy ecstasy ; while, without sitting down again after her greeting, Rachel resolutely took leave, and walked away with firm steps, ruminating on her determination not to encourage meetings in Mackarel Lane.

" Better than I expected ! " exclaimed Colonel Keith, after having ushered her to the door in the fulness of his gratitude. " I knew it was inevitable that she should be here, but that she should depart so fast was beyond hope ! "

" Yes," said Ermine, laughing, " I woke with such a certainty that she would be here and spend the first half hour n the F. U. E. E. that I wasted a great deal of resignation. But how are you, Colin? You are much thinner ! I am sure by Mrs. Tibbie's account you were much more ill than you told me."

" Only ill enough to convince me that the need of avoidng a northern winter was not a fallacy, and likewise to make Tibbie insist on coming here for fear Maister Colin should not be looked after. It is rather a responsibility to have let her come, for she has never been farther south than Edinburgh, but she would not be denied. So she has been to see you? I told her you would help her to find her underlings. I thought it might be an opening for that nice little girl who was so oppressed with lace-making."

" Ah ! she has gone to learn wood-cutting at the F. U. E. E. ; but I hope we have comfortably provided Tibbie with a damsel. She made us a long visit, and told us all about Master Colin's nursery days. Only I am afraid we did not understand half."

" Good old body," said the Colonel, in tones almost as national as Tibbie's own. " She was nursery girl when I was the spoilt child of the house, and hers was the most home-like face that met me. I wish she may be happy here. And you are well, Ermine?"

" Very well, those drives are so pleasant, and Lady Temple so kind ! It is wonderful to think how many unlooked-for delights have come to us ; how good every one is ;" and her eyes shone with happy tears as she looked up at him, and felt that he was as much her own as ever. " And you have brought your brother," she said ; " you have been too useful to him to be spared. Is he come to look after you or to be looked after ? "

" A little of both I fancy," said the Colonel, " but I suspect he is giving me up as a bad job. Ermine, there are ominous revivifications going on at home, and he has got himself rigged out in London, and had his hair cut, so that he looks ten years younger."

" Do you think he has any special views ? "

" He took such pains to show me the charms of the Benorchie property that I should have thought it would have been Jessie Douglas, the heiress thereof, only coming here does not seem the way to set about it, unless he regards this place as a bath of youth and fashion. I fancy he has learnt enough about my health to make him think me a precarious kind of heir, and that his views are general. I hope he may not be made a fool of, otherwise it is the best thing that could happen to us."

" It has been a dreary uncomfortable visit, I much fear," said Ermine.

" Less so than you think. I am glad to have been able to be of use to him, and to have lived on something like brotherly terms. We know and like each other much better

than we had a chance of doing before, and we made some
pleasant visits together, but at home there are many things
on which we can never be of one mind, and I never was
well enough at Gowanbrae to think of living there permanently."

" I was sure you had been very unwell ! You are better
though ? "

" Well, since I came into Avonmouth air," said he, " I fear
nothing but cold. I am glad to have brought him with me,
since he could not stay there, for it is very lonely for him."

" Yet you said his daughter was settled close by."

" Yes ; but that makes it the worse. In fact, Ermine, I
did not know before what a wretched affair he had made of
his daughters' marriages. Isabel he married when she was
almost a child to this Comyn Menteith, very young too at the
time, and who has turned out a good-natured, reckless, dis-
sipated fellow, who is making away with his property as fast
as he can, and to whom Keith's advice is like water on a
duck's back. It is all rack and ruin and extravagance, a
set of ill-regulated children, and Isabel smiling and looking
pretty in the midst of them, and perfectly impervious to remonstrance. He is better out of sight of them, for it is only
pain and vexation, an example of the sort of match he likes
to make. Mary, the other daughter, was the favourite, and
used to her own way, and she took it. Keith was obliged to
consent so as to prevent an absolute runaway wedding, but he
has by no means forgiven her husband, and they are living on
very small means on a Government appointment in Trinidad.
I believe it would be the bitterest pill to him that either son-
in-law should come in for any part of the estate."

" I thought it was entailed."

" Gowanbrae is, but as things stand at present that ends with me, and the other estates are at his disposal."

" Then it would be very hard on the daughters not to have them."

" So hard that the death of young Alexander may have been one of the greatest disasters of my life, as well as of poor Keith's. However, this is riding out to meet perplexities. He is most likely to outlive me ; and, moreover, may marry and put an end to the difficulty. Meantime, till my charge is relieved, I must go and see after him, and try if I can fulfil Hubert's polite request that I would take him away. Rosie, my woman, I have hardly spoken to you. I have some hyacinth roots to bring you to-morrow."

In spite of these suspicions, Colonel Keith was not prepared for what met him on his return to Myrtlewood. On opening the drawing-room door, he found Lady Temple in a low arm-chair in an agony of crying, so that she did not hear his approach till he stood before her in consternation. Often had he comforted her before ; and now, convinced that something dreadful must have befallen one of the children, he hastily, though tenderly, entreated her to tell him which, and what he could do.

" Oh, no, no ! " she exclaimed, starting up, and removing her handkerchief, so that he saw her usually pale cheeks were crimson—" Oh, no," she cried, with panting breath and heaving chest. " It is all well with them as yet. But—but —it's your brother."

He was at no loss now as to what his brother could have done, but he stood confounded, with a sense of personal share in the offence, and his first words were—" I am very sorry. I never thought of this."

"No, indeed," she exclaimed, "who could? It was too preposterous to be dreamt of by any one. At his age, too, one would have thought he might have known better."

A secret sense of amusement crossed the Colonel, as he recollected that the disparity between Fanny Curtis and Sir Stephen Temple had been far greater than that between Lady Temple and Lord Keith, but the little gentle lady was just at present more like a fury than he had thought possible, evidently regarding what had just passed as an insult to her husband and an attack on the freedom of all her sons. In answer to a few sympathising words on the haste of his brother's proceeding, she burst out again with indignation almost amusing in one so soft—"Haste! Yes! I did think that people would have had some respect for dear, dear Sir Stephen," and her gush of tears came with more of grief and less of violence, as if she for the first time felt herself unprotected by her husband's name.

"I am very much concerned," he repeated, feeling sympathy safer than reasoning. "If I could have guessed his intentions, I would have tried to spare you this; at least the suddenness of it. I could not have guessed at such presumptuous expectations on so short an acquaintance."

"He did not expect me to answer at once," said Fanny. "He said he only meant to let me know his hopes in coming here. And, oh, that's the worst of it! He won't believe me, though I said more to him than I thought I could have said to anybody! I told him," said Fanny, with her hands clasped over her knee to still her trembling, "that I cared for my dear, dear husband, and always shall—always—and then he talked about waiting, just as if anybody could leave off loving one's husband! And then when he wanted me to consider about my children, why then I told him "—and her voice grew passionate again—" the more I considered, the worse it would be for him, as if I would have my boys know me without their father's name ; and, besides, he had not been so kind to you that I should wish to let him have any-thing to do with them ! I am afraid I ought not to have said that," she added, returning to something of her meek softness ; "but indeed I was so angry, I did not know what I was about. I hope it will not make him angry with you."

" Never mind me," said Colonel Keith, kindly. " Indeed, Lady Temple, it is a wonderful compliment to you that he should have been ready to undertake such a family."

" I don't want such compliments ! And, oh ! " and here her eyes widened with fright, " what shall I do? He only said my feelings did me honour, and he would be patient and convince me. Oh, Colonel Keith, what shall I do?" and she looked almost afraid that fate and perseverance would master her after all, and that she should be married against her will.

"You need do nothing but go on your own way, and persist in your refusal," he said in the calm voice that always reassured her.

" Oh, but pray, pray never let him speak to me about it again ! "

" Not if I can help it, and I will do my best. You are quite right, Lady Temple. I do not think it would be at all advisable for yourself or the children, and hardly for him-self," he added, smiling. " I think the mischief must all have been done by that game at whist."

"Then I'll never play again in my life ! I only thought he was an old man that wanted amusing—." Then as one of the children peeped in at the window, and was called back—"O dear! how shall I ever look at Conrade again, now any one has thought I could forget his father?"

"If Conrade knew it, which I trust he never will, he ought to esteem it a testimony to his mother."

"Oh, no, for it must have been my fault! I always was so childish; and when I've got my boys with me, I can't help being happy," and the tears swelled again in her eyes. "I know I have not been as sad and serious as my aunt thought I ought to be, and now this comes of it."

"You have been true, have acted nothing," said Colonel Keith, "and that is best of all. No one who really knew you could mistake your feelings. No doubt that your conduct agrees better with what would please our dear Sir Stephen than if you drooped and depressed the children."

"Oh, I am glad you say that," she said, looking up, flushed with pleasure now, and her sweet eyes brimming over. "I have tried to think what he would like in all I have done, and you know I can't help being proud and glad of belonging to him still; and he always told me not to be shy and creeping into the nursery out of every one's way."

The tears were so happy now that he felt that the wound was healed, and that he might venture to leave her, only asking first, "And now what would you like me to do? Shall I try to persuade my brother to come away from this place?"

"Oh, but then every one would find out why, and that would be dreadful! Besides, you are only just come. And Miss Williams——"

"Do not let that stand in your way."

"No, no. You will be here to take care of me. And his

going now would make people guess; and that would be worse than anything."

"It would. The less disturbance the better; and if you upset his plans now, he might plead a sort of right to renew the attempt later. Quiet indifference will be more dignified and discouraging. Indeed, I little thought to what I was exposing you. Now I hope you are going to rest; I am sure your head is aching terribly."

She faintly smiled, and let him give her his arm to the foot of the stairs.

At first he was too indignant for any relief save walking up and down the esplanade, endeavouring to digest the unfairness towards himself of his brother's silence upon views that would have put their joint residence at Avonmouth on so different a footing; above all, when the Temple family were his own peculiar charge, and when he remembered how unsuspiciously he had answered all questions on the money matters, and told how all was left in the widow's own power. It was the more irritating, as he knew that his displeasure would be ascribed to interested motives, and regarded somewhat as he had seen Hubert's resentment treated when Francis teased his favourite rabbit. Yet not only on principle, but to avoid a quarrel, and to reserve to himself such influence as might best shield Lady Temple from further annoyance, he must school himself to meet his brother with coolness and patience. It was not, however, without strong effort that he was able to perceive that, from the outer point of view, one who, when a mere child, had become the wife of an aged general, might, in her early widowhood, be supposed open to the addresses of a man of higher rank and fewer years, and the more as it was not

in her nature to look crushed and pathetic. He, who had
known her intimately throughout her married life and in her
sorrow, was aware of the quiet force of the love that had
grown up with her, so entirely a thread in her being as to
crave little expression, and too reverent to be violent even in
her grief. The nature, always gentle, had recovered its
balance, and the difference in years had no doubt told in the
readiness with which her spirits had recovered their cheerfulness, though her heart remained unchanged. Still, retired as
her habits were, and becoming as was her whole conduct,
Colin began to see that there had been enough of liveliness
about her to lead to Lord Keith's mistake, though not to
justify his want of delicacy in the precipitation of his
suit.

These reflections enabled him at length to encounter his
brother with temper, and to find that, after all, it had been
more like the declaration of an intended siege than an actual
summons to surrender. Lord Keith was a less foolish and
more courteous man than might have been gathered from
poor Fanny's terrified account; and all he had done was to
intimate his intention of recommending himself to her, and
the view with which he had placed himself at Avonmouth;
nor was he in the slightest degree disconcerted by her vehemence, but rather entertained by it, accepting her faithful-
ness to her first husband's memory as the best augury of her
affection for a second. He did not even own that he had
been precipitate.

"Let her get accustomed to the idea," he said with a
shrewd smile. "The very outcry she makes against it will
be all in my favour when the turn comes."

"I doubt whether you will find it so."

" All the world does not live on romance like you, man.
Look on, and you will see that a pretty young widow like
her cannot fail to get into scrapes ; have offers made to her,
or at least the credit of them. I'd lay you ten pounds that
you are said to be engaged to her yourself by this time, and
it is no one's fault but your own that you are not. It is in
the very nature of things that she will be driven to shelter
herself from the persecution, with whoever has bided his
time."

" Oh, if you prefer being accepted on such terms——"

He smiled, as if the romance of the exclamation were
beneath contempt, and proceeded—" A pretty, gracious, lady-
like woman, who has seen enough of the world to know how
to take her place, and yet will be content with a quiet home.
It is an introduction I thank you for, Colin."

" And pray," said Colin, the more inwardly nettled because
he knew that his elder brother enjoyed his annoyance, " what
do you think of those seven slight encumbrances ? "

" Oh, they are your charge," returned Lord Keith, with a
twinkle in his eye. " Besides, most of them are lads, and
what with school, sea, and India, they will be easily disposed of."

" Certainly it has been so in our family," said Colin, rather
hoarsely, as he thought of the four goodly brothers who had
once risen in steps between him and the Master.

" And," added Lord Keith, still without direct answer,
" she is so handsomely provided for, that you see, Colin, I
could afford to give you up the Auchinvar property, that
should have been poor Archie's, and what with the farms
and the moor, it would bring you in towards three hundred
a year for your housekeeping."

Colin restrained himself with difficulty, but made quiet answer. " I had rather see it settled as a provision on Mary and her children."

Lord Keith growled something about minding his own concerns.

"That is all I desire," responded the Colonel, and therewith the conference ended. Nor was the subject recurred to. It was observable, however, that Lord Keith was polite and even attentive to Ermine. He called on her, sent her grouse, and though saying nothing, seemed to wish to make it evident that his opposition was withdrawn, perhaps as no longer considering his brother's affairs as his own, or else wishing to conciliate him. Lady Temple was not molested by any alarming attentions from him. But for the proclamation, the state of siege might have been unsuspected. He settled himself at the southern Gowanbrae as if he had no conquest to achieve but that of the rheumatism, and fell rapidly into sea-side habits—his morning stroll to see the fishing-boats come in, his afternoon ride, and evening's dinner party, or whist-club, which latter institution disposed of him, greatly to Colin's relief. The brothers lived together very amicably, and the younger often made himself helpful and useful to the elder, but evidently did not feel bound to be exclusively devoted to his service and companionship. All the winter residents and most of the neighbouring gentry quickly called at Gowanbrae ; and Lord Keith, in the leisure of his present life, liked society where he was the man of most consequence, and readily accepted and gave invitations. Colin, whose chest would not permit him to venture out after sunset, was a most courteous assistant host, but necessarily made fewer acquaintances, and often went his own way, sometimes riding with his brother, but more frequently scarcely seeing him between breakfast and twilight, and then often spending a solitary evening, which he much preferred either to *écarté* or to making talk.

The summer life had been very different from the winter one. There was much less intercourse with the Homestead, partly from Rachel being much engrossed with the F. U. E. E., driving over whenever the coachman would let her, to inspect progress, and spending much of her time in sending out circulars, answering letters, and writing a tale on the distresses of Woman, and how to help them, entitled "Am I not a Sister?" Tales were not much in Rachel's line; she despised reading them, and did not love writing them, but she knew that she must sugar the cup for the world, and so she diligently applied herself to the *pièce de résistance* for the destined magazine, heavily weighting her slender thread of story with disquisitions on economy and charity, and meaning to land her heroines upon various industrial asylums where their lot should be far more beatific than marriage, which was reserved for the naughty one to live unhappy in ever after. In fact, Rachel, in her stern consistency, had made up her mind to avoid and discourage the Colonel, and to prevent her own heart from relenting in his favour, or him from having any opportunity of asking an explanation, and with this determination she absented herself both from Ermine's parlour and Lady Temple's croquet ground; and if they met on the esplanade or in a morning call, took care never to give the chance of a *tête-à-tête*, which he was evidently seeking.

The croquet practice still survived. In truth, Fanny was afraid to ride lest Lord Keith should join her, and was glad

to surround herself with companions. She could not see the
enemy without a nervous trepidation, and was eager to engross
herself with anybody or thing that came to hand so as to
avoid the necessity of attending to him. More than once
did she linger among her boys "to speak to Mr. Touchett,"
that she might avoid a ten minutes' walk with his lordship;
and for nothing was she more grateful than for the quiet and
ever ready tact with which Bessie Keith threw herself into
the breach. That bright damsel was claimed by Lord Keith
as a kinswoman, and, accepting the relationship, treated him
with the pretty playfulness and coquetry that elderly men
enjoy from lively young girls, and thus often effected a
diversion in her friend's favour, to the admiration both of
the Colonel and of Lady Temple herself; all, however, by
intuition, for not a word had been hinted to her of what
had passed during that game at croquet. She certainly was
a most winning creature; the Colonel was charmed with her
conversation in its shades between archness and good sense,
and there was no one who did not look forward with dread
to the end of her visit, when after a short stay with one of
her married cousins, she must begin her residence with the
blind uncle to whose establishment she, in her humility, declared she should be such a nuisance. It was the stranger that
she should think so, as she had evidently served her appren-
ticeship to parish work at Bishopsworthy; she knew exactly
how to talk to poor people, and was not only at home in
clerical details herself, but infused them into Lady Temple;
so that to the extreme satisfaction of Mr. Touchett, the latter
organized a treat for the school-children, offered prizes for
needlework, and once or twice even came to listen to the
singing practice when anything memorable was going forward.

She was much pleased at being helped to do what she felt to be right and kind, though hitherto she had hardly known how to set about it, and had been puzzled and perplexed by Rachel's disapproval, and semi-contempt of " scratching the surface " by the commonplace Sunday-school system.

CHAPTER XII.

A CHANGE AT THE PARSONAGE.

" What could presumptuous hope inspire."—*Rokeby*.

THERE had been the usual foretaste of winter, rather sharp for Avonmouth, and though a trifle to what it was in less sheltered places, quite enough to make the heliotropes sorrowful, strip the fig-trees, and shut Colonel Keith up in the library. Then came the rain, and the result was that the lawn of Myrtlewood became too sloppy for the most ardent devotees of croquet ; indeed, as Bessie said, the great charm of the sport was that one could not play it above eight months in the year.

The sun came back again, and re-asserted the claim of Avonmouth to be a sort of English Mentone ; but drying the lawn was past its power, and Conrade and Francis were obliged to console themselves by the glory of taking Bessie Keith for a long ride.   They could not persuade their mother to go with them, perhaps because she had from her nursery-window sympathized with Cyril's admiration of the great white horse that was being led round to the door of Gowanbrae.

She said she must stay at home, and make the morning calls that the charms of croquet had led her to neglect, and in about half an hour from that time she was announced in Miss Williams' little parlour, and entered with a hurried, panting, almost pursued look, a frightened glance in her eyes, and a flush on her cheek, such as to startle both Ermine and the Colonel.

" Oh ! " she exclaimed, as if still too much perturbed to know quite what she was saying, " I—I did not mean to interrupt you."

" I'm only helping Rose to change the water of her hyacinths," said Colonel Keith, withdrawing his eyes and attention to the accommodation of the forest of white roots within the purple glass.

" I did not know you were out to-day," said Lady Temple, recovering herself a little.

" Yes, I came to claim my walking companion. Where's your hat, Rosie ? "

And as the child, who was already equipped all but the little brown hat, stood by her aunt for the few last touches to the throat of her jacket, he leant down and murmured, " I thought he was safe out riding."

" Oh no, no, it is not that," hastily answered Lady Temple, a fresh suffusion of crimson colour rushing over her face, and inspiring an amount of curiosity that rendered a considerable effort of attention necessary to be as supremely charming a companion as Rose generally found him in the walks that he made it his business to take with her.

He turned about long before Rose thought they had gone far enough, and when he re-entered the parlour there was such an expectant look on his face that Ermine's bright eyes glittered with merry mischief, when she sent Rose to take off her walking dress.

" Well ! " he said.

" Well ? Colin, have you so low an opinion of the dignity
of your charge as to expect her to pour out her secrets to the
first ear in her way ? "

" Oh, if she has told you in confidence."

" No, she has not told me in confidence ; she knew
better."

" She has told you nothing ? "

" Nothing ! " and Ermine indulged in a fit of laughter at
his discomfiture, so comical that he could not but laugh himself, as he said, " Ah ! the pleasure of disappointing me quite
consoles you."

" No; the proof of the discretion of womanhood does that!
You thought, because she tells all her troubles to you, that
she must needs do so to the rest of the world."

" There is little difference between telling you and me."

" That's the fault of your discretion, not of hers."

" I should like to know who has been annoying her.   I
suspect——"

" So do I.   And when you get the confidence at first
hand, you will receive it with a better grace than if you
had had a contraband foretaste."

He smiled.   " I thought yours a more confidence-winning
face, Ermine."

" That depends on my respect for the individual.   Now
I thought Lady Temple would much prefer my looking
another way, and talking about Conrade's Latin grammar,
to my holding out my arms and inviting her to pour into
my tender breast what another time she had rather not know
that I knew."

" That is being an honourable woman," he said, and Rose's

return ended the exchange of speculations; but it must be confessed that at their next meeting Ermine's look of suppressed inquiry quite compensated for her previous banter, more especially as neither had he any confidence to reveal or conceal, only the tidings that the riders, whose coalition had justified Lady Temple's prudence, had met Mr. Touchett wandering in the lanes in the twilight, apparently without a clear idea of what he was doing there. And on the next evening there was quite an excitement, the curate looked so ill, and had broken quite down when he was practising with the choir boys before church; he had, indeed, gone safely through the services, but at school he had been entirely at a loss as to what Sunday it was, and had still more unfortunately forgotten that to be extra civil to Miss Villars was the only hope of retaining her services, for he had walked by her with less attention than if she had been the meanest scholar. Nay, when his most faithful curatolatress had offered to submit to him a design for an illumination for Christmas, he had escaped from her with a desperate and mysterious answer that he had nothing to do with illumination, he hoped it would be as sombre as possible.

No wonder Avonmouth was astonished, and that guesses were not confined to Mackarel Lane.

" Well, Colin," said Ermine, on the Tuesday, " I have had a first-hand confidence, though from a different quarter. Poor Mr. Touchett came to announce his going away."

" Going !"

" Yes. In the very nick of time, it seems, Alick Keith has had a letter from his uncle's curate, asking him to see if he could meet with a southern clergyman to exchange duties for the winter with a London incumbent who has a delicate wife, and of course Mr. Touchett jumped at it."

" A very good thing—a great relief."

" Yes. He said he was very anxious for work, but he had lost ground in this place within the last few months, and he thought that he should do better in a fresh place, and that a fresh person would answer better here, at least for a time. I am very sorry for him ; I have a great regard for him."

" Yes ; but he is quite right to make a fresh beginning. Poor man ! he has been quite lifted off his feet, and entranced all this time, and his recovery will be much easier elsewhere. It was all that unlucky croquet."

" I believe it was. I think there was at first a reverential sort of distant admiration, too hopeless to do any one any harm, and that really might have refined him, and given him a little of the gentleman-like tone he has always wanted. But then came the croquet, and when it grew to be a passion it was an excuse for intimacy that it would have taken a stronger head than his to resist."

" Under the infection of croquet fever."

" It is what my father used to say of amusements—the instant they become passions they grow unclerical and do mischief. Now he used, though not getting on with the Curtises, to be most successful with the second-rate people ; but he has managed to offend half of them during this un-happy mania, which, of course, they all resent as mercenary, and how he is ever to win them back I don't know. After all, curatocult is a shallow motive—Rachel Curtis might triumph !"

" The higher style of clergyman does not govern by

curatocult. I hope this one may be of that description, as
he comes through Mr. Clare. I wonder if this poor man
will return?"

" Perhaps," said Ermine, with a shade of mimicry in her
voice, " when Lady Temple is married to the Colonel. There
now, I have gone and told you! I did try to resolve I would
not."

" And what did you say?"

" I thought it due to Lady Temple to tell him exactly how
she regarded you."

" Yes, Ermine, and it is due to tell others also. I cannot
go on on these terms, either here or at Myrtlewood, unless
the true state of the case is known. If you will not let me
be a married man, I must be an engaged one, either to you
or to the little Banksia."

This periphrasis was needful, because Rose was curled up
in a corner with a book, and her accessibility to outward
impressions was dubious. It might be partly for that reason,
partly from the tone of fixed resolve in his voice, that Ermine
made answer, " As you please."

It was calmly said, with the sweet, grave, confiding smile
that told how she trusted to his judgment, and accepted his
will. The look and tone brought his hand at once to press
hers in eager gratitude, but still she would not pursue this
branch of the subject; she looked up to him and said
gently, but firmly, " Yes, it may be better that the true state
of the case should be known;" and he felt that she thus
conveyed that he must not press her further, so he let her
continue, " At first I thought it would do him good, he
began pitying us so vehemently; but when he found I did
not pity myself, he was as ready to forget our troubles as—

you are to forget his," she added, catching Colin's fixed eye, more intent on herself than on her narrative.

" I beg his pardon, but there are things that come more home."

" So thought he," said Ermine.

" Did you find out," said Colin, now quite recalled, "what made him take courage ?"

" When he had once come to the subject, it seemed to be a relief to tell it all out, but he was so faltering and agitated that I did not always follow what he said. I gather, though, that Lady Temple has used him a little as a defence from other perils."

" Yes, I have seen that."

" And Miss Keith's fun has been more encouragement. than she knew ; constantly summoning him to the croquet-ground, and giving him to understand that Lady Temple liked to have him there. Then came that unlucky day, it seems, when he found Bessie mounting her horse at the door, and she called out that it was too wet for croquet, but Lady Temple was in the garden, and would be glad to see him. She was going to make visits, and he walked down with her, and somehow, in regretting the end of the croquet season, he was surprised into saying how much it had been to him. He says she was exceedingly kind, and regretted extremely that anything should have inspired the hope, said she should never marry again, and entreated him to forget it ; then I imagine she fled in here to put an end to it."

" She must have been much more gentle this time than she was with Keith. I had never conceived her capable of being so furious as she was then. I am very sorry, I wish we could spare her these things."

" I am afraid that can only be done in one way, which you are not likely at present to take," said Ermine with a serious mouth, but with light dancing in her eyes.

" I know no one less likely to marry again," he continued, " yet no one of whom the world is so unlikely to believe it. Her very gentle simplicity and tenderness tell against her ! Well, the only hope now is that the poor man has not made his disappointment conspicuous enough for her to know that it is attributed to her. It is the beginning of the fulfilment of Keith's prediction that offers and reports will harass her into the deed !"

" There is nothing so fallacious as prophecies against second marriages, but I don't believe they will. She is too quietly dignified for the full brunt of reports to reach her, and too much concentrated on her children to care about them."

" Well, I have to see her to-morrow to make her sign some papers about her pension, so I shall perhaps find out how she takes it."

He found Fanny quite her gentle composed self, as usual uncomprehending and helpless about her business affairs, and throwing the whole burthen on him of deciding on her investments ; but in such a gracious, dependent, grateful way that he could not but take pleasure in the office, and had no heart for the lesson he had been meditating on the need of learning to act for herself, if she wished to do without a protector. It was not till she had obediently written her " Frances Grace Temple " wherever her prime minister directed, that she said with a crimson blush, " Is it true that poor Mr. Touchett is going away for the winter ?"

" I believe he is even going before Sunday."

" I am very glad—I mean I am very sorry.   Do you think any one knows why it is ? "

" Very few are intimate enough to guess, and those who are, know you too well to think it was otherwise than very foolish on his part."

" I don't know," said Fanny, " I think I must have been foolish too, or he never could have thought of it.   And I was so sorry for him, he seemed so much distressed."

" I do not wonder at that, when he had once allowed himself to admit the thought."

" Yes, that is the thing.   I am afraid I can't be what I ought to be, or people would never think of such nonsense," said Fanny, with large tears welling into her eyes.   " I can't be guarding that dear memory as I ought, to have two such things happening so soon."

" Perhaps they have made you cherish it all the more."

" As if I wanted that !   Please will you tell me how I could have been more guarded.   I don't mind your knowing about this ; indeed you ought, for Sir Stephen trusted me to you, but I can't ask my aunt or any one else.   I can't talk about it, and I would not have them know that Sir Stephen's wife can't get his memory more respected."

She did not speak with anger as the first time, but with most touching sadness.

" I don't think any one could answer," he said.

" I did take my aunt's advice about the officers being here. I have not had them nearly as much as Bessie would have liked, not even Alick.   I have been sorry it was so dull for her, but I thought it could not be wrong to be intimate with one's clergyman, and Rachel was always so hard upon him."

" You did nothing but what was kind and right.   The

only possible thing that could have been wished otherwise was the making a regular habit of his playing croquet here."

" Ah ! but the boys and Bessie liked it so much. However, I dare say it was wrong. Alick never did like it."

" Not wrong, only a little overdone. You ladies want sometimes to be put in mind that, because a clergyman has to manage his own time, he is not a whit more really at liberty than a soldier or a lawyer, whose hours are fixed for him. You do not do him or his parish any kindness by engrossing him constantly in pastimes that are all very well once in a way, but which he cannot make habitual without detriment to his higher duties."

" But I thought he would have known when he had time."

" I am afraid curates are but bits of human nature after all."

" And what ought I to have done ?"

" If you had been an exceedingly prudent woman who knew the world, you would have done just as you did about the officers, been friendly, and fairly intimate, but instead of ratifying the daily appointments for croquet, have given a special invitation now and then, and so shown that you did not expect him without one."

" I see. Oh, if I had only thought in time, I need not have driven him away from his parish ! I hope he won't go on being unhappy long ! Oh, I wish there may be some very nice young lady where he is going. If he only would come back married ! "

" We would give him a vote of thanks."

" What a wedding present I would make her," proceeded Fanny, brightening perceptibly ; " I would give her my best

Indian table, only I always meant that for Ermine. I think she must have the emu's egg set in Australian gold."

"If *she* were to be induced by the bribe," said Colonel Keith, laughing, "I think Ermine would be sufficiently provided for by the emu's egg. Do you know," he added, after a pause, "I think I have made a great step in that direction."

She clasped her hands with delighted sympathy.

"She has given me leave to mention the matter," he continued, "and I take that as a sign that her resistance will give way."

"Oh, I am very glad," said Fanny, "I have so wished them to know at the Homestead," and her deepened colour revealed, against her will, that she had not been insensible to the awkwardness of the secrecy.

"I should rather like to tell your cousin Rachel myself, said the Colonel ; "she has always been very kind to Ermine, and appreciated her more than I should have expected. But she is not easily to be seen now."

"Her whole heart is in her orphan asylum," said Fanny. "I hope you will soon go with us and see it ; the little girls look so nice."

The brightening of his prospects seemed to have quite consoled her for her own perplexities.

That Avonmouth should have no suspicion of the cause of the sudden change of pastor could hardly be hoped ; but at least Lady Temple did not know how much talk was expended upon her, how quietly Lord Keith hugged himself, how many comical stories Bessie detailed in her letters to her Clare cousins, nor how Mrs. Curtis resented the presumption ; and while she shrank from a lecture, more especially as she did not see how dear Fanny was to blame, flattered herself and Grace that, for the future, Colonel Keith and Rachel would take better care of her.

Rachel did not dwell much on the subject, it was only the climax of conceit, croquet, and mere womanhood; and she was chiefly anxious to know whether Mr. Mitchell, the temporary clergyman, would support the F. U. E. E., and be liberal enough to tolerate Mr. Mauleverer. She had great hopes from a London incumbent, and, besides, Bessie Keith knew him, and spoke of him as a very sensible, agreeable, earnest man.

"Earnest enough for you, Rachel," she said, laughing.

"Is he a party man?"

"Oh, parties are getting obsolete! He works too hard for fighting battles outside."

The Sunday showed a spare, vigorous face, and a voice and pronunciation far more refined than poor Mr. Touchett's; also the sermons were far more interesting, and even Rachel granted that there were ideas in it. The change was effected with unusual celerity, for it was as needful to Mrs. Mitchell to be speedily established in a warm climate, as it was desirable to Mr. Touchett to throw himself into other scenes; and the little parsonage soon had the unusual ornaments of tiny children with small spades and wheelbarrows.

The father and mother were evidently very shy people, with a great deal beneath their timidity, and were much delighted to have an old acquaintance like Miss Keith to help them through their introductions, an office which she managed with all her usual bright tact. The discovery that Stephana Temple and Lucy Mitchell had been born within two days of one another, was the first link of a warm friendship between the two mammas ; and Mr. Mitchell fell at once into friendly intercourse with Ermine Williams, to whom Bessie herself conducted him for his first visit, when they at once discovered all manner of mutual acquaintance among his college friends ; and his next step was to make the very arrangement for Ermine's church going, for which she had long been wishing in secret, but which never having occurred to poor Mr. Touchett, she had not dared to propose, lest there should be some great inconvenience in the way.

Colonel Keith was the person, however, with whom the new comers chiefly fraternized, and he was amused with their sense of the space for breathing compared with the lanes and alleys of their own district. The schools and cottages seemed to them so wonderfully large, the children so clean, even their fishiness a form of poetical purity, the people ridiculously well off, and even Mrs. Kelland's lace-school a palace of the free maids that weave their thread with bones. Mr. Mitchell seemed almost to grudge the elbow room, as he talked of the number of cubic feet that held a dozen of his own parishioners ; and needful as the change had been for the health of both husband and wife, they almost reproached themselves for having fled and left so many pining for want of pure air, dwelling upon impossible castles for the importation of favourite patients to enjoy the balmy breezes of Avonmouth.

Rachel talked to them about the F. U. E. E., and was delighted by the flush of eager interest on Mrs. Mitchell's thin face. "Objects" swarmed in their parish, but where were the seven shillings per week to come from ? At any rate Mr. Mitchell would, the first leisure day, come over to St. Norbert's with her, and inspect. He did not fly off at the first hint of Mr. Mauleverer's "opinions," but said he would talk to him, and thereby rose steps untold in Rachel's estimation. The fact of change is dangerously pleasant to the human mind; Mr. Mitchell walked at once into popularity, and Lady Temple had almost conferred a public benefit by what she so little liked to remember. At any rate she had secured an unexceptionable companion, and many a time resorted to his wing, leaving Bessie to amuse Lord Keith, who seemed to be reduced to carry on his courtship to the widow by attentions to her guest.

CHAPTER XIII.

THE FOX AND THE CROW.

"She just gave one squall,
  When the cheese she let fall,
  And the fox ran away with his prize."
                                JANE TAYLOR.

"My dear," said Mrs. Curtis, one Monday morning, "I offered Colonel Keith a seat in the carriage to go to the annual book-club meeting with us. Mr. Spicer is going to propose him as a member of the club, you know, and I thought the close carriage would be better for him. I suppose you will be ready by eleven; we ought to set out by that time, not to hurry the horses."

"I am not going," returned Rachel, an announcement that electrified her auditors, for the family quota of books being quite insufficient for her insatiable appetite, she was a subscriber on her own account, and besides, this was the grand annual gathering for disposing of old books, when she was relied on for purchasing all the nuts that nobody else would crack. The whole affair was one of the few social gatherings that she really tolerated and enjoyed, and her mother gazed at her in amazement.

"I wrote to Mrs. Spicer a month ago to take my name off. I have no superfluous money to spend on my selfish amusement."

"But Rachel," said Grace, "did you not particularly want —oh! that fat red book which came to us uncut?"

"I did, but I must do without it."

"Poor Mr. Spicer, he reckoned on you to take it; indeed, he thought you had promised him."

"If there is anything like a promise, I suppose it must be done, but I do not believe there is. I trust to you, Grace, you know I have nothing to waste."

"You had better go yourself, my dear, and then you would be able to judge. It would be more civil by the society, too."

"No matter, indeed I cannot; in fact, Mr. Mauleverer is coming this morning to give his report and arrange our building plans. I want to introduce him to Mr. Mitchell, and fix a day for going over."

Mrs. Curtis gave up in despair, and consulted her eldest daughter in private whether there could have been any misunderstanding with Colonel Keith to lead Rachel to avoid him in a manner that was becoming pointed. Grace deemed it nothing but absorption into the F.U.E.E., and poor Mrs. Curtis sighed over this fleeting away of her sole chance of seeing Rachel like other people. Of Mr. Mauleverer personally she had no fears; he was in her eyes like a drawing or music-master, and had never pretended to be on equal terms in society with her daughters, and she had no doubts or scruples in leaving Rachel to her business interview with him, though she much regretted this further lapse from the ordinary paths of sociability.

Rachel, on the other hand, felt calmly magnanimous in the completion of a veritable sacrifice, for those books had afforded her much enjoyment, and she would much like to have pos-

sessed many of those that would be tossed aside at a cheap
rate. But the constant small expenses entailed by the first
setting on foot such an establishment as the F.U.E.E. were a
heavy drain on her private purse, as she insisted on all accounts being brought to her, and then could not bear that
these small nondescript matters should be charged upon the
general fund, which having already paid the first half-year's
rent in advance, and furnished the house, must be recruited
by some extraordinary supply before she could build. The
thing could not be done at all but by rigid economy, and she
was ready to exercise it, and happy in so doing. And the
Colonel? She thought the pain of her resolution was passing.
After all, it was not so dreadful as people would have one
believe, it was no such wrench as novels described to make
up one's mind to prefer a systematically useful life to an
agreeable man.

Mr. Mauleverer came, with a good report of the children's
progress, and talking quite enthusiastically of Lovedy's sweetness and intelligence. Perhaps she would turn out a superior
artist, now that chill penury no longer repressed her noble
rage, and he further brought a small demand for drawing
materials and blocks for engraving, to the amount of five
pounds, which Rachel defrayed from the general fund, but
sighed over its diminution.

"If I could only make the Burnaby bargain available,"
she said; "it is cruel to have it tied up to mere apprenticeships, which in the present state of things are absolutely
useless, or worse."

"Can nothing be done?"

"You shall hear. Dame Rachel Curtis, in 1605, just
when this place was taking up lace-making, an art learnt, I

believe, from some poor nuns that were turned out of St. Mary's, at Avoncester, thought she did an immense benefit to the place by buying the bit of land known as Burnaby's Bargain, and making the rents go yearly to apprentice two poor girls born of honest parents. The rent is fourteen pounds, and so the fees are so small that only the small lace-makers here will accept them. I cannot get the girls apprenticed to anything better in the towns except for a much larger premium."

" Do I understand you that such a premium is at present to be bestowed ? "

" No, not till next June. The two victims for this year have been sacrificed. But perhaps another time it might be possible to bind them to you as a wood engraver or printer ! " cried Rachel, joyfully.

" I should be most happy. But who would be the persons concerned ? "

" The trustees are the representative of our family and the rector of the parish—not Mr. Touchett (this is only a district), but poor old Mr. Linton at Avonbridge, who is barely able to sign the papers, so that practically it all comes to me."

" Extremely fortunate for the objects of the charity."

" I wish it were so ; but if it could only be made available in such a cause as ours, I am sure my good namesake's intentions would be much better carried out than by binding these poor girls down to their cushions. I did once ask about it, but I was told it could only be altered by Act of Parliament."

" Great facilities have of late been given," said Mr. Maulererer; " many old endowments have most beneficially extended their scope. May I ask where the land in question is ? "

" It is the level bit of meadow just by the river, and all the slope down to the mouth ; it has always been in our hands, and paid rent as part of the farm. You know how well it looks from the garden-seat, but it always grieves me when people admire it, for I feel as if it were thrown away."

" Ah ! I understand. Perhaps if I could see the papers I could judge of the feasibility of some change."

Rachel gladly assented, and knowing where to find the keys of the strong box, she returned in a short space with a parcel tied up with red tape, and labelled " Burnaby's Bargain."

" I have been thinking," she exclaimed, as she came in, " that that piece of land must have grown much more valuable since this rent was set on it ! Fourteen pounds a year, why we never thought of it ; but surely in such a situation, it would be worth very much more for building purposes."

" There can be no doubt. But your approach, Miss Curtis ? "

" If it is a matter of justice to the charity, of course that could not be weighed a moment. But we must consider what is to be done. Get the land valued, and pay rent for it accordingly ? I would give it up to its fate, and let it for what it would bring, but it would break my mother's heart to see it built on."

" Perhaps I had better take the papers and look over them. I see they will need much consideration."

" Very well, that will be the best way ; but we will say nothing about it till we have come to some conclusion, or we shall only startle and distress my mother. After all, then, I

do believe we have the real income of the F.U.E.E. within
our very hands ! It might be ten times what it is now."

Rachel was in higher spirits than ever. To oblige the
estate to pay 140l. a year to the F.U.E.E. was beyond measure
delightful, and though it would be in fact only taking out
of the family pocket, yet that was a pocket she could not
otherwise get at. The only thing for which she was sorry
was that Mr. Mauleverer had an appointment, and could not
come with her to call on Mr. Mitchell ; but instead of this
introduction, as she had sworn herself to secrecy rather than
worry her mother till the ways and means were matured, she
resolved, by way of compensation, upon going down to impart
to Ermine Williams this grave reformation of abuses, since
this was an afternoon when there was no chance of meeting
the Colonel.

Very happy did she feel in the hope that had come to
crown her efforts at the very moment when she had actually
and tangibly given up a pleasure, and closed a door opening
into worldly life, and she was walking along with a sense of
almost consecrated usefulness, to seek her companion in the
path of maiden devotion, when in passing the gates of Myrtlewood, she was greeted by Captain Keith and his bright-eyed
sister, just coming forth together.

A few words told that they were all bound for Mackarel
Lane, actuated by the same probability of finding Miss
Williams alone, the Colonel being absent.

"Wonderfully kind to her he is," said Rachel, glad to
praise him to convince herself that she did not feel bitter ;
"he takes that little girl out walking with him every
morning."

"I wonder if his constancy will ever be rewarded ?" said

Bessie, lightly ; then, as Rachel looked at her in wonder and almost rebuke for so direct and impertinent a jest, she exclaimed, " Surely you are not in ignorance ! What have I done ? I thought all the world knew—all the inner world, that is, that revels in a secret."

' Knew what ?" said Rachel, unavoidable intolerable colour rushing into her face.

" Why the romance of Colin and Ermine ! To live on the verge of such a—a tragi-comedy, is it ? and not be aware of it, I do pity you."

" The only wonder is how you knew it," said her brother, in a tone of repression.

" I ! Oh, it is a fine thing to be a long-eared little pitcher when one's elders imagine one hears nothing but what is addressed to oneself. There I sat, supposed to be at my lessons, when the English letters came in, and I heard papa communicating to mamma how he had a letter from old Lord Keith—not this one but one older still—-the father of him— about his son's exchange—wanted papa to know that he was exemplary and all that, and hoped he would be kind to him ; but just insinuated that leave was not desirable—in fact it was to break off an affair at home. And then, while I was all on fire to see what a lover looked like, comes another letter, this time to mamma, from Lady Alison something, who could not help recommending to her kindness her dear nephew Colin, going out broken-hearted at what was feared would prove a fatal accident, to the dearest, noblest girl in the world, for so she must call Ermine Williams. Ermine was a name to stick in one's memory if Williams was not, and so I assumed sufficient certainty to draw it all out of dear Lady Temple."

" She knows then ?" said Rachel, breathlessly, but on her guard.

" Know ? Yes, or she could hardly make such a brother of the Colonel. In fact, I think it is a bit of treachery to us all to keep such an affair concealed, don't you ?" with a vivid flash out of the corner of her eyes.

" Treachery not to post up a list of all one's ——"

" One's conquests ?" said Bessie, snatching the word out of her brother's mouth. " Did you ever hear a more ingenious intimation of the number *one* has to boast ?"

" Only in character," calmly returned Alick.

" But do not laugh," said Rachel, who had by this time collected herself; " if this is so, it must be far too sad and melancholy to be laughed about."

" So it is," said Alick, with a tone of feeling. " It has been a mournful business from the first, and I do not see how it is to end."

" Why, I suppose Colonel Colin is his own master now," said Bessie ; " and if he has no objection I do not see who else can make any."

" There are people in the world who are what Tennyson calls ' selfless,' " returned Alick.

" Then the objection comes from her ?" said Rachel, anxiously.

" So saith Lady Temple," returned Bessie.

They were by this time in Mackarel Lane. Rachel would have given much to have been able to turn back and look this strange news in the face, but consciousness and fear of the construction that might be put on her change of purpose forced her on, and in a few moments the three were in the little parlour, where Ermine's station was now by the fire.

There could be no doubt, as Rachel owned to herself instantly, that there was a change since she first had studied that face. The bright colouring, and far more, the active intellect and lively spirit, had always obviated any expression of pining or invalidism ; but to the air of cheerfulness was added a look of freshened health and thorough happiness, that rendered the always striking features absolutely beautiful ; more so, perhaps, than in their earliest bloom ; and the hair and dress, though always neat, and still as simply arranged as possible, had an indescribable air of care and taste that added to the effect of grace and pleasantness, and made Rachel feel convinced in a moment that the wonder would have been not in constancy to such a creature but in inconstancy. The notion that any one could turn from that brilliant, beaming, refined face to her own, struck her with a sudden humiliation. There was plenty of conversation, and her voice was not immediately wanted ; indeed, she hardly attended to what was passing, and really dreaded outstaying the brother and sister. When Ermine turned to her, and asked after Lovedy Kelland in her new home, she replied like one in a dream, then gathered herself up and answered to the point ; but feeling the restraint intolerable, soon rose to take leave.

" So soon ?" said Ermine ; " I have not seen you for a long time."

" I—I was afraid of being in the way," said Rachel, the first time probably that such a fear had ever suggested itself to her, and blushing as Ermine did not blush.

" We are sure to be alone after twilight," said Ermine, " if that is not too late for you ; but I know you are much occupied now."

Somehow that invalid in her chair had the dignity of a queen appointing her levee, and Rachel followed the impulse of thanking and promising, but then quickly made her escape to her own thoughts.

" Her whole soul is in that asylum," said Ermine, smiling as she went. " I should like to hear that it is going on satisfactorily, but she does not seem to have time even to talk."

" The most wonderful consummation of all," observed Bessie.

" No," said Ermine, " the previous talk was not chatter, but real effervescence from the unsatisfied craving for something to do."

" And has she anything to do now ?" said Bessie.

" That is exactly what I want to know. It would be a great pity if all this real self-devotion were thrown away."

" It cannot be thrown away," said Alick.

" Not on herself," said Ermine, " but one would not see it misdirected, both for the waste of good energy and the bitter disappointment."

" Well," said Bessie, " I can't bear people to be so dreadfully in earnest !"

" You are accountable for the introduction, are not you ?" said Ermine.

" I'm quite willing ! I think a good downfall plump would be the most wholesome thing that could happen to her ; and besides, I never told her to take the man for her almoner and counsellor ! I may have pointed to the gulf, but I never bade Curtia leap into it."

" I wish there were any one to make inquiries about this person," said Ermine ; " but when Colonel Keith came it was too late. I hoped she might consult him, but she has been so much absorbed that she really has never come in his way."

" She would never consult any one," said Bessie.

" I am not sure of that," replied Ermine. " I think that her real simplicity is what makes her appear so opinionated. I verily believe that there is a great capability of humility at the bottom."

"Of the gulf," laughed Bessie ; but her brother said, " Quite true. She has always been told she is the clever woman of the family, and what can she do but accept the position ? "

"Exactly," said Ermine ; "every one has given way to her, and, of course, she walks over their bodies, but there is something so noble about her that I cannot but believe that she will one day shake herself clear of her little absurdities."

" That is contrary to the usual destiny of strong-minded women," said Bessie.

"She is not a strong-minded woman, she only has been made to believe herself one," said Ermine, warmly.

With this last encounter, Bessie and her brother took leave, and the last at once exclaimed, in sentimental tones, " Generous rivals ! I never saw so good a comedy in all my days ! To disclose the fatal truth, and then bring the rival fair ones face to face ! "

" If that were your belief, Bessie, the demon of teasing has fuller possession of you than I knew."

" Ah ! I forgot," exclaimed Bessie, "it is tender ground with you likewise. Alas ! Alick, sisterly affection cannot blind me to the fact of that unrequited admiration for your honourable rival."

" What, from the strong-minded Curtia ? "

" Ah ! but have we not just heard that this is not the genuine article, only a country-made imitation ? No wonder it was not proof against an honourable colonel in a brown beard."

" So much the better ; only unluckily there has been a marked avoidance of him."

" Yes ; the Colonel was sacrificed with all other trivial incidents at the shrine of the F.U.L.E.—E. E, I mean. And only think of finding out that one has been sacrificing empty air after all—and to empty air ! "

" Better than to sacrifice everything to oneself," said Alick.

" Not at all. The latter practice is the only way to be agreeable ! By the bye, Alick, I wonder if she will deign to come to the ball ? "

" What ball ? "

" Your ball at Avoncester. It is what I am staying on for ! Major M'Donald all but promised me one ; and you know you must give one before you leave this place."

" Don't you know that poor Fraser has just been sent for home on his sister's death ? "

" But I conclude the whole regiment does not go into mourning ? "

" No, but Fraser is the one fellow to whom this would be real enjoyment. Indeed, I particularly wish no hints may be given about it. Don't deny, I know you have ways of bringing about what you wish, and I will not have them used here. I know something of the kind must be done before we leave Avoncester, but to give one this autumn would be much sooner than needful. I believe there is hardly an officer but myself and Fraser to whom the expense would not be a serious consideration, and when I tell you my father had strong opinions about overdoing reciprocities of gaiety, and drawing heavily on the officers' purses for them, I do not think you will allow their regard for him to take that manifestation towards you."

"Of course not," said Bessie, warmly; "I will not think of it again. Only when the fate does overtake you, you will have me here for it, Alick?"

He readily promised, feeling gratified at the effect of having spoken to his sister with full recognition of her good sense.

Meantime Rachel was feeling something of what Bessie ascribed to her, as if her sacrifice had been snatched away, and a cloud placed in its stead. Mortification was certainly present, and a pained feeling of having been made a fool of, whether by the Colonel or herself, her candid mind could hardly decide; but she was afraid it was by herself. She knew she had never felt sure enough of his attentions to do more than speculate on what she would do if they should become more pointed, and yet she felt angry and sore at having been exposed to so absurd a blunder by the silence of the parties concerned. "After all," she said to herself, "there can be no great harm done; I have not been weak enough to commit my heart to the error. I am unscathed, and I will show it by sympathy for Ermine. Only—only, why could not she have told me?"

An ordeal was coming for which Rachel was thus in some degree prepared. On the return of the party from the book club, Mrs. Curtis came into Rachel's sitting-room, and hung lingering over the fire as if she had something to say, but did not know how to begin. At last, however, she said, "I do really think it is very unfair, but it was not his fault, he says."

"Who?" said Rachel, dreamily.

"Why, Colonel Keith, my dear," said good Mrs. Curtis, conceiving that her pronominal speech had "broken" her intelligence; "it seems we were mistaken in him all this time."

"What, about Miss Williams?" said Rachel, perceiving how the land lay; "how did you hear it?"

"You knew it, my dear child," cried her mother in accents of extreme relief.

"Only this afternoon, from Bessie Keith."

"And Fanny knew it all this time," continued Mrs. Curtis. "I cannot imagine how she could keep it from me, but it seems Miss Williams was resolved it should not be known. Colonel Keith said he felt it was wrong to go on longer without mentioning it, and I could not but say that it would have been a great relief to have known it earlier."

"As far as Fanny was concerned it would," said Rachel, looking into the fire, but not without a sense of rehabilitating satisfaction, as the wistful looks and tone of her mother convinced her that this semi-delusion had not been confined to herself.

"I could not help being extremely sorry for him when he was telling me," continued Mrs. Curtis, as much resolved against uttering the idea as Rachel herself could be. "It has been such a very long attachment, and now he says he has not yet been able to overcome her scruples about accepting him in her state. It is quite right of her, I can't say but it is; but it is a very awkward situation."

"I do not see that," said Rachel, feeling the need of

decision in order to reassure her mother ; " it is very sad and distressing in some ways, but no one can look at Miss Williams without seeing that his return has done her a great deal of good ; and whether they marry or not, one can only be full of admiration and respect for them."

" Yes, yes," faltered Mrs. Curtis ; " only I must say I think it was due to us to have mentioned it sooner."

" Not at all, mother. Fanny knew it, and it was nobody's concern but hers. Pray am I to have Owen's ' Palæontology ' ? "

" No, Colonel Keith bought that, and some more of the solid books. My dear, he is going to settle here ; he tells me he has actually bought that house he and his brother are in."

" Bought it ! "

" Yes ; he says, any way, his object is to be near Miss Williams. Well, I cannot think how it is to end, so near the title as he is, and her sister a governess ; and then that dreadful business about her brother, and the little girl upon her hands. Dear me, I wish Fanny had any one else for a governess."

" So do not I," said Rachel. " I have the greatest possible admiration for Ermine Williams, and I do not know which I esteem most, her for her brave, cheerful, unrepining unselfishness, or him for his constancy and superiority to all those trumpery considerations. I am glad to have the watching of them. I honour them both."

Yes, and Rachel honoured herself still more for being able to speak all this freely and truly out of the innermost depths of her candid heart.

CHAPTER XIV.

THE GOWANBRAE BALL.

> " Your honour's pardon,
> I'd rather have my wounds to heal again,
> Than hear say how I got them."—*Coriolanus.*

" YES, I go the week after next."

" So soon ?   I thought you were to stay for our ball."

" Till this time next year ?   No, no, I can't quite do that, thank you."

" This very winter."

" Oh, no—no such thing !   Why, half the beauty and fashion of the neighbourhood is not come into winter quarters yet.   Besides, the very essence of a military ball is that it should be a parting—the brightest and the last.   Good morning."

And Meg's head, nothing loth, was turned away from the wide view of the broad vale of the Avon, with the Avoncester Cathedral towers in the midst, and the moors rising beyond in purple distance.   The two young lieutenants could only wave their farewells, as Bessie cantered merrily over the soft smooth turf of the racecourse, in company with Lord Keith, the Colonel, and Conrade.

" Do you not like dancing ? " inquired Lord Keith, when the canter was over, and they were splashing through a lane with high hedges.

"I'm not so unnatural," returned Bessie, with a merry smile; "but it would never do to let the Highlanders give one now. Alick has been telling me that the expense would fall seriously on a good many of them."

"True," said Colonel Keith; "too many *fêtes* come to be a heavy tax."

"That is more consideration than is common in so young a lad," added Lord Keith.

"Yes, but dear Alick is so full of consideration," said the sister, eagerly. "He does not get half the credit for it that he deserves, because, you know, he is so quiet and reserved, and has that unlucky ironical way with him that people don't like; especially rattlepates like those," pointing with her whip in the direction of the two young officers.

"It is a pity," said the Colonel, "it lessens his influence. And it is strange I never perceived it before his return to England."

"Oh! there's much owing to the habitual languor of that long illness. That satirical mumble is the only trouble he will take to lift up his testimony, except when a thing is most decidedly his duty, and then he does it as England expects."

"And he considered it his duty to make you decline this ball?" said Lord Keith.

"Oh, not his more than mine," said Bessie. "I don't forget that I am the Colonel's daughter."

No more was said on that occasion, but three days after cards were going about the county with invitations from Lord Keith to an evening party, with "Dancing." Lord Keith averred, with the full concurrence of his brother, that he owed many civilities to the ladies of the neighbourhood, and it was a good time to return them when he could gratify the young kinswoman who had showed such generous forbearance about the regimental ball. It was no unfavourable moment either, when he had his brother to help him, for the ordering of balls had been so much a part of Colin's staff duties, that it came quite naturally to him, especially with Coombe within reach to assist. There was some question whether the place should be the public rooms or Gowanbrae, but Bessie's vote decided on the latter, in consideration of the Colonel's chest. She was rather shocked, while very grateful, at the consequences of the little conversation on the hill top, but she threw herself into all the counsels with bright, ardent pleasure, though carefully refraining from any presumption that she was queen of the evening.

Lady Temple received an invitation, but never for one moment thought of going, or even supposed that any one could imagine she could. Indeed, if she had accepted it, it would have been a decisive encouragement to her ancient suitor, and Colin saw that he regarded her refusal, in its broad black edges, as a further clenching of the reply to his addresses.

Bessie was to be chaperoned by Mrs. Curtis. As to Rachel, she had resolved against youthful gaieties for this winter and all others, but she felt that to show any reluctance to accept the Keith invitation might be a contradiction to her indifference to the Colonel, and so construed by her mother, Grace, and Bessie. So all she held out for was, that as she had no money to spend upon adornments, her blue silk dinner dress, and her birthday wreath, should and must do duty ; and as to her mother's giving her finery, she was far too impressive and decided for Mrs. Curtis to venture

upon such presumption. She was willing to walk through
her part for an evening, and indeed the county was pretty
well accustomed to Miss Rachel Curtis's ball-room ways, and
took them as a matter of course.

Gowanbrae had two drawing-rooms with folding doors
between, quite practicable for dancing, and the further one
ending in a conservatory, that likewise extended along the
end of the entrance hall and dining-room. The small library,
where Colonel Keith usually sat, became the cloak-room, and
contained, when Mrs. Curtis and her daughters arrived, so
large a number of bright cashmere cloaklets, scarlet, white,
and blue, that they began to sigh prospectively at the crowd
which Mrs. Curtis would have encountered with such joyful
valour save for that confidence on the way home from the
book club.

They were little prepared for the resources of a practised
staff-officer. Never had a ball even to them looked so well
arranged, or in such thorough style, as a little dexterous
arrangement of flowers, lights, and sofas, had rendered those
two rooms. The two hosts worked extremely well. Lord
Keith had shaken off much of his careless stoop and air of
age, and there was something in his old world polish and his
Scotch accent that gave a sort of romance to the manner of
his reception. His brother, with his fine brow, and thoughtful eyes, certainly appeared to Rachel rather thrown away as
master of the ceremonies, but whatever he did, he always
did in the quietest and best way ; and receptions had been
a part of his vocation, so that he infused a wonderful sense
of ease, and supplied a certain oil of good breeding that
made everything move suavely. Young ladies in white,
and mothers in all the colours of the rainbow, were there in

plenty, and, by Bessie's special command, the scene was enlivened by the Highland uniform, with the graceful tartan scarf fastened across the shoulder with the Bruce brooch.

Rachel had not been long in the room before she was seized on by Emily Grey, an enthusiastic young lady of the St. Norbert's neighbourhood, whom she met seldom, but was supposed to know intimately.

" And they say you have the hero here—the Victoria Cross man—and that you know him. You must show him to me, and get me introduced."

" There is no Victoria Cross man here," said Rachel, coldly. " Colonel Keith did not have one."

" Oh, no, I don't mean Colonel Keith, but Captain Alexander Keith, quite a young man. Oh, I am sure you remember the story—you were quite wild about it— of his carrying the lighted shell out of the hospital tent ; and they told me he was always over here, and his sister staying with Lady Temple."

" I know Captain Alexander Keith," said Rachel, slowly ; " but you must be mistaken, I am certain I should know if he had a Victoria Cross."

" It is very odd ; Charlie told me it was the same," said Miss Grey, who, like all others, was forced to bend to Rachel's decisive manner.

" Scottish names are very common," said Rachel, and at that moment a partner came and carried Emily off.

" But as Rachel stood still, an odd misgiving seized her, a certain doubt whether upon the tall lazy figure that was leaning against a wall nearly opposite to her, talking to another officer, she did not see something suspiciously bronze and eight-pointed that all did not wear. There was clearly a medal, though with fewer clasps than some owned ; but what else was there ? She thought of the lecture on heroism she had given to him, and felt hot all over. Behold, he was skirting the line of chaperons, and making his way towards their party. The thing grew more visible, and she felt more disconcerted than ever had been her lot before ; but escape there was none, here he was shaking hands.

" You don't polk ? " he said to her. " In fact, you regard all this as a delusion of weak minds. Then, will you come and have some tea ? "

" Rachel took his arm, still bewildered, and when standing before him with the tea-cup in her hand, she interrupted something he was saying, she knew not what, with, " That is not the Victoria Cross ? "

" Then it is, like all the rest, a delusion," he answered, in his usual impassive manner.

" And gained," she continued, " by saving the lives of all those officers ; the very thing I told you about ! "

" You told me that man was killed."

" Then it was not you ? "

" Perhaps they picked up the pieces of the wrong one."

" But if you would only tell me how you gained it."

" By the pursuit of conchology."

" Then it was yourself ? " again said Rachel, in her confusion.

" If I be I as I suppose I be," he replied, giving her his arm again, and as they turned towards the conservatory, adding, " Many such things have happened, and I did not know whether you meant this."

" That was the reason you made so light of it."

" What, because I thought it was somebody else ? "

" No, the contrary reason ; but I cannot understand why you let me go on without telling me."

" I never interfere when a story is so perfect in itself."

" But is my story perfect in itself ? " said Rachel, " or is it the contrary ? "

" No one knows less of the particulars than I do," he answered. " I think your version was that it was an hospital tent that the shell came into. It was not that, but a bungalow, which was supposed to be out of range. It stood on a bit of a slope, and I thought I should have been able to kick the shell down before it had time to do mischief."

" But you picked it up, and took it to the door—I mean, did you ? " said Rachel, who was beginning to discover that she must ask Alick Keith a direct question, if she wished to get an answer, and she received a gesture of assent.

" I was very blind," she said, humbly, " and now I have gone and insisted to poor Emily Grey that you never did any such thing."

" Thank you," he said ; " it was the greatest kindness you could do me."

" Ah ! your sister said you had the greatest dislike to hero worship."

" A natural sense of humbug," he said. " I don't know why they gave me this," he added, touching his cross, " unless it was that one of the party in the bungalow had a turn for glorifying whatever happened to himself. Plenty of more really gallant things happened every day, and were never heard of ; and I, who absolutely saw next to nothing of the campaign, have little right to be decorated."

" Ah ! " said Rachel, thoughtfully, " I have always wondered whether one would be happier for having accomplished an act of heroism."

" I do not know," said Alick, thoughtfully ; " then, as Rachel looked up with a smile of amazement, " Oh, you mean this; but it was mere self-preservation. I could hardly even have bolted, for I was laid up with fever, and was very shaky on my legs."

" I suppose, however," said Rachel, " that the vision of one's life in entering the army would be to win that sort of distinction, and so young."

" Win it as *some* have done," said Alick, " and deserve what is far better worth than distinction. That may be the dream, but, after all, it is the discipline and constant duty that make the soldier, and are far more really valuable than exceptional doings."

" People must always be ready for them, though," said Rachel.

" And they are," said Alick, with grave exultation in his tone.

" Then, after a pause, she led back the conversation to its personal character, by saying. " Do you mean that the reception of this cross was no gratification to you ? "

" No, I am not so absurd," he replied ; but he added sadly, " That was damped quite otherwise. The news that I was named for it came almost in the same breath with that of my father's death, and he had not heard I was to receive it."

" Ah ! I can understand."

" And you can see how intolerable was the fuss my good relations made with me just when the loss was fresh on me, and with that of my two chief friends, among my brother officers, fellows beside whom I was nobody, and there was my

uncle's blindness getting confirmed. Was not that enough
to sicken one with being stuck up for a lion, and constantly
poked up by the showwoman, under pretext of keeping up
one's spirits?"

"And you were—I mean were you—too ill to escape?"

"I was less able to help myself than Miss Williams is.
There had been a general smash of all the locomotive
machinery on this side, and the wretched monster could
do nothing but growl at his visitors."

"Should you growl very much if I introduced you to
Emily Grey? You see it is a matter of justice and truth to
tell her now, after having contradicted her so flatly. I will
wait to let you get out of the way first if you like, but I
think that would be unkind to her; and if you ever do
dance, I wish you would dance with her."

"With all my heart," he answered.

"Oh, thank you," said Rachel, warmly.

He observed with some amusement Rachel's utter absence
of small dexterities, and of even the effort to avoid the
humiliation of a confession of her error. Miss Grey and a
boy partner had wandered into the conservatory, and were
rather dismally trying to seem occupied with the camellias
when Rachel made her way to them, and though he could
not actually hear the words, he knew pretty well what they
were. "Emily, you were right after all, and I was mistaken;" and then as he drew near, "Miss Grey, Captain
Keith wishes to be introduced to you."

It had been a great shock to Rachel's infallibility, and as
she slowly began working her way in search of her mother,
after observing the felicity of Emily's bright eyes, she fell
into a musing on the advantages of early youth in its indis-

criminating powers of enthusiasm for anything distinguished for anything, and that sense of self-exaltation in any sort of contact with a person who had been publicly spoken of. "There is genuine heroism in him," thought Rachel, "but it is just in what Emily would never appreciate—it is in the feeling that he could not help doing as he did; the half-grudging his reward to himself because other deeds have passed unspoken. I wonder whether his ironical humour would allow him to see that Mr. Mauleverer is as veritable a hero in yielding hopes of consideration, prospects, honours, to his sense of truth and uprightness. If he would only look with an unprejudiced eye, I know he would be candid."

"Are you looking for Mrs. Curtis?" said Colonel Keith. "I think she is in the other room."

"Not particularly, thank you," said Rachel, and she was surprised to find how glad she was to look up freely at him.

"Would it be contrary to your principles or practice to dance with me?"

"To my practice," she said smilingly, "so let us find my mother. Is Miss Alison Williams here? I never heard whether it was settled that she should come," she added, resolved both to show him her knowledge of his situation, and to let her mother see her at her ease with him.

"No, she was obstinate, though her sister and I did our utmost to persuade her, and the boys were crazy to make her go."

"I can't understand your wishing it."

"Not as an experience of life? Alison never went to anything in her girlhood, but devoted herself solely to her sister, and it would be pleasant to see her begin her youth."

" Not as a mere young lady !" exclaimed Rachel.

" That is happily not possible."

An answer that somewhat puzzled Rachel, whose regard for him was likely to be a good deal dependent upon his contentment with Alison's station in life.

" I must say young ladyhood looks to the greatest advantage there," Rachel could not help exclaiming, as at that moment Elizabeth Keith smiled at them, as she floated past, her airy white draperies looped with scarlet ribbons ; her dark hair turned back and fastened by a snood of the same, an eagle's feather clasped in it by a large emerald, a memory of her father's last siege—that of Lucknow.

" She is a very pretty creature," said the Colonel, under the sparkle of her bright eyes.

" I never saw any one make the pursuits of young ladyhood have so much spirit and meaning," added Rachel. " Here you see she has managed to make herself sufficiently like other people, yet full of individual character and meaning."

" That is the theory of dress, I suppose," said the Colonel.

" If one chooses to cultivate it."

" Did you ever see Lady Temple in full dress ?"

" No ; we were not out when we parted as girls."

" Then you have had a loss. I think it was at our last Melbourne ball, that when she went to the nursery to wish the children good night, one of them—Hubert, I believe— told her to wear that dress when she went to heaven ; and dear old Sir Stephen was so delighted that he went straight upstairs to kiss the boy for it."

" Was that Lady Temple ?" said Alick Keith, who having found Miss Grey engaged many deep, joined them again, and at his words came back a thrill of Rachel's old fear and doubt as to the possible future.

" Yes," said the Colonel ; " I was recollecting the gracious vision she used to be at all our chief's·parties."

" Vision, you call her, who lived in the house with her ? What do you think she was to us—poor wretches—coming up from barracks where Mrs. O'Shaughnessy was our cynosure ? There was not one of us to whom she was not Queen of the East, and more, with that innocent, soft, helpless dignity of hers !"

" And Sir Stephen for the first of her vassals," said the Colonel.

" What a change it has been ! " said Alick.

" Yes ; but a change that has shown her to have been unspoilable. We were just agreeing on the ball-room perfections of her and your sister in their several lines."

" Very different lines," said Alick, smiling.

" I can't judge of Fanny's," said Rachel, " but your sister is almost enough to make one believe there can be some soul in young lady life."

" I did not bring Bessie here to convert you," was the somewhat perplexing answer.

" Nor has she," said Rachel, " except so far as I see that she can follow ordinary girls' pursuits without being frivolous iu them."

Alick bowed at the compliment.

" And she has been a sunbeam," added Rachel ; " we shall all feel graver and cloudier without her."

" Yes," said Colonel Keith, " and I am glad Mr. Clare has such a sunbeam for his parsonage. What a blessing she will be there ! " he added, as he watched Bessie's graceful way of explaining to his brother some little matter in behalf of the shy mother of a shy girl. Thinking he might be wanted, Colonel Keith went forward to assist, and Rachel continued, " I do envy that power of saying the right thing to everybody ! "

" Don't—it is the greatest snare," was his answer, much amazing her, for she had her mind full of the two direct personal blunders she had made towards him.

" It prevents many difficulties and embarrassments."

" Very desirable things."

" Yes ; for those that like to laugh, but not for those that are laughed at," said Rachel.

" More so ; the worst of all misfortunes is to wriggle too smoothly through life."

This was to Rachel the most remarkable part of the evening ; as to the rest, it was like all other balls, a weariness : Grace enjoying herself and her universal popularity, always either talking or dancing, and her mother comfortable and dutiful among other mothers ; the brilliant figure and ready grace of Bessie Keith being the one vision that perpetually flitted in her dreams, and the one ever-recurring recollection that Captain Keith, the veritable hero of the shell, had been lectured by her on his own deed ! In effect Rachel had never felt so beaten down and ashamed of herself; so doubtful of her own most positive convictions, and yet not utterly dissatisfied, and the worst of it was that Emily Grey was after all carried off without dancing with the hero ; and Rachel felt as if her own opinionativeness had defrauded the poor girl.

Other balls sent her home in a state of weariness, disgust, and contempt towards every one, but this one had resulted in displeasure with herself, yet in much interest and excitement; and, oh, passing strange ! through that same frivolous military society.

Indeed the military society was soon in better odour with her than the clerical. She had been making strenuous efforts to get to St. Norbert's, with Mr. Mitchell, for some time past, but the road was in a state of being repaired, and the coachman was determined against taking his horses there.   As to going by train, that was equally impossible, since he would still less have driven her to the station.   Finally, Rachel took the resolute step of borrowing Fanny's pony carriage, and driving herself and the clergyman to the station, where she was met by Mrs. Morris, the mother of one of the girls, to whom she had promised such a visit, as it had been agreed that it would be wisest not to unsettle the scholars by Christmas holidays.

The F.U.E.E. was in perfect order ; the little girls sat upon a bench with their copies before them, Mrs. Rawlins in the whitest of caps presided over them, and Mr. Mauleverer was very urbane, conducting the visitors over the house himself, and expatiating on his views of cleanliness, ventilation, refinement, and equality of cultivation, while Mrs. Rawlins remained to entertain Mrs. Morris.   Nothing could be more practical and satisfactory ; some admirable drawings of the children's were exhibited, and their conduct was said to be excellent ; except, Mr. Mauleverer remarked unwillingly, that there was a tendency about little Mary to fancy herself injured, and he feared that she was not always truthful ; but these were childish faults, that he hoped would pass away with further refinement, and removal from the lower influences of her home.

After this, Rachel was not surprised that poor, ignorant, and always deplorable Mrs. Morris did not seem in raptures with the state of her child, but more inclined to lament not having seen more of her, and not having her at home. That was quite in accordance with peasant shortsightedness and ingratitude, but it was much more disappointing that Mr. Mitchell said little or nothing of approbation ; asked her a few questions about her previous knowledge of Mr. Mauleverer and Mrs. Rawlins, and when she began to talk of arranging for some one or two of his London orphans, thanked her rather shortly, but said there was no way of managing it. It was evident that he was quite as prejudiced as others of his clerical brethren, and the more Rachel read of current literature, the more she became convinced of their bondage to views into which they durst not examine, for fear honesty should compel them to assert their conclusions.

She had hoped better things from the stranger, but she began to be persuaded that all her former concessions to the principles infused in her early days were vain entanglements, and that it was merely weakness and unwillingness to pain her mother that prevented her from breaking through them.

She could not talk this out with anybody, except now and then an utterance to the consenting Mr. Mauleverer, but in general she would have been shocked to put these surging thoughts into words ; and Bessie was her only intimate who would avow that there could be anything to be found fault with in a clergyman. When alone together, Bessie would sometimes regretfully, sometimes in a tone of amusement, go over bits of narrow-minded folly that had struck her in the clergy, and more especially in her uncle's curate, Mr.

Lifford, whose dryness was, she owned, very repulsive to her.

" He is a good creature," she said, " and most necessary to my uncle, but how he and I are to get through life together, I cannot tell. It must soon be tried, though ! After my visit at Bath will come my home at Bishopsworthy ! " And then she confided to Rachel all the parish ways, and took counsel on the means of usefulness that would not clash with the curate and pain her uncle. She even talked of a possible orphan for the F. U. E. E., only that unlucky prejudice against Mr. Mauleverer was sure to stand in the way.

So acceptable had Bessie Keith made herself everywhere, that all Avonmouth was grieved at her engagement to spend the winter at Bath with her married cousin, to whom she was imperatively necessary in the getting up of a musical party.

" And I must go some time or other," she said to Colonel Keith, " so it had better be when you are all here to make Myrtlewood cheerful, and I can be of most use to poor Jane ! I do think dear Lady Temple is much more full of life and brightness now ! "

Everybody seemed to consider Bessie's departure as their own personal loss : the boys were in despair for their play-fellow ; Ermine would miss those sunny visits ; Colonel Keith many a pleasant discussion, replete with delicate compliments to Ermine, veiled by tact ; and Lord Keith the pretty young clanswoman who had kept up a graceful little coquetry with him, and even to the last evening, went on walking on the esplanade with him in the sunset, so as to set his brother free to avoid the evening chill.

And, above all, Lady Temple regretted the loss of the cheery companion of her evenings. True, Bessie had lately had a good many small evening gaieties, but she always came back from them so fresh and bright, and so full of entertaining description and anecdote, that Fanny felt as if she had been there herself, and, said Bessie, " it was much better for her than staying at home with her, and bringing in no novelty."

" Pray come to me again, dearest ! Your stay has been the greatest treat. It is very kind in you to be so good to me."

" It is you who are good to me, dearest Lady Temple."

" I am afraid I shall hardly get you again. Your poor uncle will never be able to part with you, so I won't ask you to promise, but if ever you can——"

" If ever I can ! This has been a very happy time, dear Lady Temple," a confidence seemed trembling on her lips, but she suppressed it. " I shall always think of you as the kindest friend a motherless girl ever had ! I will write to you from Bath. Good-bye—"

And there were all the boys in a row, little affectionate Hubert absolutely tearful, and Conrade holding up a bouquet, on which he had spent all his money, having persuaded Coombe to ride with him to the nursery garden at Avoncester to procure it. He looked absolutely shy and blushing, when Bessie kissed him and promised to dry the leaves and keep them for ever.

END OF VOL. I.

LONDON:
R. CLAY, SON, AND TAYLOR, PRINTERS,
BREAD STREET HILL.

THE

CLEVER WOMAN OF THE FAMILY.

BY THE

AUTHOR OF "THE HEIR OF REDCLYFFE."

IN TWO VOLUMES.

VOL. II.

London and Cambridge:

MACMILLAN AND CO.

1865.

LONDON :

R. CLAY, SON, AND TAYLOR, PRINTERS,

BREAD STREET HILL.

CONTENTS.

CHAPTER VIII.

CHAPTER IX.

CHAPTER X.

CHAPTER XI.

CHAPTER XII.

CHAPTER XIII.

CHAPTER XIV.

CHAPTER XV.

CHAPTER XVI.

CLEVER WOMAN OF THE FAMILY.

CHAPTER I.

GO AND BRAY.

"Come, come, elder brother, you are too young in this!"—
As You Like It.

"ALICK, I have something to say to you."

Captain Keith did not choose to let his sister travel alone, when he could help it, and therefore was going to Bath with her, intending to return to Avoncester by the next down train. He made no secret that he thought it a great deal of trouble, and had been for some time asleep, when, at about two stations from Bath, Bessie having shut the little door in the middle of the carriage, thus addressed him, "Alick, I have something to say to you, and I suppose I may as well say it now."

She pressed upon his knee, and with an affected laziness, he drew his eyes wide open.

"Ah, well, I've been a sore plague to you, but I shall be off your hands now."

"Eh! whose head have you been turning?"

"Alick, what do you think of Lord Keith?"

Alick was awake enough now! "The old ass!" he exclaimed. "But at least you are out of his way now."

" Not at all. He is coming to Bath to-morrow to see my aunt."

" And you want me to go out to-morrow and stop him ? "

" No, Alick, not exactly. I have been cast about the world too long not to be thankful."

" Elizabeth ! "

" Do not look so very much surprised," she said, in her sweet pleading way. " May I not be supposed able to feel that noble kindness and gracious manner, and be glad to have some one to look up to ? "

" And how about Charlie Carleton ? " demanded Alick, turning round full on her.

" For shame, Alick ! " she exclaimed hotly ; " you who were the one to persecute me about him, and tell me all sorts of things about his being shallow and unprincipled, and not to be thought of, you to bring him up against me now."

" I might think all you allege," returned Alick, gravely, " and yet be much amazed at the new project."

Bessie laughed. " In fact you made a little romance, in which you acted the part of sapient brother, and the poor little sister broke her heart ever after ! You wanted such an entertainment when you were lying on the sofa, so you created a heroine and a villain, and thundered down to the rescue."

" Very pretty, Bessie, but it will not do. It was long after I was well again, and had joined."

" Then it was the well-considered effect of the musings of your convalescence ! When you have a sister to take care of, it is as well to feel that you *are* doing it."

" Now, Elizabeth," said her brother, with seriousness not to be laughed aside, and laying his hand on hers, " before I hear another word on this matter, look me in the face and tell me deliberately that you never cared for Carleton."

" I never thought for one moment of marrying him," said Bessie, haughtily. " If I ever had any sort of mercy on him, it was all to tease you. There, are you satisfied?"

" I must be, I suppose," he replied, and he sighed heavily " When was this settled?"

" Yesterday, walking up and down the esplanade. He will tell his brother to-day, and I shall write to Lady Temple. Oh, Alick, he is so kind, he spoke so highly of you."

" I must say," returned Alick, in the same grave tone, " that if you wished for the care of an old man, I should have thought my uncle the more agreeable of the two."

" He is little past fifty. You are very hard on him."

" On the contrary, I am sorry for him. You will always find it good for him to do whatever suits yourself."

" Alick?" said his sister mournfully, " you have never forgotten or forgiven my girlish bits of neglect after your wound."

" No, Bessie," he said, holding her hand kindly, " it is not the neglect or the girlishness, but the excuses to me, still more to my uncle, and most of all to yourself. They are what make me afraid for you in what you are going to take upon yourself."

She did not answer immediately, and he pursued—

" Are you driven to this by dislike to living at Bishopsworthy? If so, do not be afraid to tell me. I will make any arrangement, if you would prefer living with Jane. We agreed once that it would be too expensive, but now I could let you have another hundred a year."

" As if I would allow that, Alick ? No, indeed ! Lord Keith means you to have all my share."

" Does he ? There are more words than one to that question. And pray is he going to provide properly for his poor daughter in the West Indies ?"

" I hope to induce him to take her into favour."

" Eh ? and to make him give up to Colin Keith that Auchinvar estate that he ought to have had when Archie Keith died ?"

" You may be sure I shall do my best for the Colonel. Indeed, I do think Lord Keith will consent to the marriage now."

" You have sacrificed yourself on that account ? " he said, with irony in his tone, that he could have repented the next moment, so good-humoured was her reply, " That is understood, so give me the merit."

" The merit of, for his sake, becoming a grandmother. You have thought of the daughters ? Mrs. Comyn Menteith must be older than yourself."

" Three years," said Bessie, in his own tone of acceptance of startling facts, " and I shall have seven grandchildren in all, so you see you must respect me."

" Do you know her sentiments ?"

" I know what they will be when we have met. Never fear, Alick. If she were not married it might be serious ; being so, I have no fears."

Then came a silence, till a halt at the last station before Bath roused Alick again.

" Bessie," he said, in the low voice the stoppage permitted, " don't think me unkind. I believe you have waited on purpose to leave me no time for expostulation, and what I have said has sounded the more harsh in consequence."

"No, Alick," she said, "you are a kind brother in all but the constructions you put upon my doings. I think it would be better if there were more difference between our ages. You are a young guardian, over anxious, and often morbidly fanciful about me during your illness. I think we shall be happier together when you no longer feel yourself responsible."

"The tables turned," muttered Alick.

"I am prepared for misconstruction," added Bessie. "I know it will be supposed to be the title; the estate it cannot be, for you know how poor a property it is; but I do not mean to care for the world. Your opinion is a different thing, and I thought you would have seen that I could not be insensible to such dignified kindness, and the warmth of a nature that many people think cold."

"I don't like set speeches, Bessie."

"Then believe me, Alick. May I not love the fine old man that has been so kind to me?"

"I hope you do," said Alick, slowly.

"And you can't believe it? Not with Lady Temple before you; and hers was *really* an old man."

"Do not talk of her or Sir Stephen either. No, Bessie," he added more calmly after a time, "I may be doing great injustice to you both, but I must speak what it is my duty to say. Lord Keith is a hard, self-seeking man, who has been harsh and grasping towards his family, and I verily believe came here bent on marriage, only because his brother was no longer under his tyranny. He may not be harsh to you, because he is past his vigour, and if he really loves you, you have a power of governing; but from what I know of you, I cannot believe in your loving him enough to make

such management much better than selfish manœuvring.
Therefore I cannot think this marriage for your real welfare,
or be other than bitterly grieved at it. Do not answer,
Bessie, but think this over, and if at any time this evening
you feel the least doubt of your happiness in this matter,
telegraph to me, and I will stop him."

" Indeed, Alick," she answered, without anger, " I believe
you are very anxious for my good."

It will readily be believed that Captain Keith received no
telegram.

Nevertheless, as soon as his time was his own the next
morning, he rode to Avonmouth and sought out the Colonel,
not perhaps with very defined hopes of making any change
in his sister's intentions, but feeling that some attempt on his
own part must be made, if only to free himself from acquiescence, and thinking that Colin, as late guardian to the one
party, and brother to the other, was the most proper medium.

Colonel Keith was taken by surprise at the manner in
which his cordial greeting was met. He himself had been
far from displeased at his brother's communication ; it was a
great relief to him personally, as well as on Lady Temple's
account, and he had been much charmed at Bessie's good
sense and engaging graces. As to disparity of years, Lord
Keith had really made himself much younger of late, and
there was much to excite a girl's romance in the courtesy of
an elderly man, the chief of her clan ; moreover the perfect
affection and happiness Colin had been used to witness in his
general's family disposed him to make light of that objection ;
and he perceived that his brother was sufficiently bewitched
to be likely to be kind and indulgent to his bride.

He had not expected Alexander Keith to be as well pleased

as he was himself, but he was not prepared for his strong disapprobation, and earnest desire to find some means of prevention, and he began to reassure him upon the placability of Mrs. Comyn Menteith, the daughter, as well as upon his brother's kindness to the objects of his real affection.

"Oh, I am not afraid of that. She will manage him fast enough."

"Very likely, and for his good. Nor need you question his being a safe guide for her in higher matters. Perhaps you are prejudiced against him because his relations with me have not been happy, but candidly, in them you know the worst of him ; and no doubt he thought himself purely acting for my welfare. I know much more of him now that I have been at home with him, and I was greatly struck with his real consideration for the good of all concerned with him."

"No, I am not thinking of Lord Keith. To speak it out, I cannot believe that my sister has heart enough in this to justify her."

"Young girls often are more attracted by elderly men than by lads."

"You do not know Bessie as, I am sorry to say, I do," said Alick, speaking slowly and sadly, and with a flush of shame on his cheek. "I do not say that she says anything untrue, but the truth is not in her. She is one of those selfish people who are infinitely better liked than those five hundred times their worth, because they take care to be always pleased."

"They give as much pleasure as they take."

"Yes, they take every one in. I wish to my heart I could be taken in too, but I have seen too much of her avoidance of every service to my uncle that she did not like. I verily

believe, at this moment, that one great inducement with her
is to elude the care of him."

"Stern judgments, Alick. I know you would not speak
thus without warrant ; but take it into account that marriage
makes many a girl's selfishness dual, and at last drowns the
self."

"Yes, when it is a marriage of affection. But the truth
must be told, Colonel. There was a trumpery idle fellow
always loitering at Littleworthy, and playing croquet. I set
my face against it with all my might, and she always laughed
to scorn the notion that there was anything in it, nor do I
believe that she has heart enough to wish to marry him. I
could almost say I wish she had, but I never saw her show the
same pleasure in any one's attentions, and I believe he is gone
out to Rio in hopes of earning means to justify his addresses."

Colonel Keith sat gravely considering what he knew would
not be spoken lightly. "Do you mean that there was attachment enough to make it desirable that you should tell my
brother ?"

"No, I could say nothing that she could not instantly
contradict with perfect truth, though not with perfect sincerity."

"Let me ask you one question, Alick—not a flattering one.
May not some of these private impressions of yours have been
coloured by your long illness ?"

"That is what Bessie gives every one to understand," said
Alick, calmly. "She is right, to a certain degree, that suffering sharpened my perceptions, and helplessness gave me
time to draw conclusions. If I had been well, I might have
been as much enchanted as other people ; and if my uncle
had not needed her care, and been neglected, I could have

thought that I was rendered exacting by illness. But I imagine all I have said is not of the slightest use ; only, if you think it right to tell your brother to talk to me, I would rather stand all the vituperation that would fall on me than allow this to take place."

Colonel Keith walked up and down the room considering, whilst Alick sat in a dejected attitude, shading his face, and not uttering how very bitter it had been to him to make the accusation, nor how dear the sister really was.

" I see no purpose that would be answered," said Colonel Keith, coming to a pause at last ; " you have nothing tangible to mention, even as to the former affair that you suspect. I see a great deal in your view of her to make you uneasy, but nothing that would not be capable of explanation, above all to such a man as my brother. It would appear like mere malevolence."

" Never mind what it would appear," said Alick, who was evidently in such a ferment as his usually passive demeanour would have seemed incapable of.

" If the appearance would entirely baffle the purpose, it *must* be considered," said the Colonel ; " and in this case it could only lead to estrangement, which would be a lasting evil. I conclude that you have remonstrated with your sister."

" As much as she gave me time for ; but of course that is breath spent in vain."

" Your uncle had the same means of judging as yourself."

" No, Colonel, he could do nothing ! In the first place, there can be no correspondence with him ; and next, he is so devotedly fond of Bessie, that he would no more believe anything against her than Lady Temple would. I have tried that more than once."

"Then, Alick, there is nothing for it but to let it take its course; and even upon your own view, your sister will be much safer married than single."

"I had very little expectation of your saying anything else, but in common honesty I felt bound to let you know."

"And now the best thing to be done is to forget all you have said."

"Which you will do the more easily as you think it an amiable delusion of mine. Well, so much the better. I dare say you will never think otherwise, and I would willingly believe that my senses went after my fingers' ends."

The Colonel almost believed so himself. He was aware of the miserably sensitive condition of shattered nerve in which Alick had been sent home, and of the depression of spirits that had ensued on the news of his father's death; and he thought it extremely probable that his weary hours and solicitude for his gay young sister might have made mole-hills into mountains, and that these now weighed on his memory and conscience. At least, this seemed the only way of accounting for an impression so contrary to that which Bessie Keith made on every one else, and, by his own avowal, on the uncle whom he so much revered. Every other voice proclaimed her winning, amiable, obliging, considerate, and devoted to the service of her friends, with much drollery and shrewdness of perception, tempered by kindness of heart and unwillingness to give pain; and on that sore point of residence with the blind uncle, it was quite possibly a

bit of Alick's exaggerated feeling to imagine the arrangement so desirable—the young lady might be the better
judge.

On the whole, the expostulation left Colonel Keith more
uncomfortable on Alick's account than on that of his
brother.

CHAPTER II.

AN APPARITION.

" And there will be auld Geordie Tanner,
      Who coft a young wife wi' his gowd."
                              JOANNA BAILLIE.

"MAMMA," quoth Leoline, " I thought a woman must not
marry her grandfather.   And she called him the patriarch of
her clan."

" He is a cross old man," added Hubert.   " He said children ought not to be allowed on the esplanade, because he
got into the way as I was pushing the perambulator."

" This was the reason," said Francis, gravely, " that she
stopped me from braying at him.   I shall know what people
are at, when they talk of disrespect another time."

" Don't talk of her," cried Conrade, flinging himself round;
" women have no truth in them."

" Except the dear, darling, delightful mammy ! "   And the
larger proportion of boys precipitated themselves headlong
upon her, so that any one but a mother would have been
buffeted out of breath in their struggles for embracing
ground ; and even Lady Temple found it a relief when
Hubert, having been squeezed out, bethought himself of
extending the honourable exception to Miss Williams, and

thus effected a diversion. What would have been the young gentlemen's reception of his lordship's previous proposal !

Yet in the fulness of her gladness the inconsistent widow, who had thought Lord Keith so much too old for herself, gave her younger friend heartfelt congratulations upon the blessing of being under fatherly direction and guidance. She was entrusted with the announcement to Rachel, who received it with a simple " Indeed ! " and left her cousin unmolested in her satisfaction, having long relegated Fanny to the class of women who think having a friend about to be married, the next best thing to being married themselves, no matter to whom.

" Aspirations in women are mere delusions," was her compensating sigh to Grace. " There is no truer saying, than that a woman will receive every man."

" I have always been glad that is aprocryphal," said Grace, " and Eastern women have no choice."

" Nor are Western women better than Eastern," said Rachel. " It is all circumstances. No mental power or acuteness has in any instance that I have yet seen, been able to balance the propensity to bondage. The utmost flight is, that the attachment should not be unworthy."

" I own that I am very much surprised," said Grace.

" I am not at all," said Rachel. " I have given up hoping better things. I was beginning to have a high opinion of Bessie Keith's capabilities, but womanhood was at the root all the time ; and, as her brother says, she has had great disadvantages, and I can make excuses for her. She had not her heart filled with one definite scheme of work and usefulness, such as deters the trifling and designing."

" Like the F. U. E. E. ? "

"Yes, the more I see of the fate of other women, the more thankful I am that my vocation has taken a formed and developed shape."

And thus Rachel could afford to speak without severity of the match, though she abstained from congratulation. She did not see Captain Keith for the next few days, but at last the two sisters met him at the Cathedral door as they were getting into the carriage after a day's shopping at Avoncester; and Grace offered her congratulations, in accordance with her mother's old fashioned code.

"Thank you," he said; then turning to Rachel, "Did she write to you?"

"No."

"I thought not."

There was something marked in his tone, but his sister's silence was not of long duration, for a letter arrived containing orders for lace, entreating that a high pressure might be put on Mrs. Kelland, and containing beauteous devices for the veil, which was to be completed in a fearfully short time since the wedding was to be immediate, in order that Lord Keith might spend Christmas and the ensuing cold months abroad. It was to take place at Bath, and was to be as quiet as possible; "or else," wrote Miss Keith, "I should have been enchanted to have overcome your reluctance to witness the base surrender of female rights. I am afraid you are only too glad to be let off, only don't thank me, but circumstances."

Rachel's principles revolted at the quantity of work demanded of the victims to lace, and Grace could hardly obtain leave to consult Mrs. Kelland. But she snapped at the order, for the honour and glory of the thing, and undertook through the ramifications of her connexion to obtain the whole bridal array complete. "For such a pleasant-spoken lady as Miss Keith, she would sit up all night rather than disappoint her."

The most implacable person of all was the old house-keeper, Tibbie. She had been warmly attached to Lady Keith, and resented her having a successor, and one younger than her daughters; and above all, ever since the son and heir had died, she had reckoned on her own Master Colin coming to the honours of the family, and regarded this new marriage as a crossing of Providence. She vainly endeavoured to stir up Master Colin to remonstrate on his brother's "makin' siccan a fule's bargain wi' yon glaikit lass. My certie, but he'll hae the warst o't, honest man; rinnin' after her, wi' a' her whigmaleries an' cantrips. He'll rue the day that e'er he bowed his noble head to the likes o' her, I'm jalousin."

It was to no purpose to remind her that the bride was a Keith in blood; her great grandfather a son of the house of Gowanbrae; all the subsequent descendants brave soldiers.

"A Keith ca' ye her! It's a queer kin' o' Keiths she's comed o', nae better nor Englishers that haena sae muckle's set fit in our bonny Scotland; an' sic scriechin', skirlin' tongues as they hae, a body wad need to be gleg i' the uptak to understan' a word they say. Tak' my word for't, Maister Colin, it's no a'thegither luve for his lordship's grey hairs that gars yon gilpy lassock seek to become my Leddy Keith."

"Nay, Tibbie, if you find fault with such a sweet, winning young creature, I shall think it is all because you will not endure a mistress at Gowanbrae over you."

"His lordship 'll please himsel' wi' a leddy to be mistress

o' Gowanbrae, but auld Tibbie 'll never cross the doorstane mair."

"Indeed you will, Tibbie; here are my brother's orders that you should go down, as soon as you can conveniently make ready, and see about the new plenishing."

"They may see to the plenishin' that's to guide it after han, an' that'll no be me. My lord 'll behove to tak' his orders aff his young leddy ance he's married on her, may be a whilie afore, but that's no to bind ither folk, an' it's no to be thought that at my years I'm to be puttin' up wi' a' ther new fangled English fykes an' nonsense maggots. Na, na, Maister Colin, his lordship 'll fend weel aneugh wantin' Tibbie; an' what for suld I leave yerself, an' you settin' up wi' a house o' yer ain? Deed an' my mind's made up, I'll e'en bide wi' ye, an' nae mair about it."

"Stay, stay," cried Colin, a glow coming into his cheeks, "don't reckon without your host, Tibbie. Do you think Gowanbrae the second is never to have any mistress but yourself?"

"Haud awa' wi' ye, laddie, I ken fine what ye're ettlin' at, but yon's a braw leddy, no like thae English folk, but a woman o' understandin', an' mair by token I'm thinkin' she'll be gleg aneugh to ken a body that 'll serve her weel, an' see to the guidin' o' thae feckless queans o' servant lasses, for bad's the best o' them ye'll fin' hereawa'. Nae fear but her an' me 'll put it up weel thegither, an' a' gude be wi' ye baith."

After this Colin resigned himself and his household to Tibbie's somewhat despotic government, at least for the present. To Ermine's suggestion that her appellation hardly suited the dignity of her station, he replied that Isabel was

too romantic for southern ears ; and that her surname being
the same as his own, he was hardly prepared to have the title
of Mrs. Keith pre-occupied.   So after Mrs. Curtis's example,
the world for the most part knew the colonel's housekeeper
as Mrs. Tibbs.

She might be a tyrant, but liberties were taken with her
territory ; for almost the first use that the colonel made of
his house was to ask a rheumatic sergeant, who had lately
been invalided, to come and benefit by the Avonmouth
climate.   Scottish hospitality softened Tibbie's heart, and
when she learnt that Sergeant O'Brien had helped to carry
Master Colin into camp after his wound, she thought nothing
too good for him.   The colonel then ventured to add to the
party an exemplary consumptive tailor from Mr. Mitchell's
parish, who might yet be saved by good living and good air.
Some growls were elicited, but he proved to be so deplorably
the ninetieth rather than the ninth part of a man, that Tibbie
made it her point of honour to fatten him ; and the sergeant
found him such an intelligent auditor of the Indian exploits
of the ---th Highlanders that mutual respect was fully
established, and high politeness reigned supreme, even though
the tailor could never be induced to delight in the porridge,
on which the sergeant daily complimented the housekeeper
in original and magnificent metaphors.

Nor had the Colonel any anxieties in leaving the repre-
sentatives of the three nations together while he went to
attend his brother's wedding.   He proposed that Tibbie
should conduct Rose for the daily walk of which he had
made a great point, thinking that the child did not get
exercise enough, since she was so averse to going alone upon
the esplanade that her aunt forbore to press it.   She

manifested the same reluctance to going out with Tibbie, and this the Colonel ascribed to her fancying herself too old to be under the charge of a nurse. It was trying to laugh her out of her dignity, but without eliciting an answer, when, one afternoon just as they were entering together upon the esplanade, he felt her hand tighten upon his own with a nervous frightened clutch, as she pressed tremulously to his side.

" What is it, my dear ? That dog is not barking at you. He only wants to have a stick thrown into the sea for him."

" Oh not the dog ! It was——"

" Was, what ?"

" *Him !*" gasped Rose.

" Who ?" inquired the Colonel, far from prepared for the reply, in a terrified whisper,—

" Mr. Maddox."

" My dear child ! Which, where ?"

" He is gone ! he is past. Oh, don't turn back ! Don't let me see him again."

" You don't suppose he could hurt you, my dear."

" No," hesitated Rose, " not with you."

" Nor with any one."

" I suppose not," said Rose, common sense reviving, though her grasp was not relaxed.

" Would it distress you very much to try to point him out to me ?" said the Colonel, in his irresistibly sweet tone.

" I will. Only keep hold of my hand, pray," and the little hand trembled so much that he felt himself committing a cruel action in leading her along the esplanade, but there was no fresh start of recognition, and when they had gone the whole length, she breathed more freely, and said, "No, he was not there."

Recollecting how young she had been at the time of Maddox's treason, the Colonel began to doubt if her imagination had not raised a bugbear, and he questioned her, "My dear, why are you so much afraid of this person? What do you know about him?"

"He told wicked stories of my papa," said Rose, very low.

"True, but he could not hurt you. You don't think he goes about like Red Ridinghood's wolf?"

"No, I am not so silly now."

"Are you sure you know him? Did you often see him in your papa's house?"

"No, he was always in the laboratory, and I might not go there."

"Then you see, Rose, it must be mere fancy that you saw him, for you could not even know him by sight."

"It was not fancy," said Rose, gentle and timid as ever, but still obviously injured at the tone of reproof.

"My dear child," said Colonel Keith, with some exertion of patience, "you must try to be reasonable. How can you possibly recognise a man that you tell me you never saw?"

"I said I never saw him in the house," said Rose with a shudder; "but they said if ever I told they would give me to the lions in the Zoological Gardens."

"Who said so?"

"He, Mr. Maddox and Maria," she answered, in such trepidation that he could scarcely hear her.

"But you are old and wise enough now to know what a foolish and wicked threat that was, my dear."

"Yes, I was a little girl then, and knew no better, and

once I did tell a lie when mamma asked me, and now she is dead, and I can never tell her the truth."

Colin dreaded a public outbreak of the sobs that heaved in the poor child's throat, but she had self-control enough to restrain them till he had led her into his own library, where he let her weep out her repentance for the untruth, which, wrested from her by terror, had weighed so long on her conscience. He felt that he was sparing Ermine something by receiving the first tempest of tears, in the absolute terror and anguish of revealing the secret that had preyed on her with mysterious horror. "Now tell me all about it, my dear little girl. Who was this Maria?"

"Maria was my nurse when I lived at home. She used to take me out walking," said Rose, pressing closer to his protecting breast, and pausing as though still afraid of her own words.

"Well," he said, beginning to perceive, "and was it then that you saw this Maddox?"

"Yes, he used to come and walk with us, and sit under the trees in Kensington Gardens with her. And sometimes he gave me lemon-drops, but they said if ever I told, the lions should have me. I used to think I might be saved like Daniel; but after I told the lie, I knew I should not. Mamma asked me why my fingers were sticky, and I did say it was from a lemon-drop, but there were Maria's eyes looking at me; oh, so dreadful, and when mamma asked who gave it to me, and Maria said, 'I did, did not I, Miss Rose?' Oh, I did not seem able to help saying 'yes.'"

"Poor child! And you never dared to speak of it again?"

"Oh, no! I did long to tell; but, oh, one night it was written up in letters of fire, 'Beware of the Lions.'"

" Terror must have set you dreaming, my dear."

" No," said Rose, earnestly. " I was quite awake. Papa and mamma were gone out to dine and sleep, and Maria would put me to bed half an hour too soon. She read me to sleep, but by and by I woke up, as I always did at mamma's bed time, and the candle was gone, and there were those dreadful letters in light over the door."

She spoke with such conviction that he became persuaded that all was not delusion, and asked what she did.

" I jumped up, and screamed, and opened the door; but there they were growling in papa's dressing-room."

" They, the lions ? Oh, Rose, you must know that was impossible."

" No, I did not *see* any lions, but I heard the growl, and Mr. Maddox coughed, and said, ' Here they come,' and growled again."

" And you—— ?"

" I tumbled into bed again, and rolled up my head in the clothes, and prayed that it might be day, and it was at last !"

" Poor child ! Indeed, Rose, I do not wonder at your terror, I never heard of a more barbarous trick."

" Was it a trick ?" said Rose, raising a wonderfully relieved and hopeful face.

" Did you never hear of writing in phosphorus, a substance that shines at night as the sea sometimes does ?"

" Aunt Ailie has a book with a story about writing in fiery letters, but it frightened me so much that I never read to the end."

" Bring it to me, and we will read it together, and then you will see that such a cruel use can be made of phosphorus."

" It was unkind of them," said Rose, sadly, " I wonder if they did it for fun !"

" Where did you sleep ?"

" I had a little room that opened into mamma's."

" And where was all this growling ? "

" In papa's room. The door was just opposite to mine, and was open. All the light was there, you know. Mamma's room was dark, but there was a candle in the dressing-room."

" Did you see anything ?"

" Only the light. It was such a moment. I don't *think* I saw Mr. Maddox, but I am quite certain I heard him, for he had an odd little cough."

" Then, Rose, I have little doubt that all this cruelty to you, poor inoffensive little being, was to hide some plots against your father."

She caught his meaning with the quickness of a mind precocious on some points though childish on others. " Then if I had been brave and told the truth, he might never have hurt papa."

" Mind, I do not know, and I never thought of blaming you, the chief sufferer ! No, don't begin to cry again."

" Ah ! but I did tell a lie. And I never can confess it to mamma," she said, recurring to the sad lament so long suppressed.

She found a kind comforter, who led her to the higher sources of consolation, feeling all the time the deep self-accusation with which the sight of sweet childish penitence must always inspire a grown person.

" And now you will not fear to tell your aunt," he added, " only it should be when you can mention it without such sad crying."

"Telling you is almost as good as telling her," said Rose, "and I feel safe with you," she added, caressingly drawing his arm round her. "Please tell Aunt Ermine, for my crying does give her *such* a headache."

"I will, then, and I think when we all know it, the terrors will leave you."

"Not when I see Mr. Maddox. Oh, please now you know why, don't make me walk without you. I do *know* now that he could not 'do anything to me, but I can't help feeling the fright. And, oh! if he was to speak to me!"

"You have not seen him here before?"

"Yes I have, at least I think so. Once when Aunt Ermine sent me to the post-office, and another time on the esplanade. That is why I can't bear going out without you or Aunt Ailie. Indeed, it is not disliking Tibbie."

"I see it is not, my dear, and we will say no more about it till you have conquered your alarm; but remember, that he is not likely to know you again. You must be more changed in these three years than he is."

This consideration seemed to reassure Rose greatly, and her next inquiry was, "Please, are my eyes very red for going home?"

"Somewhat mottled—something of the York and Lancaster rose. Shall I leave you under Tibbie's care till the maiden blush complexion returns, and come back and fetch you when you have had a grand exhibition of my Indian curiosities?"

"Have you Indian curiosities? I thought they were only for ladies?"

"Perhaps they are. Is Tibbie guard enough? You know

there's an Irish sergeant in the house taller than I am, if you want a garrison ?"

" Oh, I am not afraid, only these eyes."

" I will tell her you have been frightened, and she shall take no notice."

Tibbie was an admirer of Rose and gladly made her welcome, while the Colonel repaired to Ermine, and greatly startled her by the disclosure of the miseries that had been inflicted on the sensitive child.

It had indeed been known that there had been tyranny in the nursery, and to this cause the aunts imputed the startled wistful expression in Rose's eyes ; but they had never questioned her, thinking that silence would best wear out the recollection. The only wonder was that her senses had not been permanently injured by that night of terror, which accounted for her unconquerable dread of sleeping in the dark ; and a still more inexplicable horror of the Zoological Gardens, together with many a nervous misery that Ermine had found it vain to combat. The colonel asked if the nurse's cruelty had been the cause of her dismissal ?

" No, it was not discovered till after her departure. Her fate has always been a great grief to us, though we little thought her capable of using Rose in this way. She was one of the Hathertons. You must remember the name, and the pretty picturesque hovel on the Heath."

" The squatters that were such a grievance to my uncle. Always suspected of poaching, and never caught."

" Exactly. Most of the girls turned out ill, but this one, the youngest, was remarkably intelligent and attractive at school. I remember making an excuse for calling her into the garden for you to see and confess that English beauty exceeded Scottish, and you called her a gipsy and said we had no right to her."

" So it was those big black eyes that had that fiendish malice in them ! "

" Ah ! if she fell into Maddox's hands, I wonder the less. She showed an amount of feeling about my illness that won Ailie's heart, and we had her for a little handmaid to help my nurse. Then, when we broke up from home, we still kept her, and every one used to be struck with her looks and manner. She went on as well as possible, and Lucy set her heart on having her in the nursery. And when the upper nurse went away, she had the whole care of Rose. We heard only of her praises till, to our horror, we found she had been sent away in disgrace at a moment's warning. Poor Lucy was young, and so much shocked as only to think of getting her out of the house, not of what was to become of her, and all we could learn was that she never went home."

" How long was this before the crash ? "

" It was only a few weeks before the going abroad, but they had been absent nearly a year. No doubt Maddox must have made her aid in his schemes. You say Rose saw him ? "

" So she declares, and there is an accuracy of memory about her that I should trust to. Should you or Alison know him ? "

" No, we used to think it a bad sign that Edward never showed him to us. I remember Alison being disappointed that he was not at the factory the only time she saw it."

" I do not like going away while he may be lurking about. I could send a note to-night, explaining my absence."

" No, no," exclaimed Ermine, " that would be making me
as bad as poor little Rose. If he be here ever so much he
has done his worst, and Edward is out of his reach. What
could he do to us ? The affairs were wound up long ago,
and we have literally nothing to be bullied out of. No, I
don't think he could make me believe in lions in any
shape."

" You strong-minded woman ! You want to emulate the
Rachel."

" You have brought her," laughed Ermine at the sound of
the well-known knock, and Rachel entered bag in hand.

" I was in hopes of meeting you," she said to the colonel.
" I wanted to ask you to take charge of some of these ;" and
she produced a packet of prospectuses of a " Journal of
Female Industry," an illustrated monthly magazine, destined
to contain essays, correspondence, reviews, history, tales, etc.,
to be printed and illustrated in the F. U. E. E.

" I hoped," said Rachel, " to have begun with the year,
but we are not forward enough, and indeed some of the
expenses require a subscription in advance. A subscriber in
advance will have the year's numbers for ten shillings, instead
of twelve ; and I should be much obliged if you would distribute a few of these at Bath, and ask Bessie to do the
same. I shall set her name down at the head of the list, as
soon as she has qualified it for a decoy."

" Are these printed at the F. U. E. E. ?"

" No, we have not funds as yet. Mr. Mauleverer had
them done at Bristol, where he has a large connexion as a
lecturer, and expects to get many subscribers. I brought
these down as soon as he had left them with me, in hopes
that you would kindly distribute them at the wedding. And

I wished," added she to Ermine, " to ask you to contribute to our first number."

" Thank you," and the doubtful tone induced Rachel to encourage her diffidence.

" I know you write a great deal, and I am sure you must produce something worthy to see the light. I have no scruple in making the request, as I know Colonel Keith agrees with me that womanhood need not be an extinguisher for talent."

" I am not afraid of him," Ermine managed to say without more smile than Rachel took for gratification.

" Then if you would only entrust me with some of your fugitive reflections, I have no doubt that something might be made of them. A practised hand," she added with a certain editorial dignity, " can always polish away any little roughnesses from inexperience."

Ermine was choking with laughter at the savage pulls that Colin was inflicting on his moustache, and feeling silence no longer honest, she answered in an odd under tone, " I can't plead inexperience."

" No !" cried Rachel. " You have written ; you have not published !"

" I was forced to do whatever brought grist to the mill," said Ermine. " Indeed," she added, with a look as if to ask pardon ; " our secrets have been hardly fair towards you, but we made it a rule not to spoil our breadwinner's trade by confessing my enormities."

" I assure you," said the Colonel, touched by Rachel's appalled look, " I don't know how long this cautious person would have kept me in the dark if she had not betrayed herself in the paper we discussed the first day I met you."

"The 'Traveller,'" said Rachel, her eyes widening like those of a child. "She is the 'Invalid'!"

"There, I am glad to have made a clean breast of it," said Ermine.

"The 'Invalid'!" repeated Rachel. "It is as bad as the Victoria Cross."

"There is a compliment, Ermine, for which you should make your bow," said Colin.

"Oh, I did not mean that," said Rachel; "but that it was as great a mistake as I made about Captain Keith, when I told him his own story, and denied his being the hero, till I actually saw his cross;" and she spoke with a genuine simplicity that almost looked like humour, ending with, "I wonder why I am fated to make such mistakes!"

"Preconceived notions," said Ermine, smiling; "your theory suffices you, and you don't see small indications."

"There may be something in that," said Rachel, thoughtfully, "it accounts for Grace always seeing things faster than I did."

"Did Mr. ——, your philanthropist, bring you this to-day?" said the Colonel, taking up the paper again, as if to point a practical moral to her confession of misjudgments."

"Mr. Mauleverer? Yes; I came down as soon as he had left me, only calling first upon Fanny. I am very anxious for contributions. If you would only give me a paper signed by the 'Invalid,' it would be a fortune to the institution."

Ermine made a vague answer that she doubted whether the 'Invalid' was separable from the 'Traveller,' and Rachel presently departed with her prospectus, but without having elicited a promise.

"Intolerable!" exclaimed the Colonel. "She was improving under Bessie's influence, but she has broken out worse than ever. 'Journal of Female Industry!' 'Journal of a Knight of Industry,' might be a better title. You will have nothing to do with it, Ermine?"

" Certainly not as the 'Invalid,' but I owe her something for having let her run into this scrape before you."

" As if you could have hindered her! Come, don't waste time and brains on a companion for Curatocult."

" You make me so idle and frivolous that I shall be expelled from the 'Traveller,' and obliged to take refuge in the 'Female Industry Journal.' Shall you distribute the prospectuses?"

" I shall give one to Bessie! That is if I go at all."

" No, no; there is no valid reason for staying away. Even if we were sure that Rose was right, nothing could well come of it, and your absence would be most invidious."

" I believe I am wanted to keep Master Alick in order, but if you have the least feeling that you would be more at ease with me at home——"

" That is not a fair question," said Ermine, smiling. " You know very well that you ought to go."

" And I shall try to bring back Harry Beauchamp," added the Colonel. " He would be able to identify the fellow."

" I do not know what would be gained by that."

" I should know whom to watch."

Ermine had seen so much of Rose's nervous timidity, and had known so many phantoms raised by it, that she attached little importance to the recognition, and when she went over the matter with her little niece, it was with far more thought of the effect of the terror, and of the long suppressed secret, upon the child's moral and physical nature, than with any curiosity as to the subject of her last alarm. She was surprised to observe that Alison was evidently in a state of much more restlessness and suspense than she was conscious of in herself, during Colin's absence, and attributed this to her sister's fear of Maddox's making some inroad upon her in her long solitary hours, in which case she tried to reassure her by promises to send at once for Mr. Mitchell or for Coombe.

Alison let these assurances be given to her, and felt hypocritical for receiving them in silence. Her grave set features had tutored themselves to conceal for ever one page in the life that Ermine thought was entirely revealed to her. Never had Ermine known that brotherly companionship had once suddenly assumed the unwelcome aspect of an affection against which Alison's heart had been steeled by devotion to the sister whose life she had blighted. Her resolution had been unswerving, but its full cost had been unknown to her, till her adherence to it had slackened the old tie of hereditary friendship towards others of her family ; and even when marriage should have obliterated the past, she still traced resentment in the hard judgment of her brother's conduct, and even in the one act of consideration that it galled her to accept.

There had been no meeting since the one decisive interview just before she had left her original home, and there were many more bitter feelings than could be easily assuaged in looking forward to a renewal of intercourse, when all too late, she knew that she should soon be no longer needed by her sister. She tried to feel it all just retribution ; she tried to rejoice in Ermine's coming happiness ; she tried to believe that the sight of Harry Beauchamp, as a married man, would be the best cure for her ; she blamed and struggled with herself : and after all, her distress was wasted, Harry Beauchamp had not chosen to come home with his cousin, who took his unwillingness to miss a hunting-day rather angrily and scornfully. Alison put her private interpretation on the refusal, and held aloof, while Colin owned to Ermine his vexation and surprise at the displeasure that Harry Beauchamp maintained against his old schoolfellow, and his absolute refusal to listen to any arguments as to his innocence.

This seemed to have been Colin's prominent interest in his expedition to Bath ; the particulars of the wedding were less easily drawn from him. The bride had indeed been perfection, all was charming wherever she brought her ready grace and sweetness, and she had gratified the Colonel by her affectionate messages to Ermine, and her evident intention to make all straight between Lord Keith and his daughter Mary. But the Clare relations had not made a favourable impression ; the favourite blind uncle had not been present, in spite of Bessie's boast, and it was suspected that Alick had not chosen to forward his coming. Alick had devolved the office of giving his sister away upon the Colonel, as her guardian, and had altogether comported himself with more than his usual lazy irony, especially towards the Clare cousinhood, who constantly buzzed round him, and received his rebuffs as delightful jests and compliments, making the Colonel wonder all the more at the perfect good taste and good breeding of his new sister-in-law, who had spent among them all the most critical years of her life.

She had been much amused with the prospectus of the "Journal of Female Industry," but she sent word to Rachel that she advised her not to publish any list of subscribers— the vague was far more impressive than the certain. The first number must be sent to her at Paris, and trust her for spreading its fame !

The Colonel did not add to his message her recommendation that the frontispiece should represent the Spinster's Needles, with the rescue of Don as the type of female heroism.   Nor did he tell how carefully he had questioned both her and Rachel as to the date of that interesting adventure.

CHAPTER III.

THE SIEGE.

"The counterfeit presentment."—*Hamlet.*

CHRISTMAS came, and Rachel agreed with Mr. Mauleverer that it was better not to unsettle the children at the F.U.E.E. by permitting them to come home for holidays, a decision which produced much discontent in their respective families. Alison, going to Mrs. Morris with her pupils, to take her a share of Christmas good cheer, was made the receptacle of a great lamentation over the child's absence; and, moreover, that the mother had not been allowed to see her alone, when taken by Miss Rachel to the F.U.E.E.

"Some one ought to take it up," said Alison, as she came home, in her indignation. "Who knows what may be done to those poor children? Can't Mr. Mitchell do something?"

But Mr. Mitchell was not sufficiently at home to interfere. He was indeed negotiating an exchange with Mr. Touchett, but until this was effected he could hardly meddle in the matter, and he was besides a reserved, prudent man, slow to commit himself, so that his own impression of the asylum could not be extracted from him. Here, however, Colonel Keith put himself forward. He had often been asked by Rachel to visit the F.U.E.E., and he surprised and relieved Alison by announcing his intention of going over to St.

Norbert's alone and without notice, so as to satisfy himself as far as might be as to the treatment of the inmates, and the genuineness of Mauleverer's pretensions.

He had, however, to wait for weather that would not make the adventure one of danger to him, and he regarded the cold and rain with unusual impatience, until, near the end of January, he was able to undertake his expedition.

After much knocking and ringing the door was opened to him by a rude, slatternly, half-witted looking charwoman, or rather girl, who said "Master was not in," and nearly shut the door in his face. However, he succeeded in sending in his card, backed by the mention of Lady Temple and Miss Curtis ; and this brought out Mrs. Rawlins, her white streamers floating stiff behind her, full of curtsies and regrets at having to refuse any friend of Miss Curtis, but Mr. Mauleverer's orders were precise and could not be infringed. He was gone to lecture at Bristol, but if the gentleman would call at any hour he would fix to-morrow or next day, Mr. Mauleverer would be proud to wait on him.

When he came at the appointed time, all was in the normal state of the institution. The two little girls in white pinafores sat upon their bench with their books before them, and their matron presiding over them ; Mr. Mauleverer stood near, benignantly attentive to the children and obligingly so to the visitor, volunteering information and answering all questions. Colonel Keith tried to talk to the children, but when he asked one of them whether she liked drawing better than lace-making her lips quivered, and Mrs. Rawlins replied for her, that she was never happy except with a pencil in her hand. "Show the gentleman, my dear," and out came a book of studies of cubes, globes, posts, etc., while Mr. Mauleverer talked artistically of drawing from models. Next, he observed on a certain suspicious blackness of little Mary's eye, and asked her what she had done to herself. But the child hung her head, and Mrs. Rawlins answered for her, " Ah ! Mary is ashamed to tell: but the gentleman will think nothing of it, my dear. He knows that children will be children, and I cannot bear to check them, the dears."

More briefly Mr. Mauleverer explained that Mary had fallen while playing on the stairs ; and with this superficial inspection he must needs content himself, though on making inquiry at the principal shops, he convinced himself that neither Mr Mauleverer nor the F. U. E. E. were as well known at St. Norbert's as at Avonmouth. He told Rachel of his expedition, and his interest in her work gratified her, though she would have preferred being his cicerone. She assured him that he must have been very much pleased, especially with the matron.

" She is a handsome woman, and reminds me strongly of a face I saw in India."

" There are some classes of beauty and character that have a remarkable sameness of feature," began Rachel.

" Don't push that theory, for your matron's likeness was a very handsome Sepoy havildar whom we took at Lucknow; a capital soldier before the mutiny, and then an ineffable ruffian."

" The mutiny was an infectious frenzy ; so that you establish nothing against that cast of countenance."

Never, indeed, was there more occasion for perseverance in Rachel's championship. Hitherto Mrs. Kelland had been nailed to her pillow by the exigencies of Lady Keith's outfit, and she and her minions had toiled unremittingly, without a thought beyond their bobbins, but as soon as the postponed orders were in train, and the cash for the wedding veil and flounces had been transmitted, the good woman treated herself and her daughters to a holiday at St. Norbert's, without intimating her intention to her patronesses ; and the consequence was a formal complaint of her ungrateful and violent language to Mrs. Rawlins on being refused admission to the asylum without authority from Mr. Mauleverer or Miss Curtis.

Rachel, much displeased, went down charged with reproof and representation, but failed to produce the desired effect upon the aunt.

" It was not right," Mrs. Kelland reiterated, " that the poor lone orphan should not see her that was as good as a mother, when she had no one else to look to. They that kept her from her didn't do it for no good end."

" But, Mrs. Kelland, rules are rules."

" Don't tell me of no rules, Miss Rachel, as would cut a poor child off from her friends as her mother gave her to on her death-bed. ' Sally,' says she, ' I know you will do a mother's part by that poor little maid ; ' and so I did till I was over persuaded to let her go to that there place."

" Indeed you have nothing to regret there, Mrs. Kelland ; you know, that with the kindest intentions, you could not make the child happy."

" And why was that, ma'am, but because her mother was a poor creature from town, that had never broke her to her work. I never had the trouble with a girl of my own I had with her. ' It's all for your good, Lovedy,' I says to her, and poor child, maybe she wishes herself back again."

" I assure you, I always find the children well and happy,

and it is very unfair on the matron to be angry with her for being bound by rules, to which she must submit, or she would trangress the regulations under which we have laid her ! It is not her choice to exclude you, but her duty."

" Please, ma'am, was it her duty to be coming out of the house in a 'genta coloured silk dress, and a drab bonnet with a pink feather in it ?" said Mrs. Kelland, with a certain air of simplicity, that provoked Rachel to answer sharply—

"You don't know what you are talking about, Mrs. Kelland."

" Well, ma'am, it was a very decent woman as told me, an old lady of the name of Drinkwater, as keeps a baker's shop on the other side of the way, and she never sees bread enough go in for a cat to make use of, let alone three poor hungry children. She says all is not right there, ma'am."

" Oh, that must be mere gossip and spite at not having the custom. It quite accounts for what she may say, and indeed you brought it all on yourself by not having asked me for a note. You must restrain yourself. What you may say to me is of no importance, but you must not go and attack those who are doing the very best for your niece."

Rachel made a dignified exit, but before she had gone many steps, she was assailed by tearful Mrs. Morris : " Oh, Miss Rachel, if it would not be displeasing to you, would you give me an order for my child to come home. Ours is a poor place, but I would rather make any shift for us to live than that she should be sent away to some place beyond sea."

"Some place beyond sea !"

" Yes, ma'am. I beg your pardon, ma'am, but they do say that Mr. Maw-and-liver is a kidnapper, ma'am, and that he gets them poor children to send out to Botany Bay to be wives to the convicts as are transported, Miss Rachel, if you'll excuse it. They say there's a whole shipload of them at Plymouth, and I'd rather my poor Mary came to the Union at home than to the like of that, Miss Rachel."

This alarm, being less reasonable, was even more difficult to talk down than Mrs. Kelland's, and Rachel felt as if there were a general conspiracy to drive her distracted, when on going home she found the drawing-room occupied by a pair of plump, paddy-looking old friends, who had evidently talked her mother into a state of nervous alarm. On her entrance, Mrs. Curtis begged the gentleman to tell dear Rachel what he had been saying, but this he contrived to avoid, and only on his departure was Rachel made aware that he and his wife had come, fraught with tidings that she was fostering a Jesuit in disguise, that Mrs. Rawlins was a lady abbess of a new order, Rachel herself in danger of being entrapped, and the whole family likely to be entangled in the mysterious meshes, which, as good Mrs. Curtis more than once repeated, would be " such a dreadful thing for poor Fanny and the boys."

Her daughters, by soothing and argument, allayed the alarm, though the impression was not easily done away with, and they feared that it might yet cost her a night's rest. These attacks—absurd as they were—induced Rachel to take measures for their confutation, by writing to Mr. Mauleverer, that she thought it would be well to allow the pupils to pay a short visit to their homes, so as to satisfy their friends.

She did not receive an immediate answer, and was beginning to feel vexed and anxious, though not doubtful, when Mr. Mauleverer arrived, bringing two beautiful little woodcuts, as illustrations for the " Journal of Female Industry." They were entitled " The free maids that weave their thread with bones," and one called "the Ideal," represented a latticed cottage window, with roses, honeysuckles, cat, beehives, and all conventional rural delights, around a pretty maiden singing at her lace-pillow; while the other yclept the "Real," showed a den of thin, wizened, half-starved girls, cramped over their cushions in a lace-school. The design was Mr. Mauleverer's, the execution the children's; and neatly mounted on cards, the performance did them great credit; and there was great justice in Mr. Mauleverer's view that while they were making such progress, it would be a great pity to interrupt the preparation of the first number by sending the children home even for a few hours. Rachel consented the more readily to the postponement of the holiday, as she had now something to show in evidence of the reality of their doings, and she laid hands upon the cuts, in spite of Mr. Mauleverer's unwillingness that such mere essays should be displayed as specimens of the art of the F. U. E. E. When the twenty pounds which she advanced should have been laid out in blocks, ink, and paper, there was little doubt that the illustrations of the journal would be a triumphant instance of female energy well directed.

Meantime she repaired to Ermine Williams to persuade her to write an article upon the two pictures, a paper in the lively style in which Rachel herself could not excel, pointing out the selfishness of wilfully sentimental illusions. She found Ermine alone, but her usual fate pursued her in the shape of, first, Lady Temple, then both Colonel and Captain Keith, and little Rose, who all came in before she had had time to do more than explain her intentions. Rose had had another fright, and again the Colonel had been vainly trying to distinguish the bugbear of her fancy, and she was clinging all the more closely to him because he was the only person of her acquaintance who did not treat her alarms as absolutely imaginary.

Rachel held her ground, well pleased to have so many spectators of this triumphant specimen of the skill of her asylum, and Lady Temple gave much admiration, declaring that no one ought to wear lace again without being sure that no one was tortured in making it, and that when she ordered her new black lace shawl of Mrs. Kelland, it should be on condition that the poor girls were not kept so very hard at work.

" You will think me looking for another Sepoy likeness," said the Colonel, " but I am sure I have met this young lady or her twin sister somewhere in my travels."

" It is a satire on conventional pictures," said Rachel.

" Now, I remember," he continued. " It was when I was laid up with my wound at a Dutch boer's till I could get to Cape Town. My sole reading was one number of the ' Illustrated News,' and I made too good acquaintance with that lady's head, to forget her easily."

" Of course," said Rachel, " it is a reminiscence of the painting there represented.

" What was the date ? " asked Alick Keith.

The Colonel was able to give it with some precision.

" You are all against me," said Rachel ; " I see you are perfectly determined that there shall be something wrong about every performance of the F. U. E. E."

" No, don't say so," began Fanny, with gentle argument, but Alick Keith put in with a smile, " It is a satisfaction to Miss Curtis."

" Athanasius against the world," she answered.

" Athanasius should take care that his own foot is firm, his position incontrovertible," said Ermine.

" Well ! "

" Then," said Ermine, " will you allow these little pictures to be examined into ? "

" I don't know what you mean."

" Look here," and the Colonel lifted on the table a scrap-book that Rose had been quietly opening on his knee, and which contained an etching of a child playing with a dog, much resembling the style of the drawing. " Who did that, my dear ? " he asked.

" Mamma had it," was Rose's reply ; " it was always in my old nursery scrap-book."

" Every one knows," said Rachel, " that a woodcut is often like an etching, and an etching like a woodcut. I do not know what you are driving at."

" The little dogs and all," muttered Alick, as Rachel glanced rather indignantly at Rose and her book so attentively examined by the Colonel.

" I know," repeated Rachel, " that there is a strong prejudice against Mr. Mauleverer, and that it is entertained by many whom I should have hoped to see above such weakness ; but when I brought these tangible productions of his system, as evidences of his success, I did not expect to see them received with a covert distrust, which I own I do not understand. I perceive now why good works find so much difficulty in prospering."

" I believe," said Alick Keith, " that I am to have the honour of dining at the Homestead on Monday ? "

" Yes. The Greys spend the day with us, and it is Emily's due to have a good sight of you."

"Then will you let me in the meantime take my own measures with regard to these designs. I will not hurt or injure them in any way ; they shall be deposited here in Miss Williams's hands, and I promise you that if I have been able to satisfy myself as to the means of their production, Simon Skinflint shall become a subscriber to the F. U. E. E. Is it a bargain ? "

" I never made such a bargain," said Rachel, puzzled.

" Is that a reason for not doing so ? "

" I don't know what you mean to do. Not to molest that poor Mrs. Rawlins. I will not have that done."

" Certainly not. All I ask of you is that these works of art should remain here with Miss Williams, as a safe neutral, and that you should meet me here on Monday, when I will undertake to convince myself."

" Not me ? " cried Rachel.

" Who would make it part of his terms to convince a lady ? "

" You mean to say," exclaimed Rachel, considerably nettled, " that as a woman, I am incapable of being rationally convinced ! "

" The proverb does not only apply to women," said Ermine, coming to her rescue ; but Rachel, stung by the arch smile and slight bow of Captain Keith, continued—" Let the proof be convincing, and I will meet it as candidly as it is the duty of all reasonable beings to do. Only let me first know what you mean to prove."

" The terms are these then, are they not, Miss Williams ? I am to come on Monday, February the 5th, prepared to test whether these designs are what they profess to be, and Miss Curtis undertakes to be convinced by that proof, provided it be one that should carry conviction to a clear, unbiassed mind. I undertake, on the other hand, that if the said proof should be effectual, a mythical personage called Simon Skinflint shall become a supporter of the Female Union for Englishwomen's Employment."

He spoke with his own peculiar slowness and gravity, and Rachel, uncertain whether he were making game of her or not, looked perplexed, half on the defence, half gratified. The others were greatly amused, and a great deal surprised at Alick's unwonted willingness to take trouble in the matter. After a few moment's deliberation, Rachel said, "Well, I consent, provided that my candour be met by equal candour on the other side, and you will promise that if this ordeal succeeds, you will lay aside all prejudice against Mauleverer."

A little demur as to the reasonableness of this stipulation followed, but the terms finally were established. Mr. and Mrs. Grey, old family friends, had long been engaged to spend the ensuing Monday at the Homestead. The elder daughter, an old intimate of Grace's, had married an Indian civil servant, whom Colonel Keith was invited to meet at luncheon, and Captain Keith at dinner, and Alick was further to sleep at Gowanbrae. Lady Temple, who was to have been of the party, was called away, much to her own regret, by an appointment with the dentist of St. Norbert's, who was very popular and proportionately despotic, in being only visible at his own times, after long appointment. She would therefore be obliged to miss Alick's ordeal, though as she said, when Rachel—finding it vain to try to outstay so many—had taken her leave, " I should much like to see how it will turn out. I do believe that there is some difference in the colour of the ink in the middle and at the edge, and if those people are deceiving Rachel, who knows what they may be doing to the poor children ! "

It was exactly what every one was thinking, but it seemed to have fresh force when it struck the milder and slower imagination, and Lady Temple, seeing that her observation told upon those around her, became more impressed with its weight.

"It really is dreadful to have sent those little girls there without any one knowing what anybody does to them," she repeated.

"It makes even Alick come out in a new character," said the Colonel, turning round on him.

"Why," returned Alick, "my sister had so much to do with letting the young lady in for the scrape, that it is just as well to try to get her out of it.   In fact, I think we have all sat with our hands before us in a shamefully cool manner, till we are all accountable for the humbuggery."

"When it comes to your reproaching us with coolness, Captain Keith, the matter becomes serious," returned Colin.

"It does become serious," was the answer ; "it is hard that a person without any natural adviser should have been allowed to run headlong, by force of her own best qualities, into the hands of a sharper.   I do not see how a man of any proper feeling, can stand by without doing something to prevent the predicament from becoming any worse."

"If you can," said Colonel Keith.

"I verily believe," said Alick, turning round upon him, "that the worse it is for her, the more you enjoy it !"

"Quite true," said Ermine in her mischievous way ; "it is a true case of man's detestation of clever women !   Look here, Alick, we will not have him here at the great ordeal of

the woodcuts. You and I are much more candid and unprejudiced people, and shall manage her much better."

" I have no desire to be present," returned the Colonel ;
" I have no satisfaction in seeing my friend Alick baffled.
I shall see how they both appear at luncheon afterwards."

" How will that be ?" asked Fanny, anxiously.

" The lady will be sententious and glorious, and will
recommend the F. U. E. E. more than ever, and Alick will
cover the downfall of his crest by double-edged assents to
all her propositions."

" You will not have that pleasure," said Alick. " I only
go to dinner there."

" At any rate," said the Colonel, " supposing your test
takes effect by some extraordinary chance, don't take any
further steps without letting me know."

The inference was drawn that he expected great results,
but he continued to laugh at Alick's expectations of producing any effect on the Clever Woman, and the debate of
the woodcuts was adjourned to the Monday.

In good time, Rachel made her appearance in Miss
Williams's little sitting-room. " I am ready to submit to
any test that Captain Keith may require to confute himself,"
she said to Ermine ; " and I do so the more readily that
with all his mocking language, there is a genuine candour
and honesty beneath that would be quite worth convincing.
I believe that if once persuaded of the injustice of his
suspicions he would in the reaction become a fervent supporter
of Mr. Mauleverer and of the institution ; and though I
should prefer carrying on our work entirely through women,
yet this interest would be so good a thing for him, that I
should by no means reject his assistance."

Rachel had, however, long to wait.⁎ As she said, Captain Keith was one of those inborn loiterers who, made punctual by military duty, revenge themselves by double tardiness in the common affairs of life. Impatience had nearly made her revoke her good opinion of him, and augur that, knowing himself vanquished, he had left the field to her, when at last a sound of wheels was heard, a dog-cart stopped at the door, and Captain Keith entered with an enormous blue and gold volume under his arm.

"I am sorry to be so late," he said, "but I have only now succeeded in procuring my ally."

"An ally !"

"Yes, in this book. I had to make interest at the Avoncester Library, before I could take it away with me." As he spoke he placed the book desk-fashion on a chair, and turned it so that Ermine might see it ; and she perceived that it was a bound-up volume of the " Illustrated London News." Two marks were in it, and he silently parted the leaves at the first.

It revealed the lace-making beauty in all her rural charms.

"I see," said Rachel ; "it is the same figure, but not the same shaped picture."

Without another word, Alick Keith opened the pages at the lace-school ; and here again the figures were identical, though the margin had been differently finished off.

"I perceive a great resemblance," again said Rachel ; "but none that is not fully explained by Mr. Mauleverer's accurate resemblance and desire to satirize foolish sentiment."

Alick Keith took up the woodcut. "I should say," he observed, holding it up to the light, "that it was unusual to mount a proof engraving so elaborately on a card."

" Oh, I see what your distrust is driving at ; you suspect the designs of being pasted on."

" There is such a test as water," suggested Alick.

" I should be ashamed to return the proof to its master, bearing traces of unjust suspicion."

" If the suspicion you impute to me be unjust, the water will produce no effect at all."

" And you engage to retract all your distrust and contempt, if you are convinced that this engraving is genuine ? "

" I do," he answered steadily.

With irritated magnanimity Rachel dipped her finger into the vase of flowers on the table, and let a heavy drop of water fall upon the cottage scene. The centre remained unaltered, and she looked round in exultation, saying, " There, now I suppose I may wipe it off."

Neither spoke, and she applied her pocket handkerchief.

What came peeling away under her pressure ? It was the soft paper, and as she was passing the edge of the figure of the girl, she found a large smear following her finger. The peculiar brown of Indian ink was seen upon her handkerchief, and when she took it up a narrow hem of white had become apparent between the girl's head and its surroundings. Neither spectator spoke, they scarcely looked at her, when she took another drop from the vase, and using it more boldly found the pasted figure curling up and rending under her hand, lines of newspaper type becoming apparent, and the dark cloud spreading around.

" What does it mean ? " was her first exclamation ; then suddenly turning on Ermine, " Well, do you triumph ? "

" I am very, very sorry," said Ermine.

" I do not know that it is come to that yet," said Rachel,

trying to collect herself. " I may have been pressing too
hard for results." Then looking at the mangled picture
again as they wisely left her to herself, " But it is a deception ! A deception ! Oh ! he need not have done it !
Or," with a lightened look and tone of relief, " suppose he
did it to see whether I should find it out ? "

" He is hardly on terms with you for that," said Ermine ;
while Alick could not refrain from saying, " Then he would
be a more insolent scoundrel than he has shown himself
yet."

" I know he is not quite a gentleman," said Rachel, " and
nothing else gives the instinct of the becoming. You have
conquered, Captain Keith, if it be any pleasure to you to
have given my trust and hope a cruel shock."

" With little satisfaction to myself," he began to say ; but
she continued, " A shock, a shock I say, no more ; I do not
know what conclusion I ought to draw. I do not expect
you to believe in this person till he has cleared up the deceit.
If it be only a joke in bad taste, he deserves the distrust
that is the penalty for it. If you have been opening my
eyes to a deception, perhaps I shall thank you for it some
day. I must think it over."

She rose, gathered her papers together, and took her leave
gravely, while Alick, much to Ermine's satisfaction, showed
no elation in his victory. All he said was, " There is a great
deal of dignity in the strict justice of a mind slow to con-
demn, or to withdraw the trust once given."

" There is," said Ermine, much pleased with his whole
part in the affair ; " there has been full and real candour, not
flying into the other extreme. I am afraid she has a great
deal to suffer."

" It was very wrong to have stood so still when the rascal began his machinations," repeated Alick, " Bessie absolutely helping it on ! But for her, the fellow would have had no chance even of acquaintance with her."

" Your sister hardly deserves blame for that."

" Not exactly blame ; but the responsibility remains," he replied gravely, and indeed he was altogether much graver than his wont, entirely free from irony, and evidently too sorry for Rachel, and feeling himself, through his sister, too guilty of her entanglement, to have any of that amused satisfaction that even Colin evidently felt in her discomfiture. In fact Ermine did not fully enter into Colin's present tactics ; she saw that he was more than usually excited and interested about the F. U. E. E., but he had not explained his views to her, and she could only attribute his desire, to defer the investigation, to a wish that Mr. Mitchell should have time to return from London, whither he had gone to conclude his arrangements with Mr. Touchett, leaving the duty in commission between three delicate winter visitors.

Rachel walked home in a kind of dreamy bewilderment. The first stone in her castle had been loosened, and her heart was beginning to fail her, though the tenacity of her will produced a certain incapacity of believing that she had been absolutely deceived. Her whole fabric was so compact, and had been so much solidified by her own intensity of purpose, that any hollowness of foundation was utterly beyond present credence. She was ready to be affronted with Mauleverer for perilling all for a bad joke, but wildly impossible as this explanation would have seemed to others, she preferred taking refuge in it to accepting the full brunt of the blow upon her cherished hopes.

She had just re-entered the house on her return, when Grace met her, saying, " Oh, Rachel dear, Mrs. Rossitur is here."

" I think old servants have a peculiar propensity for turning up when the house is in a state of turmoil," returned Rachel.

" I have been walking round the garden with her, and doing my best to suffice for her entertainment," said Grace, good-naturedly, " but she really wants to see you on business. She has a bill for the F. U. E. E. which she wants you to pay."

" A bill for the F. U. E. E. ? "

" Yes; she makes many apologies for troubling you, but Tom is to be apprenticed to a grocer, and they want this fifteen pounds to make up the fee."

" But I tell you, Grace, there can't have been fifteen pounds' worth of things had in this month, and they were paid on the 1st."

" She says they have never been paid at all since the 1st of December."

" I assure you, Grace, it is in the books. I made a point of having all the accounts brought to me on the 1st of every month, and giving out the money. I gave out 3*l.* 10*s.* for the Rossiturs last Friday, the 1st of February, when Mr. Mauleverer was over here. He said coals were dearer, and they had to keep more fires."

" There must be some mistake," said Grace.

" I'll show you the books. Mr. Mauleverer keeps one himself, and leaves one with me. Oh, botheration, there's the Grey carriage ! Well, you go and receive them, and I'll try to pacify Mrs. Rossitur, and then come down."

Neatly kept were these account books of the F. U. E. E., and sure enough for every month were entered the sums for coals, wood, and potatoes, tallying exactly with Mrs. Rossitur's account, and each month Mr. Mauleverer's signature attested the receipt of the sum paid over to him by Rachel for household expenses. Rachel carried them down to Mrs. Rossitur, but this evidence utterly failed to convince that worthy personage that she had ever received a farthing after the 1st of December. She was profuse in her apologies for troubling Miss Rachel, and had only been led to do so by the exigencies of her son's apprentice fee, and she reposed full confidence in Rachel's eager assurance that she should not be a loser, and that in another day the matter should be investigated.

"And, Miss Rachel," added the old servant, "you'll excuse me, but they do say very odd things of the matron at that place, and I doubt you are deceived in her. Our lads went to the *the-a-ter* the other night, and I checked them well for it ; but mother, says they, we had more call to be there than the governess up to Miss Rachel's schule in Nichol Street, dressed out in pink feathers."

"Well, Mrs. Rossitur, I will make every inquiry, and I do not think you will find anything wrong. There must be some one about very like Mrs. Rawlins. I have heard of those pink feathers before, but I know who the matron is, and all about her ! Good bye. I'll see you again before you go ; I suppose it won't be till the seven o'clock train."

Mrs. Rossitur remained expressing her opinion to the butler that dear Miss Rachel was too innocent, and then proceeded to lose all past cares in a happy return to " melting day," in the regions of her past glories as cook and housekeeper.

Rachel repaired to her room to cool her glowing cheeks, and repeat to herself, "A mistake, an error. It must be a blunder! That boy that went to the theatre may have cheated them! Mrs. Rawlins may have deceived Mr. Mauleverer. Anything must be true rather than——No, no! such a tissue of deception is impossible in a man of such sentiments! Persecuted as he has been, shall appearances make me—me, his only friend—turn against him? Oh, me? here come the whole posse purring upstairs to take off their things! I shall be invaded in a moment."

And in came Grace and the two younger ladies, and Rachel was no more her own from that moment.

CHAPTER IV.

THE FORLORN HOPE.

" She whipped two female 'prentices to death,
    And hid them in the coal-hole.   For her mind
    Shaped strictest plans of discipline, sage schemes,
    Such as Lycurgus taught."—*Canning and Frere.*

THE favourite dentist of the neighbourhood dwelt in a grand
mansion at St. Norbert's, and thither were conducted Conrade
and Francis, as victims to the symmetry of their mouths.
Their mother accompanied them to supply the element of
tenderness, Alison that of firmness ; and, in fact, Lady
Temple was in a state of much greater trepidation than either
of her sons, who had been promised five shillings each as the
reward of fortitude, and did nothing but discuss what they
should buy with it.

They escaped with a reprieve to Conrade, and the loss of
one tooth of Francis's, and when the rewards had been laid
out, and presents chosen for all the stay-at-home children,
including Rose, Lady Temple became able to think about
other matters.   The whole party were in a little den at the
pastrycook's ; the boys consuming mutton pies, and the ladies
ox-tail soup, while waiting to be taken up by the waggonette
which had of late been added to the Myrtlewood establishment, when the little lady thus spoke—

"If you don't object, Miss Williams, we will go to Rachel's asylum on our way home."

Miss Williams asked if she had made the appointment.

"No," said Lady Temple, "but you see I can't be satisfied about those woodcuts; and that poor woman, Mrs. Kelland, came to me yesterday about my lace shawl, and she is sadly distressed about the little girl. She was not allowed to see her, you know, and she heard such odd things about the place that I told her that I did not wonder she was in trouble, and that I would try to bring the child home, or at any rate see and talk to her."

"I hope we may be able to see her, but you know Colone Keith could not get in without making an appointment."

"I pay for her," said Lady Temple, "and I cannot bear its going on in this way without some one seeing about it. The Colonel was quite sure those woodcuts were mere fabrications to deceive Rachel; and there must be something very wrong about those people."

"Did she know that you were going?"

"No; I did not see her before we went. I do not think she will mind it much; and I promised." Lady Temple faltered a little, but gathered courage the next moment. "And indeed, after what Mrs. Kelland said, I could not sleep while I thought I had been the means of putting any poor child into such hands."

"Yes," said Alison, "it is very shocking to leave them there without inquiry, and it is an excellent thing to make the attempt."

And so the order was given to drive to the asylum, Alison marvelling at the courage which prompted this most unexpected assault upon the fortress that had repulsed two such warriors as Colonel Keith and Mrs. Kelland. But timid and tender as she might be, it was not for nothing that Fanny Temple had been a vice-queen, so much accustomed to be welcomed wherever she penetrated, that the notion of a rebuff never suggested itself.

Coombe rang, and his lady made him let herself and Miss Williams out, so that she was on the step when the rough charwoman opened the door, and made the usual reply that Mr. Mauleverer was not within. Lady Temple answered that it was Mrs. Rawlins, the matron, that she wished to see, and with more audacity than Alison thought her capable of, inserted herself within the doorway, so as to prevent herself from being shut out as the girl took her message. The next moment the girl came back saying, " This way, ma'am, opened the door of a small dreary, dusty, cold parlour, where she shut them in, and disappeared before a word could be said.

There they remained so long, that in spite of such encouragement as could be derived from peeping over the blinds at Coombe standing sentinel over his two young masters at the carriage window, Lady Temple began to feel some dismay, though no repentance, and with anxious iteration conjured Miss Williams to guess what could be the cause of delay.

" Making ready for our reception," was Alison's answer in various forms ; and Lady Temple repeated by turns, " I do not like it," and " it is very unsatisfactory. No, I don't like it at all," the *at all* always growing more emphatic.

The climax was, " Things must be very sad, or they would never take so much preparation. I'll tell you, Miss Williams," she added in a low confidential tone ; " there are two of us, and the woman cannot be in two places at once. Now, if you go up and see the rooms and all, which I saw long ago, I could stay and talk to the poor children."

Alison was the more surprised at the simple statecraft of the General's widow, but it was prompted by the pitiful heart yearning over the mysterious wrongs of the poor little ones.

At last Mrs. Rawlins sailed in, crape, streamers, and all, with the lowest of curtsies and fullest of apologies for having detained her Ladyship, but she had been sending out in pursuit of Mr. Mauleverer, he would be so disappointed ! Lady Temple begged to see the children, and especially Lovedy, whom she said she should like to take home for a holiday.

" Why, my lady, you see Mr. Mauleverer is very particular. I hardly know that I could answer it to him to have one of his little darlings out of his sight.   It unsettles a child so to be going home, and Lovedy has a bad cold, my lady, and I am afraid it will run through the house.   My little Alice is beginning of it."

However, Lady Temple kept to her desire of seeing Lovedy, and of letting her companion see the rest of the establishment, and they were at last ushered into the room already known to the visitors of the F. U. E. E., where the two children sat as usual in white pinafores, but it struck the ladies that all looked ill, and Lovedy was wrapped in a shawl, and sat cowering in a dull, stupified way, unlike the bright responsive manner for which she had been noted even in her lace-school days.   Mary Morris gazed for a moment at Alison with a wistful appealing glance ; then, with a start as of fright, put on a sullen stolid look, and kept her eyes on her book.   The little Alice, looking very heavy and feverish, leant against her, and Mrs. Rawlins went on talking of the colds, the gruel she had made, and her care for her pupils' ailments, and Lady Temple listened so graciously that Alison feared she was succumbing to the palaver ; and by way of reminder, asked to see the dormitory.

" Oh, yes, ma'am, certainly, though we are rather in confusion," and she tried to make both ladies precede her, but Lady Temple, for once assuming the uncomprehending nonchalance of a fine lady, seated herself languidly and motioned Alison on. The matron was evidently perplexed, she looked daggers at the children, or Ailie fancied so, but she was forced to follow the governess. Lady Temple breathed more freely, and rose. " My poor child," she said to Lovedy, " you seem very poorly. Have you any message to your aunt ? "

" Please, please !" began Lovedy, with a hoarse sob.

" Lovedy, don't, don't be a bad girl, or you know——" interposed the little one, in a warning whisper.

" She is not naughty," said Lady Temple gently, " only not well."

" Please, my lady, look," eagerly, though with a fugitive action of terror, Lovedy cried, unpinning the thin coarse shawl on her neck, and revealing the terrible stripes and weals of recent beating, such as nearly sickened Lady Temple.

" Oh, Lovedy," entreated Alice, " she'll take the big stick."

" She could not do her work," interposed Mary with furtive eagerness, " she is so poorly, and Missus said she would have the twenty sprigs if she sat up all night."

" Sprigs !"

" Yes, ma'am, we makes lace more than ever we did to home, day and night ; and if we don't she takes the stick."

"Oh, Mary," implored the child, "she said if you said one word."

"Mary," said Lady Temple, trembling all over, "where are your bonnets?"

"We haven't none, ma'am," returned Mary, "she pawned them. But, oh, ma'am, please take us away. We are used dreadful bad, and no one knows it."

Lady Temple took Lovedy in one hand, and Mary in the other; then looked at the other little girl, who stood as petrified. She handed the pair to the astonished Coomb bidding him put them into the carriage, and let Mast Temple go outside, and then faced about to defend the rear, her rustling black silk and velvet filling up the passage, just as Alison and the matron were coming down stairs. "Mrs. Rawlins," she said, in her gentle dignity, "I think Lovedy is so poorly that she ought to go home to her aunt to be nursed, and I have taken little Mary that she may not be left behind alone. Please to tell Mr. Mauleverer that I take it all upon myself. The other little girl is not at all to blame, and I hope you will take care of her, for she looks very ill."

So much for being a Governor's widow! A woman of thrice Fanny's energy and capacity would not have effected her purpose so simply, and made the virago in the matron so entirely quail. She swept forth with such a consciousness of power and ease that few could have had assurance enough to gainsay her, but no sooner was she in the carriage than she seized Mary's hand, exclaiming, "My poor, poor little dear! Francis, dear boy, the wicked people have been beating her! Oh, Miss Williams, look at her poor neck!"

Alison lifting Lovedy on her knee, glanced under the shawl, and saw indeed a sad spectacle, and she felt such a sharpness of bone as proved that there was far from being the proper amount of clothing or of flesh to protect them. Lady Temple looked at Mary's attenuated hand, and fairly sobbed, "Oh, you have been cruelly treated!"

"Please don't let her get us," cried the frightened Mary.

"Never, never, my dear. We are taking you home to your mother."

Mary Morris was the spokeswoman, and volunteered the exhibition of bruises rather older, but no less severe than those of her companion. All had been inflicted by the woman; Mr. Mauleverer had seldom or never been seen by the children, except Alice, who used often to be called into Mrs. Rawlins's parlour when he was there to be played with and petted. A charwoman was occasionally called in, but otherwise the entire work of the house was exacted from the two girls, and they had been besides kept perpetually to their lace pillows, and severely beaten if they failed in the required amount of work; the ample wardrobe with which their patronesses had provided them had been gradually taken from them; and their fare had latterly become exceedingly coarse, and very scanty. It was a sad story, and this last clause evoked from Francis's pocket a large currant bun, which Mary devoured with a famished appetite, but Lovedy held her portion untasted in her hand, and presently gave it to Mary, saying that her throat was so bad that she could not make use of anything. She had already been wrapped in Lady Temple's cloak, and Francis was desired to watch for a chemist's shop that something might be done for her relief, but the region of shops was already left behind, and even the villas were becoming scantier, so that nothing was to be done but to drive on, obtaining from time to time further doleful narratives from Mary, and perceiving more and more how ill and suffering was the other poor child.

Moreover, Lady Temple's mind became extremely uneasy as to the manner in which Rachel might accept her exploit. All her valour departed as she figured to herself that young lady discrediting the alarm, and resenting her interference. She did not repent, she knew she could not have helped it, and she had rather have been tortured by Rachel than have left the victims another hour to the F. U. E. E., but she was full of nervous anxiety, little as she yet guessed at the full price of her courage ; and she uttered more than once the fervent wish that the Colonel had been there, for he would have known what to do. And Alison each time replied, " I wish it with all my heart ! "

Wrought up at last to the pitch of nervousness that must rush on the crisis at once, and take the bull by the horns, this valiant piece of cowardice declared that she could not even return the girls to their homes till Rachel knew all about it, and gave the word to drive to the Homestead, further cheered by the recollection that Colonel Keith would probably be there, having been asked to luncheon, as he could not dine out, to meet Mr. Grey. Moreover, Mr. Grey was a magistrate and would know what was to be done.

Thus the whole party at the Homestead were assembled near the door, when, discerning them too late to avoid them, Lady Temple's equipage drew up in the peculiarly ungraceful fashion of waggonettes, when they prepare to shoot their passengers out behind.

Conrade, the only person who had the advantage of a previous view, stood up on the box, and before making his descent, shouted out, " Oh, Aunt Rachel, your F. U.

thing is as bad as the Sepoys. But we have saved the two little girls that they were whipping to death, and have got them in the carriage."

While this announcement was being delivered, Alison Williams, the nearest to the door, had emerged. She lifted out the little muffled figure of Lovedy, set her on her feet, and then looking neither to the right nor left, as if she saw and thought of no one else, made but one bound towards Colonel Keith, clasped both hands round his arm, turned him away from the rest, and with her black brows drawn close together, gasped under her breath, " O, Colin, Colin, it is Maria Hatherton."

" What ! the matron ? "

" Yes, the woman that has used these poor children like a savage. O, Colin, it is frightful."

" You should sit down, you are almost ready to faint."

" Nothing ! nothing ! But the poor girls are in such a state. And that Maria whom we taught, and——" Alison stopped.

" Did she know you ? "

" I can't tell. Perhaps ; but I did not know her till the last moment."

" I have long believed that the man that Rose recognised was Mauleverer, but I thought the uncertainty would be bad for Ermine. What is all this ? "

" You will hear. There ! Listen, I can't tell you ; Lady Temple did it all," said Alison, trying to draw away her arm from him, and to assume the staid governess. But he felt her trembling, and did not release her from his support as they turned back to the astonished group, to which, while these few words were passing, Francis, the little bareheaded white

aproned Mary Morris, and lastly Lady Temple, had by this
time been added; and Fanny, with quick but courteous
acknowledgment of all, was singling out her cousin.

"Oh, Rachel, dear, I did not mean it to have been so
sudden or before them all, but indeed I could not help it,"
she said in her gentle, imploring voice; "if you only saw
that poor dear child's neck."

Rachel had little choice what she should say or do. What
Fanny was saying tenderly and privately, the two boys were
communicating open-mouthed, and Mrs. Curtis came at once
with her nervous, "What is it, my dear; is it something very
sad? Those poor children look very cold, and half starved."

"Indeed," said Fanny, "they have been starved, and
beaten, and cruelly used. I am very sorry, Rachel, but indeed that was a dreadful woman, and I thought Colonel Keith
and Mr. Grey would tell us what ought to be done."

"Mr. Grey!" and Mrs. Curtis turned round eagerly, with
the comfort of having some one to support her, "will you
tell us what is to be done? Here has poor dear Rachel
been taken in by this wicked scheme, and these poor——"

"Mother, mother," muttered Rachel, lashed up to des-
peration; "please not out here, before the servants and
every one."

This appeal and Grace's opening of the door had the effect
of directing every one into the hall, Mr. Grey asking Mrs.
Curtis by the way, "Eh? Then this is Rachel's new female
asylum, is it?"

"Yes, I always feared there was something odd about it.
I never liked that man, and now—— Fanny, my love, what
is the matter?"

In a few simple words Fanny answered that she had contrived to be left alone with the children, and had then found signs of such shocking ill-treatment of them, that she had thought it right to bring them away at once."

"And you will commit those wretches. You will send them to prison at once, Mr. Grey. They have been deceiving my poor Rachel ever so long, and getting sums upon sums of money out of her," said Mrs. Curtis, becoming quite blood-thirsty.

" If there is sufficient occasion I will summon the persons concerned to the Bench on Wednesday," said Mr. Grey, a practical, active squire.

" Not till Wednesday !" said Mrs. Curtis, as if she thought the course of justice very tardy. But the remembrance of Mr. Curtis's magisterial days came to her aid, and she continued, " but you can take all the examinations here at once, you know ; and Grace can find you a summons paper, if you will just go into the study."

" It might save the having the children over to-morrow, certainly," said Mr. Grey, and he was inducted almost passively into the leathern chair before the library table, where Mr. Curtis had been wont to administer justice, and Grace was diving deep into a bureau for the printed forms long treasured there, her mother directing her, though Mr. Grey vainly protested that any foolscap would do as well. It was a curious scene. Mrs. Grey with her daughters had the discretion to remove themselves ; but every one else was in a state of excitement, and pressed into the room, the two boys disputing under their breath whether the civilians called it a court martial, and, with some confusion between mutineers and Englishwomen, hoping the woman would be blown from the mouth of a cannon, for hadn't she gone and worn a cap

like mamma's? They would have referred the question to
Miss Williams, but she had been deposited by the Colonel
on one of the chairs in the furthest corner of the room, and
he stood sheltering her agitation and watching the proceedings. Lady Temple still held a hand of each of her rescued
victims, as if she feared they were still in danger, and all the
time Rachel stood and looked like a statue, unable to collect
her convictions in the hubbub, and the trust, that would have
enabled her to defy all this, swept away from her by the
morning's transactions. Yet still there was a hope that appearances might be delusive, and an habitual low estimate of
Mr. Grey's powers that made her set on looking with her
own eyes, not with his.

His first question was about the children's names and
their friends, and this led to the despatching of a message
to the mother and aunt. He then inquired about the terms
on which they had been placed at St. Norbert's, and Rachel,
who was obliged to reply, felt under his clear, stringent questions, keeping close to the point, a good deal more respect for
his powers than she had hitherto entertained. That dry way
of his was rather overwhelming. When it came to the children themselves, Rachel watched, not without a hope that
the clear masculine intellect would detect Fanny in a mere
frightened woman's fancy, and bring the F. U. E. E. off with
flying colours.

Little Mary Morris stood forth valiant and excited. She
was eleven years old, and intelligent enough to make it
evident that she knew what she was about. The replies
were full. The blows were described, with terrible detail
of the occasions and implements. Still Rachel remembered
the accusation of Mary's truth. She tried to doubt.

"I saw her with a bruised eye," said the Colonel's un-expected voice in a pause. "How was that?"

"Please, sir, Mrs. Rawlins hit me with her fist because I had only done seven sprigs. She knocked me down, and I did not come to for ever so long."

And not only this, and the like sad narratives, but each child bore the marks in corroboration of the words, which were more reluctant and more hoarse from Lovedy, but even more effective. Rachel doubted no more after the piteous sight of those scarred shoulders, and the pinched feeble face; but one thing was plain, namely, that Mr. Mauleverer had no share in the cruelties. Even such severities as had been per-petrated while he was in the house, had, Mary thought, been protested against by him; but she had seldom seen him; he paid all his visits in the little parlour, and took no notice of the children except to prepare the tableau for public in-spection. Mr. Grey, looking at his notes, said that there was full evidence to justify issuing a summons against the woman for assaulting the children, and proceeded to ask her name. Then while there was a question whether her christian name was known, the Colonel again said, "I believe her name to be Maria Hatherton. Miss Williams has recognised her as a servant who once lived in her family, and who came from her father's parish at Beauchamp."

Alison on inquiry corroborated the statement, and the charge was made against Maria Rawlins, *alias* Hatherton. The depositions were read over to the children, and signed by them; with very trembling fingers by poor little Lovedy, and Mr. Grey said he would send a policeman with the summons early next day.

"But, Mr. Grey," burst out Mrs. Curtis, "you don't mean

that you are not going to do anything to that man ! Why
he has been worse than the woman ! It was he that
entrapped the poor children, and my poor Rachel here, with
his stories of magazines and illustrations, and I don't know
what all !"

" Very true, Mrs. Curtis," said the magistrate, " but where's
the charge against him ?"

It may be conceived how pleasant it was to the clever
woman of the family to hear her mother declaiming on the
arts by which she had been duped by this adventurer,
appealing continually to Grace and Fanny, and sometimes to
herself, and all before Mr. Grey, on whose old-world prejudices
she had bestowed much more antagonism than he had thought
it worth while to bestow on her new lights. Yet, at the
moment, this operation of being written down an ass, was
less acutely painful to her than the perception that was
simultaneously growing on her of the miserable condition of
poor little Lovedy, whose burning hand she held, and whose
gasping breath she heard, as the child rested feebly in the
chair in which she had been placed. Rachel had nothing
vindictive or selfish in her mood, and her longing was, above
all, to get away, and minister to the poor child's present
sufferings ; but she found herself hemmed in, and pinned
down by the investigation pushed on by her mother, in-
volving answers and explanations that she alone could make.

Mr. Grey rubbed his forehead, and looked freshly annoyed
at each revelation of the state of things. It had not been
Mauleverer, but Rachel, who had asked subscriptions for the
education of the children, he had but acted as her servant ;
the counterfeit of the woodcuts, which Lady Temple suggested,
could not be construed into an offence ; and it looked very

much as if, thanks to his cleverness, and Rachel's incaution, there was really no case to be made out against him, as if the fox had carried off the bait without even leaving his brush behind him. Sooth to say, the failure was a relief to Rachel; she had thrown so much of her will and entire self into the upholding him, that she could not yet detach herself or sympathize with those gentle souls, the mother and Fanny, in keenly hunting him down. Might he not have been as much deceived in Mrs. Rawlins as herself? At any rate she hoped for time to face the subject, and kneeling on the ground so as to support little Lovedy's sinking head on her shoulder, made the briefest replies in her power when referred to. At last, Grace recollected the morning's affair of Mrs. Rossitur's bills. Mr. Grey looked as if he saw daylight, Grace volunteered to fetch both the account-book and Mrs. Rossitur, and Rachel found the statement being extracted from her of the monthly production of the bills, with the entries in the book, and of her having given the money for their payment. Mr. Grey began to write, and she perceived that he was taking down her deposition. She beckoned Mary to support her poor little companion, and rising to her feet, said, to the horror and consternation of her mother, " Mr. Grey, pray let me speak to you!"

He rose at once, and followed her to the hall, where he looked prepared to be kind but firm.

" Must this be done to-day?" she said.

" Why not?" he answered.

" I want time to think about it. The woman has acted like a fiend, and I have not a word to say for her; but I cannot feel that it is fair, after such long and entire trust of this man, to turn on him suddenly without notice."

" Do you mean that you will not prosecute ?" said **Mr.** Grey, with a dozen notes of interjection in his voice.

" I have not said so.   I want time to make up my mind, and to hear what he has to say for himself."

" You will hear that at the Bench on Wednesday."

" It will not be the same thing."

" I should hope not ! "

" You see," said Rachel, perplexed and grievously wanting time to rally her forces, " I cannot but feel that I have trusted too easily, and perhaps been to blame myself for my implicit confidence, and after that it revolts me to throw the whole blame on another."

" If you have been a simpleton, does that make him an honest man ?" said Mr. Grey, impatiently.

" No," said Rachel, " but——"

" What ?"

" My credulity may have caused his dishonesty," she said, bringing, at last, the words to serve the idea.

" Look you here, Rachel," said Mr. Grey, constraining himself to argue patiently with his old friend's daughter ; " it does not simply lie between you and him—a silly girl who has let herself be taken in by a sharper.   That would be no more than giving a sixpence to a fellow that tells me he lost his arm at Sebastopol when he has got it sewn up in a bag. But you have been getting subscriptions from all the world, making yourself answerable to them for having these children educated, and then, for want of proper superintendence, or the merest rational precaution, leaving them to this barbarous usage.   I don't want to be hard upon you, but you are accountable for all this ; you have made yourself so ; and unless you wish to be regarded as a sharer in the iniquity, the least you can do by way of compensation, is not to make yourself an obstruction to the course of justice."

" I don't much care how I am regarded," said Rachel, with subdued tone and sunken head; "I only want to do right, and not act spitefully and vindictively before he has had warning to defend himself."

" Or to set off to delude as many equal foo—mistaken people as he can find elsewhere ? Eh, Rachel ? Don't you see, if this *friend* of yours be innocent, a summons will not hurt him, it will only give him the opportunity of clearing himself."

" Yes, I see," owned Rachel, and overpowered, though far from satisfied, she allowed herself to be brought back, and did what was required of her, to the intense relief of her mother. During her three minutes' conference no one in the study had ventured on speaking or stirring, and Mrs. Curtis would not thank her biographer for recording the wild alarms that careered through her brain, as to the object of her daughter's tête-à-tête with the magistrate.

It was over at last, and the hall of justice broke up. Mary Morris was at once in her mother's arms, and in a few minutes more making up for all past privations by a substantial meal in the kitchen. But Mrs. Kelland had gone to Avoncester to se thread, and only her daughter Susan had come up, the girl who was supposed to be a sort of spider, with no capacities beyond her web. Nor did Rachel think Lovedy capable of walking down to Mackarel Lane, nor well enough for the comfortless chairs and the third part of a bed. No, Mr. Grey's words that Rachel was accountable for the children's sufferings had gone to her heart. Pity was there and indignation, but these had brought such an anguish of

self-accusation as she could only appease by lavishing personal
care upon the chief sufferer. She carried the child to her
own sitting-room and made a couch for her before the fire,
sending Susan away with the assurance that Lovedy should
stay at the Homestead, and be nursed and fed till she was
well and strong again. Fanny, who had accompanied her,
thought the child very ill, and was urgent that the doctor
should be sent for ; but between Rachel and the faculty of
Avonmouth there was a deadly feud, and the proposal was
scouted.   Hunger and a bad cold were easily treated, and
maybe there was a spark of consolation in having a patient
all to herself and her homœopathic book.

So Fanny and her two boys walked down the hill together
in the dark.   Colonel Keith and Alison Williams had already
taken the same road, anxiously discussing the future.   Alison
asked why Colin had not given Mauleverer's alias.   " I had
no proof," he said.   " You were sure of the woman, but so
far it is only guess work with him ; though each time Rose
spoke of seeing Maddox coincided with one of Mauleverer's
visits.   Besides, Alison, on the back of that etching in
Rose's book is written, ' Mrs. Williams, from her humble
and obliged servant, R. Maddox.' "

" And you said nothing about it ? "

" No, I wished to make myself secure, and to see my way
before speaking out."

" What shall you do ?   Can you trust to Rose's identifying
him ? "

" I shall ride in to-morrow to see what is going on, and
judge if it will be well to let her see this man, if he have not
gone off, as I should fear was only too likely.   Poor little
Lady Temple, her exploit has precipitated matters."

" And you will let every one, Dr. Long and all, know what a wretch they have believed. And then——"

" Stay, Alison, I am afraid they will not take Maddox's subsequent guilt as a proof of Edward's innocence."

" It is a proof that his stories were not worth credit."

" To you and me it is, who do not need such proof. It is possible that among his papers something may be found that may implicate him and clear Edward, but we can only hold off and watch. And I greatly fear both man and woman will have slipped through our fingers, especially if she knew you."

" Poor Maria, who could have thought of such frightful barbarity ? " sighed Alison. " I knew she was a passionate girl, but this is worse than one can bear to believe."

She ceased, for she had been inexpressibly shocked, and her heart still yearned towards every Beauchamp school child.

" I suppose we must tell Ermine," she added ; " indeed, I know I could not help it."

" Nor I," he said, smiling, " though there is only too much fear that nothing will come of it but disappointment. At least, she will tell us how to meet that."

CHAPTER V.

THE BREWST SHE BREWED.

"Unwisely, not ignobly, have I given."
Timon of Athens.

UNDER the circumstances of the Curtis family, no greater
penance could have been devised than the solemn dinner
party which had to take place only an hour after the investigation was closed. Grace in especial was nearly distracted
between her desire to calm her mother and to comfort her
sister, and the necessity of attending to the Grey family, who
repaid themselves for their absence from the scene of action
by a torrent of condolences and questions, whence poor
Grace gathered to her horror and consternation that the
neighbourhood already believed that a tenderer sentiment
than philanthropy had begun to mingle in Rachel's relations
with the secretary of the F. U. E. E. Feeling it incumbent
on the whole family to be as lively and indifferent as possible,
Grace, having shut her friends into their rooms to perform
their toilette, hurried to her sister, to find her so entirely
engrossed with her patient as absolutely to have forgotten the
dinner party. No wonder ! She had had to hunt up a
housemaid to make up a bed for Lovedy in a little room
within her own, and the undressing and bathing of the poor
child had revealed injuries even in a more painful state than
those which had been shown to Mr. Grey, shocking emacia-

tion, and most scanty garments. The child was almost torpid, and spoke very little. She was most unwilling to attempt to swallow; however, Rachel thought that some of her globules had gone down, and put much faith in them, and in warmth and sleep; but incessantly occupied, and absolutely sickened by the sight of the child's hurts, she looked up with loathing at Grace's entreaty that she would dress for the dinner.

"Impossible," she said.

"You must, Rachel dear; indeed, you must."

"As if I could leave *her*."

"Nay, Rachel, but if you would only send——"

"Nonsense, Grace; if I can stay with her I can restore her far better than could an allopathist, who would not leave nature to herself. O Grace, why can't you leave me in peace? Is it not bad enough without this?"

"Dear Rachel, I am very sorry; but if you did not come down to dinner, think of the talk it would make."

"Let them talk."

"Ah, Rachel, but the mother! Think how dreadful the day's work has been to her; and how can she ever get through the evening if she is in a fright at your not coming down?"

"Dinner parties are one of the most barbarous institutions of past stupidity," said Rachel, and Grace was reassured. She hovered over Rachel while Rachel hovered over the sick child, and between her own exertions and those of two maids, had put her sister into an evening dress by the time the first carriage arrived. She then rushed to her own room, made her own toilette, and returned to find Rachel in conference with Mrs. Kelland, who had come home at last, and

was to sit with her niece during the dinner. Perhaps it was
as well for all parties that this first interview was cut very
short, but Rachel's burning cheeks did not promise much for
the impression of ease and indifference she was to make, as
Grace's whispered reminders of "the mother's" distress
dragged her down stairs among the all too curious glances of
the assembled party.

All had been bustle. Not one moment for recollection had
yet been Rachel's. Mr. Grey's words, "Accountable for all,"
throbbed in her ears and echoed in her brain—the purple
bruises, the red stripes, verging upon sores, were before her
eyes, and the lights, the flowers, the people and their greetings, were like a dizzy mist. The space before dinner was
happily but brief, and then, as last lady, she came in as a
supernumerary on the other arm of Grace's cavalier, and taking
the only vacant chair, found herself between a squire and
Captain Keith, who had duly been bestowed on Emily Grey.

Here there was a moment's interval of quiet, for the squire
was slightly deaf, and, moreover, regarded her as a little pert
girl, not to be encouraged, while Captain Keith was resigned
to the implied homage of the adorer of his cross ; so that,
though the buzz of talk and the clatter of knives and forks
roared louder than it had ever seemed to do since she had
been a child, listening from the outside, the immediate sense
of hurry and confusion, and the impossibility of seeing or
hearing anything plainly, began to diminish. She could not
think, but she began to wonder whether any one knew what
had happened ; and, above all, she perfectly dreaded the
quiet sting of her neighbour's word and eye, in this consummation of his victory. If he glanced at her, she knew she
could not bear it ; and if he never spoke to her at all,

it would be marked reprehension, which would be far better than sarcasm. He was evidently conscious of her presence; for when, in her insatiable thirst, she had drained her own supply of water, she found the little bottle quietly exchanged for that before him. It was far on in the dinner before Emily's attention was claimed by the gentleman on her other hand, and then there was a space of silence before Captain Keith almost made Rachel start, by saying—

"This has come about far more painfully than could have been expected."

"I thought you would have triumphed," she said.

"No, indeed. I feel accountable for the introduction that my sister brought upon you."

"It was no fault of hers," said Rachel, sadly.

"I wish I could feel it so."

"That was a mere chance. The rest was my own doing."

"Aided and abetted by more than one looker-on."

"No. It is I who am accountable," she said, repeating Mr. Grey's words.

"You accept the whole?"

It was his usual, cool, dry tone; but as she replied, "I must," she involuntarily looked up, with a glance of entreaty to be spared, and she met those dark, grey, heavy-lidded eyes fixed on her with so much concern as almost to unnerve her.

"You cannot," he answered; "every bystander must rue the apathy that let you be so cruelly deceived, for want of exertion on their part."

"Nay," she said; "you tried to open my eyes. I think this would have come worse, but for this morning's stroke."

"Thank you," he said, earnestly.

"I daresay you know more than I have been able to understand," she presently added ; "it is like being in the middle of an explosion, without knowing what stands or falls."

"And lobster salad as an aggravation !" said he, as the dish successively persecuted them. "This dinner is hard on you."

"Very ; but my mother would have been unhappy if I had stayed away. It is the leaving the poor child that grieves me. She is in a fearful state, between sore throat, starvation, and blows."

The picture of the effect of the blows coming before Rachel at that moment, perilled her ability even to sit through the dinner ; but her companion saw the suddening whitening of her cheek, and by a dexterous signal at once caused her glass to be filled. Habit was framing her lips to say something about never drinking wine ; but somehow she felt a certain compulsion in his look, and her compliance restored her. She returned to the subject, saying, "But it was only the woman that was cruel."

"She had not her Sepoy face for nothing."

"Did I hear that Miss Williams knew her ? "

"Yes ; it seems she was a maid who had once been very cruel to little Rose Williams. The Colonel seems to think the discovery may have important consequences. I hardly know how."

This conversation sent Rachel out of the dining-room more like herself than she had entered it ; but she ran upstairs at once to Lovedy, and remained with her till disinterred by the desperate Grace, who could not see three people talking together without blushing with indignation at the construction they were certainly putting on her sister's scarlet cheeks and absence from the drawing-room. With all Grace's efforts, however, she could not bring her truant back before the gentlemen had come in. Captain Keith had seen their entrance, and soon came up to Rachel.

"How is your patient?" he asked.

"She is very ill; and the worst of it is, that it seems such agony to her to attempt to swallow."

"Have you had advice for her?"

"No; I have often treated colds, and I thought this a case, aggravated by that wicked treatment."

"Have you looked into her mouth?"

"Yes; the skin is frightfully brown and dry."

He leant towards her, and asked, in an under tone—

"Did you ever see diphtheria?"

"No!"—her brow contracting—"did you?"

"Yes; we had it through all the children of the regiment at Woolwich."

"You think this is it?"

He asked a few more questions, and his impression was evidently confirmed.

"I must send for Mr. Frampton," said Rachel, homœopathy succumbing to her terror; but then, with a despairing glance, she beheld all the male part of the establishment handing tea.

"Where does he live? I'll send him up."

"Thank you, oh! thank you. The house with the rails, under the east cliff."

He was gone, and Rachel endured the reeling of the lights, and the surges of talk, and the musical performances that seemed to burst the drum of her ear; and, after all, people

went away, saying to each other that there was something
very much amiss, and that poor dear Mrs. Curtis was very
much to blame for not having controlled her daughters.

They departed at last, and Grace, without uttering the
terrible word, was explaining to the worn-out mother that
little Lovedy was more unwell, and that Captain Keith had
kindly offered to fetch the doctor, when the Captain himself
returned.

"I am sorry to say that Mr. Frampton is out, not likely
to be at home till morning, and his partner is with a bad accident at Avonford. The best plan will be for me to ride
back to Avoncester, and send out Macvicar, our doctor. He is
a kind-hearted man, of much experience in this kind of thing."

"But you are not going back," said polite Mrs. Curtis, far
from taking in the urgency of the case. "You were to sleep
at Colonel Keith's. I could not think of your taking the
trouble."

"I have settled that with the Colonel, thank you. My
dog-cart will be here directly."

"I can only say, thank you," said Rachel, earnestly.
"But is there nothing to be done in the meantime? Do
you know the treatment?"

He knew enough to give a few directions, which revealed
to poor Mrs. Curtis the character of the disease.

"That horrible new sore throat! Oh, Rachel, and you
have been hanging over her all this time!"

"Indeed," said Alick Keith, coming to her. "I think
you need not be alarmed. The complaint seems to me to
depend on the air and locality. I have been often with
people who had it."

"And not caught it?"

" No ; though one poor little fellow, our piper's son, would not try to take food from any one else, and died at last on my knee. I do not believe it is infectious in that way."

And hearing his carriage at the door, he shook hands, and hurried off, Mrs. Curtis observing—

" He really is a very good young man. But oh, Rachel, my dear, how could you bring her here ?"

" I did not know, mother. Any way it is better than her being in Mrs. Kelland's hive of children."

" You are not going back to her, Rachel, I entreat !"

" Mother, I must. You heard what Captain Keith said. Let that comfort you. It would be brutal cruelty and cowardice to stay away from her to-night. Good night, Grace, make mother see that it must be so."

She went, for poor Mrs. Curtis could not withstand her ; and only turned with tearful eyes to her elder daughter to say, " You do not go into the room again Grace, I insist."

Grace could not bear to leave Rachel to the misery of such a vigil, and greatly reproached herself for the hurry that had prevented her from paying any heed to the condition of the chiid in her anxiety to make her sister presentable ; but Mrs. Curtis was in a state of agitation that demanded all the care and tenderness of this " mother's child," and the sharing her room and bed made it impossible to elude the watchfulness that nervously guarded the remaining daughter.

It was eleven o'clock when Alexander Keith drove from the door. It was a moonlight night, and he was sure to spare no speed, but he could hardly be at Avoncester within an hour and a half, and the doctor would take at least two in coming out. Mrs. Kelland was the companion of Rachel's

watch. The woman was a good deal subdued. The strange-
ness of the great house tamed her, and she was shocked and
frightened by the little girl's state as well as by the young
lady's grave, awe-struck, and silent manner.

They tried all that Captain Keith had suggested, but the
child was too weak and spent to inhale the steam of vinegar,
and the attempts to make her swallow produced fruitless
anguish. They could not discover how long it was since she
had taken any nourishment, and they already knew what a
miserable pittance hers had been at the best. Mrs. Kelland
gave her up at once, and protested that she was following her
mother, and that there was death in her face. Rachel made
an imperious gesture of silence, and was obeyed so far as
voice went, but long-drawn sighs and shakes of the head
continued to impress on her the aunt's hopelessness, throughout the endeavours to change the position, the moistening of
the lips, the attempts at relief in answer to the choked effort
to cough, the weary, faint moan, the increasing faintness and
exhaustion.

One o'clock struck, and Mrs. Kelland said, in a low,
ominous voice, "It is the turn of the night, Miss Rachel.
You had best leave her to me."

" I will never leave her," said Rachel impatiently.

" You are a young lady, Miss Rachel, you ain't used to the
like of this."

"Hark !"   Rachel held up her finger.

Wheels were crashing up the hill. The horrible responsibility was over, the immediate terror gone, help seemed to
be coming at the utmost need, and tears of relief rushed into
Rachel's eyes, tears that Lovedy must have perceived, for she
spoke the first articulate words she had uttered since the night-

watch had begun, "Please, ma'am, don't fret, I'm going to poor mother."

"You will be better now, Lovedy, here is the doctor," said Rachel, though conscious that this was not the right thing, and then she hastened out on the stairs to meet the gaunt old Scotsman and bring him in. He made Mrs. Kelland raise the child, examined her mouth, felt her feet and hands, which were fast becoming chill, and desired the warm flannels still to be applied to them.

"Cannot her throat be operated on?" said Rachel, a tremor within her heart. "I think we could both be depended on if you wanted us."

"She is too far gone, poor lassie," was the answer, "it would be mere cruelty to torment her. You had better go and lie down, Miss Curtis; her mother and I can do all she is like to need."

"Is she dying?"

"I doubt if she can last an hour longer. The disease is in an advanced state, and she was in too reduced a state to have battled with it, even had it been met earlier."

"As it should have been! Twice her destroyer!" sighed Rachel, with a bursting heart, and again the kind doctor would have persuaded her to leave the room, but she turned from him and came back to Lovedy, who had been roused by what had been passing, and had been murmuring something which had set her aunt off into sobs.

"She's saying she've been a bad girl to me, poor lamb, and I tell her not to think of it! She knows it was for her good, if she had not been set against her work."

Dr. Macvicar authoritatively hushed the woman, but Lovedy looked up with flushed cheeks, and the blue eyes that had been so often noticed for their beauty. The last flush of fever had come to finish the work.

"Don't fret," she said, "there's no one to beat me up there! Please, the verse about the tears."

Dr. Macvicar and the child both looked towards Rachel, but her whole memory seemed scared away, and it was the old Scotch army surgeon that repeated—

"'The Lord God shall wipe off tears from all eyes.' Ah! poor little one, you are going from a world that has been full of woe to you."

"Oh, forgive me, forgive me, my poor child," said Rachel, kneeling by her, the tears streaming down silently.

"Please, ma'am, don't cry," said the little girl feebly; "you were very good to me. Please tell me of my Saviour," she added to Rachel. It sounded like set phraseology, and she knew not how to begin; but Dr. Macvicar's answer made the lightened look come back, and the child was again heard to whisper—"Ah! I knew they scourged Him—for me."

This was the last they did hear, except the sobbing breaths, ever more convulsive. Rachel had never before been present with death, and awe and dismay seemed to paralyse her whole frame. Even the words of hope and prayer for which the child's eyes craved from both her fellow-watchers seemed to her a strange tongue, inefficient to reach the misery of this untimely mortal agony, this work of neglect and cruelty— and she the cause.

Three o'clock had struck before the last painful gasp had been drawn, and Mrs. Kelland's sobbing cry broke forth. Dr. Macvicar told Rachel that the child was at rest. She shivered from head to foot, her teeth chattered, and she murmured, "Accountable for all."

Dr. Macvicar at once made her swallow some of the cordial brought for the poor child, and then summoning the maid whom Grace had stationed in the outer room, he desired her to put her young mistress to bed without loss of time. The sole remaining desire of which she was conscious was to be alone and in the dark, and she passively submitted.

CHAPTER VI.

THE SARACEN'S HEAD.

" Alas, he thought, how changed that mien,
  How changed those timid looks have been,
  Since years of guilt and of disguise
  Have steeled her brow and armed her eyes."
                                        Marmion.

" ARE you sleepy, Rose ?   What a yawn !"

" Not sleepy, Aunt Ailie ; only it is such a tiresome long day when the Colonel does not come in."

" Take care, Rosie ; I don't know what we shall be good for at this rate."

" We ?   O Aunt Ermine, then you think it tiresome too. I know you do ——"

" What's that, Rose ?"

" It is ! it is !   I'll open the door for him."

The next moment Rose led her Colonel in triumph into the lamp-light.   There was a bright light in his eye, and yet he looked pale, grave, and worn ; and Ermine's first observation was—

" How came Tibbie to let you out at this time of night ?"

" I have not ventured to encounter Tibbie at all.   I drove up to your door."

" You have been at St. Norbert's all this time," exclaimed Alison.

" Do you think no one can carry on a campaign at St.

Norbert's but yourself and your generalissima, Miss Ailie?"
he said, stroking down Rose's brown hair.

"Then, if you have not gone home, you have had nothing
to eat, and that is the reason you look so tired," said
Ermine.

"Yes; I had some luncheon at the Abbey."

"Then, at any rate, you shall have some tea. Rosie, run
and fetch the little kettle."

"And *the* Beauchamp cup and saucer," added Rose,
proudly producing the single relic of a well-remembered set
of olden times. "And please, please, Aunt Ermine, let me
sit up to make it for him. I have not seen him all day, you
know; and it is the first time he ever drank tea in our house,
except make-believe with Violetta and Colinette."

"No, Rose. Your aunt says I spoil that child, and I am
going to have my revenge upon you. You must see the wild
beast at his meals another time; for it just happens that I
have a good deal to say to your aunts, and it is not intended
for your ears."

Rose showed no signs of being spoilt, for she only entreated
to be allowed "just to put the tea-things in order," and then,
winking very hard, she said she would go.

"Here, Rose, if you please," said Ermine, clearing the
space of table before her.

"Why, Aunt Ermine, I did not know you could make tea!"

"There are such things as extraordinary occasions, Rose.
Now, good night, my sweet one."

"Good night, my Lady Discretion. We will make up for
it one of these days. Don't stay away, pray, Ailie," as Alison
was following the child. "I have nothing to say till you
come back."

" I know it is good news," said Ermine ; " but it has cost you something, Colin."

Instead of answering, he received his cup from her, filled up her tea-pot, and said—

" How long is it since you poured out tea for me, Ermine ? "

" Thirteen years next June, when you and Harry used to come in from the cricket field, so late and hot that you were ashamed to present yourself in civilized society at the Great House."

" As if nobody from the Parsonage ever came down to look on at the cricket."

" Yes ; being summoned by all the boys to see that nothing would teach a Scotchman cricket."

" Ah ! you have got the last word, for here comes Ailie."

" Of course," said Alison, coming in ; " Ermine has had the pith of the story, so I had better ask at once what it is."

" That the Beauchamp Eleven beat Her Majesty's —th Foot on Midsummer Day, 1846, is the pith of what I have as yet heard," said Ermine.

" And that Beauchamp ladies are every whit as full of mischief as they used to be in those days, is the sum of what I have told," added Colin.

" Yes," said Ermine, " he has most loyally kept his word of reserving all for you.   He has not even said whether Mauleverer is taken."

" My story is grave and sad enough," said Colin, laying aside all his playfulness, and a serious expression coming over his features ; but, at the same time, the landlady's sandy cat, which, like all other animals, was very fond of him, and had established herself on his knee as soon as Rose had left it vacant, was receiving a certain firm, hard, caressing stroking, which resulted in vehement purrs on her part, and was evidently an outlet of suppressed exultation.

" Is he the same ?" asked Alison.

" All in due time ; unless, like Miss Rachel, you wish to tell me my story yourselves. By-the-bye, how is that poor girl to-day ?"

" Thoroughly knocked down. There is a sort of feverish lassitude about her that makes them very anxious. They were hoping to persuade her to see Mr. Frampton when Lady Temple heard last."

" Poor thing ! it has been a sad affair for her. Well, I told you I should go over this morning and see Mr. Grey, and judge if anything could be done. I got to the Abbey at about eleven o'clock, and found the policeman had just come back after serving the summons, with the news that Mauleverer was gone."

" Gone !"

" Clean gone ! Absconded from his lodgings, and left no traces behind him. But, as to the poor woman, the policeman reported that she had been left in terrible distress, with the child extremely ill, and not a penny, not a thing to eat in the house. He came back to ask Mr. Grey what was to be done ; and as the suspicion of diphtheria made every one inclined to fight shy of the house, I thought I had better go down and see what was to be done. I knocked a good while in vain ; but at last she looked out of window, and I told her I only wanted to know what could be done for her child, and would send a doctor. Then she told me how to open the door. Poor thing ! I found her the picture of desolation, in the midst of the dreary kitchen, with the child gasping

on her lap ; all the pretence of widowhood gone, and her
hair hanging loose about her face, which was quite white
with hunger, and her great eyes looked wild, like the glare
of a wild beast's in a den. I spoke to her by her own name,
and she started and trembled, and said, ' Did Miss Alison
tell you ?' I said, ' Yes,' and explained who I was, and she
caught me up half way : ' O yes, yes, my lady's nephew, that
was engaged to Miss Ermine !' And she looked me full
and searchingly in the face, Ermine, when I answered ' Yes.'
Then she almost sobbed, ' And you are true to her ?' and put
her hands over her face in an agony. It was a very strange
examination on one's constancy, and I put an end to it by
asking if she had any friends at home that I could write to
for her ; but she cast that notion from her fiercely, and said
she had no friend, no one. He had left her to her fate,
because the child was too ill to be moved. And indeed the
poor child was in such a state that there was no thinking
of anything else, and I went at once to find a doctor and
a nurse."

" Diphtheria again ?"

" Yes ; and she, poor thing, was in no state to give it the
resolute care that is the only chance. Doctors could be easily
found, but I was at my wit's end for a nurse, till I remembered that Mr. Mitchell had told me of a Sisterhood that
have a Home at St. Norbert's, with a nursing establishment
attached to it. So, in despair, I went there, and begged to
see the Superior, and a most kind and sensible lady I found
her, ready to do anything helpful. She lent me a nice little
Sister, rather young, I thought; but who turned out thoroughly
efficient, nearly as good as a doctor. Still, whether the child
lives is very doubtful, though the mother was full of hope

when I went in last. She insisted that I had saved it, when both she and it had been deserted by Maddox, for whom she had given up everything."

" Then she owned that he was Maddox?"

" She called him so, without my even putting the question to her. She had played his game long enough; and now his desertion has evidently put an end to all her regard for him. It was confusedly and shortly told; the child was in a state that prevented attention being given to anything else; but she knows that she had been made a tool of to ruin her master and you; and the sight of you, Ailie, had evidently stirred up much old affection, and remembrance of better days."

" Is she his wife?"

" No; or the evidence she promises could not be used against him. Do you know this, Ermine?" as he gave her a cover, with a seal upon it.

" The Saracen! the Saracen's head, Colin; it was made with the lost seal-ring!"

" The ring was taken from Edward's dressing-room the night when Rose was frightened with the phosphorus. Maria declares that she did not suspect the theft, or Maddox's purpose, till long after she had left her place. He effected his practices under pretence of attachment to her, and then could not shake her off. She went abroad with him after the settlement of affairs; but he could not keep out of gambling speculation, and lost everything. Then he seems to have larked about, obtaining means she knows not how— as artist, lecturer, and what not—till the notable F. U. E. E. was started. Most likely he would have collected the subscriptions and made off with them, if Rachel Curtis had not

had just sense enough to trust him with nothing without
seeing some result; so that he was forced to set the affair
going with Maria at its head, as the only person who could
co-operate with him. They kept themselves ready for a start
whenever there should be symptoms of a discovery; but, in
the meantime, he gambled away all that he got into his
hands, and never gave her enough to feed the children.
Thus she was absolutely driven to force work from them for
subsistence; and she is a passionate creature, whom jealousy
embittered more and more, so that she became more savage
than she knew. Poor thing! she has her punishment.
Maddox only came home, yesterday, too late for any train
before the mail, and by that time the child was too ill to be
moved. He must have thought it all up with him, and
wished to be rid of both, for they quarrelled, and he left her
to her misery."

"What, gone?"

"Yes; but she told us of his haunts—haunts that he
thought she did not know—a fancy shop, kept by a Mrs.
Dench at Bristol, where, it seems, that he plays the philanthropical lecturer; and probably has been trying to secure
a snug berth for himself unknown, as he thought, to Maria;
but she pried into his letters, and kept a keen watch upon
him. He was to be inquired for there by his Mauleverer
name, and, I have little doubt, will be captured."

"And then?"

"He will be committed for trial at the sessions; and, in
the meantime, I must see Beauchamp and Dr. Long, and
arrange that he should be prosecuted for the forgery, even
though he should slip through our fingers at the sessions."

"Oh, could that be?"

"This Clever Woman has managed matters so sweetly, that they might just as well try her as him for obtaining money on false pretences; and the man seems to have been wonderfully sharp in avoiding committing himself. Mrs. Curtis's man of business has been trying all day to get up the case, but he has made out nothing but a few more debts such as that which turned up yesterday; and it is very doubtful how far a case can be made out against him."

"And then we should lose him."

"That is exactly what I wish to avoid. I want to bring up my forces at once, and have him laid hold of at once for the forgery of those letters of Edward's. How long would it take to hear from Ekaterinburg? I suppose Edward could travel as fast as a letter."

Alison fairly sprang to her feet.

"O, Colin, Colin! you do not think that Edward would be here by the next sessions."

"He ought," said Colin. "I hope to induce Dr. Long and Harry to write him such letters as to bring him home at once."

Self-restrained Alison was fairly overcome. She stretched out both hands, pressed Colin's convulsively, then turned away her face, and, bursting into tears, ran out of the room.

"Poor dear Ailie," said Ermine; "she has suffered terribly. Her heart is full of Edward. Oh, I hope he will come."

"He must. He cannot be so senseless as to stay away."

"There is that unfortunate promise to his wife; and I fear that he is become so much estranged from English ways, that he will hardly care to set himself straight here, after the pain that the universal suspicion gave him."

" He cannot but care. For the sake of all he *must* care," vehemently repeated Colin, with the punctilious honour of the nobly-born soldier. " For his child's sake, this would be enough to bring him from his grave. If he refused to return to the investigation, it would be almost enough to make me doubt him."

" I am glad you said *almost*," said Ermine, trying to smile; but he had absolutely brought tears into her eyes.

" Dear Ermine," he said, gently, " you need not fear my not trusting him to the utmost. I know that he has been too much crushed to revive easily, and that it may not be easy to make him appreciate our hopes from such a distance; but I think such a summons as this must bring him."

" I hope it will," said Ermine. " Otherwise we should not deserve that you should have any more to do with us."

" Ermine, Ermine, do you not know that nothing can make any difference between us ? "

Ermine had collected herself while he spoke.

" I know," she said, " that all you are doing makes me thank and bless you—oh ! more than I can speak."

He looked wistfully at her ; but, tearful as were her eyes, there was a resolution about her face that impressed upon him that she trusted to his promise of recurring no more within the year to the subject so near his heart ; and he could say no more than, " You forgive me, Ermine; you know I trust him as you do."

" I look to your setting him above being only *trusted*," said Ermine, trying to smile. " Oh ! if you knew what this ray of hope is in the dreary darkness that has lasted so long ! "

Therewith he was obliged to leave her, and she only saw

him for a few minutes in the morning, when he hurried in
to take leave, since, if matters went right at the magistrates'
bench, he intended to proceed at once to make such representations in person to Mr. Beauchamp and Dr. Long, as might
induce them to send an urgent recall to Edward in time for
the spring sessions, and for this no time must be lost.
Ermine remained then alone with Rose, feeling the day
strangely long and lonely, and that, perhaps, its flatness
might be a preparation for the extinction of all the bright
ness that had of late come into her life. Colin had said he
would trust as she did, but those words had made her aware
that she *must* trust as he did. If he, with his clear sense
and kindly insight into Edward's character, became convinced that his absence proceeded from anything worse than
the mere fainthearted indifference that would not wipe off a
blot, then Ermine felt that his judgment would carry her own
along with it, and that she should lose her undoubting faith
in her brother's perfect innocence, and in that case her mind
was made up ; Colin might say and do what he would, but
she would never connect him through herself with deserved
disgrace. The parting, after these months of intercourse and
increased knowlege of one another, would be infinitely more
wretched than the first ; but, cost her what it would—her
life perhaps—the break should be made rather than let his
untainted name be linked with one where dishonour justly
rested. But with her constant principle of abstinence from
dwelling on contingencies, she strove to turn away her mind,
and to exert herself ; though this was no easy task, especially
on so solitary a day as this, while Alison was in charge at
Myrtlewood in Lady Temple's absence, and Rachel Curtis
was reported far too ill to leave her room, so that Ermine saw

no one all day except her constant little companion ; nor was it till towards evening that Alison at length made her appearance, bringing a note which Colin had sent home by Lady Temple.

All had so far gone well. Maria Hatherton had been committed to take her trial at the quarter sessions for the assault upon the children ; but, as her own little girl was still living, though in extreme danger, and the Sisters promised to take charge of both for the present, Colonel Keith had thought it only common humanity to offer bail, and this had been accepted. Later in the day, Mauleverer himself had been brought down, having been taken up at a grand meeting of his Bristol friends, who had all rallied round him, expressing strong indignation at the accusation, and offering evidence as to character. He denied any knowledge of the name of Maddox, and declared that he was able to prove that his own account of himself as a popular, philanthropical lecturer was perfectly correct ; and he professed to be much amazed at the charges brought against him, which could only have arisen from some sudden alarm in the young lady's mind, excited by her friends, whom he had always observed to be prejudiced against him. He appealed strongly against the hardship of being imprisoned on so slight a charge ; but, as he could find no one to take his part, he reserved his defence for the quarter sessions, for which he was fully committed. Colin thought, however, that it was so doubtful whether the charges against him could be substantiated, that it was highly necessary to be fully prepared to press the former forgery against him, and had therefore decided upon sleeping at St. Norbert's and going on by an early train to obtain legal advice in London, and then to see Harry Beauchamp. Meantime, Ermine must write to her brother as urgently as possible, backing up Colin's own representations of the necessity of his return.

Ermine read eagerly, but Alison seemed hardly able to command her attention to listen, and scarcely waited for the end of the letter before her own disclosure was made. Francis was sickening with diphtheria ; he had been left behind in the morning on account of some outbreak of peevishness, and Alison, soon becoming convinced that temper was not solely in fault, had kept him apart from. his brothers, and at last had sent for the doctor, who had at once pronounced it to be the same deadly complaint which had already declared itself in Rachel Curtis. Alison had of course devoted herself to the little boy till his mother's return from St. Norbert's, when she had been obliged to give the first intimation of what the price of the loving little widow's exploit might be. " I don't think she realizes the extent of the illness," said Alison ; " say what I would, she would keep on thanking me breathlessly, and only wanting to escape to him. I asked if we should send to let Colin know, and she answered in her dear, unselfish way, 'By no means, it would be safer for him to be out of the way ;' and, besides, she knew how much depended on his going."

" She is right," said Ermine ; " I am thankful that he is out of reach of trying to take a share in the nursing ; it is bad enough to have *one* in the midst !"

" Yes," said Alison. " Lady Temple cannot be left to bear this grievous trouble alone. and when the Homestead cannot help her. Yet, Ermine, what can be done ? Is it safe for you and Rose ?"

" Certainly not safe that you should come backwards and

forwards," said Ermine. " Rose must not be put in danger ;
so, dear, dear Ailie, you had better take your things up, and
only look in on us now and then at the window."

Alison entirely broke down. " Oh, Ermine, Ermine, since
you began to mend, not one night have we been apart ! "

" Silly child," said Ermine, straining her quivering voice
to be cheerful, " I am strong, and Rose is my best little
handmaid."

" I know it is right," said Alison ; " I could not keep
from my boys, and, indeed, now Colin is gone, I do not
think any one at Myrtlewood will have the heart to carry
out the treatment. It will almost kill that dear young
mother to see it. No, they cannot be left ; but oh, Ermine,
it is like choosing between you and them."

" Not at all, it is choosing between right and wrong."

" And Ermine, if—if I should be ill, you must not think
of coming near me. Rose must not be left alone."

" There is no use in talking of such things," said Ermine,
resolutely ; " let us think of what must be thought of, not
of what is in the only Wise Hands. What has been done
about the other children ? "

" I have kept them away from the first ; I am afraid for
none of them but Conrade."

" It would be the wisest way to send them, nurses and
all, to Gowanbrae."

" Wise, but cool," said Alison.

" I will settle that," returned Ermine. " Tibbie shall
come and invite them, and you must make Lady Temple
consent."

The sisters durst not embrace, but gazed at one another,
feeling that it might be their last look, their hearts swelling

with unspoken prayer, but their features so restrained that neither might unnerve the other. Then it was that Alison, for the first time, felt absolute relief in the knowledge, once so bitter, that she had ceased to be the whole world to her sister. And Ermine, for one moment, felt as if it would be a way out of all troubles and perplexities if the two sisters could die together, and leave little Rose to be moulded by Colin to be all he wished ; but she resolutely put aside the future, and roused herself to send a few words in pencil, requesting Tibbie to step in and speak to her.

That worthy personage had fully adopted her, and entering, tall and stately, in her evening black silk and white apron, began by professing her anxiety to be any assistance in her power, saying, "she'd be won'erfu' proud to serve Miss Williams, while her sister was sae thrang waitin' on her young scholar in his sair trouble."

Ermine thanked her, and rejoiced that the Colonel was out of harm's way.

"'Deed, aye, ma'am, he's weel awa'. He has sic a wark wi' thae laddies an' their bit bairn o' a mither, I'll no say he'd been easy keepit out o' the thick o' the distress, an' it's may be no surprisin', after a' that's come and gane, that he seeks to take siccan a lift of the concern. I've mony a time heard tell that the auld General, Sir Stephen, was as good as a faither to him, when he was sick an' lonesome, puir lad, in yon far awa' land o' wild beasts an' savages."

"Would it not be what he might like, to take in the children out of the way of infection ?"

"'Deed, Miss Ermine," with a significant curtsey, "I'm thinkin' ye ken my maister Colin amaist as weel as I do. He's the true son of his forbears, an' Gowanbrae used to be

always open in the auld lord's time, that's his grandfather.
Foreby, that he owes so much kindness to the General."

Ermine further suggested that it was a pity to wait for a
letter from the Colonel, and Tibbie quite agreed. She "liked
the nurse as an extraordinar' douce woman, not like the fine
English madams that Miss Isabel—that's Mrs. Comyn Menteith—put about her bairns; and as to room, the sergeant
and the tailor bodie did not need much, and the masons were
only busy in the front parlour."

"Masons?" asked Ermine.

"Ou, aye? didna ye ken it's for the new room, that is to
be built out frae the further parlour, and what they ca' the
bay to the drawin'-room, just to mak' the house more conformable like wi' his name and forbears. I never thocht but
that ye'd surely seen the plans and a', Miss Ermine; an' if
so be it was Maister Colin's pleasure the thing suld be private,
I'm real vext to hae said a word; but ye'll may be no let on
to him, ma'am, that ye ken onything about it."

"Those down-stairs rooms so silently begun," thought
Ermine. "How fixed his intention must be? Oh, how will
it end? What would be best for him? And how can I
think of myself, while all, even my Ailie, are in distress and
danger?"

Ermine had, however, a good deal to think of; for not
only had she Colin's daily letter to answer, but she had
Conrade, Leoline, and Hubert with her for several hours
every day, and could not help being amused by Rose's ways
with them, little grown-up lady as she was compared to
them. Luckily girls were such uncommon beings with them
as to be rather courted than despised; and Rose, having
nothing of the tom-boy, did not forfeit the privileges of her

sex. She did not think they compensated for her Colonel's absence, and never durst introduce Violetta to them ; but she enjoyed and profited by the contact with childhood, and was a very nice little comforter to Conrade when he was taken with a fit of anxiety for the brother whom he missed every moment.

Quarantine weighed, however, most heavily upon poor Grace Curtis. Rachel had from the first insisted that she should be kept out of her room ; and the mother's piteous entreaty always implied that saddest argument, " Why should I be deprived of you both in one day ?" So Grace found herself condemned to uselessness almost as complete as Ermine's. She could only answer notes, respond to inquiries, without even venturing far enough from the house to see Ermine, or take out the Temple children for a walk. For indeed Rachel's state was extremely critical.

The feverish misery that succeeded Lovedy's death had been utterly crushing, the one load of self-accusation had prostrated her, but with a restlessness of agony, that kept her writhing as it were in her wretchedness ; and then came the gradual increase of physical suffering, bearing in upon her that she had caught the fatal disorder. To her sense of justice, and her desire to wreak vengeance on herself, the notion might be grateful ; but the instinct of self-preservation was far stronger. She could not die. The world here, the world to come, were all too dark, too confused, to enable her to bear such a doom. She saw her peril in her mother's face ; in the reiterated visits of the medical man, whom she no longer spurned; in the calling in of the Avoncester physician ; in the introduction of a professional nurse, and the strong and agonizing measures to which she had to submit,

every time with the sensation that the suffering could
not possibly be greater without exceeding the powers of
endurance.

Then arose the thought that with weakness she should
lose all chance of expressing a wish, and, obtaining pencil
and paper, she began to write a charge to her mother and
sister to provide for Mary Morris; but in the midst there
came over her the remembrance of the papers that she had
placed in Mauleverer's hands—the title-deeds of the Burnaby
Bargain; an estate that perhaps ought to be bringing in as
much as half the rental of the property. It must be made
good to the poor. If the title-deeds had been sold to any
one who could claim the property, what would be the consequence? She felt herself in a mist of ignorance and perplexity; dreading the consequences, yet feeling as if her own
removal might leave her fortune free to make up for them.
She tried to scrawl an explanation; but mind and fingers
were alike unequal to the task, and she desisted just as fresh
torture began at the doctor's hands—torture from which they
sent her mother away, and that left her exhausted, and
despairing of holding out through a repetition.

And then—and then! "Tell me of my Saviour," the
dying child had said; and the drawn face had lightened at
the words to which Rachel's oracles declared that people
attached crude or arbitrary meanings; and now she hardly
knew what they conveyed to her, and longed, as for something far away, for the reality of those simple teachings—
once realities, now all by rote! Saved by faith! What was
faith? Could all depend on a last sensation? And as to
her life. Failure, failure through headstrong blindness and
self-will, resulting in the agony of the innocent. Was this

ground of hope? She tried to think of progress and purification beyond the grave ; but this was the most speculative, insecure fabric of all. There was no habit of trust to it—no inward conviction, no outward testimony. And even when the extreme danger subsided, and Francis Temple was known to be better, Rachel found that her sorrow was not yet ended ; for Conrade had been brought home with the symptoms of the complaint—Conrade, the most beloved and loving of Fanny's little ones, the only one who really remembered his father, was in exceeding, almost hopeless, peril, watched day and night by his mother and Miss Williams.

The little Alice, Maria Hatherton's own child, had lingered and struggled long, but all the care and kindness of the good Sisters at St. Norbert's had been unavailing, she had sunk at last, and the mother remained in a dull, silent tearless misery, quietly doing all that was required of her, but never speaking nor giving the ladies any opening to try to make an impression upon her.

Rachel gleaned more intelligence than her mother meant her to obtain, and brooded over it in her weakness and her silence.

Recovery is often more trying than illness, and Rachel suffered greatly. Indeed, she was not sure that she ought to have recovered at all, and perhaps the shock to her nerves and spirits was more serious than the effect of the sharp passing disorder, which had, however, so much weakened her that she succumbed entirely to the blow. " Accountable for all," the words still rang in her ears, and the *all* for which she was accountable continually magnified itself. She had tied a dreadful knot, which Fanny, meek contemned Fanny had cut, but at the cost of grievous suffering and danger to her boys, and too late to prevent that death which continually haunted Rachel; those looks of convulsive agony came before her in all her waking and sleeping intervals. Nothing put them aside, occupation in her weakness only bewildered and distracted her, and even though she was advancing daily towards convalescence, leaving her room, and being again restored to her sister, she still continued listless, dejected, cast down, and unable to turn her mind from this one dreary contemplation. Of Fanny and her sons it was hardly possible to think, and one of the strange perturbations of the mind in illness caused her to dwell far less on them than on the minor misery of the fate of the title-deeds of the Burnaby Bargain, which she had put into Mauleverer's hand. She fancied their falling into the hands of some speculator, who, if he did not break the mother's heart by putting up a gasometer, would certainly wring it by building hideous cottages, or desirable marine residences. The value would be enhanced so as to be equal to more than half that of the Homestead, the poor would have been cheated of it, and what compensation could be made? Give up all her own share? Nay, she had nothing absolutely her own while her mother lived, only 5,000l. was settled on her if she married, and she tortured herself with devising plans that she knew to be impracticable, of stripping herself, and going forth to suffer the poverty she merited. Yes, but how would she have lived. Not like the Williamses! She had tried teaching like the one, and writing like the other, but had failed in both. The Clever Woman had no marketable or available talent. She knew very well that nothing would induce her mother and sister to let her despoil herself, but to have injured them would be even more intolerable; and more than all was the sickening uncertainty, whether any harm had been done, or what would be its extent.

Ignorant of such subjects at the best, her brain was devoid of force even to reason out her own conjectures, or to decide what must be impossible. She felt compelled to keep all to herself; to alarm her mother was out of the question, when Mrs. Curtis was distressed and shaken enough already, and to have told Grace would only have brought her soothing promises of sharing the burthen—exactly what she did not want—and would have led to the fact being known to the family man of business, Mr. Cox, the very last person to whom Rachel wished to confess the proceeding. It was not so much the humiliation of owning to him such a fatal act of piracy upon his province, as because she believed him to have been the cause that the poor had all this time been cheated of the full value of the estate. He had complacently consulted the welfare of the Curtis family, by charging them with the rent of the fields as ordinary grass land, and it had never dawned on him that it would be only just to increase the rent. Rachel had found him an antagonist to every scheme she had hatched, ever since she was fifteen years old ; her mother obeyed him with implicit faith, and it was certain that if the question were once in his hands, he would regard it as his duty to save the Curtis funds, and let the charity sink or swim. And he was the only person out of the house whom Rachel had seen.

As soon as—or rather before—she could bear it, the first day that her presence was supposed not to be perilous to others, she was obliged to have an interview with him, to enable him to prepare the case for the quarter sessions. Nothing could be much worse for her nerves and spirits,

but even the mother was absolutely convinced of the necessity, and Rachel was forced to tax her enfeebled powers to
enable her to give accurate details of her relations with
Mauleverer, and enable him to judge of the form of the
indictment. Once or twice she almost sunk back from the
exceeding distastefulness of the task, but she found herself
urged on, and when she even asked what would happen if
she were not well enough to appear, she was gravely told
that she *must* be—it would be very serious if she did not
make a great effort, and even her mother shook her head,
looked unhappy, but confirmed the admonition. A little
revenge or hatred would have been a great help to her, but
she could not feel them as impulses. If it had been the
woman, she could have gladly aided in visiting such cruelty
upon her, but this had not been directly chargeable upon
Mauleverer ; and though Rachel felt acutely that he had
bitterly abused her confidence, she drooped too much to feel
the spirit of retort. The notion of being confronted with
him before all the world at Avoncester, and being made to
bring about his punishment, was simply dreadful to her, but
when she murmured some word of this to her mother, Mrs.
Curtis fairly started, and said quite fiercely, " My dear, don't
let me hear you say any such thing. He is a very wicked
man, and you ought to be glad to have him punished ! "

She really spoke as if she had been rebuking some infringe-
ment of decorum, and Rachel was quite startled. She asked
Grace why the mother was so bent on making her vindictive,
but Grace only answered that every one must be very much
shocked, and turned away the subject.

Prudent Grace ! Her whole soul was in a tumult of wrath
and shame at what she knew to be the county gossip, but

she was aware that Rachel's total ignorance of it was the only chance of her so comporting herself in court as to silence the rumour, and she and her mother were resolutely discreet.

Mrs. Curtis, between nursing, anxiety, and worry, looked lamentably knocked up, and at last Grace and Rachel prevailed on her to take a drive, leaving Rachel on a sofa in her sitting-room, to what was no small luxury to her just at present—that of being miserable alone—without meeting any one's anxious eyes, or knowing that her listlessness was wounding the mother's heart. Yet the privilege only resulted in a fresh preturbation about the title-deeds, and longing to consult some one who could advise and sympathize. Ermine Williams would have understood and made her Colonel give help, but Ermine seemed as unattainable as Nova Zembla, and she only heard that the Colonel was absent. Her head was aching with the weary load of doubt, and she tried to cheat her woe by a restless movement to the windows. She saw Captain Keith riding to the door. It suddenly darted into her mind that here was one who could and would help her. He could see Mauleverer and ascertain what had become of the deeds ; he could guess at the amount of danger ! She could not forget his kindness on the night of Lovedy's illness, or the gentleness of his manner about the woodcuts, and with a sudden impulse she rang the bell and desired that Captain Keith might be shown in. She was still standing leaning on the table when he entered.

" This is very good in you," he said ; " I met your mother and sister on my way up, and they asked me to leave word of Conrade being better, but they did not tell me I should see you."

"Conrade is better?" said Rachel, sitting down, unable to stand longer.

"Yes, his throat is better. Miss Williams's firmness saved him. They think him quite out of danger."

"Thank Heaven! Oh, I could never have seen his mother again! Oh, she has been the heroine!"

"In the truest sense of the word," he answered. And Rachel looked up with one moment's brightening at the old allusion, but her oppression was too great for cheerfulness, and she answered—

"Dear Fanny, yes, she will be a rebuke to me for ever! But," she added, before he had time to inquire for her health, "I wanted—I wanted to beg you to do me a service. You were so kind the other night."

His reply was to lean earnestly forward, awaiting her words, and she told him briefly of her grievous perplexity about the title-deeds.

"Then," he said, "you would wish for me to see the man and ascertain how he has disposed of them."

"I should be most grateful!"

"I will do my utmost. Perhaps I may not succeed immediately, as I believe visitors are not admitted every day, and he is said to be busy preparing his defence, but I will try, and let you know."

"Thanks, thanks! The doubt is terrible, for I know worry about it would distract my mother."

"I do not imagine," he said, "that much worse consequences than worry could ensue. But there are none more trying."

"Oh not *none!*"

"Do not let worry about this increase other ills," he said,

kindly; "do not think about this again till you hear from me."

"Is that possible?"

"I should not have thought so, if I had not watched my uncle cast off troubles about his eye-sight and the keeping his living."

"Ah! but those were not of his own making."

"'There is a sparkle even in the darkest water.' That was a saying of his," said Alick, looking anxiously at her pale cheek and down-cast eye.

"Not when they are turbid."

"They will clear," he said, and smiled with a look of encouraging hope that again cheered her in spite of herself. "Meantime remember that in any way I can help you, it will be the greatest favour——" he checked himself as he observed the exceeding langour and lassitude apparent in her whole person, and only said, "My sister is too much at the bottom of it for me not to feel it the greatest kindness to me to let me try to be of the slightest use. I believe I had better go now," as he rose and looked at her wistfully; "you are too much tired to talk."

"I believe I am," she said, almost reluctantly; "but thank you, this has done me good."

"And you are really getting better?"

"Yes, I believe so. Perhaps I may feel it when this terrible day is over."

What a comfort it would be, she said to herself, when he was gone, if we had but a near relation like him, who would act for the mother, instead of our being delivered up, bound hand and foot, to Mr. Cox. It would have been refreshing to have kept him now, if I could have done it without talking; it really seemed to keep the horrible thoughts in abeyance, to hear that wonderfully gentle tone! And how kind and soft the look was! I do feel stronger for it! Will it really be better after next week? Alas! that will have undone nothing.

Yet even this perception of a possibility of hope that there would be relief after the ordeal, was new to Rachel; and it soon gave way to that trying feature of illness, the insurmountable dread of the mere physical fatigue. The Dean of Avoncester, a kind old friend of Mrs. Curtis, had insisted on the mother and daughters coming to sleep at the Deanery, on the Tuesday night, and remaining till the day after the trial; but Rachel's imagination was not even as yet equal to the endurance of the long drive, far less of the formality of a visit. Lady Temple was likewise asked to the Deanery, but Conrade was still too ill for her to think of leaving him for more than the few needful hours of the trial; nor had Alison been able to do more than pay an occasional visit at her sister's window to exchange reports, and so absorbed was she in her boys and their mother, that it was quite an effort of recollection to keep up to Ermine s accounts of Colonel Keith's doings.

It was on the Monday afternoon, the first time she had ventured into the room, taking advantage of Rose having condescended to go out with the Temple nursery establishment, when she found Ermine's transparent face all alive with expectation. "He may come any time now," she said; "his coming to-day or to-morrow was to depend on his getting his business done on Saturday or not."

And in a few minutes' time the well-known knock was heard, and Ermine, with a look half arch half gay, surprised her sister by rising with the aid of the arm of her chair, and adjusting a crutch that had been leaning against it.

" Why Ermine ! you could not bear the jarring of that crutch——"

" Five or six years ago, Ailie, when I was a much poorer creature ;" then as the door opened, " I would make you a curtsey, Colonel Keith, but I am afraid I can't quite do that," though still she moved nearer to meet him, but perhaps there was a look of helplessness which made her exultation piteous, for he responded with an exclamation of alarm, put out his arm to support her, and did not relax a frown of anxiety till he had placed her safe in her chair again, while she laughed perhaps a little less freely, and said, " See what it is to have had to shift for oneself !"

" You met me with your eyes the first time, Ermine, and I never missed anything."

" Well, I think it is hard not to have been more congratulated on my great achievement! I thought I should have had at least as much credit as Widdrington, my favourite hero and model."

" When you have an arm to support you it may be all very well, and I shall never stand it without." Then, as Ermine subsided, unprepared with a reply, " Well, Ailie, how are your boys ?"

" Both much better, Francis nearly well."

" You have had a terrible time !   And their mother !"

" Dearer and sweeter than ever," said Alison, with her voice trembling; " no one who has not seen her now can guess half what she is !"

" I hope she has not missed me. If this matter had not been so pressing, I could not have stayed away."

" The one message she always gave me was, that you were not to think of coming home ; and, indeed, those dear boys were so good, that we managed very well without you."

" Yes, I had faith in your discipline, and I think that matters are in train against Edward comes. Of course there is no letter, or you would have told me."

" He will be coming himself," said Ermine, resolved against again expressing a doubt ; while Alison added that he hated letter-writing.

" Nothing could be more satisfactory than Beauchamp's letter," added Colin. " He was so thoroughly convinced, that he immediately began to believe that he had trusted Edward all along, and had only been overruled."

" I dare say," said Ermine, laughing ; " I can quite fancy honest Harry completely persuaded that he was Edward's champion, while Maddox was turning him round his finger."

" And such is his good faith, that I hope he will make Edward believe the same ! I told you of his sending his love to you, and of his hopes that you would some day come and see the old place. He made his wife quite cordial."

Alison did not feel herself obliged to accept the message, and Ermine could freely say, " Poor Harry ! I should like to see him again ! He would be exactly the same, I dare say. And how does the old place look ?"

" Just what I do not want you to see. They have found out that the Rectory is unhealthy, and stuck up a new bald house on the top of the hill and the Hall is new furnished in colours that set one's teeth on edge.   Nothing is like itself but Harry, and he only when you get him off duty—without his wife! I was glad to get away to Belfast."

" And there, judging from Julia's letter, they must have nearly devoured you."

" They were very hospitable. Your sister is not so very unlike you, Ermine?"

" Oh, Colin!" exclaimed Alison, with an indignation of which she became ashamed, and added, by way of making it better, " Perhaps not so very."

"She was very gracious to me," said Colin, smiling, "and we had much pleasant talk of you."

" Yes," said Ermine, " it will be a great pleasure to poor Julia to be allowed to take us up again, and you thought the doctor sufficiently convinced."

" More satisfactorily so than Harry, for he reasoned out the matter, and seems to me to have gone more by his impression that a man *could* not be so imprudent as Edward in good faith than by Maddox's representation."

" That is true," said Alison, " he held out till Edward refused to come home, and then nothing would make him listen to a word on his behalf."

" And it will be so again," thought Ermine, with a throb at her heart. Then she asked, " Did you see whether there was a letter for you at home?"

" Yes, I looked in, and found only this, which I have only glanced at, from Bessie."

" From Paris?"

" Yes, they come home immediately after Easter. ' Your brother is resolved I should be presented, and submit to the whole season in style; after which he says I may judge for myself.' What people will do for pretty young wives ! Poor Mary's most brilliant season was a winter at Edinburgh ; And it must be his doing more than hers, for she goes on : ' Is it not very hard to be precluded all this time from playing the chieftainess in the halls of my forefathers ? I shall have to run down to your Gowanbrae to refresh myself, and see what you are all about, for I cannot get the fragment of a letter from Alick ; and I met an Avon-cestrian the other day, who told me that the whole county was in a state of excitement about the F. U. etc.; that every one believed that the fascinating landscape-painter was on the high road to winning one of the joint-heiresses ; but that Lady Temple—the most incredible part of the story—had blown up the whole affair, made her way into the penetralia of the asylum, and rescued two female 'prentices, so nearly whipped to death that it took an infinitesimal quantity of Rachel's homœopathy to demolish one entirely, and that the virtuous public was highly indignant that there was no inquest nor trial for manslaughter ; but that it was certain that Rachel had been extremely ill ever since. Poor Rachel, there must be some grain of truth in all this ; but one would like to be able to contradict it. I wrote to ask Alick the rights of the story, but he has not vouchsafed me a line of reply ; and I should take it as very kind in you to let me know whether he is in the land of the living or gone to Edinburgh—as I hear is to be the lot of the Highlanders—or pining for the uncroquetable lawn, to which I always told him he had an eye.' "

" She may think herself lucky he has not answered," said Ermine ; " he has always been rather unreasonably angry with her for making the introduction."

"That is the reason he has not," added Alison, "for he is certainly not far off. He has been over almost every day to inquire, and played German tactics all Saturday afternoon with Francis to our great relief. But I have stayed away long enough."

"I will walk back with you, Ailie. I must see the good little heroine of the most incredible part of the story."

Lady Temple looked a good deal paler than when he had last seen her, and her eyelids still showed that they had long arrears of sleep to make up; but she came down with outstretched hands and a sunny smile. "They are so much better, and I am so glad you were not at home in the worst of it."

"And I am sorry to have deserted you."

"Oh, no, no, it was much better that you should be away. We should all have wanted you, and that would have been dangerous; and dear, dear Miss Williams did all that could be done. Do you know, it taught me that you were right when you told me I ought never to rest till the boys learnt to obey, for obedience' sake, at a word. It showed what a bad mother I am; for I am sure if dear Conrade had been like what he was last year, even she could not have saved him," said Fanny, her eyes full of tears.

Then came her details, to which he listened, as ever, like the brotherly friend he was, and there was a good deal said about restoring the little ones, who were still at Gowanbrae, to which he would by no means as yet consent, though Fanny owned herself to have time now to pine for her Stephana, and to "hear how dismal it is to have a silent nursery."

" Yes, it has been a fearful time.   We little guessed how much risk you ran when you went to the rescue."

" Dear Con, when he thought—when we thought he could not get better, said I was not to mind that, and I don't," said Fanny.   " I thought it was right ; and though I did not know this would come of it, yet you see God has been very merciful, and brought both of my boys out of this dreadful illness, and I dare say it will do them good all their lives now it is over.   I am sure it will to me, for I shall always be more thankful."

" Everything does you good," he said.

" And another thing," she added, eagerly, " it has made me know that dear Miss Williams so much better.   She was so good, so wonderfully good, to come away from her sister to us.   I thought she was quite gone the first day, and that I was alone with my poor Francie, and presently there she was by my side, giving me strength and hope by her very look. I want to have her for good ; I want to make her my sister ! She would teach the boys still, for nobody else could make them good ; but if ever her sister could spare her, she must never go away again."

" You had better see what she says," replied the Colonel, with suppressed emotion.

That night, when Conrade and Francis were both fast asleep, their mother and their governess sat over the fire together, languid but happy, and told out their hearts to one another—told out more than Alison had ever put into words even to Ermine, for her heart was softer and more unreserved now than ever it had been since her sister's accident had crushed her youth.   There was thenceforth a bond between her and Lady Temple that gave the young widow the strong-hearted, sympathizing, sisterly friend she had looked for in Rachel, and that filled up those yearnings of the affection that had at first made Alison feel that Colin's return made the world dreary to her. Her life had a purpose, though that purpose was not Ermine! But where were Edward and his letter?

CHAPTER VII.

THE QUARTER SESSIONS.

"Is it so nominated in the bond ?"—*Merchant of Venice.*

MALGRE her disinclination, Rachel had reached the point of recovery in which the fresh air and change of scene of the drive to Avoncester could not fail to act as restoratives, and the first evening with the Dean and his gentle old sister was refreshing and comfortable to her spirits.

It was in the afternoon of the ensuing day that Mr. Grey came to tell her that her presence would soon be required, and both her mother and sister drove to the court with her. Poor Mrs. Curtis, too anxious to go away, yet too nervous to go into court, chose, in spite of all Mr. Grey's advice, to remain in the carriage with the blinds closed, far too miserable for Grace to leave her.

Rachel, though very white, called up a heroic smile, and declared that she should get on very well. Her spirit had risen to the occasion, so as to brace her nerves to go becomingly through what was inevitable ; and she replied with a ready " yes," to Mr. Grey's repetition of the advice for ever dinned into her ears, not to say a word more than needful, feeling indeed little disposed to utter anything that she could avoid.

She emerged from the dark passage into full view of faces

which were far more familiar than she could have wished. She would have greatly preferred appearing before a judge, robed, wigged, and a stranger, to coming thus before a country gentleman, slightly known to herself, but an old friend of her father, and looking only like his ordinary self.

All the world indeed was curious to see the encounter between Rachel Curtis and her impostor, and every one who had contributed so much as a dozen stamps to the F. U. E. E. felt as if under a personal wrong and grievance, while many hoped to detect other elements of excitement, so that though *all* did not overtly stare at the witness, not even the most considerate could resist the impulse to glance at her reception of the bow with which he greeted her entrance.

She bent her head instinctively, but there was no change of colour on her cheek. Her faculties were concentrated, and her resolute will had closed all avenues to sensations that might impair her powers ; she would not give way either to shame and remorse for herself, or to pity or indignation against the prisoner ; she would attend only to the accuracy of the testimony that was required of her as an expiation of her credulous incaution ; but such was the tension of her nerves, that, impassive as she looked, she heard every cough, every rustle of paper ; each voice that addressed her seemed to cut her ears like a knife ; and the chair that was given to her after the administration of the oath was indeed much needed.

She was examined upon her arrangement that the prisoner should provide for the asylum at St. Norbert's, and on her monthly payment to him of the sums entered in the account-book. In some cases she knew he had shown her the bills unreceipted ; in others, he had simply made the charge in

the book, and she had given to him the amount that he
estimated as requisite for the materials for wood-engraving.
So far she felt satisfied that she was making herself distinctly
understood ; but the prisoner, acting as his own counsel, now
turned to her and asked the question she had expected and
was prepared for, whether she could refer to any written
agreement.

"No ; it was a *vivâ voce* agreement."

Could she mention what passed at the time of making the
arrangement that she had stated as existing between himself
and her ?

"I described my plans, and you consented."

An answer at which some of the audience could have
smiled, so well did it accord with her habits. The prisoner
again insisted on her defining the mode of his becoming
bound to the agreement. Rachel took time for consideration ;
and Alison Williams, sitting between Lady Temple and
Colonel Keith, felt dizzy with anxiety for the answer. It
came at last.

"I do not remember the exact words ; but you acquiesced
in the appearance of your name as secretary and treasurer."

The prospectus was here brought forward, and Mauleverer
asked her to define the duties he had been supposed to undertake in the character in which he had there figured. It of
course came out that she had been her own treasurer, only
entrusting the nominal one with the amount required for
current expenses ; and again, in reply to his deferential
questions, she was obliged to acknowledge that he had never
in so many words declared the sums entered in the book to
have been actually paid, and not merely estimates for monthly
expenditure to be paid to the tradesmen at the usual seasons.

"I understood that they were paid," said Rachel, with some resentment.

"Will you oblige me by mentioning on what that understanding was founded?" said the prisoner, blandly.

There was a pause. Rachel knew she must say something; but memory utterly failed to recall any definite assurance that these debts had been discharged. Time passed, all eyes were upon her, there was a dire necessity of reply; and though perfectly conscious of the weakness and folly of her utterance, she could only falter forth, "I thought so." The being the Clever Woman of the family, only rendered her the more sensible both of the utter futility of her answer, and of the effect it must be producing.

Alison hung her head, and frowned in absolute shame and despair, already perceiving how matters must go, and feeling as if the hope of her brother's vindication were slipping away—reft from her by Rachel's folly. Colin gave an indignant sigh, and whispering to her, "Come out when Lady Temple does, I will meet you," he made his way out of court.

There had been a moment's pause after Rachel's "I thought so," and then the chairman spoke to the counsel for the prosecution. "Mr. Murray, can you carry the case any further by other witnesses? At present I see no case to go to the jury. You will see that the witness not only does not set up any case of embezzlement, but rather leads to an inference in the contrary direction."

"No, sir," was the answer; "I am afraid that I can add nothing to the case already presented to you."

Upon this, the chairman said,

"Gentlemen of the Jury,—The case for the prosecution

does not sustain the indictment or require me to call on the
prisoner for his defence, and it is your duty to find him not
guilty. You will observe that we are not trying a civil
action, in respect of the large sum which he has received
from the young lady, and for which he is still accountable
to her; nor by acquitting him are you pronouncing that he
has not shown himself a man of very questionable honesty,
but only that the evidence will not bring him within the
grasp of the criminal law, as guilty of embezzlement under
the statute, and this because of the looseness of the arrangements, that had been implied instead of expressed. It is
exceedingly to be regretted that with the best intentions and
kindest purposes, want of caution and experience on her
part should have enabled the prisoner thus to secure himself
from the possibility of a conviction; but there can be no
doubt that the evidence before us is such as to leave no
alternative but a verdict of not guilty."

The very tenderness and consideration of the grey-haired
Sir Edward Morden's tone were more crushing to Rachel
than severe animadversions on her folly would have been
from a stranger. Here was she, the Clever Woman of the
family, shown in open court to have been so egregious a
dupe that the deceiver could not even be punished, but
must go scot-free, leaving all her wrongs unredressed! To
her excited, morbid apprehension, magnified by past self-
sufficiency, it was as though all eyes were looking in triumph
at that object of general scorn and aversion, a woman who
had stepped out of her place. She turned with a longing
to rush into darkness and retirement when she was called
to return to her mother; and even had she still been present,
little would she have recked that when the jury had, without

many moments' delay, returned a verdict of "Not Guilty," the prisoner received a strong, stern reprimand from Sir Edward, to whom he replied with a bow that had in it more of triumph than of acceptance.

Burning tears of disappointment were upon Alison's cheek, the old hopeless blank was returning, and her brother might come back in vain, to find his enemy beyond his reach. Here was an end alike of his restoration and of Ermine's happiness!

"Oh!" whispered Lady Temple, "is it not horrid? Is nothing to be done to that dreadful man? I always thought people came here to do justice. I shall never like Sir Edward Morden again! But, oh! what can that be? Where is the Colonel?"

It was a loud, frightful roar and yell, a sound of concentrated fury that, once heard, could never be forgotten. It was from the crowd outside, many of them from Avonmouth, and all frantic with indignation at the cruelty that had been perpetrated upon the helpless children. Their groans and execrations were pursuing the prison van, from which Maria Hatherton was at that moment making her exit; and so fearful was the outcry that penetrated the court, that Fanny trembled with recollections of Indian horrors, looked wistfully for her protector the Colonel, and murmured fears that her aunt must have been very much terrified.

At that moment, however, a summons came for Lady Temple, as this was the case in which she was to bear witness. Alison followed, and was no sooner past the spectators, who gladly made way, than she found her arm drawn into Colonel Keith's. "Is he come?" she asked.

" No," was rather signed than spoken. " Oh, Colin !" she sighed, but still there was no reply, only she was dragged on, downstairs and along dark passages, into a room furnished with a table, chairs, pens, ink, and paper, and lighted with gas, which revealed to her not only Mr. Grey, but one who, though eight years had made him stouter, redder, and rougher, had one of the most familiar faces of her youthful days.   Her senses almost reeled with her as he held out his hand, saying heartily, " Well, Ailie, how are you ? and how is Ermine ?   Where can this brother of yours be ? "

" Harry !   Mr. Beauchamp !   You here !" she exclaimed, in the extremity of amazement.

" Here is Colin seeming to think that something may be done towards nailing this scoundrel for the present, so I am come at his call.   We shall have the fellow in a moment." And then, by way of getting rid of embarrassment, he began talking to Mr. Grey about the County Hall, and the room, which Mr. Grey explained to be that of the clerk of the peace, lent for this occasion while the usual justice room was occupied.   Alison heard all as in a dream, and presently Mauleverer entered, as usual spruce, artist-like, and self-possessed, and was accosted by Harry Beauchamp, " Good evening, Mr. Maddox, I am sorry to trouble you."

" I hope there is no misunderstanding, sir," was the reply. " I have not the pleasure of knowing for whom you take me."

Without regarding this reply, however, Mr. Beauchamp requested Mr. Grey to take his deposition, stating his own belief in the identity of the person before him with Richard Maddox, whom he charged with having delivered to him a letter falsely purporting to come from Edward Williams, demanding three hundred pounds, which upon this he had delivered to the accused, to be forwarded to the said Mr. Williams.

Alison's heart beat violently at the ordeal before her of speaking to the genuineness of the letter. She had seen and suspected that to her brother-in-law, but she could not guess whether the flaws in that to Mr. Beauchamp would be equally palpable, and doubt and anxiety made her scarcely able to look at it steadily. To her great relief, however, she was able to detect sufficient variations to justify her assertion that it was not authentic, and she was able to confirm her statement by comparison of the writing with that of a short, indignant denial of all knowledge of the transaction, which Harry Beauchamp had happily preserved, though little regarding it at the time. She also showed the wrong direction, with the name of the place misspelt, according to her own copy of her sister-in-law's address, at the request of Maddox himself, and pointed out that a letter to Ermine from her brother bore the right form. The seal upon that to Mr. Beauchamp she likewise asserted to be the impression of one which her brother had lost more than a year before the date of the letter.

"Indeed, sir," said the accused, turning to Mr. Grey, "this is an exceedingly hard case. Here am I, newly acquitted, after nearly six weeks' imprisonment, on so frivolous a charge that it has been dismissed without my even having occasion to defend myself, or to call my own most respectable witnesses as to character, when another charge is brought forward against me in a name that there has been an unaccountable desire to impose on me. Even if I were the person that this gentleman supposes, there is nothing proved. He may very possibly have received a forged letter, but I

perceive nothing to fix the charge upon the party he calls
Maddox. Let me call in my own witnesses, who had volunteered to come down from Bristol, and you will be convinced
how completely mistaken the gentleman is."

To this Mr. Grey replied that the case against him was not
yet closed, and cautioning him to keep his own witnesses
back ; but he was urgent to be allowed to call them at once,
as it was already late, and they were to go by the six o'clock
train. Mr. Grey consented, and a messenger was sent in
search of them. Mr. Beauchamp looked disturbed. " What
say you to this, Colin ?" he asked, uneasily. " That man's
audacity is enough to stagger one, and I only saw him three
times at the utmost."

" Never fear," said Colin, " delay is all in our favour."

At the same time Colin left them, and with him went some
hope and confidence, leaving all to feel awkward and distressed
during the delay that ensued, the accused expatiating all the
time on the unreasonableness of bringing up an offence committed so many years ago, in the absence of the only witness
who could prove the whole story, insisting, moreover, on his
entire ignorance of the names of either Maddox or Williams.

The sight of his witnesses was almost welcome. They
were a dissenting minister, and a neat, portly, respectable
widow, the owner of a fancy shop, and both knew Mr.
Mauleverer as a popular lecturer upon philanthropical subjects, who came periodically to Bristol, and made himself
very acceptable. Their faith in him was genuine, and he had
even interested them in the F. U. E. E. and the ladies that
patronized it. The widow was tearfully indignant about the
persecution that had been got up against him, and evidently
intended to return with him in triumph, and endow him with

the fancy shop if he would condescend so far. The minister, too, spoke highly of his gifts and graces, but neither of them could carry back their testimony to his character for more than three years.

Mr. Grey looked at his watch, Harry Beauchamp was restless, and Alison felt almost faint with suspense ; but at last the tramp of feet was heard in the passage. Colonel Keith came first, and leaning over Alison's chair, said, " Lady Temple will wait for us at the inn. It will soon be all right."

At that moment a tall figure in mourning entered, attended by a policeman. For the first time, Mauleverer's coolness gave way, though not his readiness, and, turning to Mr. Grey, he exclaimed, " Sir, you do not intend to be misled by the malignity of a person of this description."

" Worse than a murderess ! " gasped the scandalized widow Dench. " Well, I never ! "

Mr. Grey was obliged to be peremptory, in order to obtain silence, and enforce that, let the new witness be what she might, her evidence must be heard.

She had come in with the habitual village curtsey to Mr. Beauchamp, and putting back her veil, disclosed to Alison the piteous sight of the well-remembered features, once so bright with intelligence and innocence, and now sunk and haggard with the worst sorrows of womanhood. Her large glittering eyes did not seem to recognise Alison, but they glared upon Mauleverer with a strange terrible fixedness, as if unable to see any one else. To Alison the sight was inexpressibly painful, and she shrank back, as it were, in dread of meeting the eyes once so responsive to her own.

Mr. Grey asked the woman the name of the person before her, and looking at him with the same fearful steadiness, she

pronounced it to be Richard Maddox, though he had of late
called himself Mauleverer.

The man quailed for a moment, then collecting himself,
said, " I now understand the incredible ingratitude and
malignity that have pointed out against me these hitherto
unaccountable slanders. It is a punishment for insufficient
inquiry into character. But you, sir, in common justice, will
protect me from the aspersions of one who wishes to drag
me down in her justly merited fall.

" Sentenced for three years ! To take *her* examination ! "
muttered Mrs. Dench, and with some difficulty these exclamations were silenced, and Maria Hatherton called on for
her evidence.

Concise, but terrible in its clear brevity, was the story of
the agent tampering with her, the nursemaid, until she had
given him access to the private rooms, where he had turned
over the papers. On the following day, Mr. Williams had
been inquiring for his seal-ring, but she herself had not seen
it again till some months after, when she had left her place,
and was living in lodgings provided for her by Maddox,
when she had found the ring in the drawer of his desk ; her
suspicion had then been first excited by his displeasure at
her proposing to him to return it, thinking it merely there by
accident, and she had afterwards observed him endeavouring
to copy fragments of Mr. Williams's writing. These he had
crushed up and thrown aside, but she had preserved them,
owning that she did not know what might come of them,
and the family had been very kind to her.

The seal and the scraps of paper were here produced by
the policeman who had them in charge. The seal perfectly
coincided with that which had closed the letter to Harry

Beauchamp, and was, moreover, identified by both Alison and Colonel Keith. It was noticeable, too, that one of these fragments was the beginning of a note to Mr. Beauchamp, as " Dear H." and this, though not Edward's most usual style of addressing his friend, was repeated in the demand for the £300.

" Sir," said the accused, " of course I have no intention of intimating that a gentleman like the Honourable Colonel Keith has been in any collusion with this unhappy woman, but it must be obvious to you that his wish to exonerate his friend has induced him to give too easy credence to this person's malignant attempts to fasten upon one whom she might have had reason to regard as a benefactor the odium of the transactions that she acknowledges to have taken place between herself and this Maddox, thereto incited, no doubt, by some resemblance which must be strong, since it has likewise deceived Mr. Beauchamp." ·

Mr. Grey looked perplexed and vexed, and asked Mr. Beauchamp if he could suggest any other person able to identify Maddox. He frowned, said there must have been workmen at the factory, but knew not where they were, looked at Colin Keith, asked Alison if she or her sister had ever seen Maddox, then declared he could lay his hands on no one but Dr. Long at Belfast.

Mauleverer vehemently exclaimed against the injustice of detaining him till a witness could be summoned from that distance. Mr. Grey evidently had his doubts, and began to think of calling in some fresh opinion whether he had sufficient grounds for committal, and Alison's hopes were only sustained by Colin's undaunted looks, when there came a knock at the door, and, as much to the surprise of Alison

as of every one else, there entered an elderly maid-servant,
leading a little girl by the hand, and Colonel Keith going
to meet the latter, said, "Do not be frightened, my dear,
you have only to answer a few questions as plainly and
clearly as you can."

Awed, silent, and dazzled by the sudden gas-light, she
clung to his hand, but evidently distinguished no one else ;
and he placed her close to the magistrate saying, "This is
Mr. Grey, Rose, tell him your name."

And Mr. Grey taking her hand and repeating the question,
the clear little silvery voice answered,

"I am Rose Ermine Williams."

"And how old are you, my dear ?"

"I was eight on the last of June."

"She knows the nature of an oath ?" asked Mr. Grey
of the Colonel.

"Certainly, you can soon satisfy yourself of that."

"My dear," then said Mr. Grey, taking her by the hand
again, and looking into the brown intelligent eyes, "I am
sure you have been well taught. Can you tell me what is
meant by taking an oath before a magistrate ?"

"Yes," said Rose, colour flushing into her face, "it is
calling upon Almighty God to hear one speak the truth."
She spoke so low that she could hardly be heard, and she
looked full of startled fear and distress, turning her face up
to Colonel Keith with a terrified exclamation, "Oh please,
why am I here, what am I to say ?"

He was sorry for her; but her manifest want of preparation was all in favour of the cause, and he soothed her
by saying, "Only answer just what you are asked as clearly
as you can, and Mr. Grey will soon let you go. He knows

you would try any way to speak the truth, but as he is going to examine you as a magistrate, he must ask you to take the oath first."

Rose repeated the oath in her innocent tones, and perhaps their solemnity or the fatherly gentleness of Mr. Grey reassured her, for her voice trembled much less when she answered his next inquiry, who her parents were.

"My mother is dead," she said; "my father is Mr. Williams; he is away at Ekaterinburg."

"Do you remember any time before he was at Ekaterinburg?"

"Oh yes; when we lived at Kensington, and he had the patent glass works."

"Now, turn round and say if there is any one here whom you know?"

Rose, who had hitherto stood facing Mr. Grey, with her back to the rest of the room, obeyed, and at once exclaimed, "Aunt Alison," then suddenly recoiled, and grasped at the Colonel.

"What is it, my dear?"

"It is—it is Mr. Maddox;" and with another gasp of fright, "and Maria! Oh, let me go."

But Mr. Grey put his arm round her, and assured her that no one could harm her, Colonel Keith let his fingers be very hard pinched, and her aunt came nearer, all telling her that she had only to make her answers distinctly; and though still shrinking, she could reply to Mr. Grey's question whom she meant by Mr. Maddox.

"The agent for the glass—my father's agent."

"And who is Maria?"

"She was my nurse."

" When did you last see the person you call Mr. Maddox ? "

" Last time, I was sure of it, was when I was walking on the esplanade at Avoncester with Colonel Keith," said Rose, very anxious to turn aside and render her words inaudible.

" I suppose you can hardly tell when that was ? "

" Yes, it was the day before you went away to Lord Keith's wedding," said Rose, looking to the Colonel.

" Had you seen him before ? "

" Twice when I was out by myself, but it frightened me so that I never looked again."

" Can you give me any guide to the time ? "

She was clear that it had been after Colonel Keith's first stay at Avonmouth, but that was all ; and being asked if she had ever mentioned these meetings, " Only when Colonel Keith saw how frightened I was, and asked me."

" Why were you frightened ? " asked Mr. Grey, on a hint from the Colonel.

" Because I could not quite leave off believing the dreadful things Mr. Maddox and Maria said they would do to me if I told."

" Told what ? "

" About Mr. Maddox coming and walking with Maria when she was out with me," gasped Rose, trying to avert her head, and not comforted by hearing Mr. Grey repeat her words to these tormentors of her infancy.

A little encouragement, however, brought out the story of the phosphoric letters, the lions, and the vision of Maddox growling in the dressing-room. The date of the apparition could hardly be hoped for, but fortunately Rose remembered that it was two days before her mamma's birth-day ; because she had felt it so hard to be eaten up before the fête, and this date tallied with that given by Maria of her admitting her treacherous admirer into the private rooms.

"The young lady may be precocious, no doubt, sir," here said the accused, "but I hardly see why she has been brought here. You can attach no weight to the confused recollections of so young a child, of matters that took place so long ago."

"The question will be what weight the jury will attach to them at the assizes," said Mr. Grey.

"You will permit me to make one inquiry of the young lady, sir. Who told her whom she might expect to see here?"

Mr. Grey repeated the query, and Rose answered, "Nobody; I knew my aunt and the Colonel and Lady Temple were gone in to Avoncester, and Aunt Ermine got a note from the Colonel to say that I was to come in to him with Tibbie in a fly."

"Did you know what you were wanted for?"

"No, I could not think. I only knew they came to get the woman punished for being so cruel to the poor little girls."

"Do you know who that person was?"

"Mrs. Rawlins," was the ready answer.

"I think," said Mr. Grey to the accused, "that you must perceive that, with such coincidence of testimony as I have here, I have no alternative but to commit you for the summer assizes."

Mauleverer murmured something about an action for false imprisonment, but he did not make it clear, and he was evidently greatly crestfallen. He had no doubt hoped to brazen

out his assumed character sufficiently to disconcert Mr.
Beauchamp's faith in his own memory, and though he had
carried on the same game after being confronted with Maria,
it was already becoming desperate. He had not reckoned
upon her deserting his cause even for her own sake, and the
last chance of employing her antecedents to discredit her testimony, had been overthrown by Rose's innocent witness to
their mutual relations, a remembrance which had been burnt
in on her childish memory by the very means taken to secure
her silence. When the depositions were read over, their remarkable and independent accordance was most striking; Mrs.
Dench had already been led away by the minister, in time to
catch her train, just when her sobs of indignation at the
deception were growing too demonstrative, and the policeman
resumed the charge of Maria Hatherton.

Little Rose looked up to her, saying, "Please, Aunt Ailie,
may I speak to her?"

Alison had been sitting restless and perplexed between
impulses of pity and repulsion, and doubts about the etiquette
of the justice room; but her heart yearned over the girl she
had cherished, and she signed permission to Rose, whose
timidity had given way amid excitement and encouragement.

"Please, Maria," she said, "don't be angry with me for
telling; I never did till Colonel Keith asked me, and I could
not help it. Will you kiss me and forgive me as you
used?"

The hard fierce eyes, that had not wept over the child's
coffin, filled with tears.

"Oh, Miss Rose, Miss Rose, do not come near me. Oh, if
I had minded you—and your aunts——" And the pent-up
misery of the life that had fallen lower and lower since the

first step in evil, found its course in a convulsive sob and shriek, so grievous that Alison was thankful for Colin's promptitude in laying hold of Rose, and leading her out of the room before him. Alison felt obliged to follow, yet could not bear to leave Maria to policemen and prison warders.

"Maria, poor Maria, I am so sorry for you, I will try to come and see you——"

But her hand was seized with an imperative, "Ailie, you must come, they are all waiting for you."

How little had she thought her arm would ever be drawn into that arm, so unheeded by both.

"So that is Edward's little girl ! Why, she is the sweetest little clear-headed thing I have seen a long time. She was the saving of us."

"It was well thought of by Colin."

"Colin is a lawyer spoilt—that's a fact. A first-rate get-up of a case !"

"And you think it safe now ?"

"Nothing safer, so Edward turns up. How he can keep away from such a child as that, I can't imagine. Where is she ? Oh, here—" as they came into the porch in fuller light, where the Colonel and Rose waited for them. "Ha, my little Ailie, I must make better friends with you."

"My name is Rose, not Ailie," replied the little girl.

"Oh, aye ! Well, it ought to have been, what d'ye call her—that was a Daniel come to judgment ?"

"Portia," returned Rose ; "but I don't think that is pretty at all."

"And where is Lady Temple ?" anxiously asked Alison. "She must be grieved to be detained so long."

" Oh ! Lady Temple is well provided for," said the Colonel,
" all the magistrates and half the bar are at her feet.   They
say the grace and simplicity of her manner of giving her
evidence were the greatest contrast to poor Rachel's."

" But where is she ? " still persisted Alison.

" At the hotel ; Maria's was the last case of the day, and
she went away directly after it, with such a choice of escorts
that I only just spoke to her."

And at the hotel they found the waggonette at the gate-
way, and Lady Temple in the parlour with Sir Edward
Morden, who, late as it was, would not leave her till he had
seen her with the rest of the party.   She sprang up to meet
them, and was much relieved to hear that Mauleverer was
again secured.   " Otherwise," she said, " it would have been
all my fault for having acted without asking advice.   I hope
I shall never do so again."

She insisted that all should go home together in the
waggonette, and Rose found herself upon Mr. Beauchamp's
knee, serving as usual as a safety valve for the feelings of
her aunt's admirers.   There was no inconstancy on her part,
she would much have preferred falling to the lot of her own
Colonel, but the open carriage drive was rather a risk for him
in the night air ; and though he had undertaken it in the
excitement, he soon found it requisite to muffle himself up,
and speak as little as possible.   Harry Beauchamp talked
enough for both.   He was in high spirits, partly, as Colin
suspected, with the escape from a dull formal home, and
partly with the undoing of a wrong that had rankled in his
conscience more than he had allowed to himself.   Lady
Temple, her heart light at the convalescence of her sons,
was pleased with everything, liked him extremely, and an-

swered gaily ; and Alison enjoyed the resumption of pleasant habits of days gone by. Yet, delightful as it all was, there was a sense of disenchantment : she was marvelling all the time how she could have suffered so much on Harry Beauchamp's account. The rejection of him had weighed like a stone upon her heart, but now it seemed like freedom to have escaped his companionship for a lifetime.

Presently a horse's feet were heard on the road before them ; there was a meeting and a halt, and Alick Keith's voice called out—" How has it gone ?"

" Why, were you not in court ?"

" What ! I go to hear my friends baited ?"

" Where were you then ?"

" At Avonmouth."

" Oh, then you have seen the boys," cried Lady Temple. " How is Conrade ?"

" Quite himself. Up to a prodigious amount of indoor croquet. But how has it gone ?"

" Such a shame !" returned Lady Temple. " They acquitted the dreadful man, and the poor woman, whom he drove to it, has a year's imprisonment and hard labour !"

" Acquitted ! What, is he off ?"

" Oh, no, no ! he is safe, and waiting for the Assizes ; all owing to the Colonel and little Rose."

" He is committed for the former offence," said Colonel Keith ; " the important one."

" That's right ! Good night ! And how," he added, reining back his horse, " did your cousin get through it ?"

" Oh, they were so hard on her !" cried Lady Temple. " I could hardly bring myself to speak to Sir Edward after it ! It was as if he thought it all her fault !"

" Her evidence broke down completely," said Colonel Keith.   " Sir Edward spared her as much as he could ; but the absurdity of her whole conduct was palpable.   I hope she has had a lesson."

Alick's impatient horse flew on with him, and Colin muttered to Alison under his mufflers,—" I never could make out whether that is the coolest or the most sensitive fellow living !"

CHAPTER VIII.

THE AFTER CLAP.

" I have read in the marvellous heart of man,
    That strange and mystic scroll,
That an army of phantoms vast and wan,
    Beleaguer the human soul.

" Encamped beside life's rushing stream,
    In Fancy's misty light,
Gigantic shapes and shadows gleam
    Portentous through the night."
                    The Beleaguered City, LONGFELLOW.

A DINNER party at the Deanery in the sessions week was an
institution, but Rachel, lying on the sofa in a cool room,
had thought herself exempt from it, and was conscious for
the time of but one wish, namely, to be let alone, and to be
able to shut her eyes, without finding the lids, as it were,
lined with tiers of gazing faces, and curious looks turned on
her, and her ears from the echo of the roar of fury that had
dreadfully terrified both her and her mother, and she felt
herself to have merited ! The crush of public censure was
not at the moment so overwhelming as the strange morbid
effect of having been the focus of those many, many glances,
and if she reflected at all, it was with a weary speculating
wonder whether one pair of dark grey eyes had been
among those levelled at her. She thought that if they had,

she could not have missed either their ironical sting, or perchance some kindly gleam of sympathy, such as had sometimes surprised her from under the flaxen lashes.

There she had lain, unmolested and conscious of a certain relief in the exceeding calm; the grey pinnacle of the cathedral, and a few branches of an elm-tree alone meeting her eye through the open window, and the sole sound the cawing of the rooks, whose sailing flight amused and attracted her glance from time to time with dreamy interest. Grace had gone into court to hear Maria Hatherton's trial, and all was still.

The first break was when her mother and Miss Wellwood came in, after having wandered gently together round the warm, walled Deanery garden, comparing notes about their myrtles and geraniums. Then it was that amid all their tender inquiries after her headache, and their administration of afternoon tea, it first broke upon Rachel that they expected her to go down to dinner.

"Pray excuse me," she said imploringly, looking at her mother for support; "indeed, I don't know that I could sit out a dinner! A number of people together make me so dizzy and confused."

"Poor child!" said Miss Wellwood, kindly, but looking to Mrs. Curtis in her turn. "Perhaps, as she has been so ill, the evening might be enough."

"Oh," exclaimed Rachel, "I hope to be in bed before you have finished dinner. Indeed I am not good company for any one."

"Don't say that, my dear;" and Miss Wellwood looked puzzled.

"Indeed, my dear," said Mrs. Curtis, evidently distressed,

"I think the exertion would be good for you, if you could only think so."

"Yes, indeed, said Miss Wellwood, catching at the notion; "it is your mind that needs the distraction, my dear."

"I am distracted enough already," poor Rachel said, putting her hand up. "Indeed, I do not want to be disobliging," she said, interpreting her mother's anxious gestures to mean that she was wanting in civility; "it is very kind in you, Miss Wellwood, but this has been a very trying day, and I am sure I can give no pleasure to anybody, so if I might only be let off."

"It is not so much——" began Miss Wellwood, getting into a puzzle, and starting afresh. "Indeed, my dear, my brother and I could not bear that you should do anything you did not like, only you see it would never do for you to seem to want to shut yourself up."

"I should think all the world must feel as if I ought to be shut up for life," said Rachel, dejectedly.

"Ah! but that is the very thing. If you do not show yourself it will make such a talk."

Rachel had nearly said, "Let them talk;" but though she felt tormented to death, habitual respect to these two gentle, nervous, elderly women made her try to be courteous, and she said, "Indeed, I cannot much care, provided I don't hear them."

"Ah! but you don't know, my dear," said Mrs. Curtis, seeing her friend looked dismayed at this indifference. "Indeed, dear Miss Wellwood, she does not know; we thought it would be so awkward for her in court."

"Know what?" exclaimed Rachel, sitting upright, and

putting down her feet. "What have you been keeping from me ?"

"Only—only, my dear, people will say such things, and nobody could think it that knew you."

"What ?" demanded Rachel.

"Yes," said Mrs. Curtis, perhaps, since her daughter was to have the shock, rather glad to have a witness to the surprise it caused her : "you know people will gossip, and some one has put it about that—that this horrid man was——"

Mrs. Curtis paused, Miss Wellwood was as pink as her cap strings. Rachel grasped the meaning at last. "Oh !" she said, with less reticence than her elders, "there must needs be a spice of flirtation to give piquancy to the mess of gossip ! I don't wonder, there are plenty of people who judge others by themselves, and think that motive must underlie everything ! I wonder who imagines that I am fallen so low ?"

"There, I knew she would take it in that way," said Mrs. Curtis. "And so you understand us, my dear, we could not bear to ask you to do anything so distressing except for your own sake."

"I am far past caring for my own sake," said Rachel, "but for yours and Grace's, mother, I will give as much ocular demonstration as I can, that I am not pining for this hero with a Norman name. I own I should have thought none of the Dean's friends would have needed to be convinced."

"Oh, no ! no ! but——" Miss Wellwood made a great confusion of noes, buts, and my dears, and Mrs. Curtis came to the rescue. "After all, my love, one can't so much wonder ! You have always been very peculiar, you know, and so clever, and you took up this so eagerly. And then the Greys saw you so unwilling to prosecute. And—and I have always allowed you too much liberty—ever since your poor dear papa was taken—and now it has come upon you, my poor child! Oh, I hope dear Fanny will take warning by me," and off went poor Mrs. Curtis into a fit of sobs.

"Mother—mother! this is worse than anything," exclaimed Rachel in an agony, springing to her feet, and flying after sal volatile, but feeling frightfully helpless without Grace, the manager of all Mrs. Curtis's ailments and troubles. Grace would have let her quietly cry it out. Rachel's remedies and incoherent protestations of all being her own fault only made things worse, and perhaps those ten minutes were the most overwhelming of all the griefs that Rachel had brought on herself. However, what with Miss Wellwood's soothing, and her own sense of the becoming, Mrs. Curtis struggled herself into composure again by the time the maid came to dress them for dinner; Rachel all the while longing for Grace's return, not so much for the sake of hearing the verdict, as of knowing whether the mother ought to be allowed to go down to dinner, so shaken did she look; for indeed, besides her distress for her daughter, no small ingredient in her agitation was this recurrence to a stated custom of her husband's magisterial days.

Persuasion was unavailing. At any cost the Curtis family must present an unassailable front to the public eye, and if Mrs. Curtis had forced forward her much tried and suffering daughter, far more would she persist in devoting herself to gaiety and indifference, but her nervousness was exceeding, and betrayed itself in a continual wearying for Grace, without whom neither her own dress nor Rachel's could be arranged to her satisfaction, and she was absolutely incapable of not

worrying Rachel about every fold, every plait, every bow, in a
manner that from any one else would have been unbearable;
but those tears had frightened Rachel into a penitent submission that endured with an absolute semblance of cheerfulness each of these torments. The languor and exhaustion
had been driven away, and feverish excitement had set in,
not so much from the spirit of defiance that the two elder
ladies had expected to excite, as from the having been goaded
into a reckless determination to sustain her part. No matter
for the rest.

It often happened in these parties that the ladies would
come in from the country in reasonable time, while their
lords would be detained much later in court; so when the
cathedral clock had given notice of the half-hour, Mrs. Curtis
began to pick up fan and handkerchief, and prepare to
descend. Rachel suggested there would be no occasion so
to do till Grace's return, since it was plain that no one could
yet be released.

"Yes, my dear, but perhaps—don't you think it might be
remarked as if you chose to keep out of sight?"

"Oh, very well."

Rachel followed her mother down, sustained by one hope,
that Captain Keith would be there. No; the Deanery did
not greatly patronize the barracks; there was not much chance
of any gentleman under forty, except, perhaps, in the evening. And at present the dean himself and one canon were the
entire gentleman element among some dozen ladies. Everybody knew that the cause of delay was the trial of the cruel
matron, and added to the account of Rachel's iniquities their
famished and weary state of expectation, the good Dean
gyrating among the groups, trying to make conversation,

which every one felt too fretful and too hungry to sustain
with spirit. Rachel sat it out, trying to talk whenever she
saw her mother's anxious eyes upon her, but failing in finding
anything to say, and much doubting whether her neighbours
liked talking to her.

At last gentlemen began to appear in twos and threes, and
each made some confidence to the womankind that first
absorbed him, but no one came in Rachel's way, and the
girl beside her became too unfeignedly curious to support even
the semblance of conversation, but listened for scraps of intelligence. Something was flying about respecting " a gentleman
who came down by the train," and something about "Lady
Temple" and "admirable," and the young lady seized the
first opportunity of deserting Rachel, and plunging into the
mêlée. Rachel sat on, sick with suspense, feeling utterly
unable to quit her seat. Still they waited, the whole of the
party were not arrived, and here was the curfew ringing, and
that at the Deanery, which always felt injured if it were seven
o'clock before people were in the dining-room ! Grace must
be upstairs dressing, but to reach her was impossible !

At last Mr. Grey was announced, and he had mercy upon
Rachel ; he came up to her as soon as he could without
making her remarkable, and told her the cause of his delay
had been the necessity of committing Mauleverer upon an
accusation by a relation of Colonel Keith, of very extensive
frauds upon Miss Williams's brother. Rachel's illness and the
caution of the Williamses had prevented her from being fully
aware of the complication of their affairs with her own, and
she became paler and paler, as she listened to the partial explanation, though she was hardly able as yet to understand
it. "The woman ?" she asked.

" Sentenced to a year's imprisonment with hard labour ; and let me tell you, Rachel, you had a most narrow escape there ! If that army doctor had not come in time to see the child alive, they could not have chosen but have an inquest, and no mortal can tell what might have been the decision about your homœopathy. You might have been looking forward to a worse business than this at the next assizes."

Mr. Grey had done his work at last ! The long waiting, the weary constraint, and at last the recurrence of Lovedy's sufferings and her own share in them, entirely overcame her. Mists danced before her eyes, and the very sensation that had been so studiously avoided was produced by her fainting helplessly away in her chair, while Mr. Grey was talking to her.

To be sure it brought deliverance from the multitude, and she awoke in the quiet of her room, upon her bed, in the midst of the despairing compunction of the mother, and the tender cares of Grace, but she was too utterly overdone for even this to be much relief to her ; and downstairs poor Miss Wellwood's one desire was to hinder the spread of the report that her swoon had been caused by the tidings of Mauleverer's apprehension. It seemed as if nothing else had been wanting to make the humiliation and exposure complete. Rachel had despised fainting ladies, and had really hitherto been so superabundant in strength that she had no experience of the symptoms, or she might have escaped in time. But there she lay, publicly censured before the dignitaries of her county for moral folly, and entirely conquered before the rest of the world by the physical weakness she had most contemned.

Then the mother was so terrified and distressed that all sorts of comforting reassurances were required, and the chief

object soon became to persuade her to go downstairs and leave
Rachel to her bed. And at last the thought of civility and
of the many Mrs. Grundys prevailed, and sent her downstairs,
but there was little more comfort for Rachel even in being
left to herself—that for which she had a few minutes before
most ardently longed.

That night was perhaps the most painful one of her whole
life. The earnest desire to keep her mother from uneasiness,
and the longing to be unmolested, made her play her part
well when the mother and Grace came up to see her before
going to bed, and they thought she would sleep off her over-
fatigue and excitement, and yielded to her desire that they
should bid her good night, and leave her to rest.

But what sort of rest was it ? Sometimes even her own
personal identity was gone, and she would live over again in
the poor children, the hunger and the blows, or she would
become Mrs. Rawlins, and hear herself sentenced for the
savage cruelty, or she would actually stand in court under
sentence for manslaughter. Her pulses throbbed up to fever
pitch, head and cheeks burnt, the very power to lie still was
gone, and whether she commanded her thoughts or lapsed into
the land of dreams, they worked her equal woe.

Now it was the world of gazing faces, feverishly magnified,
multiplied, and pressing closer and closer on her, till she could
have screamed to dispel them ; now it was her mother weeping
over the reports to which she had given occasion, and ac-
cusing herself of her daughter's errors ; and now it was
Lovedy Kelland's mortal agony ; now the mob, thirsting for
vengeance, were shouting for justice on her, as the child's
murderer, and she was shrieking to Alick Keith to leave her
to her fate, and only save her mother.

It would hardly be too much to say that the positive wretchedness of actually witnessing the child's death was doubled in these its imaginary repetitions on that still more suffering night of waking dreams, when every solemn note of the cathedral clock, every resolute proclamation from its fellow in the town hall, every sharp reply from the domestic timepiece in the Deanery fell on her ears, generally recalling her at least to full consciousness of her identity and whereabouts, and dispelling the delusion.

But, then, what comfort was there? Veritably she had caused suffering and death; she had led to the peril of Fanny's children; she had covered her mother with shame and grief! Nay, in her exaggerated tone of feeling, she imagined that distress and poverty might have been entailed on that beloved mother. Those title-deeds—no intelligence. Captain Keith had taken no notice. Perhaps he heard and believed those degrading reports! He had soul enough to pity and sympathize with the failure of extended views of beneficence; he despised the hypocrisy that had made charity a cloak for a credulous debasing attachment, and to such an object! He might well avoid her! His sister had always bantered her on what had seemed too absurd to be rebutted, and, at any rate, this fainting fit would clench his belief. No doubt he believed it. And if he did, why should not every one else whose opinion she cared for: Ermine, her Colonel, even gentle Fanny—no, she would never believe any harm; she had suffered too much in her cause.

Oh, for simple genuine charity like Fanny's, with eyes clear with innocence and humility? And now what was before her? should she ever be allowed to hide her head, or should she be forced again to brave that many-eyed world?

Perhaps the title-deed business would prove utter ruin. It would have been acceptable to herself, but her mother and sister!

Chastisement! Yes, it was just chastisement for head-strong folly and conceit. She had heard of bending to the rod and finding it a cross, but here came the dreadful confusion of unreality, and of the broken habit of religious meditation except as matter of debate. She did not know till her time of need how deeply sneers had eaten into her heart. The only text that would come to her mind was, "And in that day they shall roar against them like the roaring of the sea; and if one look unto the land, behold darkness and sorrow, and the light is darkened in the heavens thereof." Every effort at prayer or at calm recall of old thoughts still ended in that desolate verse. The first relief to these miserable dreams was the cool clear morning light, and by-and-by the early cathedral bells, then Grace's kind greeting made her quite herself; no longer feverish, but full of lassitude and depression. She would not listen to Grace's entreaties that she would remain in bed. "No place was so hateful to her," she said, and she came down apparently not more unwell than had been the case for many days past, so that after breakfast her mother saw no reason against leaving her on the sofa, while going out to perform some commissions in the town, attended, of course, by Grace. Miss Wellwood promised that she should not be disturbed, and she found that she must have been asleep, for she was taken by surprise by the opening of the door, and the apologetic face of the butler, who told her that a gentleman had asked if she would see him, and presented the card of "Captain Alexander Keith."

Eagerly she desired that he should be admitted, tremu-

lously she awaited his sentence upon her mother's peace;
and, as she thought of all he must have heard, all he must
believe, she felt as if she must flee; or, if that were impossible, cower in shrinking dread of the glance of his satirical
eye !

Here he was, and she could not look or speak, nor did he;
she only felt that his clasp of greeting was kind, was anxious,
and he put forward the easy-chair, into which she sank,
unable to stand.   He said, " I saw your mother and sister
going into the town.   I thought you would like to hear of
this business at once."

" Oh yes, thank you."

" I could not see the man till the day before yesterday,"
he said, " and I could get nothing satisfactory from him.   He
said he had taken the papers to a legal friend, but was not
authorized to give his name.   Perhaps his views may be
changed by his present condition.   I will try him again if
you like."

" Thank you, thank you !   Do you think this is true ? "

" He is too cunning a scoundrel to tell unnecessary lies,
and very likely he may have disposed of them to some Jew
attorney; but I think nothing is to be feared but some
annoyance."

" And annoyance to my mother is the one thing I most
fear," sighed Rachel, helplessly.

" There might be a mode of much lessening it to her," he
said.

" Oh, what ?   Tell me, and I would do it at any cost."

" Will you ? " and he came nearer.   " At the cost of yourself ? "

She thrilled all over, and convulsively grasped the arm of
her chair.

"Would not a son be the best person to shield her from annoyance," he added, trying for his usual tone ; but failing, he exclaimed, "Rachel, Rachel, let me !"

She put her hands over her face, and cried, "Oh ! oh ! I never thought of this."

".No," he said, "and I know what you do think of it, but indeed you need not be wasted. Our women and children want so much done for them, and none of our ladies are able or willing. Will you not come and help me ?"

"Don't talk to me of helping ! I do nothing but spoil and ruin."

"Not now ! That is all gone and past. Come and begin afresh."

"No, no, I am too disagreeable."

"May not I judge for myself ?" he said, drawing nearer, and his voice falling into tremulous tenderness.

"Headstrong—overbearing."

"Try," and his smile overbore her.

"Oh no, no, nobody can bear me ! This is more than you —you ought to do—than any one should," she faltered, not knowing what she said.

"Than any one to whom you were not most dear !" was the answer, and he was now standing over her, with the dew upon his eyelashes.

"Oh, that can't be. Bessie said you always took up whatever other people hated, and I know it is only that——"

"Don't let Bessie's sayings come between us now, Rachel. This goes too deep," and he had almost taken her hand, when with a start she drew it back, saying, "But you know what they say !"

"Have they been stupid enough to tell you ?" he exclaimed.

" Confute them then, Rachel—dolts that can't believe in self-devotion ! Laugh at their beards. This is the way to put an end to it ! "

" Oh no, they would only detest you for my sake. I can't," she said again, bowed down again with shame and dejection.

" I'll take care of that ! " he said with the dry tone that perhaps was above all reassurance, and conquered her far enough to enable him to take possession of the thin and still listless hand.

" Then," he said, " you will let me take this whole matter in hand ; and if the worst comes to the worst, we will make up to the charity out of the Indian money, without vexing the mother."

" I can't let you suffer for my miserable folly."

" Too late to say that ! " he answered ; and as her eyes were raised to him in startled inquiry, he said gravely, " These last weeks have shown me that your troubles *must* be mine."

A hand was on the door, and Rachel fled, in time to screen her flight from Miss Wellwood, whom Alick met with his usual undisturbed front, and inquiries for Mrs. Curtis.

That good lady was in the town more worried than flattered by the numerous inquiries after Rachel's health, and conscious of having gone rather near the wind in making the best of it. She had begun to dread being accosted by any acquaintance, and Captain Keith, sauntering near the archway of the close, was no welcome spectacle. She would have passed him with a curt salutation, but he grasped her hand, saying, " May I have a few words with you ? "

" Not Fanny—not the children ! " cried Mrs. Curtis in dismay.

"No indeed. Only myself," and a gleam of intelligence under his eyelashes and judicious pressure of his hand conveyed volumes to Grace, who had seen him often during Rachel's illness, and was not unprepared. She merely said that she would see how her sister was, substituted Captain Keith's arm for her own as her mother's support, and hurried away, to encounter Miss Wellwood's regrets that, in spite of all her precautions, dear Rachel had been disturbed by "a young officer, I believe. We see him often at the cathedral, and somebody said it was his sister whom Lord Keith married."

"Yes, we know him well, and he is a Victoria Cross man," said Grace, beginning to assume his reflected glory.

"So some one said, but the Dean never calls on the officers unless there is some introduction, or there would be no end to it. It was a mistake letting him in to disturb Rachel. Is your mother gone up to her, my dear?"

"No, I think she is in the cathedral yard. I just came in to see about Rachel," said Grace, escaping.

Miss Wellwood intended going out to join her old friend; but, on going to put on her bonnet, she saw from the window Mrs. Curtis, leaning on the intruder's arm, conversing so confidentially that the Dean's sister flushed with amazement, and only hoped she had mentioned him with due respect. And under that southern cathedral wall good Mrs. Curtis took the longest walk she had indulged in for the last twenty years; so that Grace, and even Rachel, beholding from the window, began to fear that the mother would be walked to death.

But then she had that supporting arm, and the moral support, that was infinitely more! That daughter, the spoilt

pet of her husband, the subject of her pride, even when an
enigma and an anxiety, whom she had lately been forced to
think of as

> " A maid whom there were few to praise
> And very few to love,"

she now found loved by one at least, and praised in terms
that thrilled through and through the mother's heart in their
truth and simplicity, for that sincerity, generosity, and unselfishness. It was her own daughter, her real Rachel, no
illusion, that she heard described in those grave earnest
words; only while the whole world saw the errors and exaggerated them, here was one who sank them all in the
sterling worth that so few would recognise. The dear old
lady forgot all her prudence, and would hardly let him speak
of his means; but she soon saw that Rachel's present portion
would be more than met on his side, and that no one could
find fault with her on the score of inequality of fortune.
He would have been quite able to retire, and live at ease;
but this he said at once and with decision he did not intend.
His regiment was his hereditary home, and his father had
expressed such strong wishes that he should not lightly desert
his profession, that he felt bound to it by filial duty as well
as by other motives. Moreover, he thought the change of
life and occupation would be the best thing for Rachel, and
Mrs. Curtis could not but acquiesce, little as she had even
dreamt that a daughter of hers would marry into a marching
regiment! Her surrender of judgment was curiously complete. "Dear Alexander," as thenceforth she called him, had
assumed the mastery over her from the first turn they took
under the cathedral; and when at length he reminded her

that the clock was on the stroke of one, she accepted it on his infallible judgment, for her own sensations would have made her believe it not a quarter of an hour since the interview had begun.

Not a word had been granted on either side to the conventional vows of secrecy, always made to be broken, and perhaps each tacitly felt that the less secrecy the better for Rachel. Certain it is that Mrs. Curtis went into the Deanery with her head considerably higher, kissed Rachel vehemently, and, assuring her she knew all about it, and was happier than she had ever thought to be again, excused her from appearing at luncheon, and hurried down thereto, without giving any attention to a feeble entreaty that she would not go so fast. And when at three o'clock Rachel crept downstairs to get into the carriage for her return home, the good old Dean lay in wait for her, told her she must allow him an old friend's privilege, kissed her, congratulated her, and said he would beg to perform the ceremony.

" Oh, Mr. Dean, it is nothing like that."

He laughed, and handed her in.

" Mother, mother, how could you ? " sighed Rachel, as they drove on.

" My dear, they were so kind ; they could not help knowing ! "

" But it can't be."

" Rachel, my child; you like him ! "

" He does not know half about me yet. Mother, don't tell Fanny or any one till ' I have seen him again.' "

And the voice was so imperious with the wayward vehemence of illness that Mrs. Curtis durst not gainsay it. She did not know how Alick Keith was already silencing those who asked if he had heard of the great event at the Dean's party.   Still less did she guess at the letter at that moment in writing :—

"MY DEAR BESSIE,—Wish me joy.   I have gone in for the uncroquetable lawn, and won it.—Your affectionate brother,

"A. C. KEITH."

CHAPTER IX.

DEAR ALEXANDER.

"I pray thee now tell me, for which of my bad parts didst thou first fall in love with me ! "—*Much Ado about Nothing.*

ALICK, is this all chivalry ?" inquired Colonel Keith, sitting by his fire, suffering considerably from his late drive, and hearing reports that troubled him.

"Very chivalrous, indeed? when there's an old county property to the fore."

"For that matter, you have all been canny enough to have means enough to balance all that barren moorland. You are a richer man than I shall ever be."

"Without heiress-hunting?" said Alick, as though weighing his words.

"Come, Alick, you need not put on a mask that does not fit you ! If it is not too late, take the risk into consideration, for I own I think the price of your championship somewhat severe."

"Ask Miss Williams."

"Ermine is grateful for much kindness, and is—yes—really fond of her."

"Then, Colonel, you ought to know that a sensible woman's favourable estimate of one of her own sex outweighs the opinion men can form of her."

" I grant that there are fine qualities ; but, Alick, regarding you, as I must necessarily do, from our former relations, you must let me speak if there is still time to warn you, lest your pity and sense of injustice should be entangling you in a connexion that would hardly conduce to make you happy or popular."

"Popularity is not my line," said Alick, looking composedly into the fire.

"Tell me first," said the puzzled Colonel, " are you committed ? "

" No one can be more so."

" Engaged ! ! ! "

" I thought you would have known it from themselves ; but I find she has forbidden her mother to mention it till she has seen me again. And they talk of quiet, and shut me out ! " gloomily added Alick.

The Colonel conceived a hope that the lady would abjure matrimony, and release this devoted knight, but in a few moments Alick burst out—

"Absurd ! She cannot mend with anything on her mind ! If I could have seen Mrs. Curtis or Grace alone, they might have heard reason ; but that old woman of a doctor was prosing about quiet and strain on the nerves. I know that sort of quiet, the best receipt for distraction ! "

" Well, Alick," said his friend, smiling, " you have at least convinced me that your heart is in the matter."

" How should it not be ? " returned Alick.

" I was afraid it was only with the object of unjust vituperation."

" No such thing. Let me tell you, Colonel, my heart has been in it ever since I felt the relief of meeting real truth and unselfishness! I liked her that first evening, when she was manfully chasing us off for frivolous danglers round her cousin? I liked her for having no conventionalities, fast or slow, and especially for hating heroes! And when my sister had helped to let her get into this intolerable web, how could I look on without feeling the nobleness that has never shifted blame from herself, but bowed, owned all, suffered—suffered—oh, how grievously!"

The Colonel was moved. "With such genuine affection you should surely lead her and work upon her! I trust you will be able."

"It is less that," said Alick, rather resentfully, "than sympathy that she wants. Nobody ever gave her that except your Ermine! By-the-bye, is there any news of the brother?"

Colonel Keith shook his head. "I believe I shall have to go to Russia," he said with some dejection.

"After that, reproach one with chivalry," said Alick, lightly. "Nay, I beg your pardon. Shall I take any message down to Mackarel Lane?"

"Are you going?"

"Well, yes, though I hardly ought to venture there till this embargo is taken off; for she is the one person there will be some pleasure in talking to. Perhaps I may reckon you as the same in effect."

The Colonel responded with a less cheerful look than usual, adding, "I don't know whether to congratulate you, Alick, on having to ask no one's consent but your own at your age."

"Especially not my guardian's!" said Alick, with the desired effect of making him laugh.

"No, if you were my son, I would not interfere," he added gravely. "I only feared your not knowing what you

were about. I see you do know it, and it merely becomes a
question of every man to his taste—except for one point,
Alick. I am afraid there may have been much disturbance
of her opinions."

"Surface work," said Alick, "some of the effects of the
literature that paints contradiction as truth. It is only skin
deep, and makes me wish all the more to have her with my
uncle for a time. I wonder whether Grace would let me in
if I went back again !"

No, Grace was obdurate. Mr. Frampton had spoken of
a nervous fever, and commanded perfect quiescence ; and
Grace was the less tempted to transgress the order, because
she really thought her mother was more in love with "dear
Alexander" than Rachel was. Rachel was exceedingly depressed, restless, and feverish, and shrank from her mother's
rejoicing, declaring that she was mistaken, and that nothing
more must be said. She had never consented, and he must
not make such a sacrifice ; he would not when he knew
better. Nay, in some moods, Rachel seemed to think even
the undefined result of the interview an additional humiliation, and to feel herself falling, if not fallen, from her
supreme contempt of love and marriage. The hurry, and
the consent taken for granted, had certainly been no small
elements in her present disturbed and overwhelmed state ;
and Grace, though understanding the motive, was disposed
to resent the over-haste. Calm and time to think were
promised to Rachel, but the more she had of both the more
they hurt her. She tossed restlessly all night, and was
depressed to the lowest ebb by day ; but on the second day,
ill as she evidently was, she insisted on seeing Captain Keith,
declaring that she should never be better till she had made

him understand her. Her nurses saw that she was right; and, besides, Mrs. Curtis's pity was greatly touched by dear Alexander's entreaties. So, as a desperate experiment, he was at last allowed to go into the dressing-room, where she was lying on the sofa. He begged to enter alone, only announced by a soft knock, to which she replied with a listless " Come in," and did not look up till she suddenly became conscious of a footfall firmer though softer than those she was used to. She turned, and saw who it was, who stood at a window opposite to her feet, drawing up the Venetian blind, from whose teasing divisions of glare and shade she had been hiding her eyes from the time she had come in, fretted by the low continuous tap of its laths upon the shutters. Her first involuntary exclamation was a sigh of relief.

" Oh, thank you. I did not know what it was that was such a nuisance."

" This is too much glare. Let me turn your sofa a little way round from it."

And as he did so, and she raised herself, he shook out her cushions, and substituted a cool chintz covered one for the hot crimson damask on which her head had been resting. " Thank you ! How do you know so well ?" she said with a long breath of satisfaction.

" By long trial," he said, very quietly seating himself beside her couch, with a stillness of manner that strangely hushed all her throbbings ; and the very pleasure of lying really still was such that she did not at once break it. The lull of these few moments was inexpressibly sweet, but the pang that had crossed her so many times in the last two days and nights could not but return. She moved restlessly, and he leant towards her with a soft-toned inquiry what it was she wanted.

"Don't," she said, raising herself. "No, don't! I have thought more over what you said," she continued, as if repeating the sentence she had conned over to herself. "You have been most generous, most noble; but—but," with an effort of memory, "it would be wrong in me to accept such—oh! such a sacrifice; and when I tell you all, you will think it a duty to turn from me," she added, pressing her hands to her temples. "And mind, you are not committed—you are free."

"Tell me," he said, bending towards her.

"I know you cannot overlook it! My faith—it is all confusion," she said in a low awe-struck voice. "I do believe—I do wish to believe; but my grasp seems gone. I cannot rest or trust for thinking of the questions that have been raised! There," she added in a strange interrogative tone.

"It is a cruel thing to represent doubt as the sign of intellect," Alick said sadly; "but you will shake off the tormentors when the power of thinking and reasoning is come back."

"Oh, if I could think so! The misery of darkness here—there—everywhere—the old implicit reliance gone, and all observance seeming like hypocrisy and unreality. There is no thinking, no enduring the intolerable maze."

"Do not try to think now. You cannot bear it. We will try to face what difficulties remain when you are stronger."

She turned her eyes full on him. "You do not turn away! You know you are free."

"Turn from the sincerity that I prize?"

"You don't? I thought your views were exactly what would make you hate and loathe such bewilderment, and call it wilful;" there was something piteous in the way her eye sought his face.

"It was not wilful," he said; "it came of honest truth-seeking. And, Rachel, I think the one thing is now gone that kept that honesty from finding its way."

"Self-sufficiency!" she said with a groan; but with a sudden turn she exclaimed, "You don't trust to my surrendering my judgment. I don't think I am that kind of woman."

"Nor I that kind of man," he answered in his natural tone; then affectionately, "No, indeed I want you to aid mine."

She lay back, wearied with the effort, and disinclined to break the stillness. There was a move at the door; Mrs. Curtis, in an agony of restless anxiety, could not help coming to see that the interview was doing no harm.

"Don't go!" exclaimed Rachel, holding out her hand as he turned at the opening of the door. "Oh, mother!" and there was an evident sound of disappointment.

Mrs. Curtis was infinitely rejoiced to find her entrance thus inopportune. "I only wished just to be sure it was not too much," she said.

"Oh, mother, it is the first peace I have known for weeks! Can't you stay?" looking up to him, as her mother retreated to tell Grace that it was indeed all right.

This brought him to a footstool close beside her. "Thank you," he murmured. "I was wondering just then if it would hurt you or agitate you to give me some little satisfaction in going on with this. I know you are too true not to have told me at once if your objections were more personal than

those you have made ; but, Rachel, it is true, as you say,
that you have never consented !"

The tone of these words made Rachel raise herself, turn
towards him, and hold out both her hands.   " Oh," she said,
as he took them into his own, " it was—it could be only that
I cannot bear so much more than I deserve."

" What ! such an infliction ?" in his own dry way.

" Such rest, such kindness, such generosity !"

" No, Rachel, there is something that makes it neither
kindness nor generosity.   You know what I mean."

" And that is what overpowers me more than all," she
sighed, in the full surrender of herself.   " I ought not to
be so very happy."

" That is all I want to hear," he said, as he replaced her
on her cushions, and sat by her, holding her hand, but not
speaking till the next interruption, by one of the numerous
convalescent meals, brought in by Grace, who looked doubtful
whether she would be allowed to come in, and then was
edified by the little arrangements he made, quietly taking
all into his own hands, and wonderfully lessening a sort of
fidget that Mrs. Curtis's anxiety had attached to all that was
done for Rachel.   It was not for nothing that he had spent
a year upon the sofa in the irritably sensitive state of nerves
that Bessie had described ; and when he could speak to
Grace alone, he gave her a lecture on those little refinements
of unobtrusive care, that more demonstrative ailments had
not availed to inculcate, and which Mrs. Curtis's present
restless anxiety rendered almost impossible.   To hinder her
from constantly aggravating the fever on the nerves by her
fidgeting solicitude was beyond all power save his own, and
that when he was actually in the house.

Morning after morning he rode to the Homestead to hear that Rachel had had a very bad night, and was very low, then was admitted to find Mrs. Curtis's fluttering, flurried attentions exasperating every wearied fibre with the very effort to force down fretfulness and impatience; till, when she was left to him, a long space of the lull impressed on her by his presence was needful before he could attempt any of the quiet talk, or brief readings of poetry, by which he tried further to soothe and rest her spirits. He would leave her so calm and full of repose as to make him augur well for the next day; but the moment his back was turned, something would always happen that set all the pulses in agitation again, and consigned her to a fresh night of feverish phantoms of the past. He even grew distracted enough to scold Grace fraternally as the only person he could scold.

"You seem to nurse her on the principle of old Morris, the biggest officer among us, who kindly insisted on sitting up with me, and began by taking his seat upon my hand as it was lying spread out upon a pillow."

"Indeed, Alick," said Grace, with tears in her eyes, "I hardly know what to do. When you are not in the house, the mother is almost as much in a nervous fever as Rachel, and it is hardly in her power to keep from fretting her. It is all well when you are here."

"Then, Grace, there is only one thing to be done. The sooner I take Rachel away the better for both her and the mother."

"Oh, Alick, you will drive them both wild if you hurry it on."

"Look here. I believe I can get leave from Saturday till Tuesday. If I can get a hearing in those two days, I shall try; and depend upon it, Grace, this place is the worst that Rachel can be in."

" Can you come out here for three whole days ?   Oh, what a comfort ! "

And what a comfort ! was re-echoed by Mrs. Curtis, who had erected dear Alexander to a pedestal of infallibility, and was always treated by him with a considerate kindness that made her pity Fanny for the number of years that must pass before Stephana could give her the supreme blessing of a son-in-law.   Fanny, on her side, had sufficient present bles- sing in collecting her brood around her, after the long famine she had suffered, and regretted only that this month had rendered Stephana's babyhood more perceptibly a matter of the past; and that, in the distance, school days were advanc- ing towards Conrade, though it was at least a comfort that his diphtheria had secured him at home for another half year, and the Colonel had so much to think about that he had not begun his promised researches into schools.

The long-looked-for letters came after a weary interval of expectation, the more trying to Ermine because the weather had been so bitter that Colin could not shake off his cold, nor venture beyond his own fireside, where Rose daily visited him, and brought home accounts that did not cheer her aunt.

Edward wrote shortly to his sister, as if almost annoyed at the shower of letters that had by every post begun to recall his attention from some new invention on the means of assay- ing metals :—

" I am sorry you have stirred up Keith to the renewal of this painful subject.   You know I considered that page in my life as closed for ever ; and I see nothing that would compensate for what it costs me even to think of it.   To redeem my name before the world would be of no avail to me now, for all my English habits are broken, and all that made life valuable to me is gone. If Long and Beauchamp could reject my solemn affirmation three years ago, what would a retractation slowly wrung from them be worth to me now? It might once have been, but that is all over now. Even the desire to take care of you would no longer actuate me since you have Keith again; and in a few years I hope to make my child independent in money matters—independent of your love and care you would not wish her to be. Forget the troubles of your life, Ermine, and be happy with your faithful Keith, without further efforts on behalf of one whom they only harass and grieve."

Ermine shed some bitter tears over this letter, the more sorrowful because the refusal was a shock to her own reliance on his honour, and she felt like a traitress to his cause. And Colin would give him up after this ungrateful indifference, if nothing worse. Surely it betrayed a consciousness that the whole of his conduct would not bear inquiry, and she thought of the representations that she had so indignantly rejected, that the accounts, even without the last fatal demand, were in a state that it required an excess of charity to ascribe to mere carelessness on the part of the principal.

She was glad that Alison was absent, and Rose in the garden. She laid her head on her little table, and drew long sobs of keen suffering, the reaction from the enjoyment and hope of the last few months. And so little knew she what she ought to ask, that she could only strive to say, " Thy will be done."

" Ermine ! my Ermine, this is not a thing to be so much taken to heart. This foolish philosopher has not even read his letters. I never saw any one more consistently like himself."

Ermine looked up, and Colin was standing over her, muffled up to the eyes, and a letter of his own in his hand. Her first impulse was to cry out against his imprudence, glad as she was to see him. "My cough is nearly gone," he said, unwinding his wrappings, "and I could not stay at home after this wonderful letter—three pages about chemical analysis, which he does me the honour to think I can under-stand, two of commissions for villanous compounds, and one of protestations that 'I will be drowned ; nobody shall help me.' "

Ermine's laugh had come, even amid her tears, his tone was so great a relief to her. She did not know that he had spent some minutes in cooling down his vexation, lest he should speak ungently of her brother's indifference. " Poor Edward," she said, " you don't mean that this is all the reply you have ! "

" See for yourself," and he pointed to the divisions of the letter he had described. " There is all he vouchsafes to his own proper affairs. You see he misapprehends the whole ; indeed, I don't believe he has even read our letters."

" We often thought he did not attend to all we wrote," said Ermine. " It is very disheartening !"

" Nay, Ermine, *you* disheartened with the end in view !"

" There are certainly the letters about Maddox's committal still to reach him, but who knows if they will have more effect ! Oh, Colin, this was such a hope that—perhaps I have dwelt too much upon it !"

" It *is* such a hope," he repeated. " There is no reason for laying it aside, because Edward is his old self."

" Colin ! you still think so ?"

" I think so more than ever. If he will not read reason, he must hear it ; and if he takes no notice of the letters we sent after the sessions, I shall go and bring him back in time for the assizes."

" Oh, Colin ! it cannot be. Think of the risk ! You who are still looking so thin and ill. I cannot let you."

" It will be warm enough by the time I get there."

" The distance ! You are doing too much for us."

" No, Ermine," with a smile, " that I will never do."

She tried to answer his smile, but leant back and shed tears, not like the first, full of pain, but of affectionate gratitude, and yet of reluctance at his going. She had ever been the strength and stay of the family, but there seemed to be a source of weakness in his nearness, and this period of his indisposition and of suspense had been a strain on her spirits that told in this gentle weeping. " This is a poor welcome after you have been laid up so long," she said when she could speak again. " If I behave so ill, you will only want to run from the sight of me."

" It will be July when I come back."

" I do not think you ought to go."

" Nor I, if Edward deigns to read the account of Rose's examination."

In that calm smiling resolution Ermine read the needlessness of present argument, and spoke again of his health and his solitary hours.

" Mitchel has been very kind in coming to sit with me, and we have indulged in two or three castles in the air— hospitals in the air, perhaps, I should say. I told him he might bring me down another guest instead of the tailor, and he has brought a poor young pupil teacher, whom Tibbie calls a winsome callant, but I am afraid she won't save him. Did you ever read the 'Lady of La Garaye' ?"

"Not the poem, but I know her story."

"As soon as that parcel comes in, which Villars is always expecting, I propose to myself to read that poem with you. What's that ? It can't be Rachel as usual."

If it was not Rachel, it was the next thing to her, namely, Alick Keith. This was the last day of those that he had spent at the Homestead, and he was leaving Rachel certainly better. She had not fallen back on any evening that he had been there, but to his great regret he would not be able to come out the next day. Regimental duty would take him up nearly all the day, and then he was invited to a party at the Deanery, "which the mother would never have forgiven me for refusing," he said ; just as if the mother's desires had the very same power over him as over her daughters. "I came to make a desperate request, Miss Williams," he said. "Would it be any way possible for you to be so kind as to go up and see Rachel ? She comes downstairs now, and there are no steps if you go in by the glass doors. Do you think you could manage it ?"

"She wishes it ?" said Ermine.

"Very much. There are thorns in her mind that no one knows how to deal with so well as you do, and she told me yesterday how she longed to get to you."

"It is very good in her. I have sometimes feared she might think we had dealt unfairly by her if she did not know how very late in the business we suspected that our impostors were the same," said Ermine.

" It is not her way to blame any one but herself," said
Alick, " and, in fact, our showing her the woodcut deception
was a preparation for the rest of it. But I have said very
little to her about all that matter. She required to be led
away rather than back to it. Brooding over it is fatal work,
and yet her spirits are too much weakened and shattered to
bear over-amusement. That is the reason that I thought you
would be so very welcome to-morrow. She has seen no one
yet but Lady Temple, and shrinks from the very idea."

" I do not see why I should not manage it very well," said
Ermine, cheerfully, " if Miss Curtis will let me know in time
whether she is equal to seeing me. You know I can walk
into the house now."

Alick thanked her earnestly. His listless manner was
greatly enlivened by his anxiety, and Colonel Keith was
obliged to own that marriage would be a good thing for him ;
but *such* a marriage ! If from sheer indolence he should leave
the government to his wife, then—Colin could only shrug
his shoulders in dismay.

Nevertheless, when Ermine's wheeled chair came to the
door the next afternoon, he came with it, and walked by her
side up the hill, talking of what had been absolutely the last
call she had made—a visit when they had both been riding
with the young Beauchamps.

" Suppose any one had told me then I should make my
next visit with you to take care of me, how pleased I should
have been," said Ermine, laughing, and taking as usual an
invalid's pleasure in all the little novelties only remarked
after long seclusion. That steep, winding, pebbly road, with
the ferns and creeping plants on its rocky sides, was a
wonderful panorama to her, and she entreated for a stop at

the summit to look down on the sea and the town ; but here Grace came out to them full of thanks and hopes, little knowing that to them the event was a very great one. When at the glass doors of the garden entrance, Ermine trusted herself to the Colonel's arm, and between him and her crutch crossed the short space to the morning room, where Rachel rose from her sofa, but wisely did not come forward till her guest was safely placed in a large easy chair.

Rachel then held out her hand to the Colonel, and quietly said, "Thank you," in a subdued manner that really touched him, as he retreated quickly and left them together. Then Rachel sat down on a footstool close to Ermine, and looked up to her. "Oh, it is so good of you to come to me ! I would not have dared to think of it, but I just said I wished to get out for nothing but to go to you ; and then he— Captain Keith—would go and fetch you."

" As the nearest approach to fetching the moon, I suppose," said Ermine, brightly. " It was very kind to me, for I was longing to see you, and I am glad to find you looking better than I expected."

For in truth Rachel's complexion had been little altered by her illness ; and the subdued dejected expression was the chief change visible, except in the feebleness and tremulousness of all her movements. "Yes, I am better," she said. " I ought to be, for he is so good to me."

"Dear Rachel, I was so very glad to hear of this," said Ermine, bending down to kiss her.

" Were you ? I thought no one could be that cared for him," said Rachel.

" I cared more for him the week that you were ill than ever I had done before."

"Grace tells me of that," said Rachel, "and when he is here I believe it. But, Miss Williams, please look full at me, and tell me whether everybody would not think—I don't say that I could do it—but if every one would not think it a great escape for him if I gave him up."

"No one that could really judge."

"Because, listen," said Rachel, quickly, "the regiment is going to Scotland, and he and the mother have taken it into their heads that I shall get well faster somewhere away from home. And—and they want to have the wedding as soon as I am better; and they are going to write about settlements and all that. I have never said I would, and I don't feel as if—as if I ought to let him do it; and if ever the thing is to be stopped at all, this is the only time."

"But why? You do not wish——"

"Don't talk of what I wish," said Rachel. "Talk of what is good for him."

Ermine was struck with the still resolute determination of judging for herself—the self-sufficiency, almost redeemed by the unselfishness, and the face was most piteously in earnest.

"My dear, surely he can be trusted to judge. He is no boy, in spite of his looks. The Colonel always says that he is as much older than his age in character as he is younger in appearance."

"I know that," said Rachel, "but I don't think he ought to be trusted here; for you see," and she looked down, "all the blindness of—of his affection is enhanced by his nobleness and generosity, and he has nobody to check or stop him; and it does seem to me a shame for us all to catch at such compassion, and encumber him with me, just because I am marked for scorn and dislike. I can't get any one to help

me look at it so. My own people would fancy it was only
that I did not care for him; and he—I can't even think
about it when he is here, but I get quite distracted with
doubts if it can be right whenever he goes away. And you
are the only person who can help me! Bessie wrote very
kindly to me, and I asked to see what she said to him.
I thought I might guess her feeling from it. And he said he
knew I should fancy it worse than it was if he did not let
me see. It was droll, and just like her—not unkind; but
I could see it is the property that makes her like it. And
his uncle is blind, you know, and could only send a blessing,
and kind hopes, and all that. Oh, if I could guess whether
that uncle thinks he ought! What does Colonel Keith
think? I know you will tell me truly."

"He thinks," said Ermine, with a shaken voice, "that
real trustworthy affection outweighs all the world could
say."

"But he thinks it is a strange, misplaced liking, exaggerated
by pity for one sunk so low?" said Rachel, in an excited
manner.

"Rachel," said Ermine, "you must take my beginning as
a pledge of my speaking the whole truth. Colonel Keith is
certainly not fond of you personally, and rather wonders at
Alick, but he has never doubted that this is the genuine
feeling that is for life, and that it is capable of making you
both better and happier. Indeed, Rachel, we do both feel
that you suit Alick much more than many people who have
been far better liked."

Rachel looked cheered. "Yet you," she faltered, "you
have been an instance of resolute withstanding."

"I don't think I shall be long," murmured Ermine, a vivid

colour flashing forth upon her cheek, and leading the question from herself. "Just suppose you *did* carry out this fierce act of self-abnegation, what do you think could come next ? "

"I don't know! I would not break down or die if I could help it," added Rachel, faintly after her brave beginning.

"And for him ? Do you think being cast off would be so very pleasant to him ?"

Rachel hung her head, and her lips made a half murmur of, "Would not it be good for him ?"

"No, Rachel, it is the very sorest trial there can be when, even in the course of providence, kind intentions are coldly requited ; and it would be incalculably harder when therewith there would be rejection of love."

"Ah ! I never said I could do it. I could not tell him I did not care for him, and short of that nothing would stop it," sobbed Rachel, "only I wished to feel it was not very mean—very wrong." She laid her weary head on Ermine's lap, and Ermine bent down and kissed her.

"So happy, so bright and free, and capable, his life seems now," proceeded Rachel. "I can't understand his joining it to mine ; and if people shunned and disliked him for my sake !"

"Surely that will depend on yourself. I have never seen you in society, but if you have the fear of making him unpopular or remarkable before your eyes, you will avoid it."

"Oh, yes ; I know," said Rachel, impatiently. "I did think I should not have been a commonplace woman," and she shed a few tears.

Ermine was provoked with her, and began to think that she had been arguing on a wrong tack, and that it would be better after all for Alick to be free. Rachel looked up presently. "It must be very odd to you to hear me say so, but I can't help feeling the difference. I used to think it so poor and weak to be in love, or to want any one to take care of one. I thought marriage such ordinary drudgery, and ordinary opinions so contemptible, and had such schemes for myself. And this—and this is such a break down, my blunders and their consequences have been so unspeakably dreadful, and now instead of suffering, dying—as I felt I ought—it has only made me just like other women, for I know I could not live without him, and then all the rest of it must come for his sake."

"And will make you much more really useful and effective than ever you could have been alone," said Ermine.

"He does talk of doing things together, but, oh! I feel as if I could never dare put out my hand again!"

"Not alone perhaps."

"I like to hear him tell me about the soldiers' children, and what he wants to have done for them."

"You and I little thought what Lady Temple was to bring us," said Ermine, cheerfully, "but you see we are not the strongest creatures in the world, so we must resign ourselves to our fate, and make the best of it. *They* must judge how many imperfections they choose to endure, and we can only make the said drawbacks as little troublesome as may be. Now, I think I see Miss Curtis watching in fear that I am over-talking you."

"Oh, must you go? You have really comforted me! I wanted an external opinion very much, and I do trust yours!

Only tell me," she added, holding Ermine's hand, "is this indeed *so* with you ?"

"Not yet," said Ermine, softly, "do not speak about it, but I think you will be comforted to hear that this matter of yours, by leading to the matron's confession, may have removed an obstacle that was far more serious in my eyes than even my own helplessness, willing as Colin was to cast both aside. Oh, Rachel, there is a great deal to be thankful for."

Rachel lay down on her sofa, and fell asleep, nor did Alick find any occasion for blaming Grace when he returned the next day. The effect of the conversation had been to bring Rachel to a meek submission, very touching in its passiveness and weary peacefulness. She was growing stronger, walked out leaning on Alick's arm, and was even taken out by him in a boat, a wonderful innovation, for a dangerous accident to Mr. Curtis had given the mother such a horror of the sea that no boating excursions had ever taken place during her solitary reign, and the present were only achieved by a wonderful stretch of dear Alexander's influence. Perhaps she trusted him the more, because his maimed hand prevented him from being himself an oarsman, though he had once been devoted to rowing. At any rate, with an old fisherman at the oar, many hours were spent upon the waters of the bay, in a tranquillity that was balm to the harassed spirit, with very little talking, now and then some reading aloud, but often nothing but a dreamy repose. The novelty and absence of old association was one secret of the benefit that Rachel thus derived. Any bustle or resumption of former habits was a trial to her shattered nerves, and brought back the dreadful haunted nights. The first sight of Conrade,

still looking thin and delicate, quite overset her; a drive on
the Avoncester road renewed all she had felt on the way
thither; three or four morning visitors coming in on her
unexpectedly, made the whole morbid sense of eyes staring at
her recur all night, and when the London solicitor came
down about the settlements, she shrank in such a painful
though still submissive way, from the sight of a stranger, far
more from the semblance of a dinner party, that the mother
yielded, and let her remain in her sitting-room.

"May I come in?" said Alick, knocking at the door.
"I have something to tell you."

"What, Alick! Not Mr. Williams come?"

"Nothing so good. In fact I doubt if you will think it
good at all. I have been consulting this same solicitor about
the title-deeds; that cheese you let fall, you know," he added,
stroking her hand, and speaking so gently that the very irony
was rather pleasant.

"Oh, it is very bad."

"Now wouldn't you like to hear it was so bad that I
should have to sell out, and go to the diggings to make
it up?"

"Now, Alick, if it were not for your sake, you know
should like——"

"I know you would; but you see, unfortunately, it was
not a cheese at all, only a wooden block that the fox ran
away with. Lawyers don't put people's title-deeds into such
dangerous keeping; the true cheese is safe locked up in a
tin-box in Mr. Martin's chambers in London."

"Then what did I give Mauleverer?"

"A copy kept for reference down here."

Rachel hid her face.

" There, I knew you would think it no good news, and it is just a thunder-clap to me. All you wanted me for was to defend the mother and make up to the charity, and now there's no use in me," he said in a disconsolate tone.

" Oh, Alick, Alick, why am I so foolish ? "

" Never mind ; I took care Martin should not know it. Nobody is aware of the little affair but our two selves ; and I will take care the fox learns the worth of his prize. Only now, Rachel, answer me, is there any use left for me still ? "

" You should not ask me such things, Alick, you know it all too well."

" Not so well that I don't want to hear it. But I had more to say. This Martin is a man of very different calibre from old Cox, with a head and heart in London charities and churches, and it had struck him as it did you, that the Homestead had an easier bargain of it than that good namesake of yours had ever contemplated. If it paid treble or quadruple rent, the dear mother would never find it out, nor grow a geranium the less."

" No, she would not ! But after all, the lace apprenticeships are poor work."

" So they are, but Martin says there would be very little difficulty in getting a private bill to enable the trustees to apply the sum otherwise for the benefit of the Avonmouth girls."

" Then if I had written to him, it would have been all right ! Oh, my perverseness ! "

" And, Rachel, now that money has been once so intended ; suppose it kept its destination. About £500 would put up a tidy little industrial school, and you might not

object to have a scholarship or two for some of our little
—th Highlander lassies whose fathers won't make orphans
of them for the regular military charities. What, crying,
Rachel! Don't you like it?"

"It is my dream. The very thing I wished and managed
so vilely. If Lovedy were alive! Though perhaps that
is not the thing to wish. But I can't bear taking
your——"

"Hush! You can't do worse than separate your own
from mine. This is no part of the means I laid before
Mr. Martin by way of proving myself a responsible individual. I took care of that. Part of this is prize-money,
and the rest was a legacy that a rich old merchant put me
down for in a transport of gratitude because his son was one
of the sick in the bungalow where the shell came. I have
had it these three or four months, and wondered what to do
with it."

"This will be very beautiful, very excellent. And we can
give the ground."

"I have thought of another thing. I never heard of an
industrial school where the great want was not food for
industry. Now I know the Colonel and Mr. Mitchell have
some notion floating in their minds about getting a house
for convalescents down here, and it strikes me that this
might supply the work in cooking, washing, and so on.
I think I might try what they thought of it."

Rachel could only weep out her shame and thankfulness;
and when Alick reverently added that it was a scheme that
would require much thought and much prayer, the pang
struck her to the heart—how little she had prayed over the
F. U. E. E. The prayer of her life had been for action and

usefulness, but when she had seen the shadow in the stream, her hot and eager haste, her unconscious detachment from all that was not visible and material had made her adhere too literally to that misinterpreted motto, *laborare est orare.* How should then her eyes be clear to discern between substance and shadow ?

CHAPTER X.

THE HONEYMOON.

" Around the very place doth brood
A calm and holy quietude."—Rev. ISAAC WILLIAMS.

THE level beams of a summer sun, ending one of his longest careers, were tipping a mountain peak with an ineffable rosy purple, contrasting with the deep shades of narrow ravines that cleft the rugged sides, and gradually expanded into valleys, sloping with green pasture, or clothed with wood. The whole picture, with its clear, soft sky, was retraced on the waters of the little lake set in emerald meadows, which lay before the eyes of Rachel Keith, as she reclined in a garden chair before the windows of a pretty rustic-looking hotel ; but there was no admiration, no peaceful contemplation on her countenance, only the same weary air of depression, too wistful and startled even to be melancholy repose, and the same bewildered distressed look that had been as it were stamped on her by the gaze of the many unfriendly eyes at the Quarter Sessions, and by her two unfortunate dinner parties.

The wedding was to have been quietness itself, but though the bridegroom had refused to contribute sister, brother-in-law, or even uncle to the numbers, conventionalities had been too strong for Mrs. Curtis, and " just one more " had

been added to the guests till a sufficient multitude had been
collected to renew all Rachel's morbid sensations of distress
and bewilderment with their accompanying feverish symptoms, and she had been only able to proceed on her journey
by very short stages, taken late in the day.

Alick had not forgotten her original views as to travelling,
and as they were eventually to go to Scotland, had proposed
beginning with Dutch reformatories and Swiss cretins; but
she was so plainly unfit for extra fatigue and bustle, that the
first few weeks were to be spent in Wales, where the enjoyment of fine scenery might, it was hoped, be beneficial to
the jaded spirits, and they had been going through a course
of passes and glens as thoroughly as Rachel's powers would
permit, for any over-fatigue renewed feverishness and its
delusive miseries, and the slightest alarm told upon the
shattered nerves.

She did not easily give way at the moment, but the shock
always took revenge in subsequent suffering, which all Alick's
care could not prevent, though the exceeding charm of his
tenderness rendered even the indisposition almost precious
to her.

"What a lovely sunset!" he said, coming to lean over the
back of her chair. "Have you been watching it?"

"I don't know."

"Are you very much tired?"

"No, it is very quiet here."

"Very; but I must take you in before that curling mist
mounts into your throat."

"This is a very nice place, Alick, the only really quiet one
we have found."

"I am afraid that it will be so no longer. The landlord

tells me he has letters from three parties to order rooms."

"Oh, then, pray let us go on," said Rachel, looking alarmed.

"To-morrow afternoon then, for I find there's another waterfall."

"Very well," said Rachel, resignedly.

"Or shall we cut the waterfall, and get on to Llan—something?"

"If you don't think we ought to see it."

"Ought?" he said, smiling. "What is the ought in the case? Why are we going through all this? Is it a duty to society or to ourselves?"

"A little of both, I suppose," said Rachel.

"And, Rachel, from the bottom of your heart, is it not a trying duty?"

"I want to like what you are showing me," said Rachel.

"And you are more worried than delighted, eh?"

"I—I don't know! I see it is grand and beautiful! I did love my own moors, and the Spinsters' Needles, but—— Don't think me very ungrateful, but I can't enter into all this! All I really do care for is your kindness, and helping me about," and she was really crying like a child unable to learn a lesson.

"Well," he said, with his own languor of acquiescence, "we are perfectly agreed. Waterfalls are an uncommon bore, if one is not in a concatenation accordingly."

Rachel was beguiled into a smile.

"Come," he said, "let us be strong minded! If life should ever become painful to us because of our neglect of the waterfalls, we will set out and fulfil our tale of them.

Meantime, let me take you where you shall be really quiet, home to Bishopsworthy."

" But your uncle does not expect you so soon."

" My uncle is always ready for me, and a week or two of real rest there would make you ready for the further journey."

Rachel made no opposition. She was glad to have her mind relieved from the waterfalls, but she had rather have been quite alone with her husband. She knew that Lord and Lady Keith had taken a house at Littleworthy, while Gowanbrae was under repair, and she dreaded the return to the bewildering world, before even the first month was over ; but Alick made the proposal so eagerly that she could not help assenting with all the cordiality she could muster, thinking that it must be a wretched, disappointing wedding tour for him, and she would at least not prevent his being happy with his uncle; as happy as he could be with a person tied to him, of whom all his kindred must disapprove, and especially that paragon of an uncle, whom she heard of like an intensification of all that class of clergy who had of late been most alien to her.

Alick did not press for her real wishes, but wrote his letter, and followed it as fast as she could bear to travel. So when the train, a succession of ovens for living bodies disguised in dust, drew up at the Littleworthy Station, there was a ready response to the smart footman's inquiry, "Captain and Mrs. Keith ?" This personage by no means accorded with Rachel's preconceived notions of the Rectory establishment, but she next heard the peculiar clatter by which a grand equipage announces its importance, and saw the coronetted blinkers tossing on the other side of

the railing. A kind little note of welcome was put into
Rachel's hand as she was seated in the luxurious open
carriage, and Alick had never felt better pleased with his
sister than when he found his wife thus spared the closeness
of the cramping fly, or the dusty old rectory phaeton.
Hospitality is never more welcome than at the station, and
Bessie's letter was complacently accepted. Rachel would,
she knew, be too much tired to see her on that day, and
on the next she much regretted having an engagement in
London, but on the Sunday they would not fail to meet, and
she begged that Rachel would send word by the servant
what time Meg should be sent to the Rectory for her to
ride ; it would be a kindness to exercise her, for it was long
since she had been used.

Rachel could not help colouring with pleasure at the
notion of riding her own Meg again, and Alick freely owned
that it was well thought of. He already had a horse at his
uncle's, and was delighted to see Rachel at last looking
forward to something. But as she lay back in the carriage,
revelling in the fresh wind, she became dismayed at the
succession of cottages of gentility, with lawns and hedges of
various pretensions.

" There must be a terrible number of people here ! "

" This is only Littleworthy."

" Not very little."

" No ; I told you it was villafied and cockneyfied. There,"
as the horses tried to stop at a lodge leading to a prettily
built house, " that's Timber End, the crack place here, where.
Bessie has always said it was her ambition to live."

" How far is it from the Parsonage ? "

" Four miles."

Which was a comfort to Rachel, not that she wished to
be distant from Bessie, but the population appalled her
imagination.

"Bishopsworthy is happily defended by a Dukery," explained Alick, as coming to the end of the villas they passed
woods and fields, a bit of heathy common, and a scattering
of cottages. Labourers going home from work looked up,
and as their eyes met Alick's there was a mutual smile and
touch of the hat. He evidently felt himself coming home.
The trees of a park were beginning to rise in front, when the
carriage turned suddenly down a sharp steep hill ; the right
side of the road bounded by a park paling ; the left, by
cottages, reached by picturesque flights of brick stairs, then
came a garden wall, and a halt. Alick called out, "Thanks,"
and we will get out here," adding, "They will take in the
goods the back way. I don't like careering into the
churchyard."

Rachel, alighting, saw that the lane proceeded downwards
to a river crossed by a wooden bridge, with an expanse of
meadows beyond. To her left was a stable-yard, and below
it a white gate and white railings enclosing a graveyard, with
a very beautiful church standing behind a mushroom yew
tree. The upper boundary of the churchyard was the clipped
yew hedge of the rectory garden, whose front entrance was
through the churchyard. There was a lovely cool tranquillity
of aspect as the shadows lay sleeping on the grass ; and
Rachel could have stood and gazed, but Alick opened the
gate, and there was a movement at the seat that enclosed the
gnarled trunk of the yew tree. A couple of village lads
touched their caps and departed the opposite way ; a white
setter dog bounded forward, and, closely attended by a still

snowier cat, a gentleman came to meet them, so fearlessly treading the pathway between the graves, and so youthful in figure, that it was only the " Well, uncle, here she is," and, " Alick, my dear boy," that convinced her that this was indeed Mr. Clare. The next moment he had taken her hand, kissed her brow, and spoken a few words of fatherly blessing, then, while Alick exchanged greetings with the cat and dog, he led her to the arched yew tree entrance to his garden, up two stone steps, along a flagged path across the narrow grass-plat in front of the old two-storied house, with a tiled verandah like an eyebrow to the lower front windows.

Instead of entering by the door in the centre, he turned the corner of the house, where the eastern gable disclosed a window opening on a sloping lawn full of bright flower-beds. The room within was lined with books and stored with signs of parish work, but with a refined orderliness reigning over the various little ornaments, and almost betokening feminine habitation ; and Alick exclaimed with admiration of a large bowl of fresh roses, beautifully arranged.

" Traces of Bessie," said Mr. Clare ; " she brought them this morning, and spent nearly an hour in arranging them and entertaining me with her bright talk. I have hardly been able to keep out of the room since, they make it so delicious."

" Do you often see her ? " asked Alick.

"Yes ; dear child, she is most good-natured and attentive, and I take it most kindly of her, so courted as she is."

" How do you get on with his lordship ? "

" I don't come much in his way ; he has been a good deal laid up with sciatica, but he seems very fond of her ; and it was all her doing that they have been all this time at Littleworthy, instead of being in town for the season. She thought it better for him."

"And where is Mr. Lifford ?" asked Alick.

"Gone to M—— till Saturday."

"Unable to face the bride."

"I fear Ranger is not equally shy," said Mr. Clare, understanding a certain rustle and snort to import that the dog was pressing his chin hard upon Rachel's knee, while she declared her content with the handsome creature's black depth of eye ; and the cat executed a promenade of tenderness upon Alick.

"How are the peacocks, Alick ?" added Mr. Clare ; "they, at least, are inoffensive pets. I dreaded the shears without your superintendence, but Joe insisted that they were getting lop-sided."

Alick put his head out at the window. "All right, sir ; Joe has been a little hard on the crest of the left-hand one, but it is recovering."

Whereupon, Rachel discovered that the peacocks were creatures of yew tree, perched at either end of the garden fence. Mr. Clare had found them there, and preserved them with solicitous fidelity.

Nothing could be less like than he was to the grave, thin, stooping ascetic in a long coat, that she had expected. He was a tall, well-made man, of the same youthful cast of figure as his nephew, and a far lighter and more springy step, with features and colouring recalling those of his niece, as did the bright sunny playful sweetness of his manner ; his dark handsome eyes only betraying their want of sight by a certain glassy immobility that contrasted with the play of the expressive mouth. It was hard to guess why Bessie should

have shunned such an uncle. Alick took Rachel to the bedroom above the library, and, like it, with two windows—one
overlooking churchyard, river, and hay-fields, the other commanding, over the peacock hedge, a view of the playground,
where Mr. Clare was seen surrounded by boys, appealing to
him on some disputed matter of cricket. There was a
wonderful sense of serenity, freshness, and fragrance, inexpressibly grateful to Rachel's wearied feelings, and far more
comfortable than the fine scenery through which she had
been carried, because no effort to look and admire was incumbent on her—nay, not even an effort to talk all the evening.
Mr. Clare seemed to have perfectly imbibed the idea that
rest was what she wanted, and did not try to make small talk
with her, though she sat listening with pleased interest to
the conversation between him and his nephew—so home
like, so full of perfect understanding of one another.

"Is there anything to be read aloud?" presently asked
Alick.

"You have not by chance got 'Framley Parsonage?'"

"I wish I had. I did pick up 'Silas Marner,' at a
station, thinking you might like it;" and he glanced at
Rachel, who had, he suspected, thought his purchase an act
of weakness. "Have you met with it?"

"I have met with nothing of the sort since you were here
last;" then turning to Rachel, "Alick indulges me with
novels, for my good curate had rather read the catalogue of a
sale any day than meddle with one, and I can't set on my
pupil teacher in a book where I don't know what is coming."

"We will get 'Framley,'" said Alick.

"Bessie has it. She read me a very clever scene about a
weak young parson bent on pleasing himself; and offered to

lend me the book, but I thought it would not edify Will Walker. But, no doubt, you have read it long ago."

" No," said Rachel ; and something withheld her from disclaiming such empty employments. Indeed, she was presently much interested in the admirable portraiture of "Silas Marner," and still more by the keen, vivid enjoyment, critical, droll, and moralizing, displayed by a man who heard works of fiction so rarely that they were always fresh to him, and who looked on them as studies of life. His hands were busy all the time carving a boss for the roof of one of the side aisles of his church—the last step in its gradual restoration.

That night there was no excitement of nerve, no morbid fancy to trouble Rachel's slumbers ; she only awoke as the eight o'clock bell sounded through the open window, and for the first time for months rose less weary than she had gone to rest. Week-day though it were, the description "sweet day, so calm, so cool, so bright," constantly recurred to her mind as she watched the quiet course of occupation. Alick, after escorting his uncle to a cottage, found her searching among the stores in the music stand.

" You unmusical female," he said, " what is that for !"

" Your uncle spoke of music last night, and I thought he would like it."

" I thought you had no such propensity."

" I learnt like other people, but it was the only thing I could not do as well as Grace, and I thought it wasted time, and was a young ladyism ; but if I can recover music enough to please him, I should be glad."

" Thank you," said Alick, earnestly. " He is very much pleased with your voice in speaking. Indeed, I believe I first heard it with his ears."

"This is a thorough lady's collection of music," said Rachel, looking through it to hide her blush of pleasure. "Altogether the house has not a bachelor look."

"Did you not know that he had been married? It was when he first had the living twelve years ago. She was a very lovely young thing, half Irish, and this was the happiest place in the world for two years, till her little brother was sent home here from school without proper warning of a fever that had begun there. We all had it, but she and her baby were the only ones that did not recover! There they lie, under the yew-tree, where my uncle likes to teach the children. He was terribly struck down for years, though he went manfully to his work, and it has been remarkable how his spirits and sociability have returned since he lost his sight; indeed, he is more consistently bright than ever he was."

"I never saw any one like him," said Rachel. "I have fallen in with clergy that some call holy, and with some that others call pious, but he is not a bit like either. He is not even grave, yet there is a calming, refreshing sense of reverence towards him that would be awe, only it is so happy."

Alick's response was to bend over her, and kiss her brow. She had never seen him so much gratified.

"What a comfort your long stay with him must have been," she said presently, "in the beginning of his blindness!"

"I hope so. It was an ineffable comfort to me to come here out of Littleworthy croquet, and I think cheering me did him good. Rachel, you may do and say what you please," he added, earnestly, "since you have taken to him."

"I could not help it," said Rachel, though a slight

embarrassment came over her at the recollection of Bessie, and at the thought of the narrow views on which she expected to differ. Then, as Alick continued to search among the music, she asked, " Will he like the piano to be used ?"

" Of all things. Bessie's singing is his delight. Look, could we get this up ?"

" You don't sing, Alick ! I mean, do you ?"

" We need not betray our talents to worldlings base."

Rachel found her accompaniment the least satisfactory part of the affair, and resolved on an hour's practice every day in Mr. Clare's absence, a wholesome purpose even as regarded her health and spirits. She had just sat down to write letters, feeling for the first time as if they would not be a toil, when Mr. Clare looked in to ask Alick to refer to a verse in the Psalms, quoting it in Greek as well as English, and after the research had been carried to the Hebrew, he told Rachel that he was going to write his sermon, and repaired to the peacock path, where he paced along with Ranger and the cat, in faithful, unobtrusive attendance.

" What, you can read Hebrew, Alick ?"

" So can you."

" Enough to appreciate the disputed passages. When did you study it ?"

" I learnt enough, when I was laid up, to look out my uncle's texts for him."

She felt a little abashed by the tone, but a message called him away, and before his return Mr. Clare came back to ask for a reference to St. Augustine. On her offer of her services, she was thanked, and directed with great precision to the right volume of the Library of the Fathers ; but spying a real St. Augustine, she could not be satisfied without a flight at

the original. It was not, however, easy to find the place ;
she was forced to account for her delay by confessing her
attempt, and then to profit by Mr. Clare's directions ; and,
after all, her false quantities, though most tenderly and
apologetically corrected, must have been dreadful to the
scholarly ear, for she was obliged to get Alick to read the
passage over to him before he arrived at the sense, and
Rachel felt her flight of clever womanhood had fallen short.
It was quite new to her to be living with people who knew
more of, and went deeper into, everything than she did, and
her husband's powers especially amazed her.

The afternoon was chiefly spent in the hay-field under a
willow-tree ; Mr. Clare tried to leave the young people to
themselves, but they would not consent ; and, after a good
deal of desultory talk and description of the minnows and
water-spiders, in whom Mr. Clare seemed to take a deep
interest, they went on with their book till the horses came,
and Alick took Rachel for a ride in Earlsworthy Park, a
private gate of which, just opposite to the Rectory, was free
to its inhabitants. The Duke was an old college friend of
Mr. Clare, and though much out of health, and hardly ever able
to reside at the Park, all its advantages were at the Rector's
service, and they were much appreciated when, on this sultry
summer's day, Rachel found shade and coolness in the deep
arcades of the beech woods, and freshness on the upland
lawns, as she rode happily on the dear old mare, by whom
she really thought herself fondly recognised. There was
something in the stillness of the whole, even in the absence
of the roll and plash of the sea waves beside which she had
grown up, that seemed to give her repose from the hurry and
throb of sensations and thoughts that had so long pre᷎᷎ ᷎

upon her; and when the ride was over she was refreshed, not tired, and the evening bell drew her to the conclusion most befitting a day spent in that atmosphere of quietude. She felt grateful to her husband for making no remark, though the only time she had been within a church since her illness had been at their wedding; he only gave her his arm, and said she should sit in the nook that used to be his in the time of his lameness; and a most sheltered nook it was, between a pillar and the open chancel screen, where no eyes could haunt her, even if the congregation had been more than a Saturday summer evening one.

She only saw the pure, clear, delicately-toned hues of the east window, and the reverent richness of the chancel, and she heard the blind pastor's deep musical voice, full of that expressive power always enhanced by the absence of a book. He led the Psalms with perfect security and a calm fervour that rendered the whole familiar service like something new and touching; the Lessons were read by Alick, and Rachel, though under any other circumstances she would have been startled to see him standing behind the Eagle, could not but feel all appropriate, and went along with each word as he read it in a tone well worthy of his uncle's scholar. Whether few or many were present, Rachel knew not, thought not; she was only sensible of the fulness of calm joy that made the Thanksgiving touch her heart and fill her eyes with unbidden tears, that came far more readily than of old.

"Yet this can't be all," she said to herself, as she wandered among the tall white lilies in the twilight; "is it a trance, or am I myself? I have not unthought or unfelt, yet I seem falling into a very sweet hypocrisy! Alick says thought will come back with strength. I don't think I wish it!"

The curate did not return till after she had gone to bed, and in the morning he proved to be indeed a very dry and serious middle-aged man, extremely silent, and so grave that there was no knowing how much to allow for shyness. He looked much worn and had a wearied voice, and Mr. Clare and Alick were contriving all they could to give him the rest which he refused, Mr. Clare insisting on taking all the service that could be performed without eyes, and Alick volunteering school-work. This Rachel was not yet able to undertake, nor would Alick even let her go to church in the morning; but the shady garden, and the echoes of the Amens, and sweet, clear tones of singing, seemed to lull her on in this same gentle, unthinking state of dreamy rest; and thence, too, in the after part of the day, she could watch the rector, with his Sunday class, on his favourite seat under the yew-tree, close to the cross that marked the resting-place of his wife and child.

She went to church in the evening, sheltered from curious eyes in her nook, and there for a moment she heard the peculiar brush and sweep of rich silk upon pavement, and wondered at so sophisticated a sound in the little homely congregation, but forgot it again in the exulting, joyous beauty of the chants and hymns, led by the rector himself, and, oh, how different from poor Mr. Touchett's best efforts! and forgot it still more in the unfettered eloquence of the preaching of a man of great natural power, and entirely accustomed to trust to his own inward stores. Like Ermine Williams, she could have said that this preaching was the first that won her attention. It certainly was the first that swept away all her spirit of criticising, and left her touched and impressed, not judging. On what north country folk call the loosing of the kirk, she, moving outwards after the throng, found her-

self close behind a gauzy white cloak over a lilac silk, that
filled the whole breadth of the central aisle, and by the dark
curl descending beneath the tiny white bonnet, as well as by
the turn of the graceful head, she knew her sister-in-law,
Lady Keith, of Gowanbrae. In the porch she was met with
outstretched hands and eager greetings—

"At last! Where did you hide yourself? I had begun to
imagine dire mischances."

"Only in the corner by the chancel."

"Alick's old nook! Keeping up honeymoon privileges!
I have kept your secret faithfully. No one knows you are
not on the top of Snowdon, or you would have had all the
world to call on you."

"There are always the Earlsworthy woods," said Alick.

"Or better still, come to Timber End. No one penetrates
to my morning room," laughed Bessie. "Now, Uncle George,"
she said, as the rector appeared, "you have had a full allow-
ance of them for three days; you must spare them to me
to-morrow morning."

"So it is you, my lady," he answered, with a pleased smile;
"I heard a sort of hail-storm of dignity sailing in! How is
Lord Keith?"

"Very stiff. I want him to have advice, but he hates
doctors. What is the last Avonmouth news? Is Ermine in
good heart, and the boys well again?"

She was the same Bessie as ever—full of exulting animation, joined to a caressing manner that her uncle evidently
delighted in; and to Rachel she was most kind and sisterly,
welcoming her so as amply to please and gratify Alick. An
arrangement was made that Rachel should be sent for early
to spend the day at Timber End, and that Mr. Clare and Alick

should walk over later. Then the two pretty ponies came with her little low carriage to the yew-tree gate, were felt and admired by Mr. Clare, and approved by Alick ; and she drove off gaily, leaving all pleased and amused, but still there was a sense that the perfect serenity had been ruffled.

" Rachel," said Alick, as they wandered in the twilight garden, " I wonder if you would be greatly disappointed if our travels ended here."

" I am only too glad of the quiet."

" Because Lifford is in great need of thorough rest. He has not been away for more than a year, and now he is getting quite knocked up. All he does care to do, is to take lodgings near his wife's asylum, poor man, and see her occasionally : sad work, but it is rest, and winds him up again ; and there is no one but myself to whom he likes to leave my uncle. Strangers always do too little or too much ; and there is a young man at Littleworthy for the long vacation who can help on a Sunday."

" Oh, pray let us stay as long as we can ! "

" Giving up the Crétins ? "

" It is no sacrifice. I am thankful not to be hunted about ; and if anything could make me better pleased to be here, it would be feeling that I was not hindering you."

" Then I will hunt him away for six weeks or two months at least. It will be a great relief to my uncle's mind."

It was so great a relief that Mr. Clare could hardly bring himself to accept the sacrifice of the honeymoon, and though there could be little doubt which way the discussion would end, he had not yielded when the ponies bore off Rachel on Monday morning.

Timber End was certainly a delightful place. Alick had

called it a cockney villa, but it was in good taste, and very
fair and sweet with flowers and shade. Bessie's own rooms,
where she made Rachel charmingly at home, were wonderful
in choiceness and elegance, exciting Rachel's surprise how it
could be possible to be so sumptuously lodged in such a temporary abode, for the house was only hired for a few months,
while Gowanbrae was under repair. It was within such easy
reach of London that Bessie had been able from thence to go
through the more needful season gaieties; and she had
thought it wise, both for herself and Lord Keith, not to enter
on their full course. It sounded very moderate and prudent,
and Rachel felt vexed with herself and Alick for recollecting
a certain hint of his, that Lady Keith felt herself more of a
star in her own old neighbourhood than she could be in London, and wisely abstained from a full flight till she had tried
her wings. It was much pleasanter to go along with Bessie's
many far better and more affectionate reasons for prudence,
and her minutely personal confidences about her habits, hopes,
and fears, given with a strong sense of her own importance
and consideration, yet with a warm sisterly tone that made
them tokens of adoption, and with an arch drollery that invested them with a sort of grace. The number of engagements
that she mentioned in town and country did indeed seem
inconsistent with the prudence she spoke of with regard to
her own health, or with her attention to that of her husband;
but it appeared that all were quite necessary and according to
his wishes, and the London ones were usually for the sake of
trying to detach his daughter, Mrs. Comyn Menteith, from
the extravagant set among whom she had fallen. Bessie was
excessively diverting in her accounts of her relations with
this scatter-brained step-daughter of hers, and altogether

showed in the most flattering manner how much more
thoroughly she felt herself belonging to her brother's wife.
If she had ever been amazed or annoyed at Alick's choice, she
had long ago surmounted the feeling, or put it out of sight,
and she judiciously managed to leap over all that had passed
since the beginning of the intimacy that had arisen at the
station door at Avoncester. It was very flattering, and would
have been perfectly delightful, if Rachel had not found herself wearying for Alick, and wondering whether at the end
of seven months she should be as contented as Bessie seemed,
to know her husband to be in the sitting-room without one
sight of him.

At luncheon, however, when Lord Keith appeared, nothing
could be prettier than his wife's manner to him—bright, sweet,
and with a touch of graceful deference, at which he always
smiled and showed himself pleased ; but Rachel thought him
looking much older than in the autumn—he had little appetite, stooped a good deal, and evidently moved with pain.
He would not go out of doors, and Bessie, after following him
to the library, and spending a quarter of an hour in ministering to his comfort, took Rachel to sit by a cool dancing
fountain in the garden, and began with some solicitude to
consult her whether he could be really suffering from sciatica,
or, as she had lately begun to suspect, from the effects of a
blow from the end of a scaffold-pole that had been run against
him when taking her through a crowded street. Rachel spoke
of advice.

" What you, Rachel ! you who despised allopathy ! "

" I have learnt not to despise advice."

And Bessie would not trench on Rachel's experiences.

" There's some old Scotch doctor to whom his faith is

given, and that I don't half believe in. If he would see
our own Mr. Harvey here it would be quite another thing;
but it is of no use telling him that Alick would never have
had an available knee but for Mr. Harvey's management.
He persists in leaving me to my personal trust in him, but
for himself he won't see him at any price! Have you seen
Mr. Harvey?"

"I have seen no one."

"Oh, I forgot, you are not arrived yet; but——"

"There's some one," exclaimed Rachel, nervously; and in
fact a young man was sauntering towards them. Bessie rose
with a sort of annoyance, and "Never mind, my dear, he is
quite inoffensive, we'll soon get rid of him." Then, as he
greeted her with "Good morning, Lady Keith, I thought I
should find you here," she quickly replied,

"If you had been proper behaved and gone to the door,
you would have known that I am not at home."

He smiled, and came nearer.

"No, I am not at home, and, what is more, I do not mean
to be. My uncle will be here directly," she added, in a fee-
faw-fum tone.

"Then it is not true that your brother and his bride are
arrived?"

"True in the same sense as that I am at home. There she
is, you see—only you are not to see her on any account," as
a bow necessarily passed between him and Rachel. "Now
mind you have *not* been introduced to Mrs. Keith, and if
you utter a breath that will bring the profane crowd in
shoals upon the Rectory, I shall never forgive you."

"Then I am afraid we must not hope to see you at the
bazaar for the idiots."

" No, indeed," Bessie answered, respecting Rachel's gesture of refusal ; " no one is to infringe her *incog.* under penalty of never coming here again."

" You are going ? " he added to Bessie ; " indeed, that was what brought me here.   My sisters sent me to ask whether they may shelter themselves under your matronly protection, for my mother dreads the crush."

" I suppose, as they put my name down, that I must go ; but you know I had much rather give the money outright. It is a farce to call a bazaar charity."

" Call it what you will, it is one device for a little sensation."

Rachel's only sensation at that moment was satisfaction at the sudden appearance of Ranger's white head, the sure harbinger of his master and Alick, and she sprang up to meet them in the shrubbery path—all her morbid shyness at the sight of a fresh face passing away when her hand was within Alick's arm.   When they came forth upon the lawn, Alick's brow darkened for a moment, and there was a formal exchange of greetings as the guest retreated.

" I am so sorry," began Bessie at once ; " I had taken precautions against invasion, but he did not go to the front door.   I do so hope Rachel has not been fluttered."

" I thought he was at Rio," said Alick.

" He could not stand the climate, and was sent home about a month ago—a regular case of bad shilling, I am afraid, poor fellow !   I am so sorry he came to startle Rachel, but I swore him over to secresy.   He is not to mention to any living creature that she is nearer than Plinlimmon till the *incog.* is laid aside !   I know how to stand up for bridal privileges, and not to abuse the confidence placed in me."

Any one who was up to the game might have perceived that the sister was trying to attribute all the brother's tone of disapprobation to his anxiety lest his wife should have been startled, while both knew as well as possible that there was a deeper ground of annoyance which was implied in Alick's answer.

" He seems extremely tame about the garden."

" Or he would not have fallen on Rachel. It was only a chance ; he just brought over a message about that tiresome bazaar that has been dinned into our ears for the last three months. A bazaar for idiots they may well call it ! They wanted a carving of yours, Uncle George ! "

" I am afraid I gave little Alice Bertie one in a weak moment, Bessie," said Mr. Clare, " but I hardly durst show my face to Lifford afterwards."

" After all, it is better than some bazaars," said Bessie ; " it is only for the idiot asylum, and I could not well refuse my name and countenance to my old neighbours, though I stood out against taking a stall.   Lord Keith would not have liked it."

" Will he be able to go with you ? " asked Alick.

" Oh, no ; it would be an intolerable bore, and his Scottish thrift would never stand the sight of people making such very bad bargains ! No, I am going to take the Carleton girls in, they are very accommodating, and I can get away whenever I please. I am much too forbearing to ask any of you to go with me, though I believe Uncle George is pining to go and see after his carving."

" No, thank you ; after what I heard of the last bazaar I

made up my mind that they are no places for an old parson, nor for his carvings either, so you are quite welcome to fall on me for my inconsistency."

"Not now, when you have a holiday from Mr. Lifford," returned Bessie. "Now come and smell the roses."

All the rest of the day Alick relapsed into the lazy frivolous young officer with whom Rachel had first been acquainted.

As he was driving home in the cool fresh summer night, he began—

"I think I must go to this idiotical bazaar!"

"You!" exclaimed Rachel.

"Yes; I don't think Bessie ought to go by herself with all this Carleton crew."

"You don't wish me to go," said Rachel, gulping down the effort.

"You? My dear Rachel, I would not take you for fifty pounds, nor could I go myself without leaving you as vice deputy curate."

"No need for that," said Mr. Clare, from the seat behind ; "young people must not talk secrets with a blind man's ears behind them."

"I make no secret," said Alick. "I could not go without leaving my wife to take care of my uncle, or my uncle to take care of my wife."

"And you think you ought to go?" said Mr. Clare. "It is certainly better that Bessie should have a gentleman with her in the crowd; but you know this is a gossiping neighbourhood, and you must be prepared for amazement at your coming into public alone not three weeks after your wedding."

"I can't help it ; she can't go, and I must."

"And you will bring down all the morning visitors that you talk of dreading."

"We will leave you to amuse them, sir. Much better that" he added between his teeth, "than to leave the very semblance of a secret trusted by her to that intolerable puppy——"

Rachel said no more, but when she was gone upstairs Mr. Clare detained his nephew to say, "I beg your pardon, Alick, but you should be quite sure that your wife likes this proposal."

"That's the value of a strong-minded wife, sir," returned Alick; "she is not given to making a fuss about small matters."

"Most ladies might not think this a small matter."

"That is because they have no perspective in their brains. Rachel understands me a great deal too well to make me explain what is better unspoken."

"You know what I think, Alick, that you are the strictest judge that ever a merry girl had."

"I had rather you continued to think so, uncle; I should like to think so myself. Good night."

Alick was right, but whether or not Rachel entered into his motives, she made no objection to his going to the bazaar with his sister, being absolutely certain that he would not have done so if he could have helped it.

Nor was her day at all dreary; Mr. Clare was most kind and attentive to her, without being oppressive, and she knew she was useful to him. She was indeed so full of admiration and reverence for him, that once or twice it crossed her whether she were not belying another of her principles by lapsing into Curatocult, but the idea passed away with scorn at the notion of comparing Mr. Clare with the objects of such devotion. He belonged to that generation which gave its choicest in intellectual, as well as in religious gifts to the ministry, when a fresh tide of enthusiasm was impelling men forward to build up, instead of breaking down, before disappointment and suspicion had thinned the ranks, and hurled back many a recruit, or doctrinal carpings had taught men to dread a search into their own tenets. He was a highly cultivated, large-minded man, and the conversation between him and his nephew was a constant novelty to her, who had always yearned after depth and thought, and seldom met with them. Still here she was constantly feeling how shallow were her acquirements, how inaccurate her knowledge, how devoid of force and solidity her reasonings compared with what here seemed to be old, well-beaten ground. Nay, the very sparkle of fun and merriment surprised and puzzled her; and all the courtesy of the one gentleman, and the affection of the other, could not prevent her sometimes feeling herself the dullest and most ignorant person present. And yet the sense was never mortifying except when here and there a spark of the old conceit had lighted itself, and lured her into pretensions where she thought herself proficient. She was becoming more and more helpful to Mr. Clare, and his gratitude for her services made them most agreeable, nor did that atmosphere of peace and sincerity that reigned round the Rectory lose its charm. She was really happy all through the solitary Wednesday, and much more contented with the results than was Alick. " A sickening place," he said, " I am glad I went."

" How glad Bessie must have been to have you ! "

" I believe she was. She has too much good taste for much of what went on there."

"I doubt," said Mr. Clare, laughing, " if you could have been an agreeable acquisition."

"I don't know. Bessie fools one into thinking oneself always doing her a favour. Oh, Rachel, I am thankful you have never taken to being agreeable."

CHAPTER XI.

THE HUNTSFORD CROQUET.

" Une femme égoïste, non seulement de cœur, mais d'esprit, ne
peut pas sortir d'elle-même. Le moi est indélible chez elle. Une
veritable égoïste ne sait même pas être fausse." — Mme. E. de
Girardin.

" I am come to prepare you," said Lady Keith, putting her
arm into her brother's, and leading him into the peacock
path.   "Mrs. Huntsford is on her way to call and make a
dead set to get you all to a garden party."

" Then we are off to the Earlsworthy Woods."

" Nay, listen, Alick.   I have let you alone and defended
you for a whole month, but if you persist in shutting up your
wife, people won't stand it."

" Which of us is the Mahometan ? "

" You are pitied !   But you see it was a strong thing our
appearing without our several incumbrances, and though an
old married woman like me may do as she pleases, yet for a
bridegroom of not three weeks' standing to resort to bazaars
solus argues some weighty cause."

" And argues rightly."

" Then you are content to be supposed to have an unpro-
duceably eccentric melancholy bride ? "

" Better they should think so than that she should be so.
She has been victimized enough already to her mother's desire
to save appearances."

"You do not half believe me, Alick, and this is really a very kind, thoughtful arrangement of Mrs. Huntsford's. She consulted me, saying there were such odd stories about you two that she was most anxious that Rachel should appear and confute them ; and she thought that an out-of-door party like this would suit best, because it would be early, and Rachel could get away if she found it too much for her."

"After being walked out to satisfy a curious neighbourhood."

"Now Alick, do consider it. This sort of thing could remind her of nothing painful ; Uncle George would enjoy it."

"And fall over the croquet traps."

"No ; if you wanted to attend to him, I could take care of Rachel."

"I cannot tell, Bessie ; I believe it is pure goodnature on Mrs. Huntsford's part ; but if we go, it must be from Rachel's spontaneous movement. I will not press her on any account. I had rather the world said she was crazy at once than expose her to the risk of one of the dreadful nights that haunted us till we came here to perfect quiet."

"But she is well now. She looks better and nicer than I ever saw her. Really, Alick, now her face is softer, and her eyes more veiled, and her chin not cocked up, I am quite proud of her. Every one will be struck with her good looks."

"Flattery, Bessie," he said, not ill pleased. "Yes, she is much better, and more like herself; but I dread all this being overthrown. If she wishes herself to go, it may be a good beginning, but she must not be persuaded."

"Then I must not even tell her that she won't be

required to croquet, and that I'll guard her from all civil speeches."

"No; for indeed, Bessie, on your own account and Lord Keith's, you should hardly spend a long afternoon from home."

"Here's the war in the enemy's quarters! As to fatigue, dawdling about Mrs. Huntsford's garden is much the same as dawdling about my own, and makes me far more entertaining."

"I cannot help thinking, Bessie, that Lord Keith is more ill than you suppose. I am sure he is in constant pain."

"So I fear," said Bessie, gravely; "but what can be done? He will see no one but his old surgeon in Edinburgh."

"Then take him there."

"Take him? You must know what it is to be in the hands of a clever woman before you make such a proposal."

"You are a cleverer woman than my wife in bringing about what you really wish."

"Just consider, Alick, our own house is uninhabitable, and this one on our hands—my aunt coming to me in a month's time. You don't ask me to do what is reasonable."

"I cannot tell, Bessie. You can be the only judge of what is regard of the right kind for your husband's health or for yourself; and see, there is Mrs. Huntsford actually arrived, and talking to my uncle."

"One moment, Alick: I am not going to insult myself so far as to suppose that poor Charlie Carleton's being at home has anything to do with your desire to deport me, but I want you to know that he did not come home till after we were settled here."

"I do not wish to enter into details, Bessie," and he

crossed the lawn towards the window where Mr. Clare and
Rachel had just received Mrs. Huntsford, a goodnatured
joyous-looking lady, a favourite with every one. Her invitation was dexterously given to meet a few friends at luncheon,
and in the garden, where the guests would be free to come
and go ; there might perhaps be a little dancing later, she had
secured some good music which would, she knew, attract Mr.
Clare, and she hoped he would bring Captain and Mrs.
Keith. She knew Mrs. Keith had not been well, but she
promised her a quiet room to rest in, and she wanted to
show her a view of the Devon coast done by a notable artist
in water-colours. Rachel readily accepted—in fact, this quiet
month had been so full of restoration that she had almost
forgotten her morbid shrinking from visitors; and Bessie
infused into her praise and congratulations a hint that a
refusal would have been much against Alick's reputation, so
that she resolved to keep up to the mark, even though he
took care that she should know that she might yet retract.

"You did not wish me to refuse, Alick," said she, struck
by his grave countenance, when she found him lying on the
slope of the lawn shortly after, in deep thought.

"No, not at all," he replied ; "it is likely to be a pleasant
affair, and my uncle will be delighted to have us with him.
No," he added, seeing that she still looked at him in-
quisitively, "it is the old story. My sister! Poor little
thing ! I always feel as though I were more unkind and unjust
to her than any one else, and yet we are never together without my feeling as if she was deceiving herself and me ; and
yet it is all so fair and well reasoned that one is always left
in the wrong. I regretted this marriage extremely at first,
and I am not the less disposed to regret it now."

"Indeed! Every one says how attentive she is to him, and how nicely they go on together."

"Pshaw, Rachel! that is just the way. A few words and pretty ways pass with her and all the world for attention, when she is wherever her fancy calls her, all for his good. It is just the attention she showed my uncle. And now it is her will and pleasure to queen it here among her old friends, and she will not open her eyes to see the poor old man's precarious state."

"Do you think him so very ill, Alick?"

"I was shocked when I saw him yesterday. As to sciatica, that is all nonsense; the blow in his side has done some serious damage, and if it is not well looked-to, who knows what will be the end of it! And then, a gay young widow with no control over her—I hate to think of it."

"Indeed," said Rachel, "she is so warm and bright, and really earnest in her kindness, that she will be sure to see her own way right at home. I don't think we can guess how obstinate Lord Keith may be in refusing to take advice."

"He cut me off pretty short," said Alick. "I am afraid he will see no one here; and, as Bessie says, the move to Scotland would not be easy just now. As I said, she leaves one in the wrong, and I don't like the future. But it is of no use to talk of it; so let us come and see if my uncle wants to go anywhere."

It was Alick's fate never to meet with sympathy in his feeling of his sister's double-mindedness. Whether it were that he was mistaken, or that she really had the gift of sincerity for the moment in whatever she was saying, the most candid and transparent people in the world—his uncle and his wife—never even succeeded in understanding his dissatisfaction with Bessie's doings, but always received them at her own valuation. Even while he had been looking forward, with hope deferred, to her residence with him as the greatest solace the world could yet afford him, Mr. Clare had always been convinced that her constant absence from his Rectory, except when his grand neighbours were at home, had been unavoidable, and had always credited the outward tokens of zealous devotion to his church and parish, and to all that was useful or good elsewhere. In effect there was a charm about her which no one but her brother ever resisted, and even he held out by an exertion that made him often appear ungracious.

However, for the present the uneasiness was set aside, in the daily avocations of the Rectory, where Alick was always a very different person from what he appeared in Lady Temple's drawing-room, constantly engaged as he was by unobtrusive watchfulness over his uncle, and active and alert in this service in a manner that was a curious contrast to his ordinary sauntering ways. As to Rachel, the whole state of existence was still a happy dream. She floated on from day to day in the tranquil activity of the Rectory, without daring to look back on the past or to think out her present frame of mind ; it was only the languor and rest of recovery after suffering, and her husband was heedfully watching her, fearing the experiment of the croquet party, though on many accounts feeling the necessity of its being made.

Ermine's hint, that with Rachel it rested to prevent her unpopularity from injuring her husband, had not been thrown away, and she never manifested any shrinking from the party, and even took some interest in arraying herself for it.

"That is what I call well turned out," exclaimed Alick, when she came down.

"Describe her dress, if you please," said Mr. Clare, "I like to hear how my nieces look."

Alick guided his hand. "There, stroke it down, a long white feather in a shady hat trimmed with dark green velvet; she is fresh and rosy, you know, sir, and looks well in green, and then, is it Grace's taste, Rachel? for it is the prettiest thing you have worn—a pale buff sort of silky thing, embroidered all over in the same colour;" and he put a fold of the dress into his uncle's hand.

"Indian, surely," said Mr. Clare, feeling the pattern; "it is too intricate and graceful for the West."

"Yes," said Alick, "I remember now, Grace showed it to me. It was one that Lady Temple brought from India, and never had made up. Poor Grace could get no sympathy from Rachel about the wedding clothes, so she was obliged to come to me."

"And I thought you did not know one of my things from another," said Rachel. "Do you really mean that you care?"

"Depend upon it, he does, my dear," said Mr. Clare. "I have heard him severely critical on his cousins."

"He has been very good in not tormenting me," said Rachel, nestling nearer to him.

"I apprehended the consequences," said Alick; "and besides, you never mounted that black lace pall, or curtain, or whatever you call it, upon your head, after your first attempt at frightening me away with it."

"A cap set against, instead of at," said Mr. Clare, laughing; and therewith his old horse was heard clattering in the yard, and Alick proceeded to drive the well-used phaeton about three miles through Earlsworthy Park, to a pleasant-looking demesne in the village beyond. As they were turning in at the gate, up came Lady Keith with her two brisk little Shetlands. She was one mass of pretty, fresh, fluttering blue and white muslin, ribbon, and lace, and looked particularly well and brilliant.

"Well met," she said ; "I called at the Rectory to take up Rachel, but you were flown before me."

"Yes, we went through the Park."

"I wish the Duke would come home. I can't go that way now till I have called. I have no end of things to say to you," she added, and her little lively ponies shot ahead of the old rectorial steed. However, she waited at the entrance. "Who do you think is come? Colin Keith made his appearance this morning. He has safely captured his Ouralian bear, though not without plenty of trouble, and he could not get him on to Avonmouth till he had been to some chemical institution about an invention. Colin thought him safe there, and rushed down by the train to see us. They go on to-morrow."

"What did he think of Lord Keith?" said Alick, in the more haste because he feared something being said to remind Rachel that this was the assize week at Avoncester.

"He has settled the matter about advice," said Bessie, seriously ; "you cannot think what a relief it is. I mean, as soon as I get home, to write and ask Mr. Harvey to come and talk to me to-morrow, and see if the journey to Edinburgh is practicable. I almost thought of sending an apology, and driving over to consult him this afternoon, but I did not like to disappoint Mrs. Huntsford, and I thought Rachel would feel herself lost."

"Thank you," said Rachel, "but could we not go away early, and go round by Mr. Harvey's?"

"Unluckily I have sent the ponies home, and told the close carriage to come for me at nine. It was all settled, and I don't want to alarm Lord Keith by coming home too soon."

Alick, who had hitherto listened with interest, here gave his arm to Rachel, as if recollecting that it was time to make their *entrée*. Bessie took her uncle's, and they were soon warmly welcomed by their kind hostess, who placed them so favourably at luncheon that Rachel was too much entertained to feel any recurrence of the old associations with "company." Afterwards, Bessie took her into the cool drawing-room, where were a few ladies, who preferred the sofa to croquet or archery, and Lady Keith accomplished a fraternization between Rachel and a plainly dressed lady, who knew all about the social science heroines of whom Rachel had longed to hear. After a time, however, a little girl darted in to call "Aunt Mary" to the aid of some playfellow, who had met with a mishap, and Rachel then perceived herself to have been deserted by her sister-in-law. She knew none of the other ladies, and they made no approaches to her; an access of self-consciousness came on, and feeling forlorn and uncomfortable, she wandered out to look for a friend.

It was not long before she saw Alick walking along the terrace above the croquet players, evidently in quest of her. "How is it with you?" he anxiously asked; "you know you can go home in a moment if you have had enough of this."

"No, I want nothing, now I have found you. Where is your uncle?"

" Fallen upon one of his oldest friends, who will take
care of him, and well out of the way of the croquet traps.
Where's my Lady? I thought you were with her."

" She disappeared while I was talking to that good Miss
Penwell! You must be pleased now, Alick, you see she is
really going to see about going to Scotland."

" I should be better pleased if she had not left that poor
old man alone till nine o'clock."

" She says that when he has his man Saunders to read to
him——"

" Don't tell me what she says; I have enough of that at
first hand."

He broke off with a start. The terrace was prolonged
into a walk beyond the screen of evergreens that shut in
the main lawn, and, becoming a shrubbery path, led to
a smooth glade, on whose turf preparations had been made
for a second field of croquet, in case there should have been
too many players for the principal arena. This, however,
had not been wanted, and no one was visible except a lady
and gentleman on a seat under a tree about half-way down
on the opposite side of the glade. The lady was in blue
and white; the gentleman would hardly have been recognised by Rachel but for the start and thrill of her husband's
arm, and the flush of colour on his usually pale cheek; but,
ere he could speak or move, the lady sprang up, and came
hastening towards them diagonally across the grass. Rachel
saw the danger, and made a warning outcry, " Bessie, the
hoop!" but it was too late, she had tripped over it, and fell
prone, and entirely unable to save herself. She was much
nearer to them than to her late companion, and was
struggling to disengage herself when Alick reached her,

lifted her up, and placed her on her feet, supporting her as she clung fast to him, while he asked if she were hurt.

"No, no," she cried. "Don't let him come; don't let him call any one, don't," she reiterated, as Mr. Carleton hovered near, evidently much terrified, but not venturing to approach.

Alick helped her to another garden chair that stood near. She had been entangled in her dress, which had been much torn by her attempt to rise, and hung in a festoon, impeding her, and she moved with difficulty, breathing heavily when she was first seated.

"I don't know if I have not twisted myself a little," she said, in answer to their anxious questions, "but it will go off. Rachel, how scared you look!"

"Don't laugh," exclaimed Rachel, in dread of hysterics, and she plunged her hand into Alick's pocket for a scent-bottle, which he had put there by way of precaution for her, and, while applying it, said, in her full, sedate voice, keeping it as steady as she could, "Shall I drive you home? Alick can walk home with his uncle when he is ready."

"Home! Thank you, Rachel, pray do. Not that I am hurt," she added in her natural voice, "only these rags would tell tales, and there would be an intolerable fuss."

"Then I will bring the carriage round to the road there," said Alick. "I told Joe to be in readiness, and you need not go back to the house."

"Thank you. But, oh, send him away!" she added, with a gasping shudder. "Only don't let him tell any one. Tell him I desire he will not."

After a few words with Mr. Carleton, Alick strode off to the stables, and Rachel asked anxiously after the twist.

"I don't feel it; I don't believe in it. My dear, your strong mind is all humbug, or you would not look so frightened," and again she was on the verge of hysterical laughing; "it is only that I can't stand a chorus of old ladies in commotion. How happy Alick must be to have his prediction verified by some one tumbling over a hoop!" Just then, however, seeing Mr. Carleton still lingering near, she caught hold of Rachel with a little cry, "Don't let him come, dear Rachel; go to him, tell him I am well, but keep him away, and mind he tells no one!"

Rachel's cold, repellent manner was in full force, and she went towards the poor little man, whose girlish face was blanched with fright.

She told him that Lady Keith did not seem to be hurt, and only wished to be alone, and to go home without attracting notice. He stammered out something about quite understanding, and retreated; while Rachel returned to find Bessie sitting upright, anxiously watching, and she was at once drawn down to sit beside her on the bench, to listen to the excited whisper. "The miserable simpleton! Rachel, Alick was right. I thought, I little thought he would forget how things stand now; but he got back to the old strain, as if—I shall make Lord Keith go to Scotland any way now. I was so thankful to see you and Alick." She proceeded with the agitated vehemence of one who, under a great shock, was saying more than she would have betrayed in a cooler and more guarded mood, "What could possess him! For years he had followed me about like a little dog, and never said more than I let him; and now what folly was in his head, just because I could not walk as far as the ruin with the others. When I said I was going to Scotland, what business had he to—— Oh ! the others will be coming back, Rachel ; could we not go to meet the carriage ?"

The attempt to move, however, brought back the feeling of the strain of which she had complained, but she would not give way, and by the help of Rachel's arm, proceeded across the grass to the carriage-drive, where Alick was to meet them. It seemed very far and very hot, and her alternately excited and shame-stricken manner, and sobbing breath, much alarmed Rachel ; but when Alick met them, all this seemed to pass away—she controlled herself entirely, declaring herself unhurt, and giving him cheerful messages and excuses for her hostess. Alick put the reins into Rachel's hands, and, after watching her drive off, returned to the party, and delivered the apologies of the ladies ; then went in search of his uncle. He did not, however, find him quickly, and then he was so happy with his old friend among a cluster of merry young people, that Alick would not say a word to hasten him home, especially as Rachel would have driven Bessie to Timber End, so that it would only be returning to an empty house. And such was Mr. Clare's sociableness and disability of detaching himself from pleasant conversation, that the uncle and nephew scarcely started for their walk across the park in time for the seven o'clock service. Mr. Clare had never been so completely belated, and, as Alick's assistance was necessary, he could only augur from his wife's absence that she was still at Timber End with his sister.

CHAPTER XII.

THE END OF CLEVERNESS.

" Where am I ?
O vanity,
We are not what we deem,
The sins that hold my heart in thrall,
They are more real than all."—REV. I. WILLIAMS.

As the uncle and nephew came out of church, and approached
the yew-tree gate, Rachel came swiftly to meet them. "Oh,
Alick! oh, uncle!" she said breathlessly. "Bessie says she
is shocked to have turned your house upside down, but we
could not go any further. And her baby is born!" Then in
answer to exclamations, half-dismayed, half-wondering, "Yes,
it is all right, so Nurse Jones says. I could not send to you,
for we had to send everywhere at once. Mr. Harvey was not
at home, and we telegraphed to London, but no one has come
yet, and now I have just written a note to Lord Keith with
the news of his son and heir. And, uncle, she has set her
heart on your baptizing him directly."

There was some demur, for though the child had made so
sudden a rush into the world, there seemed to be no ground
for immediate alarm ; and Mr. Clare being always at hand,
did not think it expedient to give the name without knowing
the father's wishes with regard to that hereditary Alexander
which had been borne by the dead son of the first marriage.
A message, however, came down to hasten him, and when—

as he had often before done in cottages—he demanded of
Nurse Jones whether private baptism were immediately necessary, she allowed that she saw no pressing danger, but added,
"that the lady was in a way about it," and this both Rachel
and her maid strongly corroborated. Rachel's maid was an
experienced person, whom Mrs. Curtis had selected with a
view to Rachel's weak state at the time of her marriage, and
she showed herself anxious for anything that might abate
Lady Keith's excitement, to which they at length yielded,
feeling that resistance might be dangerous to her. She further
insisted that the rite should be performed in her presence ;
nor was she satisfied when Rachel had brought in her uncle,
but insisted on likewise calling in her brother, who vaguely
anxious, and fully conscious of the small size of the room,
had remained down-stairs.

Mr. Clare always baptized his infant parishioners, and no
one was anxious about his manner of handling the little one,
the touch of whose garments might be familiar, as being no
other than his own parish baby linen. He could do no
otherwise than give the child the name reiterated by the
mother, in weak but impatient accents, " Alexander Clare,"
her brother's own name, and when the short service was concluded, she called out triumphantly, " Make Alick kiss him,
Rachel, and do homage to his young chieftain."

They obeyed her, as she lay watching them, and a very
pretty sight she was with her dark hair lying round her, a
rosy colour on her cheeks, and light in her eyes ; but Mr.
Clare thought both her touch and voice feverish, and entreated Rachel not to let her talk. Indeed Alick longed to
take Rachel away, but this was not at present feasible, since
her maid was occupied with the infant, and Nurse Jones was

so entirely a cottage practitioner that she was scarcely an available attendant elsewhere. Bessie herself would by no means have parted with her sister-in-law, nor was it possible to reduce her to silence. "Alexander!" she said joyfully, "I always promised my child that he should not have a stupid second son's name. I had a right to my own father's and brother's name, and now it can't be altered," then catching a shade of disapproval upon Rachel's face, "not that I would have hurried it on if I had not thought it right, poor little fellow, but now I trust he will do nicely, and I do think we have managed it all with less trouble than might have been expected."

Sure by this time that she was talking too much, Rachel was glad to hear that Mr. Harvey was come. He was a friendly, elderly man, who knew them all intimately, having attended Alick through his tedious recovery, and his first measure was to clear the room. Rachel thought that "at her age" he might have accepted her services, rather than her maid's, but she suspected Alick of instigating her exclusion, so eagerly did he pounce on her to make her eat, drink, and lie on the sofa, and so supremely scornful was he of her views of sitting up, a measure which *might* be the more needful for want of a bed.

On the whole, however, he was satisfied about her; alarm and excitement had restrung her powers, and she knew herself to have done her part, so that she was ready to be both cheerful and important over the evening meal. Mr. Clare was by no means annoyed at this vicissitude, but rather amused at it, and specially diverted at the thought of what would be Mr. Lifford's consternation. Lord Keith's servant had come over, reporting his master to be a good deal worn out by the

afternoon's anxiety, and recommending that he should not be
again disturbed that night, so he was off their minds, and the
only drawback to the pleasantness of the evening was surprise
at seeing and hearing nothing from Mr. Harvey. The London doctor arrived, he met him and took him up-stairs at
once; and then ensued a long stillness, all attempts at conversation died away, and Alick only now and then made
attempts to send his companions to bed. Mr. Clare went out
to the hall to listen, or Rachel stole up to the extemporary
nursery to consult Nurse Jones, whom she found very gruff
at having been turned out in favour of the stranger maid.

It was a strange time of suspense. Alick made Rachel lie
on the sofa, and she almost heard the beating of her own
heart; he sat by her, trying to seem to read, and his uncle
stood by the open window, where the tinkle of a sheep bell
came softly in from the meadows, and now and then the hoot
of the owl round the church tower made the watchers start.
To watch that calm and earnest face was their great help in
that hour of alarm; those sightless eyes, and broad, upraised
spiritual brow seemed so replete with steadfast trust and peace,
that the very sight was soothing and supporting to the young
husband and wife; and when the long strokes of twelve re-
sounded from the church tower, Mr. Clare, turning towards
them, began in his full, musical voice to repeat Bishop Ken's
noble midnight hymn—

> " My God, now I from sleep awake,
> The sole possession of me take;
> From midnight terrors me secure,
> And guard my soul from thoughts impure."

To Rachel, who had so often heard that hour strike amid a
tumult of midnight miseries, there was something in these

words inexpressibly gentle and soothing; the tears sprang into her eyes, as if she had found the spell to chase the grisly phantoms, and she clasped her husband's hand, as though to communicate her comfort.

> " Oh may I always ready stand,
> With my lamp burning in my hand ;
> May I in sight of Heaven rejoice,
> Whene'er I hear the Bridegroom's voice."

Mr. Clare had just repeated this verse, when he paused, saying, "They are coming down," and moved quickly to meet them in the hall. Alick followed him to the door, but as they entered the dining-room, after a moment's hesitation, returned to Rachel, as she sat upright and eager. "After all, this may mean nothing," he said.

"Oh, we don't make it better by fancying it nothing," said Rachel. "Let us try to meet it like your uncle. Oh, Alick, it seemed all this time as if I could pray again, as I never could since those sad times. He seemed so sure, such a rock to help and lean on."

He drew her close to him. "You are praying for her!" he murmured, his soul so much absorbed in his sister that he could not admit other thoughts, and still they waited and watched till other sounds were heard. The London doctor was going away. Alick sprang to the door, and opened it as his uncle's hand was on the lock. There was a mournful, solemn expression on his face, as they gazed mutely up in expectation. "Children," he said, "it is as we feared. This great sorrow is coming on us."

"Then there is danger," said Alick with stunned calmness.

"More than danger," said his uncle; "they have tried all that skill can do."

"Was it the fall?" said Alick.

"It was my bad management, it always is," said Rachel, ever affirmative.

"No, dear child," said Mr. Clare, "there was fatal injury in the fall, and even absolute stillness for the last few hours could hardly have saved her. You have nothing to reproach yourself with."

"And now?" asked Alick, hoarsely.

"Much more exhausted than when we were with her; sometimes faint, but still feverish. They think it may last many hours yet, poor dear child; she has so much youth and strength."

"Does she know?"

"Harvey thought some of their measures alarmed her, but they soothed and encouraged her while they saw hope, and he thinks she has no real fears."

"And how is it to be——?" said Alick. "She ought——"

"Yes; Harvey thinks she ought, she is fully herself, and it can make no difference now. He is gone to judge about coming up at once; but Alick, my poor boy, you must speak to her. I have found that without seeing the face I cannot judge what my words may be doing."

Rachel asked about poor Lord Keith, and was told that he was to be left in quiet that night, unless his wife should be very anxious for him at once. Mr. Harvey came down, bringing word that his patient was asking urgently for Mrs. Keith.

"You had better let me go in first," said Alick, his face changed by the firm but tender awe-struck look.

" Not if she is asking for me," said Rachel, moving on, her heart feeling as if it would rend asunder, but her looks composed.

Bessie's face was in shade, but her voice had the old ring of coaxing archness. " I thought you would stay to see the doctors off. They had their revenge for our stealing a march on them, and have prowled about me till I was quite faint; and now I don't feel a bit like sleep, though I am so tired. Would Alick think me very wicked if I kept you a little while ? Don't I see Alick's shadow ? Dear old fellow, are you come to wish me good-night ? That is good of you. I am not going to plague you any more, Alick, I shall be so good now ! But what ?" as he held back the curtain, and the light fell on his face, " Oh ! there is nothing wrong with the baby ? "

" No, dear Bessie, not with the *baby*," said Alick, with strong emphasis.

" What, myself ?" she said quickly, turning her eyes from one face to the other.

Alick told her the state of the case. Hers was a resolute character, or perhaps the double nature that had perplexed and chafed her brother was so integral that nothing could put it off. She fully comprehended, but as if she and herself were two separate persons. She asked how much time might be left to her, and hearing the doctor's opinion, said, " Then I think my poor old Lord Keith had better have his night's rest in peace. But, oh ! I should like to speak to Colin. Send for him, Alick ; telegraph, Alick ; he is at the Paddington Hotel. Send directly."

She was only tranquillized by her brother beginning to write a telegraphic message.

" Rachel," she said, presently, " Ermine must marry him now, and see to Lord Keith, and the little one—tell her so, please ;" then with her unfailing courtesy, " he will seem like your own child, dear Rachel, and you should have him ; but you'll have a wandering home with the dear old High-landers.   Oh! I wonder if he will ever go into them, there must always be a Keith there, and they say he is sure of the Victoria Cross, though papa will not send up his name because of being his own son."   Then passing her hand over her face, she exclaimed—" Wasn't I talking great nonsense, Rachel ? I don't seem able to say what I mean."

" It is weakness, dearest," said Rachel, " perhaps you might gain a little strength if you were quite still and listened to my uncle."

" Presently.   O Rachel ! I like the sound of your voice ; I am glad Alick has got you.   You suit him better than his wicked little sister ever did.   You have been so kind to me to-night, Rachel ; I never thought I should have loved you so well, when I quizzed you.   I did use you ill then, Rachel, but I think you won Alick by it just by force of contrast," —she was verging into the dreamy voice, and Rachel requested her to rest and be silent.

" It can't make any difference," said Bessie, " and I'll try to be quiet and do all right, if you'll just let me have my child again.   I do want to know who he is like.   I am so glad it is not he that was hurt.   Oh ! I did so want to have brought him up to be like Alick."

The infant was brought, and she insisted on being lifted to see its face, which she declared to resemble her brother ; but here her real self seemed to gain the mastery, and calling it a poor little motherless thing, she fell into a fit of violent convulsive weeping, which ended in a fainting fit, and this was a fearfully perceptible stage on her way to the dark valley.

She was, however, conscious when she revived, and sent for her uncle, whom she begged to let her be laid in his churchyard, "near the willow-tree ; not next to my aunt, I'm not good enough," she said, "but I could not bear that old ruined abbey, where all the Keiths go, and Alick always wanted me to be here—Alick was right !"

The dreamy mist was coming on, nor was it ever wholly dispelled again. She listened, or seemed to listen, to her uncle's prayers, but whenever he ceased, she began to talk—perhaps sensibly at first, but soon losing the thread—sometimes about her child or husband, sometimes going back to those expressions of Charles Carleton that had been so dire a shock to her. "He ought not ! I thought he knew better ! Alick was right ! Come away, Rachel, I'll never see him again. I have done nothing that he should insult me. Alick was right !"

Then would come the sobs, terrible in themselves, and ending in fainting, and the whole scene was especially grievous to Alick, even more than to either of the others ; for as her perception failed her, association carried her back to old arguments with him, and sometimes it was, "Alick, indeed you do like to attribute motives," sometimes "Indeed it is not all self-deception," or the recurring wail, "Alick is right, only don't let him be so angry !" If he told her how far he was from anger, she would make him kiss her, or return to some playful rejoinder, more piteous to hear than all, or in the midst would come on the deadly swoon.

Morning light was streaming into the room when one of

these swoons had fallen on her, and no means of restoration availed to bring her back to anything but a gasping condition, in which she lay supported in Rachel's arms. The doctor had his hand on her pulse, the only sounds outside were the twittering of the birds, and within, the ticking of the clock, Alick's deep-drawn breaths, and his uncle's prayer. Rachel felt a thrill pass through the form she was supporting, she looked at Mr. Harvey, and understood his glance, but neither moved till Mr. Clare's voice finished, when the doctor said, " I feared she would have suffered much more. Thank God !"

He gently relieved Rachel from the now lifeless weight, and they knelt on for some moments in complete stillness, except that Alick's breath became more laboured, and his shuddering and shivering could no longer be repressed. Rachel was excessively terrified to perceive that his whole frame was trembling like an aspen leaf. He rose, however, bent to kiss his sister's brow, and steadying himself by the furniture, made for the door. The others followed him, and in a few rapid words Rachel was assured that her fears were ungrounded, it was only an attack of his old Indian fever, which was apt to recur on any shock, but was by no means alarming, though for the present it must be given way to. Indeed, his teeth were chattering too much for him to speak intelligibly, when he tried to tell Rachel to rest and not think of him.

This of course was impossible, and the sun had scarcely risen before he was placed in his old quarters, the bed in the little inner study, and Rachel watched over him while Mr. Clare had driven off with the doctor to await the awakening of Lord Keith.

Rachel had never so much needed strength. It was hard to believe the assurances of Alick, the doctor, and the whole house, that his condition was not critical, for he was exceedingly ill for some hours, the ailment having been coming on all night, though it was forced back by the resolute will, and it was aggravated by the intensity of his grief, which on the other hand broke forth the more violently from the failure of the physical powers. The brother and sister had been so long alone in the world together, and with all her faults she had been so winning, that it was a grievous loss to him, coming too in the full bloom of her beauty and prosperity, when he was conscious of having dealt severely with her foibles. All was at an end—that double thread of brilliant good-nature and worldly selfishness, with the one strand of sound principle sometimes coming into sight. The life was gone from the earth in its incompleteness, without an unravelling of its complicated texture, and the wandering utterances that revealed how entirely the brother stood first with her, added poignancy to his regret for having been harsh with her. It could hardly be otherwise than that his censures, however just, should now recoil upon him, and in vain did Rachel try to point out that every word of his sister's had proved that her better sense had all along acquiesced—he only felt what it might have been if he had been more indulgent and less ironical, and gave himself infinitely harder measure than he ever could have shown to her. It was long before the suffering, either mental or bodily, by any means abated, and Rachel felt extremely lonely, deserted, and doubtful whether she were in any way ministering to his relief; but at last a gleam of satisfaction came upon her. He evidently did like her attendance on him, and he began to say something about Bessie's real love and esteem for her—softer grief was setting in, and the ailment was lessening.

The summer morning was advancing, and the knell rung out its two deep notes from the church tower. Rachel had been dreading the effect on him, but he lay still, as if he had been waiting for it, and was evidently counting the twenty-three strokes that told the age of the deceased. Then he said he was mending, and that he should fall asleep if Rachel would leave him, see after the poor child, and if his uncle should not come home within the next quarter of an hour, take measures to silence the bell for the morning service; after which, he laid his injunctions on her to rest, or what should he say to her mother? And the approach to a smile with which these last words were spoken, enabled Rachel to obey in some comfort.

After satisfying herself that the child was doing well, Rachel was obliged to go into her former room, and there to stand face to face with the white, still countenance so lately beaming with life. She was glad to be alone. The marble calm above all counteracted and drove aside the painful phantom left by Lovedy's agony, and yet the words of that poor, persecuted, suffering child came surging into her mind full of peace and hope. Perhaps it was the first time she had entered into what it is for weak things to confound the wise, or how things hidden from the intellectual can be revealed to babes; and she hid her face in her hands, and was thankful for the familiar words of old, " That we may embrace and ever hold fast the blessed hope of everlasting life."

The continued clang of the bell warned her. She looked round at the still uncleared room, poor Bessie's rings and bracelets lying mingled with her own on the toilet table, and her little clock, Bessie's own gift, standing ticking on as it had done at her peaceful rising only yesterday morning.

She took out her hat, and was on her way to silence the bell-ringer, when Mr. Clare was driven up to the churchyard gate.

Lord Keith had been greatly shocked, but not over-powered; he had spoken calmly, and made minute inquiries, and Mr. Clare was evidently a little disappointed, repeating that age and health made a difference, and that people showed their feelings in various ways. Colonel Keith had been met at the station, and was with his brother, but would come to make arrangements in the course of the day. Rachel begged to stop the bell, representing that the assembled congregation included no male person capable of reading the lessons; but Mr. Clare answered, "No, my dear, this is not a day to do without such a beginning. We must do what we can. Or stay, it is the last chapter of St. John. I could hardly fail in that. Sit near me, and give me the word if I do, unless you want to be with Alick."

As Rachel knelt that day, the scales of self-conceit seemed to have gone. She had her childhood's heart again. Her bitter remorse, her afterthoughts of perplexity had been lulled in the long calm of the respite, and when roused again, even by this sudden sorrow, she woke to her old trust and hope. And when she listened to the expressive though calm rehearsal of that solemn sunrise-greeting to the weary darkling fishers on the shore of the mountain lake, it was to her as if the form so long hidden from her by mists of her own raising, once more shone forth, smoothing the vexed waters of her soul, and she could say with a new thrill of recognition, "It is the Lord."

Once Mr. Clare missed a word, and paused for aid. She was crying too much to be ready, and, through her tears, could not recover the passage so as to prompt him before he had himself recalled the verse. Perhaps a sense of failure was always good for Rachel, but she was much concerned, and her apologies quite distressed Mr. Clare.

"Dear child, no one could be expected to keep the place when there was so much to dwell on in the very comfort of the chapter. And now if you are not in haste, would you take me to the place that dear Bessie spoke of, by the willow-tree. I am almost afraid little Mary Lawrence's grave may have left too little space."

Rachel guided him to a lovely spot, almost overhanging the stream, with the dark calm pools beneath the high bank, and the willow casting a long morning shadow over it. Her mind went back to the merry drive from Avoncester, when she had first seen Elizabeth Keith, and had little dreamt that in one short year she should be choosing the spot for her grave. Mr. Clare paced the green nook and was satisfied, asking if it were not a very pretty place.

"Yes," said Rachel, "there is such a quiet freshness, and the willow-tree seems to guard it."

"Is there not a white foxglove on the bank?"

"Yes, but with only a bell or two left at the top of the side spikes."

"Your aunt sowed the seed. It is strange that I was very near choosing this place nine years ago, but it could not be seen from my window, which was an object with me then."

Just then his quick ear detected that some one was at the parsonage door, and Rachel, turning round, exclaimed with horror, "It is that unhappy Mr. Carleton."

" Poor young fellow," said Mr. Clare, with more of pity than of anger, " I had better speak to him."

But they were far from the path, and it was not possible to guide the blind steps rapidly between the graves and head stones; so that before the pathway was reached young Carleton must have received the sad reply to his inquiries, for hurrying from the door he threw himself on his horse, and rode off at full speed.

By the afternoon, when Colonel Keith came to Bishops-worthy, Alick was lying on the sofa with such a headache that he could neither see nor spell, and Rachel was writing letters for him, both in the frame of mind in which the Colonel's genuine warm affection and admiration for Bessie was very comforting, assisting them in putting all past mis-givings out of sight. He had induced his brother to see Mr. Harvey, and the result had been that Lord Keith had consented to a consultation the next day with an eminent London surgeon, since it was clear that the blow, not the sciatica, was answerable for the suffering which was evidently becoming severe. The Colonel of course intended to remain with his brother, at least till after the funeral.

" Can you ? " exclaimed Alick. " Ought you not to be at Avoncester ? "

" I am not a witness, and the case is in excellent hands."

" Could you not run down ? I shall be available to-morrow, and I could be with Lord Keith."

" Thank you, Alick, it is impossible for me to leave him," said Colin, so quietly that no one could have guessed how keenly he felt the being deprived of bringing her brother to Ermine, and being present at the crisis to which all his thoughts and endeavours had so long been directed.

That assize day had long been a dream of dread to Rachel, and perhaps even more so to her husband. Yet how remote its interest actually seemed ! They scarcely thought of it for the chief part of the day. Alick looking very pale, though calling himself well, went early to Timber End, and he had not long been gone before a card was brought in, with an urgent entreaty that Mrs. Keith would see Mrs. Carleton. Rachel longed to consult Mr. Clare, but he had gone out to a sick person, and she was obliged to decide that Alick could scarcely wish her to refuse, reluctant and indignant as she felt. But her wrath lessened as she saw the lady's tears and agitation, so great that for a moment no words were possible, and the first were broken apologies for intruding, " Nothing should have induced her, but her poor son was in such a dreadful state."

Rachel again became cold and stern, and did not relent at the description of Charlie's horror and agony ; for she was wondering at the audacity of mentioning his grief to the wife of Lady Keith's brother, and thinking that this weak, indulgent mother was the very person to make a foolish, mischievous son, and it was on her tongue's end that she did not see to what she was indebted for the favour of such a visit. Perhaps Mrs. Carleton perceived her resentment, for she broke off, and urgently asked if poor dear Lady Keith had alluded to anything that had passed. "Yes," Rachel was forced to say ; and when again pressed as to the manner of alluding, replied, that " she was exceedingly distressed and displeased," with difficulty refraining from saying who had done all the mischief. Mrs. Carleton was in no need of hearing it. "Ah !" she said, "it was right, quite right. It was very wrong of my poor boy. Indeed I am not excusing him, but if you only knew how he blames himself."

"I am sure he ought," Rachel could not help saying.

Mrs. Carleton here entreated her to listen, and seized her hand, so that there was no escape. The tale was broken and confused, but there could be little doubt of its correctness. Poor Bessie had been the bane of young Carleton's life. She had never either decidedly accepted or repelled his affection, but, as she had truly said, let him follow her like a little dog, and amused herself with him in the absence of better game. He was in his father's office, but her charms disturbed his application to business and kept him trifling among the croquet lawns of Littleworthy, whence his mother never had the resolution to banish her spoilt child. At last Miss Keith's refusal of him, softened by a half-implied hope, sent him forth to his uncle at Rio, on the promise that if he did his utmost there, he should in three years be enabled to offer Miss Keith more than a competence. With this hope he had for the first time applied himself to business in earnest, when he received the tidings of her marriage, and like a true spoilt child broke down at once in resolution, capacity, and health, so that his uncle was only too glad to ship him off for England. And when Lady Keith made her temporary home in her old neighbourhood, the companionship began again, permitted by her in good nature, and almost contempt, and allowed by his family in confidence of the rectitude of both parties ; and indeed nothing could be more true than that no harm had been intended. But it was perilous ground ; ladies, however highly principled, cannot leave off self-pleasing habits all at once, and the old terms returned sufficiently to render the barrier but slightly felt. When Lady

Keith had spoken of her intention of leaving Timber End,
the reply had been the old complaint of her brother's harshness and jealousy of his ardent and lasting affection, and
reproof had not at once silenced him. This it was that had
so startled her as to make her hurry to her brother's side,
unheeding of her steps.

As far as Rachel could make out, the poor young man's
grief and despair had been poured out to his mother, and
she, unable to soothe, had come to try to extract some assurance that the catastrophe had been unconnected with his
folly. A very slight foundation would have served her, but
this Rachel would not give, honestly believing him the cause
of the accident, and also that the shock to the sense of duty
higher than he could understand had occasioned the excitement which had destroyed the slender possibility of recovery.
She pitied the unhappy man more than she had done at first,
and she was much pained by his mother's endeavours to
obtain a palliative for him, but she could not be untrue.
" Indeed," she said, " I fear no one can say it was not
so ; I don't think anything is made better by blinking the
reality."

" Oh, Mrs. Keith, it is so dreadful. I cannot tell my poor
son. I don't know what might be the consequence."

Tears came into Rachel's eyes. " Indeed," she said, " I
am very sorry for you. I believe every one knows that I
have felt what it is to be guilty of fatal mischief ; but, indeed, indeed I am sure that to realize it all is the only way
to endure it, so as to be the better for it. Believe me, I am
very sorry ; but I don't think it would be any real comfort
to your son to hear that poor Bessie had never been careful,
or that I was inexperienced, or the nurse ignorant. It is

better to look at it fairly. I hear Mr. Clare coming in. Will
you see him?" she added suddenly, much relieved.

But Mrs. Carleton did not wish to see him, and departed,
thinking Alick Keith's wife as bad as had ever been reported,
and preparing an account of her mismanagement wherewith
to remove her son's remorse.

She was scarcely gone, and Rachel had not had time to
speak to Mr. Clare, before another visitor was upon her, no
other than Lord Keith's daughter, Mrs. Comyn Menteith;
or, as she introduced herself, "I'm Isabel. I came down
from London to-day because it was so very shocking and
deplorable, and I am dying to see my poor little brother and
uncle Colin. I must keep away from poor papa till the
doctors are gone, so I came here."

She was a little woman in the delicately featured style of
sandy prettiness, and exceedingly talkative and good-natured.
The rapid tongue, though low and modulated, jarred painfully
on Rachel's feelings in the shaded staircase, and she was glad
to shut the door of the temporary nursery, when Mrs.
Menteith pounced upon the poor little baby, pitying him
with all her might, comparing him with her own children,
and asking authoritative questions, coupled with demonstrations of her intention of carrying him off to her own
nursery establishment, which had been left in Scotland with
a head nurse, whose name came in with every fourth word
—that is, if he lived at all, which she seemed to think a
hopeless matter.

She spoke of "poor dear Bessie," with such affection as
was implied in "Oh, she was such a darling! I got on with
her immensely. Why didn't you send to me, though I don't
know that Donald would have let me come;" and she in-

sisted on learning the whole history, illustrating it profusely
with personal experiences.   Rachel was constantly hoping to
be released from a subject so intensely painful ; but curiosity
prevailed through the chatter, and kept hold of the thread of
the story. Mrs. Menteith decidedly thought herself defrauded
of a summons. " It was very odd of them all not to telegraph
for me.   Those telegrams are such a dreadful shock.   There
came one just as I set out from Timber End, and I made
sure little Sandie was ill at home, for you know the child is
very delicate, and there are so many things going about, and
what with all this dreadful business, I was ready to faint,
and after all it was only a stupid thing for Uncle Colin from
those people at Avoncester."

" You do not know what it was ? "

" Somebody was convicted or acquitted, I forget which,
but I know it had something to do with Uncle Colin's
journey to Russia ; so ridiculous of him at his age, when he
ought to know better, and so unlucky for all the family, his
engagement to that swindler's sister. By-the-bye, did he not
cheat you out of ever so much money ? "

" Oh, that had nothing to do with it—it was not Miss
Williams's brother—it was not he that was tried."

" Wasn't he ? I thought he was found guilty or something ; but it is very unfortunate for the family, for Uncle
Colin won't give her up, though she is a terrible cripple, too.
And to tell you a secret, it was his obstinacy that made
papa marry again ; and now it is of no use, this poor little
fellow will never live, and this sharper's sister will be
Lady Keith after all ! So unlucky ! Papa says she is very
handsome, and poor Bessie declares she is quite lady-
like."

"The most superior person I ever knew," said Rachel, indignantly.

"Ah, yes, of course she must be very clever and artful if her brother is a swindler."

"But indeed he is not, he was cheated; the swindler was Maddox."

"Oh, but he was a glass-blower, or something, I know, and her sister is a governess. I am sure it is no fault of mine! The parties I gave to get him and Jessie Douglas together! Donald was quite savage about the bills. And after all Uncle Colin went and caught cold, and would not come! I would not have minded half so much if it had been Jessie Douglas; but to have her at Gowanbrae—a glass-blower's daughter—isn't it too bad?"

"Her father was a clergyman of a good Welsh family."

"Was he? Then her brother or somebody had something to do with glass."

Attempts at explanation were vain, the good lady had an incapacity of attention, and was resolved on her grievance. She went away at last because "those horrid doctors will be gone now, and I will be able to see poor papa, and tell him when I will take home the baby, though I don't believe he will live to be taken anywhere, poor dear little man."

She handled him so much more scientifically than Rachel could do, that it was quite humiliating, and yet to listen to her talk, and think of committing any child to her charge was sickening, and Rachel already felt a love and pity for her little charge that made her wretched at the thoughts of the prognostic about him.

"You are tired with your visitors, my dear," said Mr.

Clare, holding out his hand towards her, when she returned to him.

"How do you know?" she asked.

"By the sound of your move across the room, and the stream of talk I heard above must be enough to exhaust any one."

"She thinks badly of that poor child," said Rachel, her voice trembling.

"My dear, it would take a good deal to make me uneasy about anything I heard in that voice."

"And if he lives, she is to have the charge of him," added Rachel.

"That is another matter on which I would suspend my fears," said Mr. Clare. "Come out, and take a· turn in the peacock path. You want air more than rest. So you have been talked to death."

"And I am afraid she is gone to talk Alick to death! I wonder when Alick will come home," she proceeded, as they entered on the path. "She says Colonel Keith had a telegram about the result of the trial, but she does not know what it was, nor indeed who was tried."

"Alick will not keep you in doubt longer than he can help," said Mr. Clare.

"You know all about it;" said Rachel. "The facts every one must know, but I mean that which led to them."

"Alick told me you had suffered very much."

"I don't know whether it is a right question, but if it is, I should much like to know what Alick did say. I begged him to tell you all, or it would not have been fair towards you to bring me here."

"He told me that he knew you had been blind and wilful,

but that your confidence had been cruelly abused, and you had been most unselfish throughout."

"I did not mean so much what I had done as what I am—what I was."

"The first time he mentioned you, it was as one of the reasons that he wished to take our dear Bessie to Avonmouth. He said there was a girl there of a strong spirit, independent and thorough-going, and thinking for herself. He said, 'to be sure, she generally thinks wrong, but there's a candour and simplicity about her that make her wildest blunders better than parrot commonplace,' and he thought your reality might impress his sister. Even then I gathered what was coming."

"And how wrong and foolish you must have thought it."

"I hoped I might trust my boy's judgment."

"Indeed, you could not think it worse for him than I did; but I was ill and weak, and could not help letting Alick do what he would; but I have never understood it. I told him how unsettled my views were, and he did not seem to mind——"

"My dear, may I ask if this sense of being unsettled is with you still?"

"I don't know! I had no power to read or think for a long time; and now, since I have been here, I hope it has not been hypocrisy, for going on in your way and his has been very sweet to me, and made me feel as I used when I was a young girl, with only an ugly dream between. I don't like to look at it, and yet that dream was my real life that I made for myself."

"Dear child, I have little doubt that Alick knew it would come to this."

Rachel paused. "What, you and he think a woman's doubts so vague and shallow as to be always mastered by a husband's influence?"

Mr. Clare was embarrassed. If he had thought so he had not expected her to make the inference. He asked her if she could venture to look back on her dream so as to mention what had chiefly distressed her. He could not see her frowning effort at recollection, but after a pause, she said, "Things will seem to you like trifles, indeed, individual criticisms appear so to me; but the difficulty to my mind is that I don't see these objections fairly grappled with. There is either denunciation or weak argument; but I can better recollect the impression on my own mind than what made it."

"Yes, I know that feeling; but are you sure you have seen all the arguments?"

"I cannot tell—perhaps not. Whenever I get a book with anything in it, somebody says it is not sound."

"And you therefore conclude that a sound book can have nothing in it?" he asked, smiling.

"Well, most of the new 'sound' books that I have met are just what my mother and sister like—either dull, or sentimental and trashy."

"Perhaps those that get into popular circulation do deserve some of your terms for them. Illogical replies break down and carry off some who have pinned their faith to them; but are you sure that though you have read much, you have read deep?"

"I have read more deeply than any one I know—women, I mean—or than any man ever showed me he had read. Indeed, I am trying not to say it in conceit, but Ermine

Williams does not read argumentative books, and gentlemen almost always make as if they knew nothing about them."

" I think you may be of great use to me, my dear, if you will help me. The bishop has desired me to preach the next visitation sermon, and he wishes it to be on some of these subjects. Now, if you will help me with the book work, it will be very kind in you, and might serve to clear your mind about some of the details, though you must be prepared for some questions being unanswered."

" Best so," replied Rachel, " I don't like small answers to great questions."

" Nor I. Only let us take care not to get absorbed in admiring the boldness that picks out stones to be stumbled over."

" Do you object to my having read, and thought, and tried ? "

" Certainly not. Those who have the capability should, if they feel disturbed, work out the argument. Nothing is gained while it is felt that both sides have not been heard. I do not myself believe that a humble, patient, earnest spirit can go far wrong, though it may for a time be tried, and people often cry out at the first stumbling block, and then feel committed to the exclamations they have made."

The conversation was here ended by the sight of Alick coming slowly and wearily in from the churchyard, looking as if some fresh weight were upon him, and he soon told them that the doctors had pronounced that Lord Keith was in a critical state, and would probably have much to suffer from the formation that had begun where he had received the neglected bruise in the side. No word of censure of

poor Bessie had been breathed, nor did Alick mention her
name, but he deeply suffered under the fulfilment of his
own predictions, and his subdued, dejected manner expressed
far more than did his words. Rachel asked how Lord Keith
seemed.

"Oh, there's no getting at his feelings. He was very civil
to me—asked after you, Rachel—told me to give you his
thanks, but not a single word about anything nearer. Then
I had to read the paper to him—all that dinner at Liverpool,
and he made remarks, and expected me to know what it was
about. I suppose he does feel; the Colonel says he is exceedingly cut up, and he looks like a man of eighty, infinitely
worse than last time I saw him, but I don't know what to
make of him."

"And, Alick, did you hear the verdict?"

"What verdict?"

"That man at Avoncester. Mrs. Menteith said there had
been a telegram."

Alick looked startled. "This has put everything out of
my head!" he said. "What was the verdict?"

"That was just what she could not tell. She did not
quite know who was tried."

"And she came here and harassed you with it," he said,
looking at her anxiously. "As if you had not gone through
enough already."

"Never mind that now. It seems so long ago now that
I can hardly think much about it; and I have had another
visitor," she added, as Mr. Clare left them to themselves,
"Mrs. Carleton—that poor son of hers is in such distress."

"She has been palavering you over," he said, in a tone
more like displeasure than he had ever used towards her.

" Indeed, Alick, if you would listen, you would find him very much to be pitied."

" I only wish never to hear of any of them again." He did not speak like himself, and Rachel was aghast.

" I thought you would not object to my letting her in," she began.

" I never said I did," he answered ; " I can never think of him but as having caused her death, and it was no thanks to him that there was nothing worse."

The sternness of his manner would have silenced Rachel but for her strong sense of truth and justice, which made her persevere in saying, " There may have been more excuse than you believe."

" Do you suppose that is any satisfaction to me ?" He walked decidedly away, and entered by the library window, and she stood grieved and wondering whether she had been wrong in pitying, or whether he were too harsh in his indignation. It was a sign that her tone and spirit had recovered, that she did not succumb in judgment, though she felt utterly puzzled and miserable till she recollected how unwell, weary, and unhappy he was, and that every fresh perception of his sister's errors was like a poisoned arrow to him ; and then she felt shocked at having obtruded the subject on him at all, and when she found him leaning back in his chair, spent and worn out, she waited on him in the quietest, gentlest way she could accomplish, and tried to show that she had put the subject entirely aside. However, when they were next alone together, he turned his face away and muttered, " What did that woman say to you ?"

" Oh, Alick, I am sorry I began ! It only gives you pain."

" Go on——"

She did go on till she had told all, and he uttered no word of comment. She longed to ask whether he disapproved of her having permitted the interview ; but as he did not again recur to the topic, it was making a real and legitimate use of strength of mind to abstain from teazing him on the matter. Yet when she recollected what worldly honour would once have exacted of a military man, and the conflicts between religion and public opinion, she felt thankful indeed that half a century lay between her and that terrible code, and even as it was, perceiving the strong hold that just resentment had taken on her husband's silently determined nature, she could not think of the neighbourhood of the Carleton family without dread.

CHAPTER XIII.

THE POST BAG.

" Thefts, like ivy on a ruin, make the rifts they seem to shade."—
C. G. DUFFY.

" *August 3d,* 7 A.M.

" MY DEAR COLONEL KEITH,—Papa is come, and I have got
up so early in the morning that I have nothing to do but to
write to you before we go in to Avoncester. Papa and Mr.
Beechum came by the six o'clock train, and Lady Temple
sent me in the waggonette to meet them. Aunt Ailie would
not go, because she was afraid Aunt Ermine would get anxious
whilst she was waiting. I saw papa directly, and yet I did
not think it could be papa, because you were not there, and
he looked quite past me, and I do not think he would have
found me or the carriage at all if Mr. Beechum had not
known me. And then, I am afraid I was very naughty, but
I could not help crying just a little when I found you had
not come ; but perhaps Lady Keith may be better, and you
may come before I go into court to-day, and then I shall tear
up this letter. I am afraid papa thought I was unkind to
cry when he was just come home, for he did not talk to
me near so much as Mr. Beechum did, and his eyes
kept looking out as if he did not see anything near, only
quite far away. And I suppose Russian coats must be made
of some sort of sheep that eats tobacco."

"DEAREST COLIN,—I have just lighted on poor little Rosie's before-breakfast composition, and I can't refrain from sending you her first impressions, poor child, though no doubt they will alter, as she sees more of her father. All are gone to Avoncester now, though with some doubts whether this be indeed the critical day ; I hope it may be, the sooner this is over the better ; but I am full of hope. I cannot believe but that the Providence that has done so much to discover Edward's innocence to the world, will finish the work ! I have little expectation though of your coming down in time to see it ; the copy of the telegraphic message, which you sent by Harry, looks as bad as possible, and even allowing something for inexperience and fright, things must be in a state in which you could hardly leave your brother, so unwell as he seems.

" 2 p.m. I was interrupted by Lady Temple, who was soon followed by Mrs. Curtis, burning to know whether I had any more intelligence than had floated to them. Pray, if you can say anything to exonerate poor Rachel from mismanagement, say it strongly ; her best friends are so engaged in wishing themselves there, and pitying poor Bessie for being in her charge, that I long to confute them, for I fully believe in her sense and spirit in any real emergency that she had not ridden out to encounter.

" And I have written so far without a word on the great subject of all, the joy untold for which our hearts had ached so long, and which we owe entirely to you ; for Edward owns that nothing but your personal representations would have brought him, and, as I suppose you already know—he so much hated the whole subject of Maddox's treachery that

he had flung aside, unread, all that he saw related to it.
Dear Colin, whatever else you have done, you have filled a
famished heart. Could you but have seen Ailie's face all last
evening as she sat by his side, you would have felt your
reward—it was as if the worn, anxious, almost stern mask
had been taken away, and our Ailie's face was beaming out
as of old when she was the family pet, before Julia took her
away to be finished. She sees no change; she is in an
ecstacy of glamour that makes her constantly repeat her
rejoicings that Edward is so much himself, so unchanged, till
I almost feel unsisterly for seeing in him the traces that these
sad years have left, and that poor little Rose herself has
detected. No, he is not so much changed as exaggerated.
The living to himself, and with so cruel a past, has greatly
increased the old dreaminess that we always tried to combat,
and he seems less able than before to turn his mind into any
channel but the one immediately before him. He is most
loving when roused, but infinitely more inclined to fall off into
a muse. I am afraid you must have had a troublesome charge
in him, judging by the uproar Harry makes about the difficulty of getting him safe from Paddington. It is good to
see him and Harry together—the old schoolboy ways are so
renewed, all bitterness so entirely forgotten, only Harry
rages a little that he is not more wrapped up in Rose. To
say the truth, so do I; but if it were not for Harry's feeling
the same, I should believe that you had taught me to be
exacting about my rosebud. Partly, it is that he is disappointed that she is not like her mother; he had made up his
mind to another Lucy, and her Williams face took him by
surprise, and, partly, he is not a man to adapt himself to
a child. She must be trained to help unobtrusively in his

occupations ; the unknowing little plaything her mother was, she never can be.   I am afraid he will never adapt himself to English life again—his soul seems to be in his mines, and if as you say he is happy and valued there—though it is folly to look forward to the wrench again, instead of rejoicing in the present gladness ; but often as I had fashioned that arrival in my fancy, it was never that Harry's voice, not yours, should say the ' Here he is.'

" They all went this morning in the waggonnette, and the two boys with Miss Curtis in the carriage.   Lady Temple is very kind in coming in and out to enliven me.   I am afraid I must close and send this before their return.   What a day it is !   And how are you passing it ?   I fear, even at the best, in much anxiety.   Lady Temple asks to put in a line.— Yours ever,   " E. W."

" *August* 3*d*, 5 P.M.

" MY DEAR COLONEL,—This is just to tell you that dear Ermine is very well, and bearing the excitement and sus-pense wonderfully.   We were all dreadfully shocked to hear about poor dear Bessie ; it is so sad her having no mother nor anyone but Rachel to take care of her, though Rachel would do her best, I know.   If she would like to have me, or if you think I could do any good, pray telegraph for me the instant you get this letter.   I would have come this morning, only I thought, perhaps, she had her aunt.   That stupid telegram never said whether her baby was alive, or what it was ; I do hope it is all right.   I should like to send nurse up at once—I always thought she saved little Cyril when he was so ill.   Pray send for nurse or me, or anything I can send : anyway, I know nobody can be such a comfort as you; but the only thing there is to wish about you is, that you could be in two places at once.

"The two boys are gone in to the trial, they were very eager about it; and dear Grace promises to take care of Conrade's throat. Poor boys! they had got up a triumphal arch for your return; but I am afraid I am telling secrets. Dear Ermine is so good and resolutely composed—quite an example.—Yours affectionately,

"F. G. TEMPLE."

"AVONCESTER, *August 3d,* 2 P.M.

"MY DEAR COLONEL KEITH,—I am just come out of court, and I am to wait at the inn, for Aunt Ailie does not like for me to hear the trial, but she says I may write to you to pass away the time. I am sorry I left my letter out to go this morning, for Aunt Ailie says it is very undutiful to say anything about the sheep's wool in Russia smelling of tobacco. Conrade says it is all smoking, and that every one does it who has seen the world. Papa never stops smoking but when he is with Aunt Ermine; he sat on the box and did it all the way to Avoncester, and Mr. Beechum said it was to compose his mind. After we got to Avoncester we had a long, long time to wait, and first one was called, and then another, and then they wanted me. I was not nearly so frightened as I was that time when you sent for me, though there were so many more people; but it was daylight, and the judge looked so kind, and the lawyer spoke so gently to me, and Mr. Maddox did not look horrid like that first time. I think he must be sorry now he has seen how much he has hurt papa. The lawyer asked me all about the noises, and the lions, and the letters of light, just as Mr. Grey did;

and they showed me papa's old seal ring, and asked if I knew
it, and a seal that was made with the new one that he got
when the other was lost! and I knew them because I used
to make impressions on my arms with them when I was a
little girl.   There was another lawyer that asked how old I
was, and why I had not told before ; and I thought he was
going to laugh at me for a silly little girl, but the judge would
not let him, and said I was a clear-headed little maiden ; and
Mr. Beechum came with Aunt Ailie, and took me out of
court, and told me to choose anything in the whole world he
should give me, so I chose the little writing case I am writing
with now, and 'The Heroes' besides, so I shall be able to
read till the others come back, and we go home.—Your
affectionate little friend,

" ROSE ERMINE WILLIAMS."

"THE HOMESTEAD, August 3d, 9 P.M.

" MY DEAR ALEXANDER,—You made me promise to send
you the full account of this day's proceedings, or I do not
think I should attempt it, when you may be so sadly engaged.
Indeed, I should hardly have gone to Avoncester had the
sad intelligence reached me before I had set out, when I
thought my sudden return would be a greater alarm to my
mother, and I knew that dear Fanny would do all she could
for her.   Still she has had a very nervous day, thinking
constantly of your dear sister, and of Rachel's alarm and
inexperience ; but her unlimited confidence in your care of
Rachel is some comfort, and I am hoping that the alarm may
have subsided, and you may be all rejoicing.   I have always
thought that, with dear Rachel, some new event or sensation
would best efface the terrible memories of last spring.   My

mother is now taking her evening nap, and I am using the time for telling you of the day's doings. I took with me Fanny's two eldest, who were very good and manageable ; and we met Mr. Grey, who put us in very good places, and told us the case was just coming on. You will see the report in detail in the paper, so I will only try to give you what you would not find there. I should tell you that Maddox has entirely dropped his *alias*. Mr. Grey is convinced that was only a bold stroke to gain time and prevent the committal, so as to be able to escape, and that he 'reckoned upon bullying a dense old country magistrate ;' but that he knew it was quite untenable before a body of unexceptionable witnesses. Altogether the man looked greatly altered and crest-fallen, and there was a meanness and vulgarity in his appearance that made me wonder at our ever having credited his account of himself. He had an abject look, very unlike his confident manner at the sessions, nor did he attempt his own defence. Mr. Grey kept on saying he must know that he had not a leg to stand upon.

"The counsel for the prosecution told the whole story, and it was very touching. I had never known the whole before ; the sisters are so resolute and uncomplaining : but how they must have suffered when every one thought them ruined by their brother's fraud ! I grieve to think how we neglected them, and only noticed them when it suited our convenience. Then he called Mr. Beechum, and you will understand better than I can all about the concern in which they were embarked, and Maddox coming to him for an advance of 300*l*., giving him a note from Mr. Williams, asking for it to carry out an invention. The order for the sum was put into

Maddox's hands, and the banker proved the paying it to him by an order on a German bank.

"Then came Mr. Williams. I had seen him for a moment in setting out, and was struck with his strange, lost, dreamy look. There is something very haggard and mournful in his countenance; and, though he has naturally the same fine features as his eldest sister, his cheeks are hollow, his eyes almost glassy, and his beard, which is longer than the Colonel's, very grey. He gave me the notion of the wreck of a man, stunned and crushed, and never thoroughly alive again; but when he stood in the witness-box, face to face with the traitor, he was very different; he lifted up his head, his eyes brightened, his voice became clear, and his language terse and concentrated, so that I could believe in his having been the very able man he was described to be. I am sure Maddox must have quailed under his glance, there was something so loftily innocent in it, yet so wistful, as much as to say, 'how could you abuse my perfect confidence?' Mr. Williams denied having received the money, written the letter, or even thought of making the request. They showed him the impression of two seals. He said one was made with a seal-ring given him by Colonel Keith, and lost some time before he went abroad; the other, with one with which he had replaced it, and which he produced, he had always worn it on his finger. They matched exactly with the impressions; and there was a little difference in the hair of the head upon the seal that was evident to every one. It amused the boys extremely to see some of the old jurymen peering at them with their glasses. He was asked where he was on the 7th of September (the date of the letter), and he referred to some notes of his own, which enabled him to state that on the 5th

he had come back to Prague from a village with a horrible
Bohemian name—all cs and zs—which I will not attempt
to write, though much depended on the number of the said
letters.

"The rest of the examination must have been very distressing, for Maddox's counsel pushed him hard about his
reasons for not returning to defend himself, and he was
obliged to tell how ill his wife was, and how terrified; and
they endeavoured to make that into an admission that he
thought himself liable. They tried him with bits of the
handwriting, and he could not always tell which were his
own ;—but I think every one must have been struck with his
honourable scrupulosity in explaining every doubt he had.

"Other people were called in about the writing, but Alison
Williams was the clearest of all. She was never puzzled by
any scrap they showed her, and, moreover, she told of Maddox
having sent for her brother's address, and her having copied
it from a letter of Mrs. Williams's, which she produced, with
the wrong spelling, just as it was in the forgery. The next
day had come a letter from the brother, which she showed,
saying that they were going to leave the place sooner than
they had intended, and spelling it right. She gave the same
account of the seals, and nothing ever seemed to disconcert
her. My boys were so much excited about their 'own Miss
Williams,' that I was quite afraid they would explode into
a cheer.

"That poor woman whom we used to call Mrs. Rawlins
told her sad story next. She is much worn and subdued, and
Mr. Grey was struck with the change from the fierce excitement she showed when she was first confronted with Maddox
after her own trial ; but she held fast to the same evidence,

giving it not resentfully, but sadly and firmly, as if she felt
it to be her duty. She, as you know, explained how Maddox
had obtained access to Mr. Williams's private papers, and how
she had, afterwards, found in his possession the seal ring, and
the scraps of paper in his patron's writing. A policeman
produced them, and the seal perfectly filled the wax upon the
forged letter. The bits of paper showed that Maddox had
been practising imitating Mr. Williams's writing. It all
seemed most distinct, but still there was some sharp cross-
examination of her on her own part in the matter, and Mr.
Grey said it was well that little Rose could so exactly confirm
the facts she mentioned.

"Poor, dear little Rose looked very sweet and innocent,
and not so much frightened as at her first examination. She
told her story of the savage way in which she had been
frightened into silence. Half the people in the court were
crying, and I am sure it was a mercy that she was not driven
out of her senses, or even murdered that night. It seems
that she was sent to bed early, but the wretches knowing that
she always woke and talked while her mother was going to
bed, the phosphoric letters were prepared to frighten her, and
detain her in her room, and then Maddox growled at her
when she tried to pass the door. She was asked how she
knew the growl to be Maddox's, and she answered that she
heard him cough. Rachel will, I am sure, remember
the sound of that little dry cough. Nothing could make
it clearer than that the woman had spoken the truth.
The child identified the two seals with great readiness, and
then was sent back to the inn that she might not be perplexed
with hearing the defence. This, of course, was very trying
to us all, since the best the counsel could do for his client

was to try to pick holes in the evidence, and make the most
of the general acquiescence in Mr. Williams's guilt for all
these years. He brought forward letters that showed that
Mr. Williams had been very sanguine about the project, and
had written about the possibility that an advance might be
needed. Some of the letters, which both Mr. Williams and his
sister owned to be in his own writing, spoke in most flourishing
terms of his plans; and it was proved by documents and
witnesses that the affairs were in such a state that bankruptcy
was inevitable, so that there was every motive for securing a
sum to live upon. It was very miserable all the time this
was going on; the whole interpretation of Mr. Williams's
conduct seemed to be so cruelly twisted aside, and it was
what every one had all along believed, his absence was made
so much of, and all these little circumstances that had seemed
so important were held so cheap—one knew it was only the
counsel's representation, and yet Alison grew whiter and
whiter under it. I wish you could have heard the reply :
drawing the picture of the student's absorption and generous
confidence, and his agent's treachery, creeping into his household, and brutally playing on the terrors of his child.

"Well, I cannot tell you all, but the judge summed up
strongly for a conviction, though he said a good deal about
culpable negligence almost inviting fraud, and I fear it must
have been very distressing to the Williamses ; but the end
was that Maddox was found guilty, and sentenced to fourteen
years' penal servitude, though I am afraid they will not follow
Conrade's suggestion, and chain up a lion by his bed every
night of his life.

"We were very happy when we met at the inn, and all
shook hands. Dr. Long was, I think, the least at ease. He

had come in case this indictment had in any way failed, to
bring his own matter forward, so that Maddox should not get
off.   I do not like him very much, he seemed unable to be
really hearty, and I think he must have once been harsh and
now ashamed of it.   Then he was displeased at Colonel
Keith's absence, and could hardly conceal how much he was
put out by the cause, as if he thought the Colonel had
imposed himself on the family as next heir.   I hardly know
how to send all this in the present state of things, but I
believe you will wish to have it, and will judge how much
Rachel will bear to hear.   Good night.—Your affectionate
Sister,

                                  " GRACE CURTIS."

               "GOWANBRAE, AVONMOUTH, *August* 3d, 11 P.M.

    " DEAR   KEITH,—Before this day has ended you must have
a few lines from the man whom your exertions have relieved
from a stigma, the full misery of which I only know by the
comfort of its removal.   I told you there was much that
could never be restored.   I feel this all the more in the
presence of all that now remains to me, but I did not know
how much could still be given back.   The oppression of the
load of suspicion under which I laboured now seems to me to
have been intolerable since I have been freed from it.   I
cannot describe how changed a man I have felt, since
Beechum shook hands with me.   The full blackness of
Maddox's treachery I had not known, far less his cruelty to
my child.   Had I been aware of all I could not have refrained
from trying to bring him to justice ; but there is no need to
enter into the past.   It is enough that I owe to you a freed
spirit, and new life, and that my gratitude is not lessened by

the knowledge that something besides friendship urged you. Ermine is indeed as attractive as ever, and has improved in health far more than I durst expect. I suppose it is your all-powerful influence. You are first with all here, as you well deserve ; even my child, who is as lovely and intelligent as you told me, has every thought pervaded with ' the Colonel.' She is a sweet creature ; but there was one who will never be retraced, and forgive me, Keith, without her, even triumph must be bitterness.—Still ever most gratefully yours,

" EDWARD WILLIAMS."

" *August 3d,* 11 P.M.

"DEAREST COLIN,—The one sound in my ears, the one song of my heart is, ' Let them give thanks.' It is as if we had passed from a dungeon into sunshine. I suppose it would be too much if you were here to share it. They sent Rose in first to tell me, but I knew in the sound of their wheels that all was well. What an evening we have had, but I must not write more. Ailie is watching me like a dragon, and will not rest till I am in bed ; but I can't tell how to lose one minute of gladness in sleep. Oh, Colin, Colin, truest of all true knights, what an achievement yours has been !"

"*August 4th.*

" That was a crazy bit that I wrote last night, but I will not make away with it. I don't care how crazy you think me. It would have been a pity not to have slept to wake to the knowledge that all was not a dream, but then came the contrast with the sorrow you are watching. And I have just had your letter. What a sudden close to that joyous life ! She was one of the most winning beings, as you truly say, that ever flashed across one's course ; and if she had faults, they were those of her day and her training. I suppose, by what you say, that she was too girlish to be all the companion your brother required, and that this may account for his being more shocked than sorrow-stricken ; and his child, since he can dwell on the thought, is such a new beginning of hope, that I wonder less than you do at his bearing up so well. Besides, pain dulls the feelings, and is a great occupation. I wish you could have seen that dear Bessie, but I gather that the end came on much more rapidly than had been expected. It seemed as if she were one of those to whom even suffering was strangely lightened and shortened, as if she had met only the flowers of life, and even the thorns and stings were almost lost in their bright blossoms. And she could hardly have lived on without much either of temptation or sorrow. I am glad of your testimony to Rachel's effectiveness, I wrote it out and sent it up to the Homestead. There was a note this morning requesting Edward to come in to see Maddox, and Ailie is gone with him, thinking she may get leave to see poor Maria. Think of writing ' Edward and Ailie ' again ! Dr. Long and Harry are gone with them. The broken thread is better pieced by Harry than by the Doctor ; but he wants Ailie and me to go and stay at Belfast. Now I must hear Rose read, in order to bring both her and myself to our reasonable senses."

"5 P.M.

" They have been returned about an hour, and I must try to give you Edward's account of his interview. Maddox has quite dropped his mask, and seems to have been really touched by being brought into contact with Edward again, and, now it is all up with him, seemed to take a kind of pleasure in explaining the whole web, almost, Edward said,

with vanity at his own ingenuity. His earlier history was as
he used to represent it to Edward. He was a respectable iron-
monger's son, with a taste for art; he was not allowed to
indulge it, and then came rebellion, and breaking away from
home. He studied at the Academy for a few years, but
wanted application, and fancied he had begun too late, tried
many things and spent a shifty life, but never was con-
sciously dishonest till after he had fallen in with Edward;
and the large sums left uninquired for in his hands became
a temptation to one already inclined to gambling. His own
difficulties drove him on, and before he ventured on the
grand stroke, he had been in a course of using the sums in
his hands for his own purposes. The finding poor Maria
open to the admiration he gave her beauty, put it into his
head to make a tool of her; and this was not the first time he
had used Edward's seal, or imitated his writing. No wonder
there was such a confusion in the accounts as told so much
against Edward. He told the particulars, Edward says, with
the strangest mixture of remorse and exultation. At last
came the journey to Bohemia, and his frauds became the more
easy, until he saw there must be a bankruptcy, and made
the last bold stroke, investing the money abroad in his own
name, so that he would have been ready to escape if Edward
had come home again. He never expected but that Edward
would have returned, and finding the affairs hopeless, did this
deed in order to have a resource. As to regret, he seemed to
feel some when he said the effects had gone farther than he
anticipated; but 'I could not let him get into that subject,'
Edward said, and he soon came back to his amused compla-
cency in his complete hoodwinking of all concerned at home,
almost thanking Edward for the facilities his absence had

given him. After this, he went abroad, taking Maria lest she
should betray him on being cast off; and they lived in such
style at German gambling places that destitution brought
them back again to England, where he could better play the
lecturer, and the artist in search of subscriptions.   Edward
could not help smiling over some of his good stories, rather as
‘ the lord ’ may have ‘ commended the wisdom of his unjust
steward.’   Well, here he came, and, as he said, he really could
hardly have helped himself; he had only to stand still and let
poor Rachel deceive herself, and the whole concern was in a
manner thrust upon him.   He was always expecting to be
able to get the main sum into his hands, as he obtained more
confidence from Rachel, and the woodcuts were an over-bold
stroke for the purpose ; he had not intended her to keep or
show them, but her ready credulity tempted him too far ; and
I cannot help laughing now at poor Edward’s reproofs to us for
having been all so easily cheated, now that he has been admitted
behind the scenes.   Maddox never suspected our neighbourhood, he had imagined us to be still in London, and though
he heard Alison’s name, he did not connect it with us. After
all, what you thought would have been fatal to your hopes of
tracing him, was really what gave him into our hands—Lady
Temple’s sudden descent upon their F. U. E. E.   If he had not
been so hurried and distressed as to be forced to leave Maria
and the poor child to her fate, Maria would have held by him
to the last and without her testimony where should we have
been ?   But with a summons out against him, and hearing that
Maria had been recognised, he could only fly to the place at
Bristol that he thought unknown to Maria.   Even when
seized by the police, he did not know it was she who directed
them, and had not expected her evidence till he actually saw
and heard her on the night of the sessions.   It was all Colonel

Keith's doing, he said ; every other adversary he would have
despised, but your array of forces met him at every corner
where he hoped to escape, and the dear little Rosie gave him
check-mate, like a gallant little knight's pawn as she is. 'Who
could have guessed that child would have such a confounded
memory?' he said, for Edward had listened with a sort of
interest that had made him quite forget that he was Rose's
father, and that this wicked cunning Colonel was working in
his cause. So off he goes to penal servitude, and Edward is
so much impressed and touched with his sharpness as to predict
that he will be the model prisoner before long, if he do not
make his escape. As to poor Maria, that was a much more sad
meeting, though perhaps less really melancholy, for there can
be no doubt that she repents entirely ; she speaks of every
one as being very good to her, and indeed the old influences
only needed revival, they had never quite died out. Even
that poor child's name was given for love of Ailie, and the
perception of having been used to bring about her master's
ruin had always preyed upon her, and further embittered her
temper. The barbarity seemed like a dream in connexion
with her, but, as she told Ailie, when she once began something came over her, and she could not help striking harder.
It reminded me of horrible stories of the Hathertons' usage of
animals. Enough of this. I believe the Sisterhood will find
a safe shelter for her when her imprisonment is over, and that
temptation will not again be put in her way. We should
never have trusted her in poor dear Lucy's household. Rose
calls for the letters. Good bye, dearest Colin and conqueror.
I know all this will cheer you, for it is your own doing.
I can't stop saying so, it is such a pleasant sound—Your own,

"E. W."

CHAPTER XIV.

VANITY OF VANITIES.

" Unfaith in aught is want of faith in all."
                                        TENNYSON.

THE funeral was very quiet.   By Colonel Keith's considerate
arrangement the attendants met at Timber End, so that the
stillness of the Parsonage was not invaded ; a measure the
more expedient, as Alick was suffering from a return of his
old enemy, intermitting fever, and only was able to leave his
room in time to join the procession.

  Many were present, for poor Bessie had been a general
favourite, and her untimely fate had stirred up feelings that
had created her into a saint upon earth ; but there was no
one whose token of respect she would have more esteemed
than Colonel Hammond's, who in all the bustle of the
remove to Edinburgh had found time to come to Bishopsworthy to do honour to the daughter of his old commanding
officer.   A flush of gratitude came over Alick's pale face
when he became aware of his colonel's presence, and when
the choristers' hymn had pealed low and sweetly over the
tranquil meadows, and the mourners had turned away, Alick
paused at the Parsonage gate to hold out his hand, and bring
in this one guest to hear how near to Bessie's heart the
father's Highland regiment had been in all the wanderings
of her last moments.

The visit was prolonged for nearly an hour, while recollections of Alick's parents were talked over, and Rachel thought him more cheered and gratified than by any other tribute that had been paid to his sister. He was promised an extension of leave, if it were required on account of Lord Keith's state, though under protest that he would have the aguish fever as long as he remained overlooking the water meadows, and did not put himself under Dr. M'Vicar. Through these meadows Colonel Hammond meant to walk back to the station, and Alick and Rachel conducted him far enough to put him into the right path, and in going back again, they could not but go towards the stile leading to that corner of the churchyard where the sexton had finished his work, and smoothed the sods over that new grave.

Some one was standing at the foot—not the sexton—but a young man bending as with an intolerable load of grief. Rachel saw him first, when Alick was helping her down the step, and her start of dismay made him turn and look round. His brow contracted, and she clutched his arm with an involuntary cry of, " Oh, don't," but he, with a gesture that at once awed and tranquillized her, unclasped her hold and put her back, while he stepped forward.

She could hear every word, though his voice was low and deep with emotion. " Carleton, if I have ever been harsh or unjust in my dealings towards you, I am sorry for it. We have both had the saddest of all lessons. May we both take it as we ought."

He wrung the surprised and unwilling hand, and before the youth, startled and overcome, had recovered enough to attempt a reply, he had come back to Rachel, resumed her arm, and crossed the churchyard, still shivering and trem-

bling with the agitation, and the force he had put on himself.
Rachel neither could nor durst speak; she only squeezed his
hand, and when he had shut himself up in his own room,
she could not help repairing to his uncle, and telling him the
whole.   Mr. Clare's "God bless you, my boy," had double
meaning in it that night.

Not long after, Alick told Rachel of his having met poor
young Carleton in the meadows, pretending to occupy himself with his fishing-rod, but too wretched to do anything.
And in a short time Mrs. Carleton again called to pour out
to Mrs. Keith her warm thanks to the Captain, for having
roused her son from his moody, unmanageable despair, and
made him consent to accept a situation in a new field of
labour, in a spirit of manful duty that he had never evinced
before.

This was a grave and subdued, but not wholly mournful,
period at Bishopsworthy—a time very precious to Rachel in
the retrospect—though there was much to render it anxious.
Alick continued to suffer from recurrences of the fever, not
very severe in themselves after the first two or three, but
laying him prostrate with shivering and headache every third
day, and telling heavily on his strength and looks when he
called himself well.   On these good days he was always at
Timber End, where his services were much needed.   Lord
Keith liked and esteemed him as a sensible prudent young
man, and his qualities as a first-rate nurse were of great
assistance to the Colonel.   Lord Keith's illness was tedious
and painful; the necessity of a dangerous operation became
increasingly manifest, but the progress towards such a crisis
was slow and the pain and discomfort great; the patient
never moved beyond his dressing-room, and needed incessant

attention to support his spirits and assist his endeavours to occupy himself. It was impossible to leave him for long together, and Colonel Keith was never set at liberty for exercise or rest except when Alick came to his assistance, and fortunately this young brother-in-law was an especial favourite, partly from Lord Keith's esteem for his prudence, partly from his experience in this especial species of suffering. At any rate the days of Alick's enforced absence were always times of greater restlessness and uneasiness at Timber End.

Meantime Rachel was constantly thrown with Mr. Clare, supplying Alick's place to him, and living in a round of duties that suited her well, details of parish work, walking with, writing for, and reading to Mr Clare, and reaping much benefit from intercourse with such a mind. Many of her errors had chiefly arisen from the want of some one whose superiority she could feel, and her old presumptions withered up to nothing when she measured her own powers with those of a highly educated man, while all the time he gave her thanks and credit for all she had effected, but such as taught her humility by very force of infection.

Working in earnest at his visitation sermon, she was drawn up into the real principles and bearings of the controversy, and Mr. Clare failed not to give full time and patience to pick out all her difficulties, removing scruples at troubling him, by declaring that it was good for his own purpose to unwind every tangle even if he did not use every thread. It was wonderful how many puzzles were absolutely intangible, not even tangled threads, but a sort of nebulous matter that dispersed itself on investigation. And after all, unwilling as she would have been to own it, a woman's tone of thought is commonly moulded by the masculine intellect, which, under one form or another, becomes the master of her soul. Those opinions, once made her own, may be acted and improved upon, often carried to lengths never thought of by their inspirer, or ·held with noble constancy and perseverance even when he himself may have fallen from them, but from some living medium they are almost always adopted, and thus, happily for herself, a woman's efforts at scepticism are but blind faith in her chosen leader, or, at the utmost, in the spirit of the age. And Rachel having been more than usually removed from the immediate influence of superior man, had been affected by the more feeble and distant power, a leading that appeared to her the light of her independent mind ; but it was not in the nature of things that, from her husband and his uncle, her character should not receive that tincture for which it had so long waited, strong and thorough in proportion to her nature, not rapid in receiving impressions, but steadfast and uncompromising in retaining and working on them when once accepted, a nature that Alick Keith had discerned and valued amid its worst errors far more than mere attractiveness, of which his sister had perhaps made him weary and distrustful. Nor, indeed, under the force of the present influences, was attractiveness wanting, and she suited Alick's peculiarities far better than many a more charming person would have done, and his uncle, knowing her only by her clear mellow voice, her consideration, helpfulness, and desire to think and do rightly, never understood the doubtful amazement now and then expressed in talking of Alick's choice. One great bond between Rachel and Mr. Clare was affection for the little babe, who continued to be Rachel's special charge, and was a great deal dearer to her already than all the seven Temples put together. She studied all the books on infant management that she could obtain, constantly listened for his voice, and filled her letters to her mother with questions and details on his health, and descriptions of his small person. Alick was amused whenever he glanced at his strong-minded woman's correspondence, and now and then used to divert himself with rousing her into emphatic declarations of her preference of this delicate little being to " great, stout, coarse creatures that people call fine children." In fact, Alick's sensitive tenderness towards his sister's motherless child took the form of avoiding the sight of it, and being ironical when it was discussed ; but with Mr. Clare, Rachel was sure of sympathy, ever since the afternoon when he had said how the sounds upstairs reminded him of his own little daughter ; and sitting under the yew-tree, he had told Rachel all the long stored-up memories of the little life that had been closed a few days after he had first heard himself called papa by the baby lips. He had described all these events calmly, and not without smiles, and had said how his own blindness had made him feel thankful that he had safely laid his little Una on her mother's bosom under the church's shade ; but when Rachel spoke of this conversation to her husband, she learnt that it was the first time that he had ever talked of those buried hopes. He had often spoken of his wife, but though always fond of children, few who had not read little Una's name beneath her mother's cross, knew that he was a childless father. And yet it was beautiful to see the pleasure he took in the touch of Bessie's infant, and how skilfully and tenderly he would hold it, so that Rachel in full faith averred that the little Alexander was never so happy as with him. The chief alarms came from Mrs.

Comyn Menteith, who used to descend on the Rectory like
a whirlwind, when the Colonel had politely expelled her
from her father's room at Timber End.   Possessed with the
idea of Rachel's being very dull at Bishopsworthy, she
sedulously enlivened her with melancholy prognostics as to
the life, limbs, and senses of the young heir, who would
never live, poor little darling, even with the utmost care
of herself and her nurse, and it was very perverse of papa
and the doctors still to keep him from her—poor little darling—not that it mattered, for he was certain not to thrive,
wherever he was, and the Gowanbrae family would end with
Uncle Colin and the glassblower's daughter; a disaster on
which she met with such condolence from Alick (N.B. the
next heir) that Rachel was once reduced to the depths of
genuine despair by the conviction that his opinion of his
nephew's life was equally desponding; and another time was
very angry with him for not defending Ermine's gentility.
She had not entirely learnt what Alick's assent might mean.

Once, when Mrs. Menteith had been besetting her father
with entreaties for the keys of Lady Keith's private possessions, she was decisively silenced, and the next day these
same keys were given to Alick, with a request that his wife
would as soon as possible look over and take to herself all
that had belonged to his sister, except a few heirloom jewels
that must return to Scotland.   Alick demurred greatly, but
the old man would not brook contradiction, and Rachel was
very unwillingly despatched upon the mission on one of
Alick's days of prostration at home.   His absence was the
most consoling part of this sad day's work.   Any way it
could not be otherwise than piteous to dismantle what had
been lately so bright and luxurious, and the contrast of the

present state of things with that in which these dainty new
wedding presents had been brought together, could not but
give many a pang ; but beside this, there was a more than
ordinary impression of "vanity of vanities, all is vanity,"
very painful to affection that was striving to lose the conviction that it had been a self-indulgent, plausible life. The
accumulation of expensive trinkets and small luxuries, was
as surprising as perplexing to a person of Rachel's severely
simple and practical tastes. It was not only since the
marriage ; for Bessie had always had at her disposal means
rather ample, and had used them not exactly foolishly, but
evidently for her own gratification. Everything had some
intrinsic worth, and was tasteful or useful, but the multitude
was perfectly amazing, and the constant echo in Rachel's
ears was, " he heapeth up riches and cannot tell who shall
gather them." Lord Keith could hardly have found an
executrix for his poor young wife, to whom her properties
would have done so little harm. Rachel set many aside for
the cousins, and for Mrs. Menteith, others she tried to persuade the Colonel to call Gowanbrae belongings, and failing
in this, she hoped through Grace, to smuggle some of them
into *his* Gowanbrae ; but when all was done, there was a
mass of things that Lord Keith never wished to see again,
and that seemed to Rachel to consist of more ornaments
than she could ever wear, and more knick-knacks than a
captain's wife could ever carry about with her.

She was putting aside the various packets of letters and
papers to be looked over more at leisure, when the Colonel
knocked at the morning-room door, and told her that his
brother would like to see her, when her work was done.
" But first," he said, " I must ask you to be kind enough to

look over some of these papers, and try to find receipts for some of these bills."

" Here they are," said Rachel ; " I was going to look them over at home."

" If you have time to examine them here with me," said Colonel Keith, gently, " I think it might save Alick some pain and vexation."

Rachel was entirely unaware of his meaning, and supposed he only thought of the mere thrilling of the recent wound ; but when he sat down and took a long account out of a tradesman's envelope, a chill of dismay came over her, followed by a glow of hope as she recollected a possible explanation : " Have these wretched tradesmen been sending in bills over again at such a time as this ?" she exclaimed.

" I should be very glad to find their receipts," returned the Colonel.

They opened the most business-like looking bundles, all of them, though neatly kept, really in hopeless confusion.   In vain was the search, and notes came forth which rendered it but too plain that there had been a considerable amount of debt even before the marriage, and that she had made partial payments and promises of clearing all off gradually, but that her new expenses were still growing upon her, and the few payments "on account," since she had been Lady Keith, by no means tallied with the amount of new purchases and orders.   No one had suspected her money matters of being in disorder, and Rachel was very slow to comprehend ; her simple, country life had made her utterly unaware of the difficulties and ways and means of a young lady of fashion. Even the direct evidence before her eyes would not at first persuade her that it was not " all those wicked tradesmen ;" she had always heard that fashionable shops were not to be trusted.

" I am afraid," said Colonel Keith, "that the whole can scarcely be shifted on the tradesmen. I fear poor Bessie was scarcely free from blame in this matter."

" Not paying ! Going on in debt ! Oh she could not have meant it ;" said Rachel, still too much astonished to understand. " Of course one hears of gay, thoughtless people doing such things, but Bessie—who had so much thought and sense. It must be a mistake ! Can't you go and speak to the people ?"

" It is very sad and painful to make such discoveries," said Colonel Keith ; " but I am afraid such things are not uncommon in the set she was too much thrown amongst."

" But she knew so well—she was so superior ; and with Alick and her uncle to keep her above them," said Rachel ; " I cannot think she could have done such things."

" I could not *think*, but I see it was so," said Colonel Keith, gravely. " As I am obliged to understand these things, she must have greatly exceeded her means, and have used much cleverness and ingenuity in keeping the tradesmen quiet, and preventing all from coming to light."

" How miserable ! I can't fancy living in such a predicament."

" I am much afraid," added the Colonel, looking over the papers, " that it explains the marriage—and then Keith did not allow her as much as she expected."

" Oh, Colonel Keith, don't !" cried Rachel ; " it is just the one thing where I could not bear to believe Alick. She was so dear and beautiful, and spoke so rightly."

" To believe Alick ! " repeated the Colonel, as Rachel's voice broke down.

" I thought—I ought not to have thought—he was hard upon her—but he knew better," said Rachel ; " of course he did not know of all this dreadful business !"

" Assuredly not," said the Colonel, " that is self-evident ; but as you say, I am afraid he did know his poor sister's character better than we did, when he came to warn me against the marriage."

" Did he ? Oh how much it must have cost him."

" I am afraid I did not make it cost him less.   I thought he judged her harshly, and that his illness had made him magnify trifles, but though our interference would have been perfectly useless, he was quite right in his warning.   Now that, poor thing, she is no longer here to enchant us with her witcheries, I see that my brother greatly suffered from being kept away from home, and detained in this place, and that she left him far more alone than she ought to have done."

" Yes, Alick thought so, but she had such good reasons ; I am sure she believed them herself."

"If she had not believed them, she could not have had such perfect sincerity of manner," said the Colonel ; " she must have persuaded at least one half of herself that she was acting for every one's good except her own."

" And Mr. Clare, whom Alick always thought she neglected, never felt it.   Alick says he was too unselfish to claim attention."

" *I* never doubted her for one moment till I came home, on that unhappy day, and found how ill Keith was.   I did think then, that considering how much she had seen of Alick while the splinters were working out, she ought to have

known better than to talk of sciatica ; but she made me quite
believe in her extreme anxiety, and that she was only going
out because it was necessary for her to take care of you on
your first appearance. How bright she looked, and how
little I thought I should never see her again !"

"Oh, she meant what she said ! She always was kind to
me ! Most kind !" repeated Rachel ; "so considerate about all
the dreadful spring—not one word did she say to vex me
about the past ! I am sure she did go out on that day as
much to shelter me as for anything else. I can't bear to
think all this—here in this pretty room that she had such
pleasure in ; where she made me so welcome, after all my
disagreeableness and foolishness."

The Colonel could almost have said, "Better such foolishness than such wisdom, such repulsion than such attraction."
He was much struck by Rachel's distress, and the absence of
all female spite and triumph, made him understand Ermine's
defence of her as really large-minded and generous.

"It is a very sad moment to be undeceived," he said ;
"one would rather have one's faults come to light in one's
life than afterwards."

They were simple words, so simple that the terrible truth with
which they were connected, did not come upon Rachel at the
first moment ; but as if to veil her agitation, she drew towards
her a book, an ivory-bound Prayer-book, full of illuminations,
of Bessie's own doing, and her eye fell upon the awful verse,
"So long as thou doest well unto thyself, men will speak
good of thee." It was almost more than Rachel could bear,
sitting in the midst of the hoards, for which poor Bessie had
sold herself. She rose up, with a sob of oppressive grief,
and broke out, "Oh ! at least it is a comfort that Alick was

really the kindest and rightest!   Only too right! but you
can settle all this without him," she added imploringly ;
"need he know of this ?   I can't bear that he should."

"Nor I," said Colonel Keith, "it was the reason that I am
glad you are here alone."

"Oh, thank you! No one need ever know," added Rachel.

"I fear my brother must see the accounts, as they have to
be paid, but that need not be immediately."

"Is there anything else that is dreadful ?" said Rachel,
looking at the remaining papers, as if they were a nest of
adders.   "I don't like to take them home now, if they will
grieve Alick."

"You need not be afraid of that packet," said the Colonel ;
"I see his father's handwriting. They look like his letters
from India."

Rachel looked into one or two, and her face lighted up.
"Oh !" she exclaimed, "this is enough to make up for all.
This is his letter to tell about Alick's wound.   Oh how
beautifully he speaks of him," and Rachel, with no voice to
read, handed the thin paper to her companion, that he might
see the full commendation, that had been wrung from the reserved father's heart by his son's extremity.

"You must be prepared to hear that all is over," wrote the
father to his daughter ; " in fact, I doubt whether he can live
till morning, though M'Vicar declares that nothing vital has
been touched.   Be it as it may, the boy has been in all
respects, even more than I dared to wish, and the comfort he
has been ever since he came out to me has been unspeakable.
We must not grudge him such a soldier's death after his
joyous life.   But for you, my poor girl, I could only wish
the same for myself to-morrow.   You will, at least, if you

lose a brother's care, have a memory of him, to which to live up. The thought of such a dead brother will be more to you than many a living one can ever be to a sister."

Rachel's heart beat high, and her eyes were full of tears of exultation. And the Colonel was well pleased to compensate for all the pain he had inflicted by giving her all the details he could recollect of her husband's short campaign. They had become excellent friends over their mournful work, and were sorry to have their *tête-à-tête* interrupted when a message was brought that his Lordship was ready, if Mrs. Keith would be so good as to come into his sitting-room.

She wiped away the tears, and awe-struck and grave, followed the Colonel; a great contrast to Lord Keith's more frequent lady-visitor, as she silently received the polished greeting, its peculiar stateliness of courtesy, enhanced by the feeble state of the shattered old man, unable to rise from his pillowed chair, and his face deeply lined by suffering. He would not let her give him any account of her labours, nor refer any question to him, he only entreated that everything might be taken away, and that he might hear nothing about it. He spoke warmly of Alick's kindness and attention, and showed much solicitude about his indisposition, and at last he inquired for Rachel's " little charge," hoping he was not clamorous or obnoxious to her, or to Mr. Clare's household. Her eager description of his charms provoked a look of interest and a sad smile, followed by a request, that weather and doctor permitting, she would bring the child to be seen for a few minutes. The next day there was an appointment, at which both the Colonel and Alick were wanted, but on the following one, the carriage should be sent to bring her and the little one to Timber End.

The effect of this invitation amused Alick. The first thing he heard in the morning was a decided announcement from Rachel that she must go up to London to procure equipments for the baby to be presented in !

"You know I can't go with you to-day."

"Of course, but I must make him fit to be seen. You know he has been wearing little Una's things all this time, and that will not do out of the nursery."

"A superior woman ought to know that his Lordship will never find out what his son has on."

"Then it is all the more reason that I should not let the poor dear little fellow. go about wrapped up in somebody's old shawl !"

"What will you do then—take your maid ? "

"Certainly not.   I can't have him left."

"Then take him with you ? "

"What, Alick, a little unvaccinated baby ! Where have you ever lived ? I don't see the least reason why I should not go alone."

"You need not begin beating about the world yet, Rachel. How many times did you say you had been in London ? "

"Three ; once with my father when I was a child, once in the time of the Great Exhibition, and passing through it now with you.   But any one of common sense can manage."

"If you will wait till five o'clock I will come with you," said Alick, wearily.

"No, indeed, I had rather not go, than that you should ; you are quite tired out enough at the end of the day."

"Then do not go."

"Alick, why will you have no proper feeling for that poor dear child ? " said Rachel with tears in her eyes.

If he winced he did not show it. "My proper feeling takes the direction of my wife," he said.

"You don't really mean to forbid me to go," she exclaimed.

"I don't *mean* it, for I do so, unless you find some one to go with you."

It was the first real collision that had taken place, but Alick's quiet, almost languid tone had an absolute determination in it from the very absence of argument; and Rachel, though extremely annoyed, felt the uselessness of battling the point. She paused for a few moments, then said with an effort, "May I take the housekeeper?"

"Yes, certainly," and then he added some advice about taking a brougham, and thus lightened her heart; so that she presently said humbly,

"Have I been self-willed and overbearing, Alick?"

He laughed. "Not at all; you have persevered just where you ought. I dare say this is all more essential than shows on the surface. And," he added, with a shaken voice, "if you were not myself, Rachel, you know how I should thank you for caring for my poor Bessie's child." He was gone almost as he spoke the words, but Rachel still felt the kiss and the hot tears that had fallen on her face.

Mr. Clare readily consented to spare his housekeeper, but the housekeeper was untoward, she was "busied in her housewife skep," and would not stir. Alick was gone to Timber End, and Rachel was just talking of getting the schoolmaster's wife as an escort, when Mr. Clare said—

"Pray are you above accepting my services?"

"You! Oh, uncle; thank you, but——"

"What were your orders? Anybody with you, was it not? I flatter myself that I have some *body*, at least."

"If Alick will not think I ought not!"

"The boy will not presume to object to what I do with you."

"I do wish it very much," said candid Rachel.

"Of course you do, my dear. Alick is not cured of a young man's notion that babies are a sort of puppies. He is quite right not to let you run about London by yourself, but he will be quite satisfied if you find eyes and I find discretion."

"But is it not very troublesome to you?"

"It is a capital lark!" said Mr. Clare, with a zest that only the slang word could imply, removing all Rachel's scruples; and in effect Mr. Clare did enjoy the spice of adventure in a most amusing way. He knew perfectly well how to manage, laid out the plan of operations, gave orders to the driver, went into all the shops, and was an effective assistant in the choice of material and even of embroidery. His touch and ear seemed to do more for him than many men's eyes do for them; he heard odd scraps of conversation and retailed them with so much character; he had such pleasant colloquies with all in whose way he fell, and so thoroughly enjoyed the flow and babble of the full stream of life, that Rachel marvelled that the seclusion of his parsonage was bearable to him. He took her to lunch with an old friend, a lady who had devoted herself to the care of poor girls to be trained as servants, and Rachel had the first real sight of one of the many great and good works set on foot by personal and direct labour.

"If I had been sensible, I might have come to something like this!" she said.

"Do you wish to undo these last three months?"

" No ; I am not fit to be anything but an ordinary married woman, with an Alick to take care of me ; but I am glad some people can be what I meant to be."

" And you need not regret not being useful *now*," said Mr. Clare. " Where should any of us be without you ? "

It had not occurred to Rachel, but she was certainly of far more positive use in the world at the present moment than ever she had been in her most assuming maiden days.

Little Alexander was arrayed in all that could enhance his baby dignity, and Rachel was more than ever resolved to assert his superiority over " great frightful fine children," resenting vehemently an innocent observation from Alick, that the small features and white skin promised sandiness of hair. Perhaps Alick delighted in saying such things for the sake of proving the ' very womanhood ' of his Clever Woman.

Rachel hung back, afraid of the presentation, and would have sent her maid into the room with the child if Colonel Keith had not taken her in himself. Even yet she was not dexterous in handling the baby ; her hands were both occupied, and her attention absorbed, and she could not speak, she felt it so mournful to show this frail motherless creature to a father more like its grandfather, and already almost on the verge of the grave. She came up to Lord Keith, and held the child to him in silence. He said, " Thank you," and kissed not only the little one, but her own brow, and she kept the tears back with difficulty.

Colonel Keith gave her a chair and footstool, and she sat with the baby on her lap, while very few words were spoken. It was the Colonel who asked her to take off the hood that hid the head and brow, and who chiefly hazarded opinions as to likeness and colour of eyes. Lord Keith looked earnestly and sadly, but hardly made any observation, except that it looked healthier than he had been led to expect. He was sure it owed much to Mrs. Keith's great care and kindness.

Rachel feared he would not be able to part with his little son, and began to mention the arrangements she had contemplated in case he wished to keep the child at Timber End. On this, Lord Keith asked with some anxiety, if its presence were inconvenient to Mr. Clare; and being assured of the contrary, said, "Then while you are so kind as to watch over him, I much prefer that things should remain in their present state, than to bring him to a house like this. You do not object?"

"Oh, no; I am so glad. I was only dreading the losing him. I thought Mrs. Menteith wished for him when he is old enough to travel."

"Colin!" said Lord Keith, looking up sharply, "will nothing make the Menteiths understand that I would rather put out the child to nurse in a Highland hut than in that Babel of a nursery of theirs?"

Colin smiled and said, "Isabel does not easily accept an answer she dislikes."

"But remember, both of you," continued Lord Keith, "that happen what may, this poor child is not to be in her charge. I've seen enough of her children left alone in perambulators in the sun. You will be in Edinburgh?" he added, turning to Rachel.

"Yes, when Alick's leave ends."

"I shall return thither when this matter is over, I know I shall be better at home in Scotland, and if I winter in Edinburgh, may be we could make some arrangement for his being still under your eye."

Rachel went home more elevated than she had been for months past.

CHAPTER XV.

AT LAST.

> " I bid thee hail, not as in former days,
>   Not as my chosen only, but my bride,
>   My very bride, coming to make my house
>   A glorious temple."   A. H. HALLAM.

" Timber End, Littleworthy, September 10th.

"DEAR MISS WILLIAMS,—I must begin by entreating your
forgiveness for addressing you in a manner for which perhaps
you may be unprepared; but I trust you have always been
aware, that any objections that I may have offered to my
brother Colin's attachment to yourself have never been personal, or owing to anything but an unfortunate complication
of circumstances. These difficulties are, as no doubt he will
explain to you, in great measure removed by the present
condition of my family, which will enable me to make such
settlements as I could wish in the case of one so nearly connected with me; so that I am enabled to entreat of you at
length to reward the persevering constancy so well deserved.
I have a further, and a personal cause for wishing that the
event should not be deferred, as regard for my feelings might
have led you to propose. You are aware of the present state
of my health, and that it has become expedient to make
immediate arrangements for the future guardianship of my
little boy. His uncles are of course his natural guardians,

and I have unbounded confidence in both; but Alexander Keith's profession renders it probable that he may not always be at hand, and I am therefore desirous of being able to nominate yourself, together with my brother, among the personal guardians. Indeed, I understand from Alexander Keith, that such was the express wish of his sister. I mention this as an additional motive to induce you to consent. For my own part, even without so stringent a cause, all that I have ever seen or known of yourself would inspire me with the desire that you should take a mother's place towards my son. But you must be aware that such an appointment could only be made when you are already one of the family, and this it is that leads me to entreat you to overlook any appearance of precipitancy on my brother's part, and return a favourable reply to the request, which with my complete sanction, he is about to address to you.

"Yes, Ermine Williams, forgive all that is past, and feel for an old, it may be, a dying man, and for a motherless infant. There is much to forget, but I trust to your overcoming any scruples, and giving me all the comfort in your power, in thinking of the poor child who has come into the world under such melancholy circumstances.

"Yours most truly,

"KEITH OF GOWANBRAE."

"Poor Keith, he has given me his letter open, his real anxiety has been too much at last for his dignity; and now, my Ermine, what do you say to his entreaty? The state of the case is this. How soon this abscess may be ready for the operation is still uncertain, the surgeons think it will be in about three weeks, and in this interval he wishes to complete all

his arrangements.   In plain English, his strongest desire is to
secure the poor little boy from falling into Menteith's hands.
Now, mine is a precarious life, and Alick and Rachel may
of course be at the ends of the earth, so the point is that
you shall be 'one of the family,' before the will is signed.
Alick's leave has been extended to the 1st of October, no-
more is possible, and he undertakes to nurse poor Keith for
a fortnight from to-morrow, if you will consent to fulfil this
same request within that time.   After the 1st, I should have
to leave you, but as soon as Keith is well enough to bear the
journey, he wishes to return to Edinburgh, where he would
be kindly attended to by Alick and Rachel all the winter.
There, Ermine, your victory is come, your consent has been
entreated at last by my brother, not for my sake, but as
a personal favour to himself, because there is no woman in
the world of whom he thinks so highly.   For myself I say
little.   I grieve that you should be thus hurried and fluttered,
and if Ailie thinks it would harm you, she must telegraph
back to me not to come down, and I will try to teach myself
patience by preaching it to Keith, but otherwise you will see
me by four o'clock to-morrow.   Every time I hear Rachel's
name, I think it ought to have been yours, and surely in
this fourteenth year, lesser objections may give way.   But
persuasions are out of the question, you must be entirely led
by your own feeling.   If I could have seen you in July, this
should not have come so suddenly at last.

> "Yours, more than ever, decide as you may,
> "COLIN A. KEITH.

> "P.S.—I am afraid Rose would hardly answer this purpose
equally well."

Colonel Keith followed his letter at four o'clock, and entering his own study, found it in a cloud of smoke, in the midst of which he dimly discerned a long beard and thin visage absorbed in calculation.

" Edward ! How is Ermine ? "

" Oh ? " (inquiringly) " Keith ! " (as taken by surprise) " ah ! you were to come home to-day. How are you ? "

" How is she ? Has she had my letter ? "

" What letter ? You write every day, I thought."

" The letter of yesterday. Have you heard nothing of it ? "

" Not that I know of. Look here, Keith, I told you I was sure the platinum——"

" Your brain is becoming platinum. I must go," and the chemist remained with merely a general impression of having been interrupted.

Next the Colonel met Rose, watching at his own gate, and this time his answer was more explicit.

" Yes, Aunt Ermine said you were coming, and that I might meet you, but that I must let you come in alone, for she had not seen you so long, that she wanted you all to herself."

" And how is she ; how has she been ? "

" She is well now," said Rose, in the grave, grown-up way she always assumed when speaking of her aunt's health ; " but she has been having a good deal of her nervous head- ache this summer, and Lady Temple wanted her to see Mr. Frampton, but Aunt Ailie said it was only excitement and wear of spirits. Oh, I am glad you have come back ! We have so wearied after you."

Nevertheless Rose duteously loosed the hand to which she

had been clinging till they came to the door; and as Colin
Keith opened it, again he was met by the welcoming glances
of the bright eyes. This time he did not pause till he was
close to her, and kneeling on one knee beside her, he put
his arm round her, and held her hands in his.

The first words that passed were, "You had the
letters?"

"Colin, Colin, my one prayer has been, 'Make Thy way
plain before my face.'"

"And now it is?"

"The suspicion is gone; the displeasure is gone; the
doubts are gone; and now there is nothing—nothing but
the lameness and the poverty; and if you like the old
cinder, Colin, that is your concern;" and she hid her face,
with a sort of sobbing laugh.

"And even the haste; you consent to that?"

"I don't feel it like haste," she said, looking up with a
smile, and then crimsoning.

"And Ailie gives leave, and thinks the hurry will not
harm you?"

"Ailie! O Colin, did you think I could tell any one of
your letter, before you had had your answer?"

"Then Edward is not so moonstruck as I thought him!
And when shall it be, dearest? Give me as much time as
you can. I must go back this day fortnight."

"I suppose your expectations are not high in the matter
of finery," said Ermine, with a certain archness of voice.

"Those eyes are all the finery I ever see."

"Then if you will not be scandalized at my natural
Sunday dress, I don't see why this day week should not
do as well as any other time."

" Ermine, you are the only woman I ever met totally free from nonsense."

" Take care, it is very unfeminine and disagreeable to be devoid of nonsense."

" Very, and therefore you are talking it now! Ermine, how shall I thank you? Not only for the sake of the ease of mind to my poor brother; but in the scenes we are going through, a drop of happiness is wanted as a stimulant. When I looked at the young couple at Bishopsworthy, I often felt as if another half-year of suspense was more than I could bear, and that I must ask you to help me through with at least a definite hope."

" Ah! you have gone through a great deal. I am sure it has been a time of great trouble."

" Indeed it has. The suffering has become unceasing and often most severe, and there is grievous depression of spirits; I could not have left him even for a day, if he had not been so fervently bent on this."

" Is he feeling his loss more acutely than at first?"

" Not so much that, as for the poor little boy, who is a heavy burthen on his mind. He has lived in such a state of shrewd distrust that he has no power of confidence, and his complications for making all the boy's guardians check one another till we come to a dead lock, and to make provision for Isabel out of Menteith's reach, are enough to distract the brain of a man in health."

" Is he fond of the child?"

" It is an oppressive care to him, and he only once has made up his mind to see it, though it is never off his mind, and it is very curious how from the first he has been resolved on your taking charge of it. It is the most real testimony he could give you."

"It is very comfortable not to be brought in like an enemy in spite of him, as even a year ago I could have been proud to do."

"And I to have brought you," he answered, "but it is far better as it is. He is very cordial, and wants to give up the Auchinvar estate to me; indeed, he told me that he always meant me to have it as soon as I had washed my hands of you—you wicked syren—but I think you will agree with me that he had better leave it to his daughter Mary, who has nothing. We never reckoned on it."

"Nor on anything else," said Ermine, smiling.

"You have never heard my ways and means," he said, "and as a prudent woman you ought, you know. See," taking out his tablets, "here is my calculation."

"All that !"

"On the staff in India there were good opportunities of saving; then out of that sum I bought the house, and with my half-pay, our income will be very fair, and there would be a pension afterwards for you. This seems to me all we can reasonably want."

"Unless I became like *die Ilsebill* in the German tale. After four years of living from hand to mouth, this will be like untold gold. To wish to be above strict economy in wheeled chairs has seemed like perilous discontent in Rose and me."

"I have ventured on the extravagance of taking the ponies and little carriage off my brother's hands, it is low enough for you, and I shall teach Rose to ride one of the ponies with me."

"The dear little Rose ! But, Colin, there is a dreadful

"And indeed, Ailie, he is so wedded to smoke and calculations, and so averse to this sublunary world, that though your being with him might be beneficial, still I greatly question whether the risk of carrying poor little Rose to so remote a place in such a climate, would be desirable. If he were pining to have a home made for him, it would be worth doing ; as it is, the sacrifice would be disproportioned."

"It would be no sacrifice if he only wanted us."

"Where you are wanted is here. Ermine wants you. I want you. The Temples want you."

"Now, Colin, tell me truly. Edward feels as I do, and Dr. Long spoke seriously of it. Will not my present position do you and Ermine harm among your friends ?"

"With no friend we wish to make or keep !"

"If I do remain," continued Alison, "it must be as I am. I would not live upon you, even if you asked me, which you have too much sense to do ; and though dear Lady Temple is everything to me, and wants me to forget that I am her governess, that would be a mere shuffle, but if it is best for you that I should give it up, and go out, say so at once."

"Best for me to have eight Temples thrown on my hands, all in despair ? To have you at Myrtlewood is an infinite relief to me, both on their account and Ermine's. You should not suspect a penniless Scotsman of such airs, Ailie."

"Not you, Colin, but your family."

"Isabel Menteith thinks a glass-blower was your father, and Mauleverer your brother, so yours is by far the most respectable profession. No, indeed, my family might be thankful to have any one in it who could do as you have done."

Alison's scruples were thus disposed of, and when Edward's

brain cleared itself from platinum, he showed himself satisfied with the decision, though he insisted on henceforth
sending home a sum sufficient for his daughter's expenses,
and once said something that could be construed into a hope
of spending a quiet old age with her and his sister; but at
present he was manifestly out of his element, and was bent
on returning to Ekaterinburg immediately after the marriage.

His presence was but a qualified pleasure. Naturally shy
and absent, his broken spirits and removal from domestic
life, and from society, had exaggerated his peculiarities; and
under the pressure of misfortune, caused in a great measure
by his own negligence, he had completely given way, without
a particle of his sister's patience or buoyancy, and had
merely striven to drown his troubles in engrossing problems
of his favourite pursuit, till the habit of abstraction had
become too confirmed to be shaken off. When the blot on
his name was removed, he was indeed sensible that he was
no longer an exile, but he could not resume his old standing;
friendships rudely severed could not be re-united; his absorption had grown by indulgence; old interests had passed
away; needful conformity to social habits was irksome, and
even his foreign manner and appearance testified to his entire
unfitness for English life.

Tibbie was in constant dread of his burning the house
down, so incalculable and preposterous were his hours, and
the Colonel, longing to render the house a perfect shrine for
his bride, found it hard to tolerate the fumes with which her
brother saturated it. If he had been sure that opium formed
no portion of Edward's solace, his counsel to Alison would
have been less decisive. To poor little Rose, her father was
an abiding perplexity and distress; she wanted to love him,

and felt it absolute naughtiness to be constantly disappointed
by his insensibility to her approaches, or else repelled and
disgusted by that vice of the Russian sheep. And a vague
hint of being transported to the Ural mountains, away from
Aunt Ermine, had haunted her of late more dreadfully than
even the lions of old; so that the relief was ineffable when
her dear Colonel confided to her that she was to be his niece
and Aunt Ermine's handmaid, sent her to consult with Tibbie
on her new apartment, and invited Augustus to the most
eligible hole in the garden. The grotto that Rose, Conrade,
and Francis proceeded to erect with pebbles and shells, was
likely to prove as alarming to that respectable reptile as a
model cottage to an Irish peasant.

Ermine had dropped all scruples about Rose's intercourse
with other children, and the feeling that she might associate
with them on equal terms, perhaps, was the most complete
assurance of Edward's restoration. She was glad that companionship should render the little maiden more active and
childlike, for Edward's abstraction had made her believe that
there might be danger in indulging the dreaminess of the
imaginative child.

No one welcomed the removal of these restraints more
warmly than Lady Temple. She was perhaps the happiest of
the happy, for with her there was no drawback, no sorrow, no
parting to fear. Her first impulse, when Colonel Keith came
to tell her his plans, was to seize on hat and shawl, and rush
down to Mackarel Lane to kiss Ermine with all her heart,
and tell her that "it was the most delightful thing of her to
have consented at last, for nobody deserved so well to be
happy as that dear Colonel;" and then she clung to Alison,
declaring that now she should have her all to herself, and if

she would only come to Myrtlewood, she would do her very best to make her comfortable there, and it should be her home—her home always.

"In fact," said Ermine, afterwards to the Colonel, "when you go to Avoncester, I think you may as well get a licence for the wedding of Alison Williams and Fanny Temple at the same time. There has been quite a courtship on the lady's part."

The courtship had been the more ardent from Fanny's alarm lest the brother should deprive her of Alison; and when she found her fears groundless, she thanked him with such fervour, and talked so eagerly of his sister's excellences that she roused him into a lucid interval, in which he told Colonel Keith that Lady Temple might give him an idea of the style of woman that Lucy had been. Indeed, Colin began to think that it was as well that he was so well wrapped up in smoke and chemistry, otherwise another might have been added to the list of Lady Temple's hopeless adorers.

The person least satisfied was Tibbie, who could not get over the speediness of the marriage, nor forgive the injury to Miss Williams; " of bringing her hame like any pleughman's wife, wantin' a honeymoon trip, forbye providin' hersel' with weddin' braws conformable. Gin folk tak' sic daft notions aff the English, they'd be mair wise like to bide at hame, an' that's my way o' thinkin'."

Crusty as she was, there was no danger of her not giving her warmest welcome; and thus the morning came. Tibbie had donned her cap, with white satin ribbons, and made of lace once belonging to the only heiress who had ever brought wealth to the Keiths. Edward Williams, all his goods packed up, had gone to join his sisters, and the Colonel, only

perceptibly differing from his daily aspect in having a hat
free from crape, was opening all the windows in hopes that a
thorough draft would remove the last of the tobacco, when
the letters were brought in, and among them one of the black
bordered bulletins from Littleworthy, which ordinarily arrived
by the second post. It was a hurried note, evidently dashed
off to catch the morning mail.

MY DEAR COLONEL,—Alick tells me to write in haste to
catch the morning post, and beg you to telegraph the instant
your wedding is over. The doctors see cause to hasten their
measures, but your brother will have nothing done till the
will is signed. He and Alick both desire you will not come,
but it is getting to be far too much for Alick. I would tell
you more if there were time before the post goes. Love to
dear Ermine.

Very sincerely yours,

R. KEITH.

There was so shocked and startled a look on Colin's face,
that Tibbie believed that his brother must be dead, and when
in a few almost inaudible words he told her that he must start
for Bishopsworthy by the afternoon train, she fairly began to
scold, partly by way of working off the irritation left by her
alarm. "The lad's clean demented! Heard ye ever the
like, to rin awa' frae his new-made wife afore the blessin's
been weel spoke; an' a' for the whimsie of that daft English
lassie that made siccan a piece of work wi' her cantrips."

"I am afraid she is right now," said the Colonel, "and my
brother must not be left any longer."

"Hout awa, Maister Colin, his lordship has come between
you and your luve oft enough already, without partin' ye at

the very church door. Ye would na have the English cast up
to us, that one of your name did na ken better what was
fittin by his bride ! "

"My bride must be the judge, Tibbie. You shall see
whether she bids me stay," said Colin, a little restored by his
amusement at her anxiety for his honour among the English.
" Now desire Smith to meet me at the church door, and ride
at once from thence to Avoncester ; and get your face ready
to give a cheerful welcome, Tibbie. Let her have that, at
least, whatever may come after."

Tibbie looked after him, and shook her head, understanding from her ain laddie's pallid cheek, and resolute lip, nay,
in the very sound of his footfall, how sore was his trial, and
with one-sided compassion she muttered, "Telegrafted awa on
his vera weddin' day. His Lordship 'll be the death o' them
baith before he's done."

As it was in every way desirable that the wedding should
be unexpected by Avonmouth in general, it was to take place
at the close of the ordinary morning service, and Ermine in
her usual seat within the vestry, was screened from knowing
how late was Colin's entrance, or seeing the determined composure that would have to her eyes betrayed how much
shaken he was. He was completely himself again by the
time the congregation dispersed, leaving only Grace Curtis,
Lady Temple, and the little best man, Conrade, a goodly sight
in his grey suit and scarlet hose. Then came the slow movement from the vestry, the only really bridal-looking figure
being Rose in white muslin and white ribbons ; walking
timidly and somewhat in awe beside her younger aunt ; while
her father upheld and guided the elder. Both were in quiet,
soft, dark dresses, and straw bonnets, but over hers Ermine

wore the small though exquisite Brussels lace veil that had
first appeared at her mother's wedding; and thankful joy and
peaceful awe looked so lovely on her noble brow, deep, soft
dark eyes, and the more finely moulded, because somewhat
worn, features; and so beauteously deepened was the carna-
tion on her cheek, that Mr. Mitchell ever after maintained
that he had never married any one to compare with that thirty-
three years' old bride upon crutches, and, as he reported to
his wife, in no dress at all.

Her brother, who supported her all the time she stood, was
infinitely more nervous than she was. Her native grace and
dignity, and absence of all false shame entirely covered her
helplessness; and in her earnestness, she had no room for
confusion ; her only quivering of voice was caught for one
moment from the tremulous intensity of feeling that Colin
Keith could not wholly keep from thrilling in his tones, as he
at last proclaimed his right to love and to cherish her for
whom he had so long persevered.

Unobserved, he filled up the half-written despatch with the
same pen with which he signed the register, and sent Conrade
to the door with it to his already mounted messenger. Then
assuming Edward's place as Ermine's supporter, he led her to
the door, seated her in her wheeled chair, and silently handing Rachel's note as his explanation to Alison, he turned
away, and walked alone by Ermine's side to his own house.
Still silent, he took her into the bright drawing-room he had
so long planned for her, and seated her in her own peculiar
chair. Then his first words were, "Thank God for this!"

She knew his face. "Colin, your brother is worse?" He
bent his head, he could not speak.

"And you have to go to him ! This very day?"

"Ermine, you must decide. You are at last my first duty!"

"That means that you know you ought to go. Tell me what it is."

He told the substance of the note, ending with, "If you could come with me!"

"I would if I should not be a tie and hindrance. No, I must not do that; but here I am, Colin, here I am. And it is all true—it has all come right at last! All we waited for. Nothing has ever been like this."

She was the stronger. Tears, as much of loving thankfulness as of overflowing disappointment, rushed into his eyes at such a fulfilment of the purpose that he had carried with him by sea and land, in battle and sickness, through all the years of his manhood. And withal her one thought was to infuse in its strongest measure the drop of happiness that was to sustain him through the scenes that awaited him, to make him feel her indeed his wife, and to brighten him with the sunbeam face that she knew had power to cheer him. Rallying her playfulness, she took off her bonnet, and said, as she settled her hair, "There, that is being at home! Take my shawl, yes, and these white gloves, and put them out of sight, that I may not feel like a visitor, and that you may see how I shall look when you come back. Do you know, I think your being out of the way will be rather a gain, for there will be a tremendous feminine bustle with the flitting of our possessions."

Her smile awoke a responsive look, and she began to gaze round and admire, feeling it safest to skim on the surface; and he could not but be gratified by her appreciation of the pains spent upon this, her especial home. He had recovered

himself again by the time these few sentences had passed ;
they discussed the few needful arrangements required by his
departure, and Tibbie presently found them so cheerful that
she was quite scandalized, and when Ermine held out her
hands, saying, " What Tibbie, won't you come and kiss me,
and wish me joy ?" she exclaimed—

"Wish ye joy ! It's like me to wish ye joy an yer lad
hurled awa frae yer side i' the blink o' an ee, by thae wild
telegrams. I dinna see what joy's to come o't ; it's clean
again the Scripture !"

"I told you I had left it to her to decide, Tibbie," said
the Colonel.

"Weel, an what wad ye hae the puir leddy say ? She
kens what sorts ye, when the head of yer name is sick an
lyin' among thae English loons that hae brocht him to siccan
a pass."

"Right, Tibbie," exclaimed Ermine, greatly amused at the
unexpected turn, purely for the sake of putting Maister Colin
in the wrong. " If a gentleman won't be content without a
bride who can't walk, he must take the consequence, and
take his wedding trip by himself ! It is my belief, Tibbie,
as I have just been telling him, that you and I shall get the
house in all the better order for having him off our hands,
just at first," she added, with a look of intelligence.

"Deed, an maybe we shall," responded Tibbie, with profound satisfaction. " He was aye a camsteary child when
there was any wark on hand."

Colin could not help laughing, and when once this had
been effected, Ermine felt that his depression had been
sufficiently met, and that she might venture on deeper, and
more serious sympathy, befitting the chastened, thankful

feelings with which they hailed the crowning of their youthful love, the fulfilment of the hopes and prayers that the one had persisted in through doubt and change, the other had striven to resign into the All-wise Hands.

They had an early meal together, chiefly for the sake of his wheeling her to the head of his table, and "seeing how she looked there," and then the inexorable hour was come, and he left her, with the echo of her last words in his ear, "Goodbye, Colin, stay as long as you ought. It will make the meeting all the sweeter, and you have your wife to come back to now. Give a sister's love to your brother, and thanks for having spared you;" and his last look at the door was answered with her sunshiny smile.

But when, a few minutes after, Edward came up with Alison for his farewell, they found her lying back in her chair, half fainting, and her startled look told almost too plainly that she had not thought of her brother. "Never mind," said Edward, affectionately, as much to console Alison as Ermine for this oblivion; "of course it must be so, and I don't deserve otherwise. Nothing brought me home but Colin Keith's telling me that he saw you would not have him till my character was cleared up; and now he has repaired so much of the evil I did you, all I can do is to work to make it up to you in other ways. Goodbye, Ermine, I leave you all in much better hands than mine ever were, you are right enough in feeling that a week of his absence outweighs a year of mine. Bless you for all that you and he have done for my child. She, at least, is a comfort to you."

Ermine's powers were absolutely exhausted; she could only answer him by embraces and tears; and all the rest of the day she was, to use her own expression, "good for nothing but to be let alone." Nor, though she exerted herself that she might with truth write that she was well and happy, was she good for much more on the next, and her jealous guardians allowed her to see no one but soft, fondling Lady Temple ; who insisted on a relationship (through Rachel), and whose tender pensive quietness could not fail to be refreshment to the strained spirits, and wearied physical powers, and who better than anybody could talk of the Colonel ; nay, who could understand, and even help Ermine herself to understand, that these ever-welling tears came from a source by no means akin to grief or repining.

The whole aspect of the rooms was full of tokens of his love and thought for her. The ground-floor had been altered for her accommodation, the furniture chosen in accordance with her known tastes or with old memories, all undemonstratively prepared while yet she had not decided on her consent. And what touched her above all, was the collection of treasures that he had year by year gathered together for her throughout the weary waiting, purchases at which Lady Temple remembered her mother's banter, with his quiet evasions of explanation. No wonder Ermine laid her head on her hand, and could not retain her tears, as she recalled the white, dismayed face of the youth, who had printed that one sad earnest kiss on her brow, as she lay fire-seathed and apparently dying ; and who had cherished the dream unbroken and unwaveringly, had denied himself consistently, had garnered up these choice tokens when ignorant even whether she still lived ; had relied on her trust, and come back, heart-whole, to claim and win her, undaunted by her crippled state, her poverty, and her brother's blotted name. " How can such love ever be met ? Why am I favoured beyond all I could have dared to image to myself?" she thought, and wept again; because, as she murmured to Fanny, " I do thank God for it with all my heart, and I do long to tell him all. I don't think my married life ought to begin by being sillier than ever I was before, but I can't help it."

" And I do love you so much the better for it," said Fanny; a better companion to-day than the grave, strong Alison, who would have been kind, but would have had to suppress some marvel at the break down, and some resentment that Edward had no greater share in it.

The morning's post brought her the first letter from her husband, and in the midst of all her anxiety as to the contents, she could not but linger a moment on the aspect of the Honourable Mrs. Colin Keith in his handwriting; there was a carefulness in the penmanship that assured her that, let him have to tell her what he would, the very inditing of that address had been enjoyment to him. That the border was black told nothing, but the intelligence was such as she had been fully prepared for. Colin had arrived to find the surgeon's work over, but the patient fast sinking. Even his recognition of his brother had been uncertain, and within twenty-four hours of the morning that had given Colin a home of his own, the last remnant of the home circle of his childhood had passed from him.

Still Ermine had to continue a widowed bride for full a fortnight, whilst the funeral and subsequent arrangements necessitated Colin's presence in Scotland. It was on a crisp, beautiful October evening that Rose, her chesnut hair flying about her brow, stood, lighted up by the sunbeams in the porch, with upraised face and outstretched hands, and as the Colonel bent down to receive her joyous embrace, said,

"Aunt Ermine gave me leave to bring you to the door. Then I am going to Myrtlewood till bed-time. And after that I shall always have you."

The open door showed Ermine, too tremulous to trust to her crutch, but leaning forward, her eyes liquid with tears of thankfulness. The patient spirits had reached their home and haven, the earthly haven of loving hearts, the likeness of the heavenly haven, and as her head leant, at last, upon his shoulder, and his guardian arm encircled her, there was such a sense of rest and calm that even the utterance of their inward thanksgiving, or of a word of tenderness would have jarred upon them. It was not till a knock and message at the door interrupted them, that they could break the blessed stillness.

"And there you are, my Ermine!" said Colin, standing on the hearth-rug, and surveying her with satisfied eyes. "You are a queenly looking dame in your black draperies, and you look really well, much better than Rachel led me to expect."

"Ah! when she was here I had no fixed day to look forward to. And receiving our poor little orphan baby was not exactly like receiving his uncle, though Rachel seemed to think it ought to make up for anything."

"She was thoroughly softened by that child! It was a spirited thing her bringing him down here on the Monday when we started for Scotland, and then coming all the way alone with her maid. I did not think Alick would have consented, but he said she would always be the happier for having deposited her charge in your hands."

"It was a great wrench to her. I felt it like robbery when she put the little fellow down on my lap and knelt over him, not able to get herself away, but saying that she

was not fit to have him ; she could not bear it if she made
him hate her as Conrade did ! I am glad she has had his
first smile, she deserves it."

" Is Tibbie in charity with him ? "

" Oh, more than in charity ! She did not take the first
announcement of his coming very amiably ; but when I told
her she was to reign in the nursery, and take care the poor
little chief knew the sound of a Scots' tongue, she began to
thaw ; and when he came into the house, pity or loyalty, or
both, flamed up hotly, and have quite relieved me ; for at
first she made a baby of me, and was a perfect dragon of
jealousy at poor Ailie's doing anything for me. It was a rich
scene when Rachel began giving her directions out of ' Hints
for the Management of Infants,' just in the old voice, and
Tibbie swept round indignantly, ' His Lordship, Lord Keith
of Gowanbrae, suld hae the best tendance she could gie him.
She did na lippen to thae English buiks, as though she
couldna rear a wean without buik learning.' Poor Rachel
nearly cried, and was not half comforted by my promising to
study the book as much as she pleased."

" It will never do to interfere with Tibbie, and I own I am
much of her opinion, I had rather trust to her than to
Rachel, or the book ! "

" Well, the more Rachel talked book, the more amiable
surprise passed between her mother and Lady Temple that
the poor little fellow should have lived at all, and I believe
they were very angry with me for thinking her views very
sensible. Lady Temple is so happy with him. She says it
is so melancholy to have a house without a baby, that she
comes in twice or three times a day to console herself with
this one."

" Did you not tell me that she and the Curtises spent the evening with you?"

" Yes, it was rather shocking to receive them without you, but it was the only way of being altogether on Rachel's one evening here ; and it was very amusing, Mrs. Curtis so happy with her daughter looking well and bright, and Rachel with so much to tell about Bishopsworthy, till at last Grace, in her sly odd way, said she thought dear Alexander had even taught Rachel curatolatry; whereupon Rachel fired up at such an idea being named in connexion with Mr. Clare ; then came suddenly, and very prettily, down, and added, ' Living with Alick and Mr. Clare has taught me what nonsense I talked in those days.' "

" Well done, Rachel ! It proves what Alick always said, that her great characteristic is candour !"

" I hope she was not knocked up by the long night journey all at one stretch. Mrs. Curtis was very uneasy about it, but nothing would move her; she owned that Alick did not expect her, for she had taken care he should not object, by saying nothing of her intention, but she was sure he would be ill on Wednesday morning, and then Mrs. Curtis not only gave in directly, but all we married women turned upon poor Grace for hinting that Alick might prefer a day's solitary illness to her being over-tired."

" She was extremely welcome ! Alick was quite done for by all he had gone through ; he was miserably ill, and I hardly knew what to do with him, and he mended from the moment his face lightened up at the sight of her."

" There's the use of strength of mind ! How is Alick ?"

" Getting better under M'Vicar and Edinburgh winds. It was hard on him to have borne the brunt of all the nursing

that terrible last week, and in fact I never knew how much
he was going through rather than summon me.   His sauntering manner always conceals how much he is doing, and poor
Keith was so fond of him, and liked his care so much that
almost the whole fell upon him at last.   And I believe he
said more that was good for Keith, and brought in Mr. Clare
more than perhaps I should ever have been able to do.   So
though I must regret having been away, it may have been the
best thing."

" And it was by your brother's earnest wish," said Ermine ;
" it was not as if you had stayed away for your own pleasure."

" No !   Poor Keith repeatedly said he could not die in
peace till he had secured our having the sole charge of his
son.   It was a strong instinct that conquered inveterate prejudice !   Did I tell you about the will ? "

" You said I should hear particulars when you came."

" The personal guardianship is left to us first, then to Alick
and Rachel, with £300 a year for the expenses.   Then we
have Auchinvar.   The estate is charged with an equivalent
settlement upon Mary, a better plan, which I durst not propose, but with so long a minority the estate will bear it.
Alick has his sister's fortune back again, and the Menteith
children a few hundreds ; but Menteith is rabid about the
guardianship, and would hardly speak to Alick."

" And you ? "

" They always keep the peace with me.   Isabel even made
us a wedding present—a pair of miniatures of my father and
mother, that I am very glad to rescue, though, as she politely
told me, I was welcome to them, for they were hideously
dressed, and she wanted the frames for two sweet photographs
of Garibaldi and the Queen of Naples."

Then looking up as if to find a place for them—

"Why, Ermine, what have you done to the room? It is the old parsonage drawing-room!"

"Did not you mean it, when you took the very proportions of the bay window, and chose just such a carpet?"

"But what have you done to it?"

"Ailie and Rose, and Lady Temple and her boys, have done it. I have sat looking on, and suggesting. Old things that we kept packed up have seen the light, and your beautiful Indian curiosities have found their corners."

"And the room has exactly the old geranium scent!"

"I think the Curtises must have brought half their greenhouse down. Do you remember the old oak-leaf geranium that you used to gather a leaf of whenever you passed our old conservatory?"

"I have been wondering where the fragrance came from that made the likeness complete. I have smelt nothing like it since!"

"I said that I wished for one, and Grace set off without a word, and searched everywhere at Avoncester till she found one in a corner of the Dean's greenhouse. There, now you have a leaf in your fingers, I think you do feel at home."

"Not quite, Ermine. It still has the dizziness of a dream. I have so often conjured up all this as a vision, that now there is nothing to take me away from it, I can hardly feel it a reality."

"Then I shall ring. Tibbie and the poor little Lord upstairs are substantial witnesses to the cares and troubles of real life."

CHAPTER XVI.

WHO IS THE CLEVER WOMAN?

" Half-grown as yet, a child and vain,
    She cannot fight the fight of death.
    What is she cut from love and faith ? "
            Knowledge and Wisdom, TENNYSON.

IT was long before the two Mrs. Keiths met again. Mrs.
Curtis and Grace were persuaded to spend the spring and
summer in Scotland, and Alick's leave of absence was felt
to be due to Mr. Clare, and thus it was that the first real
family gathering took place on occasion of the opening of the
institution that had grown out of the Burnaby Bargain.
This work had cost Colonel Keith and Mr. Mitchell an
infinity of labour and perseverance before even the preliminaries could be arranged, but they contrived at length to
carry it out, and by the fourth spring after the downfall of
the F. U. E. E. a house had been erected for the convalescents, whose wants were to be attended to by a matron,
assisted by a dozen young girls in training for service.

The male convalescents were under the discipline of
Sergeant O'Brien, and the whole was to be superintended by
Colonel and Mrs. Keith. Ermine undertook to hear a class
of the girls two or three times a week, and lower rooms had
been constructed with a special view to her being wheeled
into them, so as to visit the convalescents, and give them her
attention and sympathy. Mary Morris was head girl, most

of the others were from Avonmouth, but two pale Londoners
came from Mr. Touchett's district, and a little motherless
lassie from the —th Highlanders was brought down with the
nursery establishment, on which Mrs. Alexander Keith now
practised the "Hints on the management of Infants."

May was unusually propitious, and after an orthodox
tea-drinking, the new pupils and all the Sunday-schools were
turned out to play on the Homestead slopes, with all the
world to look on at them.   It was a warm, brilliant day, of
joyous blossom and lively green, and long laughing streaks of
sunlight on the sea, and no one enjoyed it more than did
Ermine, as she sat in her chair delighting in the fresh
sweetness of the old thorns, laughing at the freaks of the
scampering groups of children, gaily exchanging pleasant
talk with one friend after another; and most of all with
Rachel, who seemed to gravitate back to her whenever any
summons had for a time interrupted their affluence of
conversation.

And all the time Ermine's footstool was serving as a table
for the various flowers that two children were constantly
gathering in the grass and presenting to her, to Rachel, or to
each other, with a constant stream of not very comprehen-
sible prattle, full of pretty gesticulation that seemed to make
up for the want of distinctness. The yellow-haired, slenderly-
made, delicately-featured boy, whose personal pronouns were
just developing, and his consonants very scanty, though the
elder of the two, dutifully and admiringly obeyed the more
distinct, though less connected, utterances of the little dark-
eyed girl, eked out by pretty imperious gestures, that seemed
already to enchain the little white-frocked cavalier to her
service.   All the time it was droll to see how the two ladies

could pay full attention to the children, while going on with
their own unbroken stream of talk.

"I am not overwhelming you," suddenly exclaimed
Rachel, checking herself in mid-career about the mothers'
meetings for the soldiers' wives.

"Far from it. Was I inattentive—— ?"

"Oh no—(Yes, Una dear, very pretty)—but I found
myself talking in the voice that always makes Alick shut his
eyes."

"I should not think he often had to do so," said Ermine,
much amused by this gentle remedy—("Mind, Keith, that
is a nettle. It will sting—")

"Less often than before," said Rachel—("Never mind the
butterfly, Una)—I don't think I have had more than one
thorough fit of what he calls leaping into the gulf. It was
about the soldiers' wives married without leave, who, poor
things, are the most miserable creatures in the world ; and
when I first found out about them I was in the sort of mood
I was in about the lace, and raved about the system, and was
resolved to employ one poor woman, and Alick looked
meeker and meeker, and assented to all I said, as if he was
half asleep, and at last he quietly took up a sheet of paper,
and said he must write and sell out, since I was bent on my
gulf, and an officer's wife must be bound by the regulations
of the service. I was nearly as bad as ever ; I could have
written an article on the injustice of the army regulations,
indeed I did begin, but what do you think the end was ? I
got a letter from a good lady, who is always looking after the
poor, to thank Mrs. Alexander Keith for the help that had
been sent for this poor woman, to be given as if from the
general fund. After that I could not help listening to him,

and then I found it was so impossible to know about character, or to be sure that one was not doing more harm than — What is it, boys ? " as three or four Temples rushed up.

" Aunt Rachel, Mr. Clare is going to teach us a new game, and he says you know it. Pray come."

" Come, Una. What, Keith, will you come too ? I'll take care of him, Ermine."

And with a child in each hand Rachel followed the deputation, and had scarcely disappeared before the light gracious figure of Rose glanced through the thorn trees. " Aunt Ermine, you must come nearer ; it is so wonderful to see Mr. Clare teaching this game."

" Don't push my chair, my dear ; it is much too heavy for you uphill."

" As if I could not drive you anywhere, and here is Conrade coming."

Conrade was in search of the deserter, but he applied himself heartily to the propulsion of aunt Ermine, informing Rose that Mr. Clare was no end of a man, much better than if he could see, and aunt Rachel was grown quite jolly.

" I think she has left off her long words," said Rose.

" She is not a civilian now," said Conrade, quite unconscious of Ermine's amusement at his confidences as he pushed behind her. " I did think it a most benighted thing to marry her, but that's what it is. Military discipline has made her conformable." Having placed the chair on a spot which commanded the scene, the boy and girl rushed off to take their part in the sport, leaving Ermine looking down a steep bank at the huge ring of performers, with linked hands, advancing and receding to the measure of a chanted verse

round a figure in the centre, who made gesticulations, pursued
and caught different individuals in the ring, and put them
through a formula which provoked shouts of mirth.   Ermine
much enjoyed the sight ; it was pretty to watch the *prononcé*
dresses of the parish children, interspersed with the more
graceful forms of the little gentry, and here and there a taller
lady.   Then Ermine smiled to recognise Alison as usual
among her boys, and Lady Temple's soft greys and whites,
and gentle floating movements, as she advanced and receded
with Stephana in one hand, and a shy infant school-child in
the other.   But Ermine's eye roamed anxiously ; for though
Rachel's animated, characteristic gestures were fully dis-
cernible, and her little Una's arch toss of the head marked
her out, yet the companion whom she had beguiled away, and
who had become more to Ermine than any other of the
frisking little ones of the flock, was neither with her nor
with his chief protector, Rose.   In a second or two, however,
the step that to her had most " music in't " of all footfalls
that ever were trodden, was sounding on the path that led
circuitously up the path, and the Colonel appeared with the
little runaway holding his hand.

"Why, baby, you are soon come away !"

" I did not like it,—sit on mamma's knee," said the little
fellow, scrambling to his place then as one who felt it his
own nest and throne.

" He was very soon frightened," said the Colonel ; " it was
only that little witch Una who could have deluded him into
such a crowd, and, as soon as she saw a bigger boy to
beguile, she instantly deserted Keith, so I relieved Rachel of
him."

" See Rachel now ; Mr. Clare is interrogating her.   How

she is making them laugh! I did not think she could ever have so entered into fun."

"Alick must have made it a part of her education. When the Invalid has time for another essay, Ermine, it should be on the Benefits of Ridicule."

"Against Clever Womanhood? But then the subject must have Rachel's perfect good humour."

"And the weapon must be in the most delicately skilful hands," added the Colonel. "Properly wielded, it saves blunting the superior weapon by over-frequent use. Here the success is complete."

"It has been irony rather than ridicule," said Ermine, "though, when he taught her to laugh, he won half the battle. It is beautiful to see her holding herself back, and most forbearing where she feels most positive. I am glad to see him looking so much stronger and more substantial. Where is he?"

"On the further bank, supposed by Mrs. Curtis to be asleep, but watching uncle, wife, and child through his eyelashes. Did you ever see any one so like his sister as that child?"

"Much more so than this one. I am glad he may one day see such a shadow of his bright-faced mother."

"You are mother!" said the the little orphan, looking up into Ermine's face with a startled, wistful look, as having caught more of her meaning than she had intended, and she met his look with a kiss, the time was not yet come for gainsaying the belief more than in the words, "Yes, always a mother to you, my precious little man."

"Nor could you have had a bonnier face to look into," added the Colonel. "There, the game breaks up. We should

collect our flock, and get them back to Les Invalides, as
Alick calls it."

"Take care no one else does so," said Ermine, laughing.
"It has been a most happy day, and chief of all the pleasures
has been the sight of Rachel just what I hoped, a thorough
wife and mother, all the more so for her being awake to larger
interests, and doing common things better for being the
Clever Woman of the family. Where is she? I don't see
her now."

Where is she? was asked by more than one of the party,
but the next to see her was Alick, who found her standing
at the window of her own room, with her long-robed, two
months old baby in her arms. "Tired?" he asked.

"No; I only sent down nurse to drink tea with the other
grandees. What a delightful day it has been! I never
hoped that such good fruit would rise out of my unhappy
blunders."

"The blunders that brought so much good to me."

"Ah! the old places bring them back again. I have been
recollecting how it used to seem to me the depth of my fall
that you were marrying me out of pure pity, without my
having the spirit to resent or prevent it; and now I just like
to think how kind and noble it was in you."

"I am glad to hear it! I thought I was so foolishly in
love, that I was very glad of any excuse for pressing it on."

"Are the people dispersing? Where is your uncle?"

"He went home with the Colonel and his wife; he has
quite lost his heart to Ermine."

"And Una—did you leave her with Grace?"

"No; she trotted down hand in hand with his little lordship; promising to lead her uncle back."

" My dear Alick, you don't mean that you trust to that ? "

" Why, hardly implicitly."

" Is that the way you say so ? They may be both over the cliffs. If you will just stay in the room with baby, I will go down and fetch.them up."

Alick very obediently held out his arms for his son, but when Rachel proceeded to take up her hat, he added, " You have run miles enough to-day. I am going down as soon as my uncle has had time to pay his visit in peace, without being hunted."

" Does he know that ? "

" The Colonel does, which comes to the same thing. Is not this boy just of the age that little Keith was when you gave him up ? "

" Yes ; and is it not delightful to see how much larger and heavier he is ! "

" Hardly, considering your objections to fine children."

" Oh, that was only to coarse, over-grown ones. Una is really quite as tall as little Keith, and much more active. You saw he could not play at the game at all, and she was all life and enjoyment, with no notion of shyness."

" It does not enter into her composition."

" And she speaks much plainer. I never miss a word she says, and I don't understand Keith a bit, though he tells such long stories."

" How backward ! "

" Then she knows all her letters by sight—almost all, and Ermine can never get him to tell *b* from *d*; and you *know* how she can repeat so many little verses, while he could not even say, ' Thank you, pretty cow,' this morning, when I wanted to hear him."

" Vast interval ! "

" It is only eight months ; but then Una is such a bright, forward child."

" Highly-developed precocity ! "

" Now, Alick, what am I about ?   Why are you agreeing with me ? "

" I am between the horns of a dilemma.   Either our young chieftain must be a dunce, or we are rearing the Clever Woman of the family."

" I hope not ! " exclaimed Rachel.

" Indeed ?   I would not grudge her a superior implement, even if I had sometimes cut my own fingers."

" But, Alick, I really do not think I ever was such a Clever Woman."

" I never thought you one," he quietly returned.

She smiled.   This faculty had much changed her countenance.   " I see," she said, thoughtfully, " I had a few intellectual tastes, and liked to think and read, which was supposed to be cleverness ; and my wilfulness made me fancy myself superior in force of character, in a way I could never have imagined if I had lived more in the world.   Contact with really clever people has shown me that I am slow and unready."

" It was a rusty implement, and you tried weight instead of edge.   Now it is infinitely brighter."

" But, Alick," she said, leaving the thought of herself for that of her child, " I believe you may be right about Una ; for," she added in low voice, " she is like the most practically clever person I ever saw."

" True," he answered gravely, " I see it every day, in every saucy gesture and coaxing smile, when she tries to turn away displeasure in her naughty fits. I hardly knew how to look on at her airs with Keith, it was so exactly like the little sister I first knew. Rachel, such cleverness as that is a far more perilous gift to woman than your plodding intellectuality could ever be. God grant," he added, with one of the effusions which sometimes broke through his phlegmatic temperament, "that this little fellow may be a kinder, wiser brother than ever I was, and that we may bring her up to your own truth and unselfishness. Then such power would be a happy endowment."

"Yes," said Rachel, "may she never be out of your influence, or be left to untrustworthy hands. I should have been much better if I had had either father or brother to keep me in order. Poor child, she has a wonderful charm, not all my fancy, Alick. And yet there is one whose real working talent has been more than that of any of us, who has made it effective for herself and others, and has let it do her only good, not harm."

"You are right. If we are to show Una how intellect and brilliant power can be no snares, but only blessings helping the spirits in infirmity and trouble, serving as a real engine for independence and usefulness, winning love and influence for good, genuine talents in the highest sense of the word, then commend me to such a Clever Woman of the family as Ermine Keith."

THE END.

LONDON :
R. CLAY, SON, AND TAYLOR, PRINTERS,
BREAD STREET HILL.